Whither from Aulis

Anke Weihs

Whither from Aulis

A Childhood Autobiography

Floris Books

First published in 1989 by Floris Books.

© 1990 Estate of Anke Weihs

All rights reserved. No part of this publication may be reproduced without the prior permission of Floris Books, 21 Napier Road, Edinburgh.

British Library CIP Data available

ISBN 0-86315-098-5

Printed in Great Britain
by Billing & Sons, Worcester

To Thomas
who pulled out the thorns

No One is my name: for
everyone calls me No One,
my father and my mother
and all my companions
  Odyssey, Stanza 9

Preface

Anke Weihs concludes this childhood autobiography with the words: "I was 13; my childhood was at an end. What would I be able to make of it? Where would I go from there?" The answers to these existential questions were not long in being conceived — although the gestation period lasted twelve years.

That same autumn Dr Karl König witnessed for the first time an "Advent Garden" in one of the Anthroposophical homes for handicapped children in Switzerland. There and then he decided to work towards establishing a community based on the teachings of Rudolf Steiner, where children with handicaps would receive the care, education and guidance they needed to fulfil their potential, where the co-workers would develop new social forms of living with the children and where the celebration of the seasonal and Christian festivals would play a central role.

This challenge lived with Karl König for the next twelve years as he gained experience at a large home for handicapped children in East Germany, and subsequently as a private physician in Vienna. During this latter period leading up to the Second World War, in response to his public lectures and study group, a number of young men and women gathered round him and commonly decided to support his ideals — one of them was Anke.

Anke's somewhat tortuous path during the same period is described in her addendum: Her voyage to Europe at 16 years, and the first glimpse of the English coastline through rising fog engendered a vision that recurred as she entered Camphill nine years later. Initial contact with members of Dr König's youth group occurred in 1934 and shortly thereafter, on their recommendation, she met and sought treatment from him. Between 1938 and 1939, as the Second World War was about to break out, the majority of the group left Austria and made their way to the United Kingdom which was willing to offer asylum to victims of Nazi persecution and others fleeing the tyranny of National-Socialism.

Out of this flux of idealism and darkness the Camphill Movement was born. Dr König, his family and a few of the group, were given a temporary home at Kirkton House, a manse at Insch in Aberdeenshire. On June 1, 1940, whilst all the males were interned, Anke, Mrs König and Alix Roth were able to accomplish the move to Camphill House, the estate on Lower Deeside that was to give the Movement its name.

Anke's life thereafter is inextricably bound up with the physical, social and spiritual development of the Camphill Movement with which she unreservedly allied all her gifts and strength over the ensuing 47 years. Her contribution during those early years centred partly on her willingness and enthusiasm to take on the most basic domestic chores, such as the estate laundry, cooking and cleaning. But with her wonderful gift for language, and as the only member of the initial group whose native tongue was English, she also conducted many of the negotiations with authorities and others on behalf of Camphill. Later this gift for language was highlighted in her ability to hold large groups of disturbed adolescents spellbound during her story lessons, as she unfolded myths, fairy tales and legends in a most evocative manner. And again, in the mid-fifties, at Dr König's request, she was the founder editor of *The Cresset*, the Camphill Journal that accompanied the national and international growth of the Movement at that time and until 1972. The realms of child guidance and of home care were also Anke's strengths and, as Camphill expanded locally through the acquisition of further properties in the area, she was often at the forefront, as the Matron, in establishing the house communities. But her activities, in those early years, were not restricted to "house mothering" for in 1948, after a short period at the Waldorf School in Stuttgart to gain experience, she, along with two colleagues, took up the challenge of starting St John's School — the educational stream within Camphill. Three years later the school was opened to all the pupils at Camphill, thus pioneering Dr König's impulse: the birthright of every child to a full education, irrespective of their handicap. During this period the Camphill Seminar in Curative Education was also started to which Anke made a significant contribution in later years, a contribution vividly remembered by many of the hundreds of young people who have completed their training in Curative Education at Camphill.

In 1951 Anke married Dr Thomas Weihs and, for the next 32 years until his death, they were in the vanguard of Camphill's development, as inspired by Dr König. They were the only founder members of the Camphill Community who did not move out to support the development of other Centres of the Movement in the United Kingdom and abroad, as Dr König himself did in 1964 for the last two years of his life, although in 1959 Anke did spend some months in the United States preparing for the development of the Camphill Movement on that continent. For ten years from the mid-fifties, as Deputy Superintendent of the Camphill-Rudolf Steiner-Schools, she supported Thomas in his task as Superintendent with Dr König acting as Consultant and they, following his move to Germany and his subsequent death, together continued in these capacities until 1972. During these years Anke also accompanied Thomas on numerous lecture tours of the United Kingdom, Southern Africa and Australia.

Anke's creativity for exploring and developing new visions and new horizons, for bringing new impulses into being, bore fruit in the further development of the Scottish Neighbourhood of the Camphill Movement; the Templehill Community for Mutual Help was founded in 1972, work at Camphill Blair Drummond started in 1975, and in 1978 Corbenic College opened its doors for the work of Camphill. This culminated in the first Convention of Councils of Camphill Communities in Scotland in 1979. These developments were very much linked to a recognition of the importance of early historical Celtic and Christian streams in Scotland and the need for Anthroposophical impulses in the widest possible context to unfold — in Biodynamic Agriculture, in the Waldorf School stream, and in Anthroposophical medicine, all of which have, to a greater or lesser degree, grown with the growth of Camphill in this area. Through Anke, Camphill's work was also linked to the founding of the Six Circle Group in the late 1960s and early 1970s — an activity involving the mutual support of prison and borstal provisions with those for mentally and physically handicapped youngsters and others.

Much of Anke's energy during the last ten years of her life was given to inspiring growth and transformation of the social and spiritual fabric of Camphill. She made central contributions to the annual New Year Assemblies of the British Region of the Movement, focusing on the redemption of Lord Stanhope's part in the destiny of Caspar Hauser — a destiny very much linked to that of Camphill. She travelled widely in the Camphill and Anthroposophical Movements nationally and internationally, lecturing and supporting their manifold activities in diverse ways. She was intimately associated with the founding and progress of the first Camphill Youth Guidance Seminars of the British Region and with the developments leading to the founding of the Seminars on Psychological Disturbances. All of this work intensified following the death of her husband, Thomas, in 1983 and continued, in an ever more inspiring manner through much of her own final illness, an illness she bore with remarkable fortitude and modesty for many years.

Anke's destiny is linked to the destiny of Camphill. From its beginnings in Scotland in 1940, it has now developed nationally and internationally to encompass seventy centres in fifteen other countries spanning Europe, Africa and the Americas. The social impulse behind Camphill finds its many expressions through the initiatives of its co-workers who see local needs and respond to them in an individual way. Thus the activities of the Movement include the various Schools, Training Centres and "Villages" with diversely handicapped children, adolescents and adults. In most of them the responsible care for the land through biodynamic horticulture and agriculture, and activity centred on a variety of craft workshops, provide a source of work and growth. Adult education is an important area of activity too, focusing on Curative Education but including other activities as well. Camphill is also engaged in the provision of residential care facilities for the elderly and counselling services for people with mental illness and handicaps, and their families.

In the Camphill Movement, communities come about such that the members, whatever their abilities, can help to support the needs of their fellows, while they themselves are supported in turn. The handicapped, retarded or socially difficult person is accepted as an individual whose needs of body, soul and spirit are recognized by the whole community, and all live, work and learn together to form one community. This demands faith, love and hope. By making a commitment to a Camphill community each person makes a sacrifice, giving something of himself to help another. Out of this attitude the community grows stronger and all are helped. Within the economic life, one of the pillars of the Camphill Movement rests on a Fundamental Social Law expressed by Rudolf Steiner:

> The well-being of a community of people working together becomes greater, the less each individual demands for himself the products of his own achievements; that is, the more of those products he passes on to his fellow workers and the more his own needs are satisfied, not out of his own achievements, but out of the achievements of others.

But such communities can maintain themselves only if they also uphold spiritual and social values and in those Anke was a pillar of strength and inspiration.

The Camphill Movement is far from static. Its very name suggests its openness to change and its history over fifty years is witness to this. New challenges are always being presented: many are taken up either by new developments in existing centres or by the founding of new communities — activities very close to Anke's heart. The social ideal found in Camphill could find its expression in many ways. To date, the principle task has been with mentally and socially handicapped people, but the modern world throws up many disadvantaged groups. There is a growing concern for how land is used and for the environment. People are more conscious of the need for better education, health care and nutrition. There are new ways of expressing the arts. No one can predict what Camphill may be asked to respond to in the future. As a social movement Camphill was founded ahead of its time, but it has achieved much in a short time and has helped to change public awareness of certain problems and to influence changes in government policy. Dr Karl König conceived of Camphill in 1927 at the point when Anke stepped out of the childhood described in this autobiography. She, and a small group of others, through their life commitment, supported Dr König in realizing his ideal and establishing Camphill, which has since developed into a worldwide Movement. His earnest call that:

> Only the help from man to man, the encounter of ego with ego — the awareness of the other person's individuality — without enquiring into his creed or his world conception or his political affiliation, but simply the meeting, eye to eye, of two individualities — only this creates the kind of Curative Education which may counter and heal the threat to our innermost humanity.

This was a call to which Anke was able to respond and give her life.

>   Nick Blitz
>   Friedwart Bock
>   Camphill
>   November 1989

PART 1

1

My father's father came from a long line of Friesian peasant nobility; my father's mother came from the Prussian House of Brandenburg. My father was tall and fair and although he had a badly-set broken nose from his early youth, he was very good-looking. He was in no way erudite and in spite of his ability to adapt to any situation, or just because of it, he seemed somewhat sanguine and superficial. He had an air about him that made people want to spoil him, or at least further him as though their own well-being depended on his well-being and as a result of this and probably his own ambition, he was at the age of twenty-three the managing director of an export-import firm with offices in Rotterdam, Shanghai, Tokyo, Melbourne, New York and Los Angeles. He traded mainly in jade.

My mother was English, born in Melbourne of a father of obscure antecedents and a beautiful mother who maintained her family after its move to Australia by making ladies' hats and painting rural scenes of bovine tranquillity on screens, because my grandfather could never reconcile himself with his move to Australia and became an alcoholic.

My mother was entirely self-educated, musically highly sensitive, widely read, witty and fastidious in her tastes, but owing to the impecuniosity of the family circumstances, there being two older sisters who were sent back to England to school, she was both unschooled as well as untrained. She was tiny, dark, intense and imperious in manner. When my father met her while on his travels, he wrote to his mother in Holland: "She just reaches up to my heart."

Even now I feel my long deceased parents as distinct components in my make-up: my father in my body and physical reactivity, in a certain woodenness of common intelligence, in a basic passivity or indolence, and there have been many who have wanted to spoil me as well.

I feel my mother in the texture of my mind which tends to be restless, to some extent fastidious, to all appearances imperious and equally untrained, and finally in my musical nerve.

My Self was not derived from parental sources, but had a different genesis and an own moment of emergence.

My father and mother married after only three weeks of acquaintance. My mother maintained she married him solely to escape from Australia. She lingered there, however, until I was born while my father continued his round of the world.

I was born two days after the heir to the Austrian Throne was assassinated at Sarajevo. The inexplicably shattering effect the news of the assassination had on my mother was the signal that started my own laborious and protracted entry into this world.

My parents' marriage began to crumble with my birth, but they had both looked forward to my arrival and my mother named me before I was born. We left Australia for good when I was eighteen months old.

(Gliding on currents of rushing noise through yellow land until the earth raised up its arms and hugged the yellow land and crumpled it in its titanic embrace, making it writhe into cliffs bearing twisted pines on their jagged shoulders moaning in the wind.

Terraced fields, minute, mounted stepwise into secret places in the vale where the cliffs narrowed, spiking into the blue air. Deep below ran a river hidden from sight but emanating chilly sweetness. A monastery with a winged roof clung to a crag higher up among the pines like an eagle scanning distances no other creature could sight in the rare ether.

The narrowing vale mounted high and higher until there was no way on because of the wall ahead which towered above everything else on earth. High up where there is no sound, above the roseate fringe of the breath of the earth in ineffable serenity shone the unearthly peaks, hovering above gravity — the gleaming hems of the garments of gods, treading eternity.

Thus the dreamlike memory of the Himalayas at the feet of which we spent six months lingered on in the mind of the child.)

I was a fat infant, for the most part placid, and made no attempt to speak at the time a young child should do so. This was doubtless due to the fact that although my father insisted that I speak Dutch first, my mother regarded Dutch as "that peasant language" and undermined my father's dispositions where she could in favour of English, while the object of their contention maintained its mute existence.

We stayed by the seaside at Yokohama, but my father had to leave on business. The day we were to sail for Los Angeles, I took ill with whooping cough and was not allowed on board ship nor could my mother accompany my father because of me. She was always inordinately gentle and intuitive when I was ill and was what I clung to when my mind wandered in fever; she was my motive for living.

When I recovered from an illness, she would often say that I was not her child but that she had picked me up somewhere. This made me howl with rage and smash things or become so totally stubborn that nothing could move me save the trunk strap applied to my bottom by my father.

My mother did not wait for my full recovery but joined my father wherever he was, leaving me with my nanny in Yokohama.

When I was acutely ill with whooping cough. I saw the whoops in my room at night. They arched in the darkness over my bed in thin trembling rounds, cold, menacing, hoarse violin strings, while I became a massive stone statue lying on its side, each finger as ponderous as a tree trunk, torso and legs gigantic. With a sense of acute regret, the little spark of Self within abandoned its place and flitted out into a no-man's land beyond the pale of the headache that bored into the huge stone skull on the pillow, until the hugeness began to abate and the stony colossus on the bed shrank to familiar proportions and the little spark slipped back inside like a cat into a warm basket.

Normally the body was a tiny plumb dangling neatly down from Me; Me was a forward-going arrow of force. The little plumb experienced a distinct downward pull which was pleasurable but by no means primary. Either I gave in to the pull and walked firmly on the ground with a sensation of gladness in the arch of my foot or — I stayed up aloft in the air where I

was free and not even very young; up there I was older than I was — wiser and knowing. I was before I was.
There were moments when the body had no weight at all and had no hold on me. I rose out of it and looked down on to the top of my head where the hair formed a tiny flaxen whirl. It was like leading a little dog on a leash, the little dog running ahead and my Self following comfortably behind.
I was often invisible. Down on the beach, I was like the soft wind, sighing but unseen; I passed unnoticed and was often not recognized. This was my anonymity, my undeclared presence.

When my parents returned to Japan, they found me babbling uninhibitedly in Japanese to which my mother reacted in disgust as though every word were a dirty sweet picked up from the street, but we left Yokohama soon after and stayed for a while in California, although I didn't know where that was. We occupied a big house standing in heavy, oppressive shade. Oranges grew in at the windows and outside there was a pool of huge forget-me-nots. The river moved along like a gigantic snake and sired enormous mosquitoes.

My father had business in Washington. We walked down marble steps, I between my parents. To my delight, my mother said: "We are the cats that walked alone."
Something from behind tore the moment away. The cupola was ablaze with dazzling light against a deep blue sky. A nightmarish white thing drew upwards on thin spiky wings, ripping up the sky and filling the air with shrieks of silent laughter.
Something terrible scorched my mind; light was not what relieved darkness — light was glare, blinding, blanching, consuming. Ligħt seemed to be light, but it had a hard core of darkness. It engendered appearances, distortions, caricatures. It exposed what was vulnerable. It deviated from the vibrant essence of things. At dusk the jasmine bushes breathed out their sweetness; their truth could be smelled. The night is resonant, redolent with the sound and fragrance and the touch and truth of things. All this retreats before the advance of the day, and truth and fragrance and vibrant being are imprisoned behind the bars of the sun, and a deceptive arrangement of surfaces falls silently and stealthily over the essential world. When day-

light comes creeping up behind the night, another wisp of Eden is lost.

The enemy lurked in the phantom carnival of flashing advertisements that seared the nights over cities, in the coloured electric bulbs that blistered along the thin wire snake coiling in and out of the helpless branches of the Christmas Tree in our hotel bedroom, magnified in the colossal tree at the hub of flashing lights in Times Square on the way to the docks. But the most vicious sign of the enemy was the naked electric bulb hanging, shadeless, over my bed like a drop of poison about to fall.

Very early on I developed a preference for dimness, shade, coolness and the minor moments at the edge of the day, for the unseen, the long slant shadows cast by the sinking sun, for mists and steel grey folds of cloud low over hills, for the andante of rain dripping from the eaves.

On winter days the sun would be black, a single staring hollow eye in the ashen sky, baleful, and when the thin sharp shrieking angel rose up out of the leaden snow on spiked wings, it was a secret declaration of war.

At times my forehead was a curtainless window through which everything could be seen; nothing could be shut out. Everything was transparent. This was often before an illness. All warmth and goodness shrivelled up in a sterile landscape through which barbed wire stretched between fence posts standing in a straggled line like gravestones, continuing on beyond the horizon into nothingness.

Alone at night in the dark room wherever it was, a descent began into shadowy orphic caverns filled with blue mists through which a path wound downwards into hidden places in the depths where an inward blue light quivered in the expectant dark, falling around me like a cloak and giving me back to myself with a gesture of unspeakable comfort, because the nature of that light is other than anything else in the world.

It began with a sunset that was like a universal wound pouring its blood out on to the wet sands and into the curling clutches of the waves coming in all down the shore.

O Yuki-san came over the sands calling. The Other was busy alone on the beach bringing forth castles, mountain ranges, pools, rivers and dams in the sand in the intensifying dark.

The hand of the Maker passed once more over his creation, determined to establish a kingdom in occupied territory, while the real sovereign was coming nearer with every long sigh of the tide.

O Yuki-san's sandals and the hem of her kimono entered the kingdom and the wet sand responded to the weight of her tread. In the twilight she was smiling, unseen. She coaxed: "Come, it's time to go up to the hotel." But the Other went on patting the sand into shapes no longer quite visible yet communicating to the touch its true allegiance to that great lapping Presence out there in the dark. O Yuki-san bent down and grasped the hand that lay upon mountains and pulled up gently. Destruction followed and mountains, castles, dams dissolved all too willingly towards the incoming surge of the sea.

In that moment a swift shaft of light was hurled silently across the sky to pierce a tiny target. What was Before retreated out into the dark and the Now advanced to stake its claim. The pricked target quivered like a droplet of molten glass at the end of a blow-pipe. This droplet was I — a girl aged three.

A fierce sensation of bliss mingled with grief was injected into my blood stream. My conscious Self began its uncertain course and there was no turning back to the state such as it was before the prick. I went meekly up to the hotel clinging to O Yuki-san's hand, the new element establishing itself with every step.

At each end of the beach red sandstone cliffs jutted out into the sea. They were the Jachin and Boaz of the lovely day that was a brimming cup of expectation never quite drained when bedtime came, but always retaining a golden droplet of enthusiasm for the next day.

The cliffs did not like to be looked at because you couldn't look at both at the same time and to prefer one before the other was perilous. The gaze was best fastened to the things on the sand in front of one — the red tin sand bucket, the shells, seaweeds and the nameless bleached fragments of some remote existence cast up by the sea and forgotten.

Yet the cliffs looked at Me and observed every movent however stealthy, the passing shadows inside, the unborn intentions.

They never relaxed their forbidding scrutiny and their distant hostility was there all the time.

The safest place on the beach was the middle. O Yuki-san was a middle person. She would never coax me too far in any one extreme away from safety. But my mother was not a middle person. She challenged peril like the wind in her face and would suddenly let my hand go and not be there. The cliffs would then heave themselves loose from their roots with a harsh groan and come grinding along the beach from either side and there would be no escape from their brazen embrace.

Our hotel was a long low building on the upper edge of a grove of pines, with balconies and french windows opening out towards the sea. During breakfast in the dining room there were earth tremors which swung the pictures awry on the walls and jangled the cutlery and made the parrot in his cage say: "Damn!" There was a faint sense of being out of touch with the universe for a moment, whether it was because of the tremor or because of what the parrot said. In any case, the grown-ups wore startled embarrassed faces.

I knew the tremors were caused by the giant in the earth who was just waking up and stretching himself for a new day. He would rouse his children who were asleep behind his big floppy ears and they would swarm up through the cracks in the earth to play in the sun. They were as big as my father's thumb and they hopped about and over the gnarled roots of the pines and were hard to focus on because they got into one's eyes and made them water.

Further down in the cavernous belly of the earth lay monsters blinking their hooded eyes in the sudden flood of sunlight. The little men clambered over their encrusted bodies up on to your shoulders, if you stood still enough, and whispered into your ear something of the greatest significance; nothing must get in the way of finding out what it was. There would be no real power to prevent me from running outside to where the little men were dancing — only if I was too late, they would do something silly and spoil everything because they would think I wasn't coming or didn't know they were there. But — if I said I-have-to-go-to-the-bathroom-please — and went outside instead, if I said it to my parents, even if I said it to O Yuki-san, I would be struck dead.

The sky was leaden from cliff to cliff. The air was rigid and the birds stopped twittering in the pines. The old man who holds the sea in his hands tipped it up and the horizon went right up into the sky. The hotel tottered and broken things strewed the floor. The tennis court in front was cracked from end to end. The open french windows stared down into the fissure below. The rent skin of the turf hung along the gash and the little men were already surging up out of the broken earth into the daylight.

O Yuki-san was fussing in the room sorting out clothing. "Why just now, O Yuki-san?" She came over to the window to chatter. The crack in the tennis court below was speechless like a mouth with parched lips. "You must go away now, O Yuki-san; please go away."

"Why should I go away?" O Yuki-san laughed, her voice rising.

"Ssssssst! O Yuki-san, you don't understand."

Something was bobbing along the edge of the fissure, dancing in green or red jackets — I couldn't tell for the tiny figures were almost transparent. I dashed to the door of the room. O Yuki-san stood there with her back pressed against the door: "Your mother said you are not to go out just now."

"But I must! Let me go!"

"I can't let you go."

"Please, O Yuki-san, I must go! I must, I MUST!"

"I shall not let you go."

"Damn you, O Yuki-san!"

There was a shot in the room like a thunderclap and O Yuki-san was badly hurt. She went out of the room with her mouth hanging limp. A great lump of sorrow rose up in my throat.

"What did you say to O Yuki-san?" My shoulder was gripped in a vice of iron. "I said what did you say to O Yuki-san?"

I couldn't repeat what I said to O Yuki-san so I said: "I'm going to stay out on the balcony all day."

"Then stay out on the balcony all day if you can't be civil to O Yuki-san."

He pushed me out and shut the french window firmly on the inside. The soft white muslin curtains were behind glass and out of reach. The knobbly squat pillars along the balcony were musty. Between their knobbed knees the ravaged tennis court was desolate and hostile, so were the people walking about, taking stock of the damage below.

The wind crept around the eaves with a thin sharp whine and rattled petulantly at the brittle glass door. The shadows shifted from one place to the next silently all the time and although I put my hands and legs in their way, they still went on passing over me. Weren't the knobbly knees wobbly? The fattest one in the middle was surely loose and would leave a huge gap when it fell out and would suck me after it. There was nothing to hold on to — the handle of the french window was too small and too smooth to grip and save myself from falling off into the dark below. All light was gone and I could no longer see if the knobbly knees — if the knobbly knees — were — there at all —.

There was a deafening pounding in my ears and the chilly wind stuck pins into my chest. The wind couldn't be pushed away like O Yuki-san when she came to give me a goodnight kiss. Her skin tasted like gall, but I wouldn't want to push O Yuki-san away now — she was warm and soft and would hold me fast, would not let me fall — but the wind shook and rattled angrily at the door and whined and would sweep me up into the dark and let me go and I would hurtle to the ground and bruise my whole existence and would never recover from the horrible thud . . .

The long light fingers of the sun-rays passed down the muslin folds of the mosquito net draped like a tent over my bed and my pillow and bed-covers were invested with its gentleness. O Yuki-san stepped to my bedside with a tray: "I've brought you strawberry jam for your toast today."

Along the horizon out over the sea lay the thick luminous coil of a giant serpent between the edge of the ocean and the empty sky. Ships cut right through the body of the serpent when they passed out of sight. Beyond the horizon, tier upon tier of seats rose up, the top row dissolving into infinity. *They* sat on the seats and watched everything that happened on the beach with unbendingly austere mien. They stared down at Me when I was doing nothing — sitting in the sand with that silly red-and-white sunhat O Yuki-san said I must wear, or transfixed by the sight of the beach fleas hopping up and down.

The luminous coil of the serpent was elastic, and on some days it retreated out over the edge where it vanished and you caught a glimpse of the big bright forms in the distance, passing over glistening meadows on into silver shadows along the shores at the end of the world.

Suddenly and imperceptibly it lay there again, hemming in everything and the sea was grey and surly.

I cradled in the sun-warm sand, but water always seeped up from below and made the base of my spine itch unbearably inside my rompers, and my mother said you must never scratch in public. No day was ever quite perfect because of the wet sand and other things that ached and prickled or were too tight.

The wind snuffled along the beach like a vagrant dog. The waves levelled their interminable attack on the edge of the shore, sometimes mildly, sometimes impatiently, and the beach yielded to the want of the water with a sigh and let its grains of sand slip willingly out into the great gulping belly of the ocean.

I was a silver-blue fish, streaking through a warm sea of diffused light, darting across broad shafts of luminescent swaying green water, caressed by the trailing tendrils of seaweeds, the sleeves of unseen wearers. Shooting headlong and fearlessly into silent deeper depths, I came to rest among the huge shadows of whales gathered in a great universal cluster, obscuring everything, casting up a ponderous womb of protection around me so that nothing could happen to me . . . O Yuki-san's shrill call pierced the impregnable walls and my mind returned to the beach like a tiny bird before the storm.

My world was like those glass balls made in Czechoslovakia which, when shaken, produce a snow flurry or a fall of autumn leaves. There was always a shake, a flurry and a gradual subsiding — all inside the glass ball.

My mother and my father lived in the glass ball with me — although they were often away outside somewhere and there was only O Yuki-san left. Or I was alone and there were long hours with nothing but the sea and the sky and gulls mounting the wind. When the rain tapped steadily on the hotel roof, the wash of the waves became rhythmical and gentle, assuaged by the touch of sweet water on their bitter manes.

The white muslin folds of the mosquito-netting falling down over my bed was my diaphanous tabernacle from the inner sunlit sanctum of which everything outside was transfigured, and my mother, when she occasionally came into my room, appeared with an aureole of light around her that sent a thrill of bliss through me.

As soon as my mother went out of the room, it darkened a little and a physical ache for her presence took possession of me. When she would tuck me in at night before going out for the evening, I remained in the same hallowed position till dawn although every muscle ached, but when she was there again, the room would be charged with alien currents of suffocating intensity at the outer edge of which my father hovered uncertainly.

O Yuki-san's smile went before her. It was irritating because she showed her teeth when she smiled. It was best not to look at her at all, to do as though she were not there. But O Yuki-san was impervious and went on existing. She would pick me up at odd moments and kiss me all over my face, and my spine would wriggle because she tasted of gall, but this did not make her put me down. In her arms, I felt as heavy as the whole world.

"I won't have any sugar on my boiled egg this morning, thank you O Yuki-san."

"Oh, but you may have some" and with the quickness of a bird she sprinkled sugar on my boiled egg because she thought I wanted it in spite of my protests, protests being expressions of politeness, leaving me to choke the sweet boiled egg down with rising revulsion.

O Yuki-san was as undifferentiated as the snow — her name meant "Snow" — which falls over everything and is both soft and chilling. She was there the whole day and during the night as well and kept constant vigil over me. Although she was exasperating, she was never completely stifling for she was compassionate, and things always came to an end with her even though my mother insisted that she never give in.

I had to wear a stony face most of the time so that O Yuki-san couldn't see what was inside. The more stony my face became, the more it ached and wouldn't let even the most urgent smile break through the crust and it took a whole night's sleep to soften it up again. Even so, it would harden the next morning out of habit.

In the evenings when everyone else had left the beach for the hotel, I lingered with O Yuki-san until the fishermen came along to haul in their nets, their russet bodies stripped down to their black loin cloths. The twisted trunks of the pines, the wet sands, the ruffled sea were infused with dull red. The fateful gash left by the departing sun had opened up again and its bleak blood was pouring out over everything. From the east came a blue wind, cooling the hectic fever of the day still hanging in the air and brushed on beyond, leaving sadness in its wake.

O Yuki-san urged: "Come, it's getting late."

"Wait, O Yuki-san, just a minute."

On the sand the fishermen were labouring, shouting hoarse harsh cries to one another. Their nets emerged slowly out of the darkening sea and were hauled up on to the shore. They contained huge turtles lying like mounds on the beach. Their ugly slightly swaying heads reminded me of thumbs and their eyes of tiny windows looking back into the beginnings of creation.

There were always some fish in the nets with the turtles, flapping violently on their sides, gasping for life in the agonizing air. I began to sob. The fishermen bent over the nets to extract the turtles and their muscles were balled with cruelty as they flung the unwanted fish aside. In the falling darkness, the feeble convulsions of their bodies caught the dying light.

"O Yuki-san, why must they take them from the sea? Why, O Yuki-san?"

The Diabutusu loomed through the trees. Crowds of people walked in the gardens beneath the outspread branches of the pines. They all passed by the Diabutusu. He towered over everything. The dust under foot was musty after a rain. The massive body of the Diabutusu was slaten like musty dust.

"O Yuki-san, let's not go that way, let's go another way." He loomed through the trees. I didn't want to go past him because his flat calm face, the symmetrical fold of his garment beneath his belly, the precise meeting of his thumbs, the basket of red apples placed before him — roused a deep itch of irritation inside me that made me want to giggle and be silly.

"You, Diabutusu, can you see me? What if I would stick out my tongue at you, Diabutusu?" I never stuck out my tongue at anyone.

The Diabutusu's mammoth serenity was undisturbed by my threats of impudence. Had he but frowned or shaken his head in disapproval, I would have been put in my place and would have been relieved (when later on, Zeus frowned, I felt the fear of God like sobering steel). There was no ire in the Diabutusu's broad breast, no wild moment of danger in his presence, no wrath roaring like the wind down from the mountains at night.

"Diabutusu, stop looking down! Look at me!"

Great calm smiles filtered through the foliage in the gardens from the double upward-carved temple gates that let people pass through them into the courtyards and the lacquered stillness inside, to release them out again into labyrinths of tiny paths and ponds and little arched stone bridges, on the humps of which they paused and glimpsed the reflection of the winged temple roofs trembling in the water lilies. Out on the horizon, an ocean-going liner trailed smoke from its funnels as it passed into invisibility.

A dream shimmered in the bright distance over the rice fields. We stood on a shaky, little bridge of sticks tied with frayed ropes which came from nowhere and led to nowhere — fragment of a hempen dirge. The water below was dull brown and reflected the earth beneath rather than the sky above. Peasants with their kimonos hitched up were at work in the rippling furrows of rice. All the more radiant, Fujiyama tapered down from its glistening crown, broadening out at the base like a benediction, not quite touching the profane earth, but hovering a little on white mists. I trembled with awe — the frail hempen bridge vibrated uncertainly.

"Why are we packing, Mummy? Where are we going?" My father was strapping up our big pigskin trunks — there were thirteen of them. Rickshaws were waiting outside the hotel. We proceeded down the main staircase, my father dispensing tips to the left and to the right where the hotel staff stood at attention like the front row of an army. It was always like running the gauntlet to check out of a hotel.

O Yuki-san was nowhere to be seen. On the way to the point of departure to wherever we were going, we stopped at O Yuki-san's mother's house in town. She and O Yuki-san were standing in the doorway, smiling. My father lifted me out of the rickshaw and a few of our bags were carried in after me. The rickshaws with the big pigskin trunks and my mother and father went off down the street and out of sight.

O Yuki-san and her mother took me in. I badly wanted to cry, but there was nowhere one could cry by oneself because all the rooms in O Yuki-san's house led into each other and the fragile paper walls were almost transparent. I was to sleep on a mat in an alcove off O Yuki-san's sleeping place.

They said that O Yuki-san's mother was a princess but that her family had become poor and that was the reason why O Yuki-san had to go out and look after European children. I discerned no trace of gold about O Yuki-san's mother's person, no starlight in the folds of her dark blue kimono, no moonlight in her coarse iron-coloured hair, although I peeled her person like an onion as I followed her around the house. She was short and broad and her face was wrinkled like the sand when the tide has gone out, and when she laughed in her deep voice which she did readily, she shook like a jelly pudding and everyone else had to laugh with her. Her hands felt good — they were impersonal and at the same time warm and firm.

O Yuki-san's mother arranged blossoms in delicate vases — one twig for above, one twig bending towards you, and a third twig slanting downwards with a faintly ominous gesture. I stood at her side, watching her silently.

Her house was in the centre of the town. The beach, the cliffs, the horizon between the sea and the sky receded out of sight and instead, there were busy streets with rickshaw men running this way and that, crying out when someone was in their way and smiling as they flashed by barefoot and panting. Sometimes a neat little heap of horse's dung lay steaming on the cobbles in the wake of a carriage — the diligent rickshaw men ran their race undeterred.

I ambled behind O Yuki-san's mother past rows of shops in the narrow streets and peered into the interior where coloured ware and brass gleamed in the dimness within. Out in front there were big round baskets of vegetables and fruits and fish. O Yuki-san's mother gave me a little basket to carry, into which she put bundles of herbs or vegetables so that I would feel useful, provided the basket did not become too heavy. When she met her friends, they would all stop at the crossings and talk and would spoil me with their gracious compliments and I would feel significant and central for a bit as though I were the young heir to a throne.

O Yuki-san bought me a kite in the form of a bulbous paper fish with bulging eyes that wobbled in flight, and blue and red cheeks like a gargoyle's and a long trailing blue and red tail. It was the most beautiful thing in the whole world.

I skipped along the paths in the gardens with the lovely fish bobbing up and down in the breeze and surrendered my will to its wayward course, and through its globular eyes I looked down upon the dusty earth and rejoiced in giddy freedom. As I panted along in the wake of the colourful lover of the wind, each little tug on the string sent a thrill down the arm that clutched it, and I played a secret game with the wind, gently because the wind can get annoyed very quickly. It was best to pretend to give in and to let the wind have the fish a little and lift it higher and higher on his wings, that great invisible bird whose all-scanning eyes see the earth as a speck of dust in indigo space — or I pulled the reins of what after all, was *my* fish and sensed the false acquiescence of the wind, but was far too intoxicated by my fleeting supremacy to realize that I was being punished — because the wind had exacted his due — my exquisite blue and red fish was impaled on the hook of a naked pine twig and hung, its mouth agape, the breeze tugging at the paper tatters making sure that nothing was left. I stood beneath the tree too appalled to sob.

I had been left behind by my parents the year before in Yokohama. This time in Kamakura, I was conscious of my dark blue kimono with its white markings and the broad butterfly girdle around my still inarticulate middle but I was not conscious of any difference between myself and those around me and the fear of the taste of the gall on skin that was yellow had vanished.

I found O Yuki-san beautiful and gazed on the cast of her face with growing adoration. She assumed a dignity in her own home which was not in evidence in the hotel in the presence of my parents to whom she was always deferential. It was now my turn to seek her affections and I suffered pangs of jealousy because she had many friends and five brothers with their families besides and I was often alone with her mother. O Yuki-san did not want me to meet her friends too often lest they spoil me like her mother's older friends did. Her brothers were dark and heavy and preoccupied and took no notice of me at all when they came to visit. On these occasions the whole family seemed darker and more serious, and I had no place in their midst.

O Yuki-san could be gone for entire days. When evening drew on, I would listen to the sounds in the street and for O Yuki-san's voice on the threshold. When she came in at last and the light fell on her shining face with its quick black eyes, I ached so much for relief that I could hardly rise to greet her. She would take my hand in hers and hold it while she told her mother what her day had been like, and I waited until she turned to me and, with a radiant smile, led me into the next room.

She would take tea with me kneeling on the mat opposite and would tell me stories and laugh with me until the tears rolled down our cheeks. Afterwards she would fetch a big basin of warm water and set it down on the mat and would be firm about the way I washed and folded up my clothes for the night.

My father was very tall and to see him towering in O Yuki-san's fragile house with its paper partitions was foreboding. He had to bend to pass from one room to another and did not like it, to judge from the expression on his face. I was frightened lest the delicate structure suffer damage and wanted to warn him, but he seemed not to have noticed my presence.

My mother followed him into the house. Her greeting was cursory as though she had just returned from shopping; there was an atmosphere of distant cities around her. She was looking cold and displeased with O Yuki-san's mother whom she hardly deigned to address as though she were a servant. (O Mummy, what has happened?)

O Yuki-san herself looked distressed and sad and I was aware of growing tension between her and my mother. They all went in to an inner room leaving me by myself and after a few minutes of low murmuring, a storm burst. I heard my mother saying in her iciest voice something about O Yuki-san's having encouraged me to speak Japanese as though it were the tongue of pariahs (my father spoke it fluently). I heard O Yuki-san's voice rise shrill with despair.

With a hot head I blundered into the room where they were all standing and clung to O Yuki-san, anguished because she had to defend herself because of me and taken aback at the stern aloof expression on my mother's face. My mother cut in: "Take her away."

My father picked me up like a piece of luggage and carried me out to a waiting taxi. When my mother joined us later in the hotel, she said to my father: "Well, I've cleared that mess up."

A tense world followed of new and strange hotels and ships and docks and nannies without names.

I was careful never to mention O Yuki-san to my parents although her name was always hovering just behind my teeth ready to spring out in a whisper, sometimes in a shout. But at night when I was alone I searched for her in the temple gardens, in the bright streets crowded with people, sometimes along the forsaken beach in the grey light before dawn.

O Yuki-san, I couldn't say Good-bye to you — O Yuki-san? I wanted to tell you I'm sorry I was unkind to you in the hotel. O Yuki-san, Good-bye . . .

In the crowd that passed through my mind at night when I lay in a strange bed, I saw her bright kimono, saw her hurrying along or passing by in severity or not seeing me as I tried, yearning for her, to press through the crowd to reach her side before she would be gone. And then — just as I would be falling asleep, she would be coming towards me laughing, her arms outstretched, and I would slip to her feet — I wanted to say Good-bye to you and couldn't, O Yuki-san. O Yuki-san?

Sleep swallowed the utmost endeavour to communicate, and later on, time.

2

My father was reading the newspaper, my mother a book. I was looking out of the window at the passing meadows on either side of the train. All at once there was a violent lurch and the train was wrenched around as though a giant were twisting rope. There was confusion and screaming as suitcases fell off the luggage racks on to the ladies who were thrown into a heap of skirts, and everything came to a dead stop. A conductor appeared from somewhere, still managing to walk upright in his uniform and, boosted up my father and the other men, pushed open one of the carriage doors which was facing upward into the sky. Everyone scrambled up to the open door and was helped to slither out and down over the huge gap between the side of the train and the tracks below.

Just before the bend ahead, the locomotive lay on its side like a sick horse panting steam and a few of the carriages including ours had turned over with it. No one was hurt but everyone was shocked and excited. After standing around and talking about the accident, the passengers climbed the embankment and settled down on the grass. Sandwiches were passed around and everyone picnicked in groups.

A flock of lambs and their dams was grazing on the rounded hummocks of grass in the constant play of sun and cloud. The viridescence of the meadows was unearthly. Oyster-catchers veered down in their tortuous flight to fly steeply up again crying their piercing minor lament. In the distance, rounded purple and russet hills heaved in layers along the horizon overhung by shifting folds of cloud containing the brown hue of the earth and casting great shadows over the crofts up on the edge of the bracken.

I fell asleep on the ground wrapped up in a rug. When I woke up, the sun seemed to have gone into the interior of the earth to shine on from within. Lambs were bleating and the homing cry of seagulls streaked through the silence.

Over the crest of a hill I saw a great crown of stone set in a sea of twinkling lights against a luminous evening sky.

"What's that?"

"Edinburgh," someone said.

3

We couldn't get bookings on a larger ship, my father said. The ship we were now on was indeed much smaller than any of the others and was manned by friendly Chinese sailors. I knew all the crew by sight after a day at sea.

A gale blew up. The sea responded wildly and my father told me to go down to the cabin and play there, for the waves were now rearing over the railings and washing down along the decks and everything had to be cleared.

Our cabin was tiny and stuffy and right next to the engine room. I was too elated by the roll of the ship and the whistling of the wind in the rigging to so easily accept confinement. In an auspicious moment, I reached the upper deck again where a small group of passengers clung to the railing and were watching the crew struggling with ropes and poles in the blast.

I did not see exactly what happened but some of the passengers cried out in horror and their words were whipped like tatters in the wind across the deck. A sailor lay limply on the lower deck, his body oddly awry. Two sailors lifted away a pole. The wind kept sweeping it around as though it were possessed by rage. In the stunned faces of the passengers I saw that something awful had happened to the sailor lying on the deck. I suddenly felt that I should have been downstairs in the protection of our cabin and as I edged past the tense little group at the railing, I heard one of the women say: "He's dead."

Alone in the cabin where it was curiously still in spite of the chugging of the engines, I whispered to myself: "He's dead." The engines chugged, the boat dipped and rose and turned from side to side in the heaving seas. I began to play.

The storm had abated. I was up on deck at the stern of the ship. The sun was obscured behind a sheet of pale grey and the glare of defused light was harsh. The sea was choppy with restrained fury and the atmosphere ravaged by storm.

Down below a group of sailors came out on deck carrying a long bundle wrapped in whitish canvas. In a flash I knew that the dead sailor was inside. With senses a-tingle, I watched as the captain at whose table we dined followed and took up his place in front of the sailors who were standing around the white bundle. The captain opened a little book and read something rapidly under his breath while the sailors listened with bowed heads. Some passengers stood along the railings on the upper deck.

Then the awful thing happened. The long white bundle was lifted up and lowered by ropes over the side of the ship where the wash at the stern churned up and closed over it with a gesture of finality.

No! No! No! I sped along the deck and downstairs to our cabin where my parents were. "Please, please, save him. Don't let the fishes eat him! Please!" I flung myself at their feet and pleaded: "Please, please!"

My mother raised me up and laid me on her bunk (mine was always the top one) and put a cool compress on my forehead. "Don't, Pan, you'll get a headache if you go on like this."

"But Mummy, the fishes will eat him!" I rolled over and beat the pillow in despair. "Why did they have to give him to the fishes?"

My father said everyone has to die sometime and this was the way they buried people who died at sea. I shouldn't think that a person could feel anything at all once he was dead and, he joked (my father was a great joker and you could always tell when a joke was coming by the significant look on his face), "What about the fishes' lunchtime?"

I do not know what made him say this. I deafened myself to anything more and withdrew into the agony inside. In my head the ugly throb of a sick headache had already begun to drum.

Alone in the darkened cabin I tossed about on the narrow hot bunk. Down below the keel of the ship the sailor's body was twisting and turning around in the deeper currents of the ocean and the canvas wrapping was coming loose. Fishes sped through the dim water like a host of arrows and nosed into the drifting folds of canvas and began to nibble, nibble . . . Oh, no! No! DON'T! My whole existence wailed.

However far the ship travelled from that spot — you could never fix a spot on the ocean — however seemingly unconcerned the hours of daylight spent playing on the upper deck in a sheltered place, at night the Terrible returned the moment my parents turned off the light and left the cabin, and legions of howling wraiths chased after the ship and hauled it back to the bad place where the sailor's body was twisting and swaying in the loosening canvas folds under the keel, its features nibbled . . . nibbled . . . away . . .

I was so desperately sorry for the sailor. Everything that was *he* was being nibbled at bit by bit, he the sailor in his living moving body delivered by his companions to the sea to be nibbled to bits, to become less and less every day until . . . I couldn't think of it.

In my small world Death was still firmly enclosed in his larva, and had not yet begun his inexorable approach to my conscious mind. I did not know that he was coming from the hour I was born.

The sailor's burial at sea opened the first chink in my wall of protection against any notion of subversion and it loosened foundations which would never be wholly firm again. A draught of fear crept in that, behind everything that was lovely and brimming with life and movement, there was a subjacent force which disintegrated all Form, ultimately the Form of the body itself. Until then, the body was Life — it could not die — it was the primary evidence of eternity. If the body disintegrated, the world itself would fall to pieces . . . No!

No! No! I woke up every morning wondering that I had come through the night.

We arrived in Honolulu. The beach there was much wider and longer and less defined than the beach held in the grip of the two deadly cliffs, and it swarmed with people, bath-chairs and multi-coloured parasols.

My aunt joined us from England. She was as diminutive as my mother but whereas my mother had small deep-set steely grey eyes, my aunt's eyes were brimming pools of violet and kindliness, instantly noticeable and much admired. She had a soothing effect on my parents, especially on my father who showed her open respect and affection.

The day after she arrived from England, my aunt began to knit me a bathing-suit out of fluffy butter-yellow and powder-blue wool in broad alternating bands. My mother remarked: "She's hardly more than a baby — she can easily run around with nothing on; no one will mind." But my aunt sensed how I longed to be like others and covered. Sitting under a gaudy parasol in a voluminous black sateen bathing costume, she flicked the knitting needles so rapidly that I could not follow what they were doing, while down over her lap flowed the flood of fluff until the finished garment was put into my hands. I buried my nose in the faintly fragrant tickling softness, sneezed, kissed my aunt enthusiastically and dashed to our bathing cabin to put the garment on.

The fluffy bathing-suit caressed my skin as I emerged triumphantly to conform with the rest of bathing humanity on the beach. My aunt and my mother waved as I proceeded down to the edge of the water at some distance where I dabbled my toes for a while because I did not like cold water and was undecided as to my further course. Then — lest anyone might be looking and thinking me finical, I stepped resolutely into the water, squatted and let a wave break over me.

The wave receded in embarrassment for suddenly I was bare. A sodden mass of yellow and blue swaying in the tide clung to my ankles. Appalled, I gathered it up to hide my nakedness, but the garment seemed to be possessed by a demon of elongation against which I was no match. Flinging the wet thing over my head so as not to witness my own shame, I sat down in the hot sand. All around there was a profusion of sound — shouts and laughter, and the breaking of waves along the shore with the deep drawn out sigh that follows. Tears welled up and caught on the fine fibres of the drying wool in a bunch on my knees to hang like dewdrops until they were sucked up and replenished by more.

"Hello. Pan, why are you sticking around in the sand like that?" I looked up and saw my father. A blush spread from my face down over my shoulders. "Come on, Pan, come with me."

Cool drops of water sprang from his body on to mine and communicated a sense of abandon. I rose, the bathing-suit draped around my neck and put my hand into his. A few yards along, he loosened a little boat from a barnacled post by the pier and secured a surfboard at the back of it. He helped me into the boat, climbed in after me and pushed off, the bottom of the boat scraping on the pebbles for a moment as though one's very existence were scraping along the bottom of the world, until it was waterborne.

As my father rowed away from the shore, the swell of the waves increased and a brisk breeze was blowing. I was excited to see the beach recede into a colourful blur when I turned around from watching my father who was laughing and beautiful with his muscles playing under his fine fawn skin.

When we reached the end of the long pier, my father hailed an attendant to come and take our boat while he loosened the surfboard and slithered on to it, instructing me to climb on to his back. I parted from the rocking row-boat with a thrill of apprehension because I could not swim and had never been in deep water. The swell of the water felt alien and unaccountable but I achieved my position with some wriggling and squealing and clung breathlessly to my father's shoulders trying to keep my toes out of the cold water.

"Hold tight, Pan, we're going to ride the waves!" The ingoing sea took possession of us and swept us shorewards. A splash of brine whipped across my eyes and stung them. I let go to rub them . . .

The green water was infinitely still. Broad shafts of opaque luminescence swayed around me and as I sank into dimmer depths dark ponderous gentle forms of whales gathered forming a wall around me, closing out the last vestiges of daylight from above . . .

Back on the sun-scorched beach I opened my eyes. A crowd was standing around. The sun was a gaping hole in a vacuous sky. I shuddered. Someone laid a rug over me that was sodden with sand. Then I saw my mother.

"You idiot, did you want to drown the child?" her words cut across me like a whip. Without turning my head, I knew my father was standing on the other side and that his face was ashen.

I began to be morbid about ships and the sea. The ill omen was the appearance of our huge pigskin trunks in the hotel bedroom. While my mother and the maid packed our belongings, the pounding in my bloodstream thundered in the room even if my mother and the maid did as if they couldn't hear it. Choked down waves of terror at the impending journey to the docks would gather into a whirlpool of nausea and the bathroom door would come open just in time. I was never seasick at sea — only on land.

Outside in the street, a fleet of taxis would be lined up and the procession downstairs would begin with the departure from rooms one had just got used to, and the pigskin trunks would be lifted up like coffins containing dying existence and passed me by on the staircase out to the taxis gravely waiting for the last pieces.

My mother usually went alone to the docks in the leading taxi. How would I know where to find her again? The bulk of our luggage went unaccompanied in other taxis, which worried me into a state of feverish anxiety because — How would the taxis know the way to the docks by themselves?

I went with my father in the taxi which took up the rear of the procession and perched on top of a pile of smaller suitcases, hat-boxes, typewriters and indeterminate bags, my legs getting crushed between them as the taxi lurched around corners. I was not supposed to speak to my father on the way to the docks because he had all our papers and passports and tickets fanned out in his hand and repeatedly looked through them to assure himself that everything was in order, and when I would at last ask him to free my legs from the unbearable weight of suitcases, he would become uncertain and examine our papers all over again. "Your mother would be furious if I overlooked anything."

At the docks, I followed closely in the wake of my parents, who would be too preoccupied to take my hand through the long-drawn-out ritual of the passport and customs examination, with a tight mouth trying not to inhale the acrid smell of horses' urine in the sawdust underfoot, trying not to take in the broadside of our ship looming all down the wharf. Then, at the foot of the gangplank, terror erupted. My father would put down his bags with an oath and carry me, screaming, on to the ship.

Soon from the throbbing interior of the ship came the deafening blast from the funnel with which the ship proclaimed its impending doom, and the ominous jerk away from the ropes that held it fast to the blunt iron posts planted all down the wharf. Up on deck, I watched the tugboat pilot the ship out of the harbour which did not add to my peace of mind, for I supposed the ship was too stupid to find its way out by itself. Clinging to the railing, I waved my handkerchief enthusiastically to the crowd of people on the fading wharf although there was never anyone we knew among them because we never came from anywhere where we knew anyone.

I now performed the rites of getting to know the lay-out of the ship without being seen by my father, for the moment he caught sight of me, he put me through an examination on our ship's flags and the flags of all the other ships coming in or going out or anchored in the harbour wherever it was. He taught me that ships have a language of their own; their flags will tell you what they are going to do, where they have come from and what they carry, whether they have just come in or are about to leave or how long they are intending to stay, what their nationality is and whether they are in quarantine.

"Nationality" and "quarantine" were terms too big to fit into my head and I preferred to avoid the whole examination if I could because it forced me to take an interest in things I secretly dreaded, so I developed some skill and cunning in keeping out of my father's way until all other ships were at such a distance that their flags were no longer discernible and we were safely out on the open sea.

My mother constantly reproved me for staring at people, but left to myself day after day, I persisted in the inexhaustible occupation of staring at the passengers or the stewards who brought around the broth and biscuits halfway through the morning, or the crew when they scrubbed the decks and polished the brass on the railings. I could tell by looking at a passenger's feet whether he or she was going to remind me of an owl or a codfish or a fox, and by a face whether the ankles that belonged to it were going to be slender, cushioned or knobbly.

The auburn-haired lady in the deck-chair next to ours had hands that seemed to come straight out of her armpits. I studied her physique with care and could not dispel the curious impression that she had no arms. Her auburn hair was piled up on top of her head but there was enough left to hang down in a massive coil over the nape of her neck and between her shoulder blades and anyone could see that she looked exactly like a squirrel.

I kept the auburn-haired lady tracked. Wherever she went, I contrived to follow at a distance, maintaining a favourable vantage point whence I scrutinised her every move. Poor lady — she was seasick and hung limply over the railing, her white hands fluttering over her chest and her auburn tail heavy on her back — while I regarded what followed with clinical attention.

When at last she lay back wanly in her deck-chair, I addressed the squirrel-lady and offered to read to her to make her better. She was surprisingly indignant for someone in her plight and muttered that little girls should not pretend they can read when anyone could see that they were far too small to be able to read. The squirrel-lady was right — I could not read — I was only going on for four.

On the tiny shelf in our cabin next to my bunk lay *Peter Rabbit*, one of my most treasured possessions because of its exquisite pictures. The only flaw in *Peter Rabbit* were the pages of heavy black markings between the pictures which for some reason I could not fathom, and which occupied too much precious space in the little book.

Reading was a deadly boring habit of grown-ups, especially of my mother, and it could only be done if everyone else kept quiet. Even so, you couldn't hear what was going on because it worked like a silent clock inside her head. When my mother sat up on deck reading a book, she could have been a statue. She didn't even notice when the breeze stirred the ruffle just by her ear which *must* have tickled, which would have driven me frantic like a buzzing fly. She was so closed off when she was reading that I rebounded as though from a hard surface when I tried to gain her attention.

But now the squirrel lady was lying in her deck-chair up on deck and wasn't feeling at all well and I was fired by an urge to be of help to her. I snatched up *Peter Rabbit* and opened it. The balance of something shifted in an infinitesimal earthquake. The pictures I loved moved back away from me a little while the black markings suddenly became assertive and suggestive. I stared at them with incredulous eyes as they swam into my field of sight and at this end and that, fell into place and advanced to meet me as I marched down the line like a general taking the salute.

The squirrel lady was lying in her chair with a peaked nose and closed eyes. I landed at her side with a bounce and breathlessly read the opening words of *Peter Rabbit*. News of the miracle soon reached my parent's ears and I basked in the rare sunlight of their proud attention. There was much speculation as to how I was suddenly able to read (I hadn't yet been to nursery school). My mother thought it was from seeing so many luggage labels and names of streets and railway stations and from asking ceaseless questions. I left the analysis of my new ability to the grown-ups' findings and set myself to the practice of reading, sensing I had been given something by an invisible agent which contained untold increase if pursued with passion.

My mind was now in constant communion with words written and heard and I tasted and pronounced the words that kept streaming in upon me from all sides. My mother helped me with all kinds of words, even the ugly ones like "Ketchup" or "Gentlemen" or "No Smoking" which had unpleasant associations but which seemed to be universal on ships and in hotels and other places. Some words were like weeds in the burgeoning garden that was waxing for my very own use. It would be at times the only plot I could call my own. I never asked my father about words

Flopsy and Mopsy were twin bears each two inches long. Because my mother had given them to me, I was obsessional about them. They had to attend meals and baths and bed-time and were otherwise habitually stuffed into the back pocket of my dungarees and went everywhere I went.

I was allowed in the ship's kitchen to play with the cook's cat. The cook was Japanese, a slender man who never appeared to be doing anything but leaned back against the shelves and smiled with a shut mouth. His cat did not look Japanese at all but was striped like any alley cat prowling the streets of New York. She was a mother cat and had a big family and needed my help to look after them. Everyone in the kitchen knew that.

One afternoon when I rose to my feet stiffly having been crouching by the cat and her kittens for some time, I reached automatically into my back pocket for my bears. They were not there. I thrust my hand under the warm mass of squirming kittens. No bears. I looked despairingly around in the hot kitchen. The cook said nothing but smiled his bottled-up smile. I dashed out of the kitchen with a red face and frantically retraced my steps all over the ship, becoming more and more panic-stricken. Finally I sat down on one of the main staircases and burst into great shuddering sobs: "They're overboard!"

Passengers reported that there was talk of a man overboard. My mother appeared and whisked me down to the cabin, not wanting to have me exposed to another morbid experience, and disappeared again. The ship's engines were throttled, roll-call took place, no one was missing, but the cook opened his mouth and explained that I had not been able to find my bears.

Trusting that Flopsy and Mopsy would be restored to me after the alarm I had given, I had begun to play in the cabin. My father stepped in through the narrow doorway. He always had to bend his head to get in.

"Do you know what you have done?" His voice was

trembling with rage. I was confused. "You nearly had the captain stop the ship and all for nothing!"

I began to gasp: "Not for nothing, daddy, I couldn't find Flopsy and Mopsy . . . " My last words were lost. He swept me off my feet and spanked me, and the day ended with a sick headache.

The next morning, after a subdued breakfast at our table in the dining-room, my mother handed me Flopsy and Mopsy with a faint twinkle in her eyes, but the anguish I had undergone on their behalf suddenly seemed ill-matched with their mean two-inch bodies and tiny beady eyes. I seized the bears with loathing in my fingertips and hurled them across the dining-room. Ostracism followed. My parents disowned me, didn't know me any more before the people on the ship.

To be on a ship at sea was to be suspended in a vacuum of nothingness. Existence was only resumed at first sight of land. To be cut off from everything — from one's parents even at night at bedtime — on a ship was to die a second time over.

I stood at the stern licking the bitter salt from the life-belt fastened to the railing and peering through at the leaden sea and vacant sky. The enormity of what I had done — not hurling the bears across the dining-room, the bears my mother had given me — suddenly overwhelmed me in an onrush of shame which made me feel as though I were on fire. I had committed the ultimately impermissible — I nearly had the ship stopped! It was not because I was a child; it was because I was I that it was impermissible. By some kind of pre-natal command, prerogatives were not to be used. There was an authority in one of which one was not to make use, an adult power charged to remain incognito. In having nearly had the ship stopped, I had come dangerously near to betraying a charge, to overstepping some existential limit. Wave after wave of shame swept over me.

I heard a step behind me and straightened up. A youngish lady was looking down at me with mild contempt. Did she know my mother? "Are you a little boy or a little girl?" (I was habitually dressed in navy dungarees and my straight fair hair was cut in a fringe). Perhaps I sensed that the lady's question was rhetorical, perhaps it was a protest or a sudden disorientation or an imp that made me answer the young lady: "I'm a little boy."

The words tasted as bitter as the salt on the life-belt and fire flared up in my cheeks with renewed vehemence and exposed me to the stranger. With a look of calculated disdain she turned away leaving me alone by the railing benumbed by my double sinfulness — betrayal and untruth.

A nanny once told me that the stain of a lie would never wash out.

I bowed my head with this new trouble and suddenly felt forgiven, restored to my pristine innocence. But I remained sensitive to the incognito imposed on me from before, often to the extent of foregoing things that would have been there for me to take.

Interspersed between ships and ports and cities, there were the interminable trans-continental train journeys which not only made my body ache because of the constricted space to move about in, but which made my very existence ache. With the thud of the iron wheels along the tracks my life rubbed and thudded along the bottom: Da-dum, dadum, da-dum, dadum, lum-da, dum-da lud, mud and blood, dadud — with nose pressed against the grimy carriage window, I hummed this dirge over and over.

At certain times of the day my mother took a newspaper and with a little smirk on her face which made other passengers respond with their own smirks, she formed an unmistakeable receptacle over which I was held in front of everyone to suffer indescribably from embarrassment. When I was put back on my place, I could not raise my eyes and look around.

From the observation platform at the rear of the train where I was oddly enough allowed to be alone, I observed the landscape contract along the narrowing tube of shining steel rails in the distance and puzzled how the big wide country on either side of the train could squeeze into the tiny receding, then vanishing, point at the end. I stared so long at the vanishing point to catch the mystery of the moment that a bad headache almost always followed.

To free myself from the ache in my legs, my imagination

went out through the window of the train and clung to a farmhouse on a sunlit slope or crept into a gully between rocks and moss where a hidden brook gurgled or entered a woodlet with mottled shadows and a carpet of anemones — to turn and look back on the puffing train carrying my tortured body along in one of its many coaches. Or — I flitted along the upper edge of a cornfield gleaming in the late sun to a farmyard where the cows were coming in, their broad muzzles dripping and tails whisking, and sat down at the big table in the kitchen where a lamp was lit, yearning to sink into the huge bed upstairs that smelt of hay — whilst the train would be disappearing around a bend, shrieking, with clouds of steam rolling over its exit.

In the stuffy hotel, I stood at the window in the passage close to musty curtains:
>   Little dancing dust,
>   I-o, I-o ust,
>   Fingers and tiptoes,
>   Little dancing dust.

– my song of airlessness and vacant moments of uncertain waiting.

Music of any kind was searing. The rise and fall of a melody especially in minor shook and squeezed my heart and made it as heavy as a stone. Stringed instruments were like the sharpened blades of knives drawn over raw and open parts of one's existence. The plaintive sound of a barrel organ at the end of the street summoned up all that was dreary and bleak at the edge of the world and the military band in the park was a blunt and blatant attack on a broad front against which I had no defences. When the orchestra struck up in the hotel diningroom, a sick headache would always follow. For a long time, I was unable to establish any immunity against music. But at night in bed in the hotel when I was alone and the light was put out, I hummed songs into the pillow until it became a vibrant soundbox expanding over a threshold into a shining infinitude of sound and harmony into which I fell asleep.

Although my parents' struggles and contentions with one another went on for the most silently in ships' cabins, hotel rooms next to mine, on station platforms in the nameless moments between arrivals and departures, they were the dull persistent undertone, the subterranean river bed through which my own existence sought its course. At times I floundered and choked in their Lethe.

I loved them painfully and anxiously. At the bare thought of them, tears darted into my eyes. I yearned for them when they were in the next room and when they went out in the evenings, so beautifully dressed, either together or separately, I imagined macabre things happening to them and woke sobbing from nightmares. Every time my parents left me even briefly, I steeled myself to face the excruciating possibility of their not returning.

Yet when we were together my own existence was obliterated, my Self fragmented. The pendulum swung from my being a mere incident in the lives of my parents to their being the backdrop for my own central existence. In the one extreme I was extinguished. In the other it was I who extinguished. Only in rare moments did we form a warm and unquestionable amalgam and the pendulum came to rest like a gull in the trough of a wave.

4

We went to Holland to visit my father's mother in Friesland. It was the first time my father returned to his home since he met my mother and had me.

My grandmother still occupied the old family home, living all alone in the dim rooms in which gleamed the family silver embossed with its ancient coat-of-arms. My grandfather had died when my father was an infant, leaving my grandmother to bring up five children all of whom left the land when they grew up. The eldest became an inventor of some repute in Holland, but he lost his reason when his best friend had one of his inventions relating to traffic signalling patented under his own name, and spent the rest of his life as a mental invalid. My father's oldest sister studied law, married a wealthy theosophical tea planter in Java and died in a Japanese prison camp during the Second World War. Her twins, a son and a daughter, became lawyers as well and assisted in the Nürnberg trials of Nazi war criminals.

My father's second sister had five sons, one of whom I met later when we were both young adults. He was outstandingly handsome and had an attractive personality, and this cousin of mine and I formed a mutual attachment for a while before the War when I spent some time in Holland. When the Nazis occupied the country, he entered the Dutch Resistant Movement and worked with a married uncle until he was captured by the Nazis and tortured — his teeth and all his nails were pulled out one by one. He broke and did some desultory work for the Nazis only to be tried as a traitor to his own country after the War. He died as a broken old man at the age of thirty-three.

My father's youngest and favourite sister married an architect who became prominent in Holland, first as a hero in the Resistance, then as an architect who did a great amount of rebuilding in eastern Holland when the War was over.

My father, whom my grandmother adored, ran away from home at the age of fourteen taking all kinds of jobs, first in Holland and then overseas, picking up languages as he went. When he was seventeen, he met a wealthy South American who engaged him to be his companion and male nurse during bouts of madness and violence to which this otherwise charming man was subject. My father looked after him devotedly until the man died four years later and he always spoke of him with deepest respect and affection. In spite of his madness he must have been the father figure my own father had not had. My father inherited his export-and-import firm.

When we arrived at the village in Friesland where my grandmother's estate was, she and my father's favourite sister were at the tiny station to meet us. As we walked across the immaculate little village square, I asked: "Mummy, is this San Francisco?" a variant of the endless question: "Where are we now?"

From the first moment my mother took an undisguised dislike to my grandmother, perhaps because of her Prussian background — and our stay in Friesland was terminated not long after we arrived. I only have fragmentary memories of my grandmother's place, indeed of my grandmother herself. A blue-and-white tiled dairy smelling faintly of milk and of sea; very high ceilings; flat country near the sea; a courtyard reminiscent of a fortress; and globular silver jugs shining in singular purity on the shelves in the house; and then my grandmother's black-clad upright figure and dignified bearing, somewhat slight and unsmiling. Her full name was given to me at birth and I often wished I could have enjoyed her influence as well.

From Friesland we went down to Haarlem where my grandmother and one of her sisters-in-law owned a large house. The latter occupied the ground floor and we the middle storey. We had little or no communication with my great aunt and my grandmother herself never came to visit us.

The house in Haarlem was dark and rambling and ponderously furnished with heavily carved oaken objects. It had the distinction of having a lift, though, a large square cage with thick walls of dismally coloured glass which reminded me of disgorged carrots and invariably aroused in me a sense of dismay whenever we entered it.

My father now assumed command of our life and Dutch was the language of the day. I was proud that my mother enlisted my help when the housekeeper came to take an order or that I had to ask for a bunch of flowers she wanted to buy at the market, but at the same time, it was painful to witness the lost look on her face when my father and I spoke Dutch with other people in her presence. She was not the person to be excluded in any context — her place was always central. Fundamentally Dutch remained to her "that peasant language" and she always wore an expression of disdain when I babbled increasingly freely in Dutch, as though I had in some way let myself down. Even so our months in Holland were the most harmonious in our life as a family.

My parents began to talk of sending me to nursery school to "work off your energies." An immediate upsurge of the instinct of self-preservation made me try not to understand what they were talking about as though I would be protected from the ultimate as long as I had not grasped what was afoot. But the subject of nursery school raised every day at breakfast became abjectly familiar. However hard I tried I could not uphold the pretence that by now I didn't know what they were contemplating for me. A nursery school had been found and I was going to go.

I was not going to be able to endure the oncoming trial. To brave the New was always an ordeal. When I was taken for walks I was careful not to look down any unfamiliar street for fear of what might open up at the end of it, something I had never seen before. I refused to go and see the dykes outside the town because I had never seen dykes. The stacks of cheeses in the market square, the heavy medieval gates to the old town, canals that ran into distances, church spires piercing through the morning mists where other towns were, unaccustomed ware in dimly lit shops suddenly come upon as we rounded a corner — bombarded my fortress of the Known and the relentless pricks of new impressions hooked themselves into my mind and inflamed it.

At night in bed, I licked the wounds inflicted by the New by going over and over the impressions received until they were assuaged and I fell asleep in the embrace of the Familiar. The New was the great Predator, cruel and ruthless and always ready to pounce upon and tear to pieces my fragile little world.

Having to go to nursery school was by far the heaviest attack on my fortress so far, for it signified that I myself had advanced unwittingly on some subterranean path of time which made me ripe for things hitherto not reckoned with.

At the breakfast table I said to my parents: "But I don't even know where the nursery school is!" and scanned their faces for a sign that this argument had struck home — it did not seem possible that they could ignore it.

"Don't worry, Pan, Anna will take you there and fetch you back each morning."

The day came. I stood in the passage as stiff as a log of wood while Anna buttoned up my coat and tugged on my mittens. It was a cold day. The nursery school — Montessori — was housed in a neat one-storied red brick building at some distance from my grandmother's house. To get there we had to walk through the town along canals and over bridges. My father gave me a pair of painted *klompjes* like those the other children wore and I contributed enthusiastically to the increasing din on the cobblestones as we approached the nursery school building.

I do not know if anything untoward happened in the red brick school building. No child, no teacher emerged singly in defined contours out of a flat grey uniformity and I remember nothing other than that I was coerced into making little square baskets out of grey-blue paper which had little body and tore at the crucial moment creating a desolate atmosphere of futility around me.

And yet one morning when I crossed the street in front of the school house holding on to Anna's hand, a huge black witch rose up from behind the building and threatened me with her stick. Nothing had ever threatened me like that before. I was petrified and unable to take another step forward. Anna who was unaware of the appearance of the witch urged me to move lest I be late for nursery class. She tried persuasion, she tried argument and in the end, resorted to physical force by attempting to carry me across the street. My only chance of survival —

for the witch was now filling the sky with evil — was to wrest myself from Anna's frantic grip and fling myself on the cobblestones, screaming for help.

A deeply injured Anna took me back to my parents to whom I explained that there was a witch behind the school house and that I could not possibly go there again. "But Anna didn't see the witch" — my mother was trying to undermine my case.

"Anna's too stupid," I announced indignantly. This undoubtedly true statement brought on further disaster. My father spanked me and I was sent to bed for the rest of the day.

The next morning I felt sorry for Anna whose plump white face was set under her scarlet hat as she buttoned up my coat and pulled on my mittens. I had not wanted to be unkind. The horror of the previous day had faded like a dream and I tried to be accommodating and did not once wriggle out of the grip of Anna's podgy hand until we reached the schoolhouse. Up over the roof behind rose the witch brandishing her stick as threatening and sinister as on the day before. I was chilled to the bone with terror by the opening up of the nightmare all over again and hung back quaking and incoherent.

The identical scene took place in front of the nursery school with the same results at home only that my parents were not disposed to listen to my pleas. "Don't think that you can get away with this kind of behaviour, Pan." I took my father's spanking and went to bed relieved to have to face a lesser and more familiar evil.

A trying time began. My parents were adamant about my continuing at nursery school and pooh-poohed my "witch story" as a transparent ruse on my part to stay at home. Yet the witch was there daily behind the schoolhouse and her presence grew more deadly as her hold on my mind increased. I knew it would end with my rushing headlong into her lethal embrace and that it would then be too late to be saved. There were daily scenes in front of the schoolhouse and the daily aftermath at home. Anna gave notice and left us. I was finally withdrawn from nursery school.

My mother said that no nanny would want to look after me now and there was no one to take me for walks. My mother had met some English people and was frequently out in their company. My father went to Rotterdam for days on end on business. I was alone in the gloomy house for long tedious hours. The large forbidding rooms offered little inspiration for playing on my own, and I listened too intently for the turn of a key in the lock of the front door which meant that my mother or my father had come home to apply myself to any occupation, or rather, listening for the turn of the key *was* my occupation.

A goldfish bowl stood on the windowsill in the dining-room. The goldfish which occupied it was nominally mine for my father had given him to me, but he said that the fish's name was Shimmy (the name was associated with a kind of undergarment worn at the time) which so embarrassed me that I avoided taking real possession of the fish or having anything to do with it. But now he was the only living, moving thing in the big dim flat. I drew near to his bowl and fell to watching his streaking through the water with waxing admiration. Admiration for his abilities kindled enthusiasm and enthusiasm made me want to do something for his well-being. I would clean out his bowl and make it shine and give him fresh water as I had seen my father do.

I prepared everything in the bathroom with ritual care and took cognizance of the place in the bathroom that was never empty of water where the goldfish would be happy while I cleaned out his bowl in the basin. Stepping slowly and carefully I carried the goldfish bowl in both hands to the bathroom and gently emptied the fish into the perpetually watery place.

When after washing out the bowl and filling it with fresh water I turned to scoop up the fish and put him back in his bowl, he was not there. I stared down incredulously. The white porcelain vessel stared back with insolent emptiness. Sweat broke out all over my body. Shimmy! Shimmy! I pulled the chain to flush him to the surface but when the turbulence subsided the porcelain vessel was as empty as before. Shimmy! I wailed and wailed and pulled and pulled. A broken lavatory chain lay on the tiled floor of the bathroom and everywhere there was a terrible silence. I had drowned my goldfish! Stunned by my unwitting crime I crept into a corner of my room at the back of the flat and shuddered and sobbed and dreaded what was to come.

Later in the early evening when my parents returned, I did not run to greet them in the entrance hall, but my father soon discovered the broken lavatory chain and the empty goldfish bowl in the bathroom. To him they were evidence of unprecedented malevolence which had to be "thrashed out" of me. For days afterwards tears welled up at the slightest provocation, suddenly in the middle of a meal or out on a walk. At night when the light was turned out in my room, I sobbed into my pillow because I had drowned my goldfish and because my father could have thought I had done it on purpose.

    A new Anna came to look after me and take me for walks. I do not know who suggested that Shimmy had gone down the drainpipes to swim about in the murky canals of Haarlem, but with the new Anna, I lingered on the bridges and peered down into the brown water stirring sluggishly in the canals below and watched for Shimmy to streak past through the shadows. In the evenings when a flood of burnished sunlight poured out along the still canals, changing them into rivers of flaky molten gold, a host of goldfish rose to the surface and graced the ripples and Shimmy was among them, vibrant with life and beauty and glad to be with his own kind, and I was deeply comforted by the evidence of his continued existence.

Temper tantrums kept sweeping over me in waves, in frightening paroxysms of grief that made me want to tear myself to pieces and break up the things I loved most. I never knew when a tantrum was coming and could do nothing to ward it off. They came in dreams too and were then much worse because I was alone with their violence, rage and sorrow. My parents were openly worried and showed pity and anxiety in their handling of me. They resolved to have me seen by a child specialist.

    The man they thought of consulting lived in Ghent and we went there by train; that is, my father and I. My father sat opposite in the carriage and disappeared behind newspapers. I stared out of the window over flat country where the next town was already visible from the one we were just passing through and on the horizon all around there were steeples and towers and the great broad arms of windmills doing their cartwheels. Sometimes a town would look like an ocean going liner in the mist with smoke trailing from its chimneys as it passed.

    In Flanders the next town would be concealed behind the

long straight rows of willows with their bright orange bark stretching across the country and bent by the sea-wind, and there was an infinitesimal rising of meadow-land towards a stronger sun than in Holland. The evening mists along the rows of willows were impregnated with the afterglow of the setting sun, and hovered over the fields and over the cows with their coats on like a rosy and magical caress.

The word "Ghent" aroused intense expectancy in my mind and thrilling darts of anticipation shot through my system. I pictured the station at which we were going to arrive with golden gates and crystal lights and all the porters in red velvet. The extreme drabness of the station when the train pulled in did not disconcert me — the splendour was yet to come. As we walked through the damp streets of Ghent to the hotel, I sensed a hidden magnificence and the tingling of my nerves intensified . . .

There was a house here which I would not fail to recognize by the zodiacal signs carved on its oaken door. (I forgot my father striding at my side.) The door would open into a low-ceilinged room. A man in brown sat at the top of the bare oak table in the centre of the room. He wore a low hat — one of my family names means "low hat" — which cast a deep shadow over his face so that his features could only be guessed at. Only from very near could the gleam in his eyes be discerned . . .

Much later I dreamt about the man in brown in Ghent to whom I went for instruction about the meaning of a dream. I said in my dream: "Last night I roamed in an orchard. Ripe plums and pears and apples hung on the branches of the fruit trees and weighted them down, but there was no one there to gather them when they fell one by one to earth. Just as they fell to earth, they became tones — the purple plums, the yellow pears and the red apples. The ripened tones lay on the earth and bled into the soil. Tell me — what does this dream mean?"

The man — he was a physician — to whom I told my dream about the man in Ghent to whom I told the dream in the dream said: "The orchard was the Eden of music and the gardener was Bach who with his *wohltemperiertes Klavier* wanted to tune men's ears to hear the falling apples of Haydn, the pears of Mozart and the purple plums of Beethoven, which would be followed by ever newer harvests of music so that in times to come when men will be spiritually famished by utilitarianism, music will provide healing and nourishment. But never was the new music to break away from the original tree in the Eden of music . . . " The man in brown drew his fine strong hand out of the sleeve in which he had kept it and placed it palm downwards on the table, setting a seal on what had passed from him to myself and causing it to sink back into a long night . . .

The hotel we went to was dimly lit by gas jets and very raucous. My father and I had supper in the dingy dining-room mostly full of men. It was not easy for us to find anything to talk about and my father was markedly forced in his cheerfulness with me. As long as he was in action — skating on his slender red painted wooden skates along the frozen canals with me on a little sledge behind, flying past houses like a big bird, or carrying me high up on his shoulders as he "galloped" up the street, we were at ease in one another's company. In reflective moments we were strangers. I waited politely for what I knew was coming. After supper my father sent me to bed and went out for the evening.

Lying at rest in the big brass double bed, I listened to the clanging of the trams in the street below and to other harsh noises and the sound of voices passing by.

The strange almost sweet sensation of expectancy returned with enhanced force and took possession of me . . . I was again in the streets of Ghent riding over broad shafts of light that poured out through open doors and covered the cobblestones as with carpets. Behind there was the restrained tread of horses hooves, and silken banners hung on poles of gold at rest from the winds of the open plain. My thighs were clothed in velvet. I rode on over amber shadows through the night . . .

The brass knobbles on the ends of the bedposts caught up the light that flashed in from the streets and dull brass globes gleamed like regalia — an orb held in the cup of a hand, sceptre tilted to catch the sunray of majesty, golden symbols against folds of purple — until deep sleep obliterated the brief excursion into the wells of time.

The next day my father took me to the specialist. He and my father got on very well. They conversed in French so that I would not understand what they were talking about and laughed heartily at their own jokes. The specialist hardly took any notice of me and when he did, his eyes sidled around to different objects in the room as though he could not quite tell where I was, which made me feel tenuous and fleeting. I sat in a corner by a potted plant while my father and the specialist went on talking. At last they rose from their seats still laughing and shook hands. The specialist dangled his fingertips for a moment over my hand and looked at the wall behind me and conducted us to the door.

I followed my father down into the street. He clapped me roundly on the back and said: "There's nothing wrong with you, Pan my girl, you'll just have to learn to behave."

What had he told the specialist? Had they talked about me at all? Or was it about me that they had laughed so much? It would have been different with my mother. I would not have been paraded and then ignored to no purpose. Or had my father said something about me to the specialist that revolted him? I had once entered our cabin and found my father washing, stark naked. "Get out!" he shouted and slammed the door after me. Was it this he told the specialist?

My father said nothing more about the interview as we walked down the street but announced that we both deserved a treat. The last treat he had given me was a visit to Barnum and Bailey's in New York, a huge circus with sawdust underfoot and four arenas which couldn't be focused into one, where the ghastly white faces of clowns bobbed about and the infinitely sad faces of lions circled noiselessly round and round the arenas to the crack of the trainer's whip. Ladies in pink tights and spangles flew through the air like plucked birds with nets underneath them lest they fell to their death — a jangling market place of hidden distress and danger from beginning to end. Something age old in myself went to the circus with the child in my father.

The treat in Ghent, however, was to be of an entirely new kind. We entered a long low room in the dark and sat down in one of the rows of seats all facing the far end where there was a glaring white area of wall animated by sudden shrill flashes of black and white light in human semblance, focusing on a little man with a black moustache who couldn't keep his trousers up and was forever getting shut up in a collapsible bed that came down from the wall. His frantic undecided movements were accompanied by someone thumping on a piano somewhere in the room. My father roared with laughter and laughter came from all the rows behind and in front of us. I was in a grinding mortar of noise and glare.

After an interminable time, the lights went on and the flashing at the far end ceased. We rose stiffly from our seats and made our way to the exit. It was odd to be alive and moving after having been pulverized. I stumbled after my father with a blinding sick headache, too miserable to feel relieved that the ordeal in the dark room was over.

Outside the streets were sulphurous and damp and the smell of drains and trams and stagnant coats pressed in upon me. My father said we were going for tea. My stomach rose in revolt but I did not want to spoil things for him and did not tell him what was brewing. My mother would have known I had a headache. We sat down at a tiny table in a hot pastry shop where my father ordered chocolate and eclairs with whipped cream. I fought a losing battle with my stomach and the throb over the eye gained momentum. The visit to the pastry shop ended in disaster.

My father took me back to the hotel and saw me to bed. He wrung out a face flannel in cold water and laid it on my forehead, turned off the light and left the room. In the dark the full horror of the afternoon returned. I fought for my life with a big bed that rose up from the foot end to flatten me against the wall behind. My father was out and there was no one in the passage to hear me calling for help as the bedclothes tumbled down over my mouth and suffocated me. Sleep came while I was on the rack of the reoccurring nightmare.

For some time after the visit to Ghent, I suffered from a morbid fear of beds, especially hotel beds with crisp fresh sheets. When sheets were crumpled one had already lain in the bed and had survived.

Back in Haarlem things were no better for having been seen by the specialist. Temper tantrums became more frequent and violent. I came in from a walk one afternoon with my parents feeling as though every nerve in my body had a raw ending.

The sight of the unpleasant glass walls of the lift so irritated me that I seized hold of a bicycle that was leaning in the entrance hall and flung it against the glass walls. To the sound of splintering glass I sank down into a dark red well of oblivion.

I lay for six weeks with a silken bandage over my eyes. My mother was always in the room. I needed to make no effort to ask for anything — she knew what I wanted before it became a need. She was so gentle that I dared not think of her lest the tears came to sting my over-sensitive eyes beneath the bandage. I was submerged in a pool of love, not stirring for fear of ruffling it.

After long days of only gentle sounds in the room and the regular muted visits of the doctor who smelt like leather and had good firm hands, the bandage was removed from my eyes for a few minutes and I registered my mother's restrained joy when I named some of the objects in the room for her. She had feared that I would be blind or mentally confused as a result of very severe measles.

I had the sensation of having been through a long dark tunnel of which I only became aware when I began to emerge out of its oblivion. When the bandage came off my eyes and I looked around the room, the tunnel had begun to recede rapidly into the distance behind.

My parents and I now celebrated my return. Slowly the shapes of the furniture in the room took on definite contours, even colours, as day by day, a little more light was let in — until I was able to stand the full impact of daylight. But as the light gradually filtered back into the room where I lay, the pool of love receded too and left me on dry land where I had to begin to do things for myself and no longer enjoyed the full bliss of my mother's solicitude. Nonetheless I felt clean and new, like a snake that has sloughed a skin and lies tender and untried in the sun.

I turned with all my newborn life to my mother and my father whose welcome was a glad one and I had no doubt that a new order had been established for us all during my illness.

The doctor ceased visiting daily and I was allowed out of bed for periods of the day. I took excursions in the flat holding on to my father's hand until my head became cold and began to spin and I was caught up in his arms and carried back to my warm bed. When I was safely tucked up, my mother brought warm broth for all three of us to my bedside and afterwards, she told me about Baba Yaga and Old Peter in the forest, and then my father would sing me to sleep with Dutch nursery rhymes.

I walked around the dining-room table holding on to it with one hand. The dining-room table was round and highly polished and had thick carved legs as huge as tree trunks. I climbed up and reached the polished plateau which was as slippery as ice and where there was nothing to hold on to so that I kept sliding back to the brink, but after a final exertion I managed to stand up on tip-toe in the very centre of the table and to fly off into the room, gaining height by strenuous swimming movements, trying not to bump my head against the ceiling or scrape along the pelmets, out into the passage along to the kitchen just missing the gas jets on the way.

I flew out of the half-open kitchen window with a thrill of excitement and flitted over dark roofs and down along the canal, but not too low lest I lose height, like a bird skimming the earth in the dimness before dawn . . . until I heard the clanking of milk churns, the opening of windows and the whine of bicycles, the streets filling with people — the day beginning. Only the sun was nowhere yet and the people, the houses, the vegetable carts were colourless like an under-exposed negative.

I flew on to the playground behind the nursery school where the children were playing with their teachers like dancing grey shadows. I flew low over their heads. They caught sight of me circling above them and shouted to me without sound. The teachers did not look up but tried to regain the attention of the children and shut me out. I laughed and rose higher and dangled my shadow in front of them and knew they saw it. Higher and higher I rose in the bright morning, shaking everything off like redundant feathers, and flew away from there.

When I was fully well and strong again, we left Holland and returned to Japan. On the ship something very important to the grown-ups happened.

Earlier in a park in New York or somewhere else, a nanny said to me: "Don't be naughty or the Germans will get you."

When I sneezed in the presence of my mother, she said: "You've got a Germ." A connection evolved in my mind — a Germ-an was a tiny mosquito-like insect flying around in great masses of dark cloud somewhere beyond Haarlem, often swarming over places where people lived and even reaching out to sea and engulfing ships, causing dull chronic dread and subdued discussions among grown-ups on board on how to destroy them.

When my father tried to explain to me what Germ-ans were, I formed with a degree of prescience a picture of mechanically jointed insect-men in black, marching along harrowed horizons and exuding lethal fumes. My mother would not allow my father to speak of my Prussian grandmother as though he could be criminally implicated. But now something miraculous had happened and there was no longer any danger of Germ-ans. They had been wiped out and there were long loud parties in fancy dress on board and people danced to raucous music until dawn.

5

I rode around the park in Tokyo on my brand new wooden tricycle with newspaper photographers in my wake, for mine was the first tricycle to be seen in Japan. I demonstrated how the tricycle worked to admiring groups of people and children by lowering my head and pedalling furiously along the paths, taking the curves with the abandon the slightly wobbly wooden wheels allowed. The taste of notoriety was sweet.

Then — Iain, the fat little American boy from our hotel who was just my age, rode into the park on *his* tricycle, which had a shiny steel frame and rubber tyres on spoked wheels. Public attention swung over to Iain and I was left to make my entries into the park on my wooden contraption along side paths, unnoticed, while beyond the shrubs, Iain claimed the adulation of the crowd. My mother tried to comfort me: "Still, yours was the *first* tricycle" — and she kept the newspaper cuttings with photographs of me on my tricycle for years afterwards.

Iain's parents were actors and they and my parents immediately took to each other and spent a lot of time together. It followed that Iain and I would spend our time together.

Iain was the first child I encountered at close quarters, apart from the amorphous group in the nursery school in Haarlem. I had not been initiated in the rites, codes and taboos of children's play, whereas Iain was already a master. Then there was the modesty of my mount in comparison with the shiny magnificence of his, which set a chasm between us from the beginning. I was no match for such competence; Iain found other children in the park to play with and I spent my time watching the colourful ducks on the pond.

Not long after, tricycling came to its own end. My mother took me to a young Japanese doctor to be vaccinated against smallpox. I leaned back against her while the doctor scratched a double patch on the inside of my right calf and had a curious sensation of fate while I looked on; it was as though something in my life were coming to an end.

A night or two later, I woke with violent throbbing all down my leg and moaned with pain. My mother came in and turned on the light. There was an angry red streak all down the leg and swelling in the groin. I was seized by a chill and my teeth chattered uncontrollably. The room seemed to be full of people. My father was in the background looking anxious. I heard the word "hospital" and my mother's angry objections — she was going to look after me herself, enough harm had been done already.

After an interminable time, the room emptied and the light was turned off. My mother stayed with me in the dark. As if from a vast distance, I heard her wringing out compresses. The trickle of water into the basin sounded like torrents pouring down from steep rocky heights.

Then came dragging days in the hotel room when the swelling in the groin gradually went down and the red streak along the leg faded away. My mother was on edge; she had been up with me for nights. She now lay sleeping in the next room and my father came in to look after me. It needed a great effort to adapt to the change and to take his well-meaning jokes without crying. But he tip-toed around the room and was gentle and I fell in with his game of attending on his "little Japanese princess," to experience unspeakable relief when he was gone. When I was better, I felt old and dried up and had the sensation of my flesh rustling like tissue paper when I moved about.

As I was not allowed to walk beyond the door of my room in the hotel, my mother procured a push-pram in which she took me out to the park. These excursions were an ordeal, for I was past five and was ashamed of what people would think to see my slender little mother pushing me, a big child, around. When my mother grasped what was worrying me, she changed our daily route and we ventured further into the city through unfamiliar streets where we stood less chance of meeting any Europeans we knew by sight. My mother pretended she was my rickshaw woman and I was allowed to give her my orders when I wanted to stop and gaze into a shop window. From my push-pram, I would address people who passed by and my mother took pleasure in the surprise it elicited to hear a European child speak Japanese.

My mother and I had never been so close, nor were we ever to be so close again. This illness seemed to be more hers than mine; that is, hers was the active part in it and it made her warmer and more animated in her relation to me, whereas I was consumed by it and greatly debilitated, in spite of the closeness to my mother. But these days did not last.

My father had gone to Shanghai and had not returned when he said he would. My mother began to type for hours on end in the next room. She couldn't be disturbed, she said, because she had to earn some money or we would not be able to pay the hotel bills. I was left to myself, because there was no nanny either.

I sat in a big armchair at the window of my little room, a rug over my knees, and the butler came in, bringing my meal on a tray. My mother had gone down to the dining-room by herself, because she said she had a lot of thinking to do. The butler was excessively fat and old and too preoccupied to linger and talk with me, besides he refused to speak Japanese with hotel guests and his English was so poor that I could not follow what he said.

I tried to take a long time over my meals to fill the blankness of the hours I spent alone, confined to my room. I fingered a teaspoon which lay on the tray, twirling it round and round. To my horror, it suddenly broke, but to my greater horror, the broken spoon did not fall apart because it had a cardboard spoon inside it; it was only half dead.

A mixture of feelings took hold of me; I was ashamed and frightened at having broken a spoon belonging to the hotel for which my mother would have to pay when she didn't have any money, but I was more profoundly shocked that something that appeared to have virtue like a silver spoon would have a cardboard spoon inside it. Unquestionable trust in appearances was suddenly and rudely shattered.

I was abundantly bestowed with enthusiasm for coloured balloons, red ribbons, motley chocolate boxes, velvet surfaces and shiny beads, but the concealed cheapness within the silver spoon undermined the world of colourful and bright appearances and injected pessimism and a fear of expecting too much of things. Although I continued to crave for shiny things, it was the craving I craved for and not the object itself. I did not want what I wanted and Christmases and birthdays became complicated occasions: I could not bear being given anything by anyone except by my mother. I still trusted what came from her hands.

I sat again in the armchair by the window. It was raining. The grey curved slate tiles on the roofs outside glinted dully in the wet and stretched monotonously as far as I could see. Down the window panes ran the raindrops. Whenever a drop seemed to be winning the race, it halted without reason and another drop came darting crazily down past it. Beyond was the endless static sea of slate tiles. My gaze shifted from the dull grey outside to the futile racing of the raindrops down the window-panes and a thought formed in my head — a thought I knew I was thinking: What is the sense of it all? The moment this thought emerged, it fastened itself to my mind like a leech and at times grew fat there. It was always present, even in my most enthusiastic and zestful moments.

6

My parents came to the old farmhouse in Connecticut for occasional weekends. The large low-ceilinged bedroom upstairs with the rose-patterned wallpaper and hand-woven old-rose rugs was reserved for them. My own room was a tiny wooden cell in the attic with a narrow window looking east. The passage to my room was lined with cedar chests for keeping linen and winter clothing in and the whole attic was spiced with the fragrance of the reddish cedar wood.

For a while David was my almost constant companion. We went with the men when they gathered in the hay and sat on the edge of the field, watching them pitch the hay on to the carts, making a mountain on top of which we were allowed to climb while the horses started off on the journey back to the barn with a jerk which made us fall over and shriek with delight. David and I would see who could burrow deepest into the hay and back in the farmyard would squeal with excitement — at least I would — when the men said there were two mice in the hay.

David and I sat on the stone wall at the bottom of the garden, our arms around one another's shoulders, watching for caterpillars and worms and other creeping insects. David's black hand dangling near my cheek was as much a part of me as was my own hand dangling near his cheek. We were neither separate from one another nor were we separate from the world around us. In the summer's heat, we melted into the universal mind of the sun where everything that is separate merges into one in quivering warmth.

After a time I would weary of watching for caterpillars and would wriggle about on the stone wall, not finding comfort in its hardness any longer, waiting restlessly for something to deliver us from the primeval state of ponderous sluggishness in which worms and caterpillars loomed like leviathan harbingers of early stages of evolution when time proceeded in aeons, while David gazed on entirely abandoned to the hot humming atmosphere.

All at once, there came a shrill call from the kitchen door: "Somebody's wanted to crack nuts!" I sprang off the wall like a shot, while David gathered up his body with a veiled look in his dark eyes and followed me to the stone threshold of the back door where old Mrs White stood waiting for us with a basket of walnuts in her hands.

I began to apply my energies unrestrainedly to cracking walnuts while David, inwardly still watching for caterpillars, lethargically split a nut now and then. When we had cracked them all, our walnuts were put into the ice-cream churn with cream and sugar and churned, and we all had walnut ice-cream for supper.

David was at home in a farmhouse at the other end of the village. His adoptive mother, to whom the farmhouse belonged, was a writer who championed the negro cause. She often went to the city and was away for days, leaving David to old Mrs White to be looked after.

On days when David stayed at home with his adoptive mother, I betook myself to the pig-run in the orchard and spent hours trying to ride the pigs, chasing and hoping to be chased, for pigs have a garbled sense of things if any sense at all, or I perched on the stone wall marvelling at their pluglike snouts as they snuffled among the fallen apples, spiral tails whirling around in reverse.

Raggedy Ann accompanied me wherever I went. Her beady black shoe-button eyes saw what I saw. Her inverted hidden ears heard what I heard, but the ambiguous half-smile on her cloth face showed that she often did not think what I thought — she often disapproved. I was always slightly in her debt.

The afternoon had drawn on and I went up to the house for supper at the given time. Raggedy Ann stayed behind in the pigsty. I remembered her only the next morning. I leapt out of bed when she entered my mind, my entire skin aflame with shame and alarm: how would I be able to face her contempt at what amounted to a gross breakdown in responsibility on my part.

Anticipation of Raggedy Ann's disdain was bad enough; I had not expected her total demise, for down in the pigsty only fragments of her existence remained. Her body and clothing were in shreds, scattered in offal and mud. On the battlefield where she had been assassinated the enemy scampered madly around, wriggling tails and grunting wantonly.

How was I going to live without Raggedy Ann? I was unnerved. I retreated to the stone wall, my feelings lying like faggots on the funeral pyre in my aching heart — memories of what she had said yesterday, of her new blue dress made by old Mrs White, of her cool companionship. In the heat of my grief I hated pigs.

I raised my eyes to look upon those who had done this unspeakable thing with punishing wrath. Beneath the apple trees, the pigs were at their rooting, pigs kept by man for man to kill, wrested out of some divine order in which pigs had been kept for the glory of God. What were they guilty of? The infinite sorrow of "pighood" came to me; it spoke through their tiny knowing eyes, glistened on their flattened snouts, pricked in the coarse bristles on their naked pink bodies. A lump of compassion formed in my throat and found relief in the torrent of tears wept for pighood and Raggedy Ann and myself.

Thunderstorms were frequent and violent. When a storm was gathering, all the windows had to be shut lest a draught conduct an electric current through the house, and we would sit in the stuffy parlour while the lightning played outside in the swaying treetops and the thunder boomed overhead. Someone said that God was shifting grand pianos around in heaven. This had a bearing on my later musical preferences and for a long time, the piano remained for me God's instrument, albeit I never played it myself.

Out in the fields, the men were fetching in the last hay. A storm brewed up rapidly and on the horizon, snake lightning played wickedly against towering black clouds. David and I were lifted on to a half-empty cart and driven back to the farmhouse where we arrived just as the storm broke. My father, who had come from the city for the weekend, stood at the front door as though he had been sent before the storm and lifted me down from the cart and carried me indoors. David followed.

My father was about to shut the front door when a thunderbolt entered and proceeded up the staircase and, as was later discovered, out through an open attic window. The flowered wallpaper was seared all the way up the stairs and there was a faint acrid smell in the wake of the bolt. I took it for some kind of divine manifestation and was profoundly impressed. What did God want to say? Did God always come like this? Was God dangerous? I had no concept of God; only a numinous feeling of divinity.

In this same storm, the princely maple tree on the front lawn was struck and cloven right down to its roots. In the days that followed, my father tirelessly swung an axe, felling the tree and splitting the wood into logs. I gathered the chips that flew into burlap bags for lighting the kitchen stove and helped to stack the logs around the back of the farmhouse. It was reverent labour — putting things into order after a royal progress.

A thunderstorm broke out at night after I had gone to sleep and the stables belonging to a wealthy riding horse owner next door were struck and set on fire. I woke to see the angry reflections of flames flickering ominously and fitfully on the walls of my room like a horrible script recording an unspeakable horror, while the rain hammered furiously on the attic roof and thunder cracked like whips across the sky.

Wide awake now in my bed, I distinguished screams in the turmoil of the storm. I groped my way to the window which was sheeted with rain and discerned a terrible scene. The grooms who worked in the stables were trying to rescue the frantic animals from the burning buildings. The horses were rearing up on their hind legs, screaming with anguish and fright, their nostrils rent with terror, dragging their helpless grooms behind them. I wrestled with the latch of the window: "Help them, help!"

My father was suddenly in the room, his eyes alight with compassion. He drew me gently away from the window, laid me back in my bed and tucked me up, but how could I be consoled although he was almost more gentle than my mother ever was? His clothing was wet right through.

"Never mind, Pan, they'll be alright." He closed the shutters firmly; the room became dark and the din was excluded. But the leaping flames around the rearing horses were branded into my mind and the screams of agony echoed on inside as I flitted along the threshold of burdened sleep, starting and shuddering and taking little comfort from my father's firm warm hand on my shoulder and his voice more vibrant than usual.

The next morning I had a temperature and was ill for a few days. My father was silent about the storm and said nothing about the fate of the horses before he returned to the city. No one else said anything either but I heard bit by bit that about half the horses had to be shot because of extensive burns and very many died that night.

For a long time the hell of this storm lingered on and animated the wallpaper in my room at night, engraved there in invisible ink which only needed the dark to bring it out in blood red luminosity, and I again saw the long cruel fingers of fire tearing at the silken hides of the frenzied horses that rose up in agony and filled the sky with their dying screams.

On Thursday nights old Mrs White, the farmer's mother, harnessed the mare to the buggy and drove over the Devil's Elbow down to a small town some miles away to attend a Quaker meeting. On a few occasions she took me with her so that I would not be alone in the house at night.

The Devil's Elbow was a sharp bend over a steep decline and it was terrifying to drive down there in the buggy with the poor mare straining back on her haunches, her hip bones protruding through her muscles as she edged warily down the precipitous dirt road, the buggy creaking in its joints as though it were about to disintegrate.

Old Mrs White held the reins hard and the veins on the backs of her hands swelled like the roots of gnarled trees. The black cloth sides of the buggy flapped like raven's wings on the way to doom.

It was no less harrowing to ascend the Elbow on the way back. It would be pitch dark and abysses opened up on either side of the steep narrow road. The mare strained upwards, snorting and huffing, her head bobbing violently and her shoulders awry, just visible in the amber light of the paraffin lamp which hung crazily from the shaft.

When we arrived in the little town at the bottom of the long decline that tapered down from the Elbow, we clattered along the main street beneath the boughs of maple trees until we reached the white wooden Meeting Hall which was lit up by paraffin lamps. Old Mrs White unharnessed the mare and led her around to the stables at the back of the building, while I merged into the gathering of quiet voiced, grave and kindly women inside. I would be given a cup of hot chocolate and a piece of cake before being put to sleep on a heap of rugs behind a screen at one end of the hall where it was warm and dark. I dozed off with the sound of singing in my ears and later the low murmur of conversation, seasoned by the crackling of the logs in the great iron stove in the corner.

The women worked in groups, sewing patchwork quilts for missions out east, each at her own corner, while the younger women and girls cut fresh pieces of coloured gingham and handed them to the sewers.

The company was utterly silent for stretches of time and these silent intervals were filled with potency, and I woke up into them with alert senses . . . The night opened up like a deep well at the bottom of which the stars sparkled. My mind reached out for a silver bucket to draw the mystery from the well of the night and gazing into the profound ground of the universe, I discerned a faint texture of silver threads spun from star to star — a glistening loom upon which patterns of existence were woven in eternity, and straining my every nerve, I tried to trace my own eternal pattern . . .

Late in the night I would be roused by old Mrs White who would be in a hurry to go home. I would be given a large piece of white bread and butter and another cup of chocolate while she went round to the stables to fetch the mare and buggy.

We would set off in the dark to face the ordeal ahead — sometimes with the moon shining through the slits in the buggy's shabby black cloth bonnet.

7

We occupied a flat in an old Dutch house in the Dutch district downtown in New York. Everyone else in the house was Dutch as well; below us the "chocolate family", makers of a prominent brand of Dutch chocolate, and above us the Historian. The latter who befriended my father presented me with his *Outline of History for Children*, a large flat book with illustrations in india ink done by himself.

On the inside cover of the book, the Historian had drawn a picture especially for me: at the bottom of the left-hand corner, there was my father and me out for a walk. Diagonally a little higher, there was my grandfather wearing his golden chain of office, then came my great-grandfather ploughing in Friesland, my great-great grandfather who owned the first printing press there, and in ascending line back through the centuries, remoter ancestors followed until nearer the summit of my genealogy, features coarsened and became heavy, displaying fanglike teeth as they fished from houses on stilts in the water, then brandished clubs in the mouths of caves. Finally on the peak of my lineage, a Pretender sat on the sacred place among the gods, stealing my birthright. What grim joke had the Historian in mind when he drew that picture for me?

When my mother had guests, I had to fetch the book and show it around with the famous man's dedication inside.

Noel was eight; he looked like Ganymede, someone said. His mother was American — a short, round, honey-haired widow of an English socialist who came over on the Peace Ship. When my mother spoke of the English socialist on the Peace Ship, he seemed to stick out at right angles from decent society and I concluded from the tone of her voice when she referred to him that socialists were a particular kind of hobo.

I often spent nights with Noel and his mother when my parents were out of town or gave parties in our flat. We had breakfast in their tiny chilly kitchen on cracked plates while Noel and his mother conversed in Latin and ancient Greek across the table. Noel's mother was a private tutor in classical languages. I do not know how she and my mother met.

Noel was almost like the brother I always longed for, but not quite, yet we were a great deal together for a time and our relationship lasted intermittently into our adult years.

We assiduously practised what had not been forbidden because no one knew we were doing it. It was to satisfy Noel's insatiable curiosity as to what New York was like inside.

We travelled uptown on the subway to Central Park, visited the zoo and roamed through the Metropolitan Museum; or we went downtown on the elevated to the Battery to inspect the Aquarium, a large rotund building containing big and small fish and lots of frightening reptiles; or we went inside the Woolworth Building which was a particularly precarious venture because my father had an office in it at the time.

Not being in a position to have our excursions financed legitimately, because our mothers would never have allowed us to so roam freely in the city, we had to find capital by other means. Noel was convinced — no doubt a legacy from his English father on the Peace Ship — that society owed us something, and he would stop a stranger on the street and ask for two dimes for the elevated, and the stranger would inevitably give — probably not because his social conscience was pricked, but because Noel's golden curls and English accent were irresistible.

We took the launch over to the Statue of Liberty standing guard out in the harbour of New York, her feet washed by oily waters and her head swathed in the murky atmosphere exhaled by countless big and small boats sailing in and out every day. This was our keenest adventure and one which taxed the scope of my own ability to experience the full dimensions of New York City, which always had for me something threatening and sinister about it. But on the way over, the buoys rang out in response to our passing as though they expected us, which gave some sort of assurance that we were still contained in the order of things.

When we arrived, I was astonished to see that the Statue of Liberty was not standing on the water at all as I had always assumed she was, but was solidly planted on a star-shaped concrete island. We entered her great body which was just like a building inside with ticket booths and a lift, and mounted up into her forehead where Noel explained that we were now in the forehead of a goddess looking through her divine eyes over New York Harbour, she being well aware of our presence in her divine mind. It seemed she was in reality the goddess Athene. I had not encountered Athene yet.

Rather I was secretly and feverishly worrying how we were going to get back, for I was frightened of the turgid waters of the harbour and terrified of the Battery which was bleak and dark and filthy and where huge carthorses lumbered past from the wharves. What if Noel couldn't find the way? What if we got lost in the grimy, obliterating fog that sometimes came in from the harbour? Who would know where we were?

On Sunday mornings we sauntered up Madison Avenue in the sunshine, scrutinising the mansions of the rich and observing them getting in and out of their limousines in fur coats. Noel explained that in reality, all these people were *hoi polloi* whereas *we* were aristocrats of the spirit and dwelt in the rarefied atmosphere of the mind. I was not sure that I had a mind of my own yet, but to live up to Noel's fastidious and erudite world at the age of six certainly forced a degree of temporary precocity upon me.

We heard that there were real bathrooms at Grand Central Station where people could have baths while waiting for their trains. This was at a time when not every flat had its own bathroom and so we felt obliged to explore the unheard-of sophistications of Grand Central Station. We took the subway to our destination, wormed our way through the crowds at the Station and invested our quarters in the slots of the bathroom doors, but once inside, each of us was so over-awed at the prospect of stripping and having a bath in the middle of a big station in broad daylight that we emerged out of our bathrooms simultaneously, unabluted.

On rainy afternoons we repaired to my parents' flat when they were out and strung chocolates on black sewing thread and let them down out of the window to the pavement below where they lay waiting for someone to come along. We were all too often witness to frailties in human nature, for it was always more often than not adults who, thinking they were unobserved, stooped to pick up the chocolate. Just as they would be about to pop it into their mouths, it would be jerked upward by an invisible hand and two pairs of invisible eyes from behind voile curtains stared coolly down upon poor Tantalos below. We became expert in this pastime and exhausted ourselves in its lovelessness.

Then Noel moved out of town with his mother and I reverted to Earnest Thompson-Seton's bear stories from which I derived my mental nourishment at the time, relieved to abandon the heights of spiritual aristocracy and be a *hoi poloi*, bear loving member of the masses.

In the flat (it was now another flat) I often heard the word "Chicago" and gathered that my father frequently went there. The way my mother referred to Chicago was charged with tension and I sensed that in some obscure way, it was related to a person — a third person.

Yet on Sundays when my father was back in New York, we dressed in our best and went for dinner to the Brevoort Hotel where my father always reserved the same table for us with a single red rose in the centre for my mother in an effort to secure things, and everything swelled with hope when my mother looked across the table at him with acknowledgement in her grey eyes. But there were times when she was too withdrawn to notice the rose or, if she noticed it, to attach any meaning to it, or she was visibly bored by the Brevoort which she considered bourgeois to the extreme and was icily untouched by all my father's attentions.

On such occasions the rose was an open wound in the matrix of our togetherness which could not be assuaged, and all anxiety held down came to the surface and burst out in odd remarks and disjointed motives. My father's manner would then become warped; he would begin to crack bald jokes in a loud voice and attract the attention of people at neighbouring tables, and the look of disdain on my mother's face would become fixed.

My father would the jump up and walk jauntily over to the

band and get them to play something for me, dispensing lavish tips as he did so. He had never grasped that I experienced music of any kind as torture. The band embarked on "The March of the Tin Soldiers". I ate my ice-cream slowly, trying to seal my ears against the blast of the brass instruments, saving the large red strawberry that balanced on top of the ice-cream mound for a final consolation. I did not at first notice that my father had "stolen" the strawberry and popped it in his own mouth. When I discovered it was gone, he was grinding his jaws jocularly and patting his stomach to indicate how delicious the strawberry had tasted. Tears welled up and fell on my lap in spite of my trying to squeeze them in. My father muttered with sudden coldness that he thought I could have taken a little joke. When we went out for our coats, my mother looked as though she had nothing to do with either of us.

Weeks came without dinners at the Brevoort Hotel on Sundays. My father was absent in Chicago. My mother took me to a school uptown for the mornings where the children raced around and threw their spinach at the walls of the dining-room during meals under the clinically observant eyes of the teachers. I froze within my inhibitions and could not respond to the liberating spirit of this school. My mother withdrew me after a short while and I was back in the flat with no schooling and nothing to occupy me save my books.

My mother was worried and tense and rarely spoke to me. When she did, it was about money in a way that was frightening because it seemed that without it, we could not live. The fact of my own existence appeared to make things worse.

My father suddenly came back to the flat speaking neither to my mother nor to me. He sat in the big armchair in the sitting room behind the *Herald Tribune* as though we didn't exist. When he got up, I followed him around shyly, hoping for a sign of recognition, but I seemed to have dropped out of his world.

My mother went down to the shop for groceries at the corner of the street. My father had retired behind the newspaper again, but I was sure that he would talk to me now that we were alone: "Daddy, daddy," I whispered. He gave no sign that he knew I was there. I leaned forward and touched his knee. He sprang up, flinging the newspaper on the floor, seized me and thrashed me. My mother came in.

There was a terrible breach and everything, even the impermissible, was said. My name was tossed about between them. My father went into the next room and slammed the door. Lying face down on the sofa with a beginning sick headache, I heard him packing and later, a door slammed again — the front door.

8

Our large travel-battered pigskin trunks were out in the sitting room and their familiar smell filled the flat. "Are we going to Chicago, Mummy?"

"No, darling, we're first going to Italy which you will love" — Italy was my mother's promised land — "and on the way back, we'll stop in England to visit your aunt."

Three days before we sailed, Fate advanced.

Our trunks having been sent to the docks, my mother and I went to Brentano's to buy books to read on the boat. She said I could choose three books for myself and left me in the children's department where I began a tour of the counters until a heap of my choice of books formed at the end of the counter.

My mother came down from upstairs to fetch me. I showed her the books I had chosen; there were nine in all. She was slightly amused at the exorbitance of a six year old, but pointed out that she had said I could have three books. My head grew hot. My mother told me to hurry and not make a fuss but choose the three books I most wanted. "I want them all." I whispered. "Do as I say or you'll have no books at all."

I became confused and incoherent; the nine books could now not be taken apart — the sibylline number of nine seemed to have some binding magic of its own. To put some of them back would be like taking the bottom out of a boat before you set sail.

My mother's frown was a storm warning. I went up to a stout woman in a green tweed suit standing nearby. "Please help me; I need nine books and my mother will only let me have three."

I did not take in the answer the woman in the green tweed suit gave to this untoward plea, but only perceived that all nine books were being parcelled up by the saleswoman. Nor did I take in the fact that my mother and the woman in green were deep in conversation. The saleswoman handed the heavy parcel to me. I went to the strange woman who seemed like a nebulous green cloud to thank her and followed my mother out of the bookshop. She was silent on the way home.

When the ship pulled out of the docks and was under way past the Statue of Liberty, known to me clandestinely, I realized I was not alone with my mother. In the cabin adjoining ours, there was a florid dark-haired young woman who demanded all my mother's time. My mother explained to me that she was a well-known actress and that she, my mother, was for the present acting as her secretary to earn our living. The actress had paid our fares. I was to keep this in mind and be my "most politest self."

I had my meals by myself at a little table in a corner of the dining room and was attended by a friendly elderly waiter. My mother and the actress occupied a table in the centre. I hardly saw my mother to speak to.

I watched the crew scrubbing the decks. "Where is this ship going to dock?"

"In Plymouth, lassie."

"Where's Plymouth?"

"In England."

When one stared at the sea long enough, it became gelatinous with a thick scum like rubber that would hold you up if you slipped down the side of the ship on to it. It would bounce a little under your weight at first, but if you were careful, you could walk away towards the horizon off the edge of the earth . . .

The ship docked at Plymouth early in the morning. It was foggy. My mother had packed my things the night before. My aunt was on the pier to meet me. I went ashore, leaving my mother on the ship which was sailing on to Cherbourg. My aunt waited patiently with me while the ship was being unloaded and reloaded — because I did not want to be the first to part; I thought it would upset my mother to see me going off with my aunt.

PART 2

9

Months went by shrouded in dampness that hung over iron-fenced enclosures to and from which we marched in double column, eyes cast down as though on the pavement were to be found the only sense in existence. "Are you looking for sixpence? Head up!" I again became aware of the straw boater on my head with a sense of ignominy.

There were long chocolate brown passages, refectory tables on which the same menu appeared every week, and my lovely birthday cake baked for me by my aunt shut up in a cupboard behind glass, diminishing rapidly by some mysterious means before my eyes, and the inexplicable regimentation of things that hitherto hadn't seemed to exist. Only at weekends when my older cousins came to fetch me out to my aunt's gracious home in Cheltenham was any sense of life or meaning restored to my existence.

But with the chocolate brown passages and the dampness behind me, I now ran along the steep bank of the Hudson River with the wind in my face. The bracken on the path was light brown, frail and brittle and the faded grasses bent to the wind and dryly whispering as I passed by.

In the distance around, the woods rising on the ridges were aflame along the horizon and on the banks above the river, the scarlet berries of the sumac trees glowed like drops of blood against the deep blue sky. There was a faint smell of decay in the autumn wind that filled me with elation, and a feeling of relief that lushness and saturated life were dying back to earth, leaving the shimmer of light hovering over the earth clear and transparent.

A song sang in my blood as I ran on up the bank into the

presence of a god. I paused and took in the width of his sanctuary from the crest of the hill, breathless and awe-struck.

The sky was burning from the setting sun and the scarlet forests heaved over the ridges and down into the hollows in tidal waves of flame. Above, the sky was darkening into radiant indigo lit up from beyond, and the stars had begun to prick through like the characters of a glistening script written in that bright world beyond the blue vault above. I burst in upon his Presence like a prodigal. Who was he who manifests in the garment of autumn, in a robe of fire?

There were clay quarries in the district. The broad stream of the Hudson flowed beneath the banks in which the quarries gaped like titanic wounds. Back off the river there was open rolling country with isolated farms here and there.

I discovered a rabbit colony in a sandbank nearby which occupied a massive warren in the yellow hollow. When I first came upon it over the top of the sandy ridge, the legions of rabbits took alarm and vanished, leaving the hollow empty and desolate. The wind sighed in the tall grasses and its after-moan could be heard in the sumac trees. The red berries seemed almost as black as the tones of a dirge.

(There seemed to be no school to go to.) I headed for the rabbit warren every morning, stealing up the sandy slope from below or approaching it from above, shoes filling and becoming leaden with the weight of sand, only to see the last of the rabbits scurrying into their holes, profoundly disturbed that they feared me; they must have known who I was.

Lying flat on my stomach, I stared down into the vacant hollow and pleaded with the Spirit of the Rabbits to infuse his folk with confidence and encourage them to remain outside when I came to visit. As a result of my supplications, things changed. When I now appeared over the ridge, there would be a brief flurry of disappearance, but then, one by one, the rabbits ventured out of their holes, crouched in the entrances, sniffing, popping back again — I supposed because they had forgotten something — and reappearing to hop further afield, and gradually the silent empty hollow became alive with activity.

I attached great significance to all rabbit business — nibbling, scratching, ear-twitching, nose-twitching, chasing and hopping, chewing, preening and sitting up. The pattern of rabbit existence lay open before me like a vast animated book, passages of which I gradually knew by heart, but always when I finally arose and brushed the sand off my front to leave for the house because evening was not far off, I took an enigma with me which made me feel I was taking an alien world by violence.

Winter came. Rabbits, foxes, weasels and other creatures which abounded in the district went to earth, and deep drifts of snow crowned the ridges and filled the crevices in the quarries and levelled everything off into a white infinite. Bitter winds blew from the north.

Until now I had put off any conscious appraisal of my situation. Winter brought it home to me: I was with the woman in the green tweed suit. I learned that my mother had handed me over to her that day in Brentano's when I had asked for help in the matter of the nine books. In that moment of mental incontinence, I had caught the inexorable attention of Fate.

The woman in the green tweed suit was now "responsible" for me and was going to "support" me until I was eighteen, provided my mother would "do her part." These phrases used to chisel out my present circumstances were repeated daily. I tried hard to embark on themes of conversation which allowed for no reference to my person, but even the remotest themes had a way of veering round like the keel of a boat in an adverse wind and heading straight for the rocks. It was not that I disliked her; only with her my life took a totally alien course.

Yet I was dimly aware from the beginning that it was I who had singled her out. I sensed I had an account to settle the nature of which was buried deep in Time and that everything else was to recede out of my life until that was done. I had delivered myself into her hands to clear an existential debt which was not a matter of a mere nine books; it was an indisputable hurdle that had to be taken before life went on.

Miss Tyler had long white hair pulled back unmercifully from her face which was square and belligerent, and "done" in a heavy knot on the nape of her short thick neck. At times this hair turned a dull greenish ivory and she would wash it in laundry bluing to restore its whiteness. Her eyes were small and ice blue. Her nose was short and blunt and the skin on her cheeks hung loosely, also round her chin whence it cascaded downwards and trembled as she walked. Although she was stout, she was not properly filled out, it seemed to me, and I concluded, although I did not like to dwell on it, that her skin had stretched beyond its original elasticity leaving it like a flaccid sack with a great weight inside.

Yet she was square and her body was oddly wooden when one inadvertently came up against it. Her hands were covered with paper-like skin and she had pudgy blunt fingers with rasping fingertips. When she touched me, she was inclined to grasp and slow to let go.

Miss Tyler was commanding in appearance and bearing and when she walked, she came down heavily on her heels and walked like a man in big broad shoes. Her voice was deep and mannish. She habitually wore green — green tweed in the winter, green striped tailored dresses when it was hot.

Miss Tyler had a sister — Dorothea — who was younger than herself and who had had an "operation". Her hair was soft and brown and unkempt, her eyes a little protuberant and her cheeks often flushed and damp. When she became excited which was frequent, her voice screwed up to a high pitch and dwindled away in an indignant squeak. The "operation" from which she had an unsightly scar on her throat was a standing fact in the household and often referred to which I found both distressing and embarrassing. But Dorothea never addressed me directly and I didn't have to talk with her.

Miss Tyler's father, the General, occupied a tiny wooden room upstairs in the attic apart. He was in his nineties and had fought in a war long before anyone was born. Although he shuffled along on a stick, there was something in his carriage lacking in others.

General Tyler was now "simple" and he sometimes spoke oddly at the table, breaking off in the middle of a sentence and smiling into a corner of the room as though he would be seeing someone very dear to him, or he would cry softly into his beard, his head bowed on his chest. His skin stretched like thin brown parchment over his gaunt cheekbones and the dark blue veins on his sunken temples. When he was "foolish" his daughters would look stiff and the younger one would say: "Oh,

Father, don't you know how you're hurting us with your behaviour?" The General would suddenly raise his head and look venerable and taking nothing amiss, would rise and leave the room, closing the door infinitely gently behind him.

At times he would forget to put on his clothes and there would be an agitated scuffle upstairs in the passage and the sound of Dorothea's indignant squeaking: "Oh, why must he hurt us like this?"

I was once sent up to the attic to fetch down some dried apples, and encountered General Tyler walking along the passage stark naked looking like one of Tolstoy's three ancients on the island, with his beard hanging down over his box-like chest and his withered limbs groping an uncertain way. There was an outcry from below and his daughters rushed up with averted faces: "Father, don't you know how you're hurting us?"

There were cold clear evenings when General Tyler steered me firmly out on to the little wooden porch at the front door and pointed out the stars and their constellations, telling me their names, their relationships and habits. I shivered as I stood at his side and tried to be a receptive pupil because of the respect I held him in, but failing to retain most of the names of the aloof bodies and getting giddy from much looking up.

When a shooting star flashed across the sky and down towards the horizon, so startling in comparison to the fixed stars who knew where they belonged night after night, I was not sure whether General Tyler had not summoned it as he stood in the frosty air, his beard sparkling, knotted fingers stirring the Milky Way — an ancient Druid.

I had some unsatisfactory moments with him though. When there was a display of northern lights, I heard violins, thin and distant, played in an unearthly key. The sometimes measured, sometimes fitful dance of cold green, blue or red beams was synonymous with the sound of bows drawn over cosmic strings tuned to an extra-terrestrial pitch. But General Tyler said: "Piffle! No one ever *heard* northern lights!" I could not agree.

Miss Tyler told me to go for walks with the General in the later autumn afternoons. She did as though I were being virtuous to do so which put me in a false light because I looked forward to these walks for my own sake. I did not find his conversation "simple" and even when he recognisably wandered, I assumed he was communing with an unseen presence and did not know whether to listen or not.

General Tyler instructed me in the behaviour of trees; how the oak poisons the soil for some plants and does not let them grow in its immediate vicinity, how the crowns of trees are indicative of the configuration of their roots, how the tap root is the water seeker and must never be injured, how the sap rises and falls in the trees with the waxing and waning of the year.

As we paused at the edge of a fallow field by a stone wall, I had to guess the depth of the tap roots of trees in the distance by observing the upward or outward sweep of their crowns and tell the kind of tree by its outline traced against the pale cold sky.

Along the stone walls there grew the slender fan-shaped elms, and along the creeks the willows crouched in the twilight like huddled witches on the march. General Tyler always paused in front of a huge oak standing alone in a field on the way back, looking as gnarled as the tree with which he had some private unworded understanding, but I loved best the royal and gracious maple with its leaves like generous outspread hands and which were so quick to colour under the sweep of the wings of the autumn wind. However, we always went back to the house talking of oaks. I gathered they were only relatively poisonous — it was more that they were like some people who do not allow other people to become adult because they are so adult themselves.

Otherwise General Tyler made no claims on my person nor did he ever ask me to do anything for him although I would have happily responded to his every request. I was dimly aware that although he was too old and frail to do things for others, it was his prerogative; ultimately he seemed more responsible for us all than Miss Tyler herself. Sometimes I wept for him. Then — for weeks he would remain in his little room in the attic out of sight and hearing.

The house occupied by the Tylers was wooden and oddly tentative as though a squall could split it in the overture. It was painted white. The floorboards and slatted wooden walls were unevenly joisted so that the wind whistled, unchecked by carpets and curtains, through the house. It was like living in a cleanly scrubbed barn.

The house stood well back off the road and had no near neighbours. There was a village some distance away, but Miss Tyler possessed neither horse nor buggy and we never went anywhere.

She spent most of her time in the kitchen and Dorothea hers in her little room under the staircase. I passed most of my time by myself out doors; Miss Tyler was to begin with shy of me and tended to let me roam.

I roamed in the woods. No one knew how far I went on some days; I was outside the orbit of anyone's awareness of my existence. This gave me a feeling of desolation as well as freedom — a kind of desolate freedom.

Even in winter it was better to be outside. The woods were still. Beneath the low-spread branches of the fir trees, the blue snowdrifts were impregnated with fire when the morning sun slanted into the woods, and each snow crystal and the icicles hanging from glassy twigs were set aflame and burned with a kind of divine enthusiasm. This enthusiasm sprang over into me and I experienced the afterglow of a presence which had gone that way at dawn, leaving behind it the frosty fragrance of an unseen essence that invested the forest with grace and filled me with tingling expectancy, as though the presence were only just ahead of me, waiting.

In the big oak forest behind the house, the snow lay thinner on the ground and was laced with the filigree traces of birds in search of food, cut across by the purposeful tracks of fox. Deer stood beneath the trees mournfully pawing the snow and I watched them with held breath until they wearied of the fruitless search and walked away, gently lifting their tiny hoofs, their fragile loins springing as they went.

When blizzards raged outside, I sat in the warm kitchen while Miss Tyler baked pies and Dorothea did her sewing. Miss Tyler occasionally drew me into a conversation but never mentioned my parents or anything about my earlier life, but talked about her own earlier on as though it would hold great significance for me. I experienced a kind of suction in these moments and took refuge in extreme politeness, commenting on Miss Tyler's revelations with odd remarks, at which Dorothea would take offence and hiss and huff under her breath and the kitchen would become stuffy and oppressive.

I began to have complaints I had not had before. The smell of turpentine or creosote caused hot rashes to break out all over my body, acids brought up large swellings on my forearms which made them look as if they had been blown up. Dorothea held that all this was produced by myself to gain attention and she would leave the room with emphatic disgust when I broke out in a rash after eating something acid, saying she could not finish her meal "under such circumstances."

Once alone with Miss Tyler, a dish of preserved gooseberries in front of me, lump after lump came up on my forehead, tightening the skin like a vice around my head. She observed my discomfort closely, her expression obscure. I was delivered to her scrutiny and reacted by wave after wave of rash coming out all over. When I could no longer bear to be stripped in my discomfort, I asked to be excused and went to my room to lie down until I gathered myself together again, for these rashes made me feel as though I were breaking up in all directions.

Gradually Miss Tyler's reserve towards me began to wear off and she would show open disapproval of some of my ways, and strictness on the assumption that she could drive the allergies out of my system. She said if I could not eat this, I could not have "that", and "that" was the pies and cakes she made so well and for which I had a constant craving. When I was not allowed to have any apple pie because I had not been able to eat something with vinegar on it without breaking out in a rash, the craving for apple pie became consuming. It would drive me to Miss Tyler later on in the afternoon: "Please may I have a piece of apple pie?"

She would regard me with a slightly uncomprehending smile in one corner of her mouth, saying she had not heard me properly. So I would say it again: "Please may I have some apple pie?"

"Oh, I see. Well, the apple pie's all gone now."

This was an open door to temptation. Miss Tyler kept chocolates in a corner cupboard in the dining room and I had not been beyond begging for one now and then, never certain whether the boon would be granted. Then there was an afternoon when I was alone in the house. The dining-room door was ajar, the house silent and unwitnessing. The corner cupboard was not kept locked and inside lay a large box of chocolates. When I put the box back in the cupboard, there were three chocolates left — one for Miss Tyler, one for Dorothea and one for the General who didn't eat chocolates.

I came from the garden for supper. Miss Tyler and Dorothea were putting the evening meal on the table and the General was once again downstairs. We sat down and the meal proceeded without a ruffle on a calm surface. When I lay in bed afterwards and let the impressions of the day pass through my mind, what happened in the dining-room stayed away. Next morning I woke to a new day.

Hanging from the boughs of a tree in the garden there was a swing. The horizon rose and sank around me in regular measure as I swung higher and higher. Miss Tyler called. There was a note in her voice I had not heard before. I sprang off the swing and went in. She was standing in the open doorway of the dining-room; the sight of her in that place made me tremble violently. Out of oblivion the ugly face of reality stared and could not be wiped out. "What happened to the chocolates in the dining-room?"

I was speechless.

She repeated "What happened to the chocolates in the dining-room?" in the identical tone of voice.

I felt as though invisible cobwebs lay around me like chains and cried inwardly for help from some corner of the universe. Rising out of the subterranean pool of apprehension, imagination came to my aid: "A mouse took the chocolates."

Miss Tyler was looking at me with undisguised contempt.

"It *was* a mouse. I even saw it going into the dining-room."

In my now desperate mind, I saw the dusty little velvet creature scurrying over the floorboards and would have ventured more about it had not Miss Tyler icily cut in: "I would not have thought you would stoop to telling lies."

I hardened; I was not going to have Miss Tyler set my standards and how did she know from where I had to stoop, was made to stoop and stoop. "It was a mouse!" I shouted.

My cheeks were on fire from Miss Tyler's slaps: "March up to your room!"

As I mounted the creaky wooden steps, Dorothea's voice came from below rising to an indignant pitch at what "she had done."

The room in which I slept was bare and cold. I spent no time in it during the day — all it contained was a narrow bed and a rickety wicker chair. My few belongings were kept in a rickety wardrobe outside in the passage.

I sat down on the wicker chair. There was a presence in the room. I saw it; it sat on a like chair. It was my Self. We looked at one another.

"Do you know that you told a lie?"

"Yes, I know I did."

"It wasn't a mouse at all. Why did you blame a mouse?"

"I was afraid."

"Afraid of what?" The Other looked at me, and I bowed my head in shame.

"You're a coward."

"Yes, I know I am."

"You needn't be a coward."

"I can't help it."

"You must help it — you alone."

Through communion with the Other it grew lighter in the room and the weight oppressing my existence began to lift. In dialogue with the Other who was I, I experienced the catharsis I needed to restore my moral balance. From that day on, chastisements undergone at the hands of Miss Tyler were to me discharges of tension in her, but never had anything to do with my own moral recoveries. Recovery of moral integrity could not depend on the fear of others and the pain they could inflict on one. I alone had to re-establish moral equilibrium and set my own standards. This was to require an inner strength I did not possess in great measure nor was I inspired by examples in others. A certain moral weakness was to accompany me which stemmed from not really infallibly knowing what was wrong or right — from sucking in influences, mostly through reading, as one breathes in air. One does not ask before inhaling if the air is good or not — one simply needs air to live. I needed to be influenced by anything that came my way, and so little seemed to come my way, in order to live spiritually.

There was nothing in the Other who was in the room with me that day that was vindictive or judging or contemptuous when I later faced him in moments of moral defeat. I needed to have no fear of being exposed, because the Other was my Self and knew me as no one else would ever know me. The only condition between us was that absolute truth prevail; everything had to be spoken out without prevarication. Any attempt at deviation caused the precious symbiosis to withdraw and I was left with myself.

This day was a milestone in my personal evolution; yet I had lost ground in relation to Miss Tyler and was in a subtle way beholden to her.

Spring came. The snow melted, leaving patches of tired white in the ditches along the road. Damp-burdened winds blew low over the open fields and the smell of waiting earth filled me with melancholy and made me feel as limp as the sodden leaf mould in the woods. Yet the sap was rising in the trees and the birds singing, mounted higher and higher on the winds.

There was a country mansion in the district that belonged to a rich chocolate manufacturer called Hyler. The store in the village at some distance belonged to a Mr Fyler. Miss Tyler seemed to attach great significance to the fact that there were Hylers, Fylers and Tylers in the same neighbourhood, but on the few occasions when I was sent on errands to Mr Fyler's store, my emphatic announcements that I had been sent by Miss Tyler failed to rouse any reaction in the taciturn shop owner and I concluded he was deaf.

As far as I knew, Miss Tyler had never met any member of the Hyler family and had never been that way. As for myself, I had seen the Hyler mansion from the distance when I roamed along the ridge of an extended hill away off and had looked down from there on to the roofs of its stables.

Easter was coming. News came to Miss Tyler that all the children in the neighbourhood (I had never seen any children in our vicinity) were invited to an egg-roll at the Hyler mansion on Easter Sunday afternoon. "Am I invited too?" I was dubious.

"Why, of course, if all the other children in the district are invited, so are you."

Miss Tyler took some material out of her sewing cupboard and made me a new frock for the occasion. The material was slate blue with tiny oranges printed all over and was wonderfully soft to the touch. She put smocking all around the yoke whence the material fell freely. I expressed my delight with uninhibited enthusiasm; it was one of the rare moments of immediacy between us.

Easter Sunday was a brilliant day but a brisk wind was blowing. I shivered in my lovely frock and would have liked to remain in the house, but Miss Tyler did not want me to miss the egg-roll, so I put on my cardigan and set off over the fields after dinner, careful lest I tear my frock on the barbed wire fences I had to climb on the way.

I arrived at the front door of the Hyler mansion, my frock intact, and found crowds of children in the entrance hall. Butlers and maids were weaving their ways in and out of the noisy children, smiling partly benignly, partly restrainedly to show that they were suffering the imposition of having to look after so many children in this august place.

I edged my way over to a french window, feeling I was trespassing, and tried to gaze out over the lawn, but my eyes were red with embarrassment and I could see nothing distinctly. I knew that beyond the hollow into which the sloping lawn fell away, there rose a long wooded hill, blue in the distance, and that there were squirrels and woodpeckers and violets up there — but that did not help me now as I was caged behind the bars of the french windows in this house.

A butler jerked me by the elbow and told me to line up with the other children to shake hands with Mrs Hyler. I took a place in the long line of eager children who were already moving steadily towards a point behind the square wooden pillars in the hall.

Mrs Hyler was a portly lady. She stood very upright against a background of satin wall coverings, china dogs, striped satin upholstered chairs and a grand piano covered with a tasselled Spanish shawl. The children were filing past her looking up into her face with bright smiles. When my turn came, my face was on fire and the joints of my knees did not want to hold me up. The satin stripes on the walls undulated in my gaze like snakes. Mrs Hyler said loudly and clearly: "And who is *this* little girl?"

No one seemed to know. How were you to account for yourself? Who were you to say you were? Sweat trickled down my body underneath my vest; I feared it would drip on the carpet. Mrs Hyler was gracious: "Never mind little girl, once you're here you might as well have a *veeery* good time."

At a signal the crowd of children surged through the open french window out on to the terrace outside. I was swept along with them. On the stone portico a little above, Mrs Hyler with her grown-up sons and daughters and, somewhere, Mr Hyler, the chocolate manufacturer, were grouped. Out through the french windows behind us there issued a row of butlers carrying large round baskets of chocolate Easter eggs. Mrs Hyler blew a whistle and the butlers bent over at the waist and emptied the contents of the baskets down the grassy slope.

Hundreds of chocolate eggs bobbed down the turf and at a second piercing whistle blast from Mrs Hyler's mouth, the crowd of children surged after them to catch as many as they could before the eggs disappeared into the tufts of longer grass in the dell below. The air was filled with shouts and laughter and the family group watched benevolently from above.

I picked my way down the slope at one side and saw a number of chocolate eggs vanish unseen by anyone; the turf was alive with invisible little fingers that drew them into the deep grass and hid them there. I was not going to prevent them.

I went on down into the gully where a brook gurgled on its hidden course, teeming with life. I sprang from tuft to tuft and gained the far side of the stream whence I looked back: the Hyler mansion and the children on the slope were as remote as a painting and as I moved away, a fresh green curtain of boughs obscured the whole scene and I came to myself. Presently my feet were on a tiny meadow path leading upwards along a stone wall.

The sun was near setting as I came up on to the edge of the ridge and looked around. A farm lay in the hollow just below;

the red barn was doubly red in the fire of the westering sun. The rest of the farm lay in shadows and the lamps inside were not yet lit.

I had been that way before and knew the path that skirted the farmyard and emerged out on to a dirt track that ultimately passed Miss Tyler's house which stood beyond the oak forest to the east.

As I took this path, the stillness of the evening was rent by screams. My heart pounding with fear, I peered round the corner into the farmyard where a number of men were slaughtering pigs in the enclosure; their faces were in the dark — blood ran into the troughs. The scene had a horrible magnetic pull but then I managed to pull my feet up and gained the shoulder of the hill behind the farm from where I looked back once more. Along the wall of the barn, only dimly perceptible in the dusk, pigs hung head downwards from a thick wire cable side by side. I stared through the gathering twilight — the row of pink bodies looked human.

Out of a deep well of existence, wraiths, premonitions rose — phantoms hovering on the brink of graves, mass graves — "and they trembled but not for long" until the night came down over the dreadful vision of my first Easter.

Summer came bringing a big change. Miss Tyler was going to take a position as housemother in an orphanage near Philadelphia. Dorothea was going to teach at the orphanage and the General was going with them.

Inside I was full of melody because of my impending release; not too much had been exacted. I had not expected to be set free so soon and thought exultantly of going to my mother.

Nearer the time of departure from the house on the Hudson River, Miss Tyler clarified things. I was going to Philadelphia too; she had only taken the position in the orphanage because of me, to be able to "support" me, and my mother was in full agreement. Anyhow, my mother had not been "doing her part" as she had said she would and besides, I needed schooling, and if my mother wouldn't see to my being educated, someone else would have to.

A bolt slipped firmly into place and any false hopes of release were corrected.

10

The orphanage lay on the fringe of a suburb of Philadelphia. It had been founded by a philanthropist for totally orphaned girls. He had died just before we went there.

The main buildings were grouped loosely in a flat basin of land surrounded by low treeless hills. The central building was vast and rambling and was in reality two buildings connected by a long low passage. They were designed in chateau style and constructed out of a stone which contained much glitter that sparkled in the sunlight and invested the grey walls with grace.

In the entrance to the main building where the offices were — a low arched doorway, somewhat Gothic, opening into the connecting passage between the two parts of the building, there hung on the inner wall a replica of a Della Robia relief of the Christ Child in gold. The Child could be seen gleaming through the ivy covered windows on approach to the main building and especially on rainy days, it shone like an internal sun.

Besides the offices in the main wing, there were the older girls' classrooms and the big gymnasium which also served as an assembly hall for the entire orphanage.

Our classroom was in the other wing, in a room as big as the gymnasium but with various corners and niches and two enormous fireplaces which we sometimes used to play our plays in. At some distance along a winding asphalt drive, there were two residential houses built of the same glittering stone but all the while I was at the orphanage, I had no occasion to set foot in either.

There were seven other living houses down in the village over four miles away which were all wooden and which varied in size and ugliness. The one Miss Tyler was going to look after was the smallest and ugliest of all — a mustard-yellow slatted wooden structure of ungainly proportions, narrow-chested, with an encircling veranda overhung with ornate mustard-yellow wooden scallops, standing somewhat on its own at the edge of the village on the fringe of open country with a large garden at the back. There were nine girls of different ages in this house, and myself.

I was just seven years old when we moved to Philadelphia. Miss Tyler said that the time had come for me to call her Elizabeth and her sister Dorothea. I had not used names for people hitherto because people were always changing and names referred to something in them that placed a demand on one's feelings and caused too much chronic grief when one had to leave. "Mummy" and "Daddy" were as far as I was prepared to go, but my parents were away now and I was in a world of people with no names. All the time I was at the orphanage, I managed never to address either Miss Tyler or Dorothea by name.

Dorothea was now my teacher and I attended school proper for the first time and for the first time, was one of a group. Nonetheless, Miss Tyler made it clear from the beginning that I was an exception at the orphanage — I had parents, "They," the girls, had none; I was privileged because of my background, "they" had no backgrounds — and so on.

I was to remember that I was responsible to her alone, because she had only taken the position at the orphanage to "support" me . . . my situation was again outlined including my mother's failure to "do her part." I was not here like the other girls; I was here rather as her very own child and none of the other teachers were to have any say concerning me . . . and so on.

Our classroom had the two huge fireplaces I have mentioned. The windows were high above our heads so we could see the sky and the larks and the clouds but nothing else, not even the tops of the three tall elms just outside. Our classroom was a fortress under protection.

Back in the mustard-yellow house, I rarely saw Dorothea although I had to pass her room whenever I went to the bathroom. When she appeared, she was always distraught and her hair unkempt. She spoke only to her sister in her characteristic high trembly voice which faded away towards the end of a sentence so that her final meaning had to be guessed at. Miss Tyler was authoritative with her as though she were incapable of being responsible for herself.

I never saw Dorothea going off to school in the mornings when everyone else was busy going off nor did I ever discover how she covered the four miles from the house to the main orphanage buildings. When I arrived in our classroom having trudged all the way up in all kinds of weather, she was always there to receive us.

Dorothea was a different person in the classroom. Firm and enthusiastic, she introduced us (I don't remember the "us" at all) to the various subjects, speaking resonantly with singularly clear diction, and everything she did to demonstrate a point was precise and beautiful. She was the mentor par excellence — mediator rather than teacher. She imparted information in a way that made it become rich in experience and meaning. Each subject was a shrine before which we paused to commune with the local spirit and become inspired by it. My own enthusiasm bubbled unbounded.

What method Dorothea pursued, I cannot say. I think her own latent genius came to expression in the classroom, albeit genius which did not embrace mathematics or the scientific subjects with the same near passionate involvement she otherwise inculcated in her pupils. We entered into the histories of Babylonia, Egypt, Greece — almost spatially, as if into our own biographies. Dorothea was not interested in the doctrines of cause and effect; historical time was simultaneous — it was all around one all the time like the walls of a great house within which one's own microcosmic life had its being. History was the hotbed of one's own becoming, but at the same time, Dorothea managed to fill one with a sense of responsibility for everything that had ever happened since civilization began.

Grammar and Geography were likewise qualitative worlds of their own and exclusive to themselves while we sojourned in them, which we usually did for three or four weeks at a time. Dorothea did not teach us to be objective; she taught us to, completely and without reserve, identify with and love what we were doing.

In the afternoons, we had weaving, painting, pottery, tile-making, tie-dyeing, lino-cutting — all in the same classroom and all with Dorothea so that what filled our minds was extended to what we learned to do with our hands. Our classroom was to me an alchemical laboratory of continuous creativity and discovery, sometimes like a cathedral with many little side altars, for I had a religious experience every day I came to school.

When I chanced to catch Dorothea's eye back at the house, she looked away, or when I referred to something that had happened in the classroom, she would raise an eyebrow as though she had never seen me before and could not imagine what I was talking about. She never addressed me, and I learned about any new school arrangements solely through Miss Tyler. Dorothea did not want to exist for me outside the classroom and gradually she did not exist as I learned to accept her injunction.

The village lay along a highway coming from the city and leading roughly north. A few houses lined the straggling roads off the main road on either side. There was an accumulation of small stores down on the highway and somewhere further on, a little wooden village hall. On a steep embankment amid meagre pines there stood a small stone Episcopal church.

In my free time, I was absorbed by the garden at the back of the house. Soon after our arrival, I was given the chore of looking after the chickens. It was the first time I was entrusted with looking after anything and I was overawed by the dignity and responsibility to which I had advanced. I discharged my duties with ritual care, but after some time the lack of evolution and dynamic in hen life began to fill me with despair and profound irritation; hen life seemed utterly senseless. I concluded that the hens didn't have enough to do.

Efforts to find sensible and meaningful occupations for my charges led to squawking chaos in the hen-yard, the inhabitants fluttering and screeching into a diaspora all over the garden while I shouted my defence after them: "It's because they don't have enough to do!"

Miss Tyler tried to explain the laws of "henhood" to me and to impress me with their usefulness to mankind — I disliked eggs intensely — but I could not rid myself of my scathing opinion of their superficiality and lack of fire.

It was infinitely more gratifying to work in the vegetable garden. After a rain, a crusade had to be conducted against the weeds that sprang up in profusion in the wake of a downpour and usurped the places of the legitimate plants, albeit I felt sorry for some of the weeds. There were those that came out willingly when you pulled at them. Others came out with a tiny moan like the plantain with its rich delta of roots to which the earth clung lovingly. Other weeds were stubborn and had to be wrestled with until the right angle was found to make them give in and leave the earth. Some were graveolent and disgusting and dock with its slimy stem and dogged root was the bane of the afternoon.

Kneeling between the rows of vegetables to restore order and render the enemy impotent, I was in constant dialogue with the plants. Some vegetables aroused unreserved sympathy, admiration and compassion, some my reserve. The feathery carrot with its orange spearhead pointing keenly down into the earth was the aristocrat of the garden. Cabbages and other brassica were the crowd. Beetroot, peas, beans, onions and lettuces were all individuals with different minds and when I inadvertently pulled one up with a weed, it was as though I had committed murder with the whole row looking on.

Beyond the garden fence there was a large rhubarb patch. The stalks grew to a great height and on hot days when my feelings of responsibility towards the garden and its inhabitants became diffuse, I crept into the shade of the enormous rhubarb leaves that flapped phlegmatically like elephants ears and crouched, a crumpled colossus, in a strange world of insects, slugs and caterpillars until the pink stalks, the columns of this articulated leaf-house, brought gooseflesh out all over my skin in spite of the humidity and I emerged into the sunlight again.

For a time I had the job of sweeping the veranda after breakfast before setting off for school. The scalloped rim around the house was the daytime resting place of myriads of bats hanging head down side by side and raining a carpet of dropping. I retched as I swept the tiny black specks off into the flowerbeds and the thought that I might have to weed the flowerbeds in the afternoon after school filled me with dark despair, and I continued sweeping the veranda benumbed by the fear that the broomstick would stir the sleeping bats overhead, hanging like minute Damocles' swords ready to strike.

I could extend to bats none of the love and passionate concern aroused in me by squirrels, rabbits, woodchucks, weasels, foxes, garden snakes, not to mention cats. I felt nothing but abysmal revulsion for bats, and the notion that the world contained creatures one loathed and feared ultimately reflected back upon oneself. Only when one was able to love bats and slugs and flies would one be perfectly human but then, I did not want to be perfectly human — yet.

Over the meadows to the woods in the distance, there ran a little footpath, narrow and concise along the stone wall, but however determined the path might have been on the open meadow, at the edge of the wood it became uncertain and lost in a maze of brambles and poison ivy vines that wove a barrier between the world without and the darkness of the wood within.

There was access to the wood along an old disused cart track which led around a hollow which had been a dump. A vile smell emanated from rusty tins and scraps of leather and iron and other unnameable things that lay hidden under the nettles.

This track led through the woods to open country beyond. When I emerged out on the other side, I saw strange hamlets and farmsteads which seemed clearer and cleaner than those on our side, and the unfamiliar freshness of the landscape would start up a throb of longing to walk up to a farmhouse and be received by an apron with deep folds and the smell of hay and freshly baked bread and everyone sitting around the lamp in the middle of the table.

Then the sun would be lowering and suddenly sink as though let out of hand and the woods would be smouldering with dull red, and I would be possessed by panic lest I would not reach our side before darkness fell, and would plunge into the woods along the rutty cart track. As I sprang over half seen stones, I sensed wanton and nameless beings in the undergrowth between rotting stumps of trees and ran faster, panting heavily, to gain the nearside of the woods and the brambles stretched out their thorny arms to draw me back and deliver me to the horror within. No one would know where I fell and lay.

I would pull away from the brambles, tearing my clothes and the skin on my legs, to spurt out on to the pasture, indescribably relieved to have escaped, barely aware that my legs were sticky with blood and deeply reassured by the cows standing in the dusk, munching and smelling infinitely sweet.

This wood was called Militia Woods. It was a veritable Evilshaw, a continuous source of badness. It was from there that I first fetched the maddening outbreak of tiny watery blisters that spread all over my body from contact with poison ivy. My excursions to Militia Woods, an anti-Eden of knotted poison ivy vines that grew to the thickness of a man's arm, were followed by days swathed in bandages and zinc ointment and isolation from school and nights of unbearable itching, hands tied to the bedstead to prevent scratching.

Militia Woods was outwardly unprepossessing — an elongated area of indeterminate deciduous growth and thin spindly stems. Even in the autumn it displayed no glory. It had to be known from within to realize how sinister it was. A lion once escaped from a visiting circus and was thought to have made for the Woods. For some days, men with shotguns passed by beyond the railway track at the bottom of our garden in pursuit of the lion (I heard later that they were looking for a fox which had been looting in the hen-yards in the neighbourhood). I heard the lion prowling outside at night beneath my window and volunteered information at breakfast that he was surely crouching in the shrubbery in the front garden ready to pounce on anyone leaving for school by the front gate. When I myself went off for school, I saw his yellow body lying low in the forsythia bushes and spurted out on to the road with a thrill of fear and anticipation, but no one else seemed to sense the danger.

When I returned from school in the afternoon, I set out towards Militia Woods, scanning the edge of it for a glimpse of a tawny body, terrified and elated at the same time, longing for an encounter; but suddenly possessed by dread, I made a dash back across the meadow, charging through the barbed wire fence below the garden with the lion close behind, until I reached the kitchen door just in time to slam it in his face.

The lion's ultimate fate was lost on me or was such an anticlimax that no one had anything to say about it, but for myself his amber eyed lurking on powerful pads continued to constitute part of the sinister magic of Militia Woods.

At the far end where I seldom went, I came upon a gypsy camp. Swarthy men in torn shirts and tangled haired women crouched around a sooty pot steaming over a fire. Half naked children with squalid tatters hanging about their spare bodies ran around in the clearing, and sinister looking horses were tethered to the trees with frayed ropes, not even grazing but lost in the contemplation of unspeakably evil things.

One of the men caught sight of me transfixed in the thicket and leered, showing perfect white teeth fletched in malevolence. The horses pulled back their lips and grinned in agreement. I could not lift my leaden feet to get away. A woman rose to her feet and waved to me and the children followed suit; there was a surge in my direction. This broke through the petrification; I backed away and ran as I had never ran before.

I ran — often; I learned to anticipate the texture of the ground beneath my feet, to change gait from springing pasture land to a hard rutty track or to adapt to the asphalted road to school, to clear ditches and creeks in one bound without pausing or hesitating, equally to take a fence with as little loss of impetus as possible or to glide along in a liquid lope when there was a clear distance to be covered. Or — to spring forward from the ball of the foot when I had to extricate myself from undergrowth and to use all the gaits at my disposal when I was sent on errands and wanted to be back in record time to demonstrate my usefulness. Running in this wise was a kind of language for me.

A night came when the sky over Militia Woods was ablaze and great black columns of smoke rose up and filled the smouldering sky, and the acrid smell of burning wood came across the meadows. We watched the fire eating its way along the ridge until after midnight; for once we were not sent to bed. All the men in the village were over at the woods fighting the flames. Their tiny black forms could just be distinguished against the hot red sheet of glow that radiated from the burning woods.

The next morning black coiling columns of smoke still rose upwards from the scorched trees and the bared outlines of charred branches stood out against the dull sky. A rumour took its course that the Ku-Klux-Klan had started the fire to cover up the lynching of a negro in the woods. For days evil whispered.

I never went to Militia Woods again. I shut it out of my field of vision, which required practice and constancy because the woods formed the horizon at the back of the house where I spent most of my free time. The landscape around was otherwise flat and dull and I never felt tempted to explore it, but without Militia Woods, life became suburban.

One morning at school, I was asked to take a message to Thistle, one of the two residential houses near the main building. I waited at the front door for someone to answer the doorbell and contemplated the mosaic thistle set into the stone archway. A maid finally came and took the piece of paper out of my hand and thanked me with a bright smile on her black face. I turned to go, having discharged my mission, with a curious sense of emptiness as though something I had anticipated had not happened. Then from out of an open window upstairs there came:

— down along endless sands lay row upon row of whales basking in the long primeval afternoon of early creation, the interminable rhythm of the tide breaking over their great backs glistening in the light. Now and then in intervals, they slipped gently into the sea and others came up out of the depths to take their places . . . Along the long, long sands came the young god to count his creatures and to gaze upon them with profound satisfaction while the seas swirled and washed around his feet. As he trod the infinite beach, my infinitesimal spirit flitted in his wake in the pre-natal sunlight. Then — after me horses galloped with manes streaming in the wind and hooves of thunder and the oceans responded to their coming with a roar of exultation and flung its foam into the sky. The bare golden sands churned up as the horses reared and plunged into the sea to rise again above the crests of the waves, and to gallop with the wind upwards, leaping from star to star, from aeon to aeon, ridden by youthful gods whose laughter caused the universe to tremble in joy . . .

Silence fell. I crouched on the doorstep of the house, my head bowed on my knees. A spirit had poured itself out over me; I had been baptized by an unknown force. Music had rushed in upon me in an apocalypse of sound and joy and power and brushed me with a promethean hand; these rhythms had lifted me out of my minute cage into eternity and gave me the knowing that I had been and would always be.

Miss Tyler often went to Philadelphia to shop and frequently took me with her. We went by train, stopping at each small station on the way before arriving at the big station in the centre of the city.

She would proceed to John Wanamaker's where she bought buttons and sewing silks and fine needles and materials. She always chose green for herself and Dorothea, taking a long time to make her choices and causing the saleswoman to lay everything they had in store out on the counter before her. My legs would ache as I stood behind her, suppressing my own desire for something to buy and, at the same time, wearied by the endless multiplication of things in the big department store and the ultimate senselessness of things.

After shopping, we would go somewhere to have a cup of chocolate and if there was time enough, to the Museum or to William Penn's monument from the rim of whose colossal Hat, we viewed the city of Philadelphia. Chestnut Street, Walnut Street, Maple Street — a whole forest had petrified into the concrete plan of the city as though into an asphalted necropolis — were again and again identified from the Hat by Miss Tyler with almost religious awe.

On one of these excursions to Philadelphia when we were still wandering from counter to counter in John Wanamaker's, a group of Japanese men and women passed us chattering and laughing. I pricked my ears and tiny sparkling beads of understanding strung themselves together as the meaning of what they were saying came across to me. One of them noticed the pop-eyed child staring at them and addressed me in English. I struggled for words blushing furiously and stammered my answer in Japanese and was at once surrounded by surprised and delighted people. I could not summon the words quickly enough to answer all their eager questions. They asked Miss Tyler if they could take me for tea, but she was guarded and said we had to catch a train. Their faces fell with disappointment and I fought back my tears lest I make them still more unhappy and tried to say "Good-bye" in Japanese in a steady voice. My heart had the tangible weight of a stone as I watched them go and disappear and I experienced distinctly how the sparkling fragments of Japanese — up till then I had occasional Japanese dreams — sank back into a fathomless well for good. I remember only O Yuki-san's name: Snow.

Miss Tyler continued her shopping in the department store with myself silent and bleak in her wake.

11

Before school I carried out the chores allotted to me by Miss Tyler. I made my bed, swept and dusted my room, continued in the passage outside and down the front staircase, dusted the knobbled banisters, swept and dusted the entrance hall and the parlour. Miss Tyler had painted all the woodwork orange-and-blue or blue-and-orange and I had helped with a little brush so I knew the places where dust could settle.

When I finished my round of sweeping and dusting, I knocked at Miss Tyler's door by arrangement and asked her to inspect my work. She would raise the quilt on my bed to look for creases in the bottom sheet and would then trace her finger along all the woodwork for specks of dust. When she detected any dust on her upheld finger, I had to go over the woodwork again.

On bad days, I had to dust three or four times over before being released to go to school. On such days an almost intolerable feeling of strain took possession of me and I began to attach a sensation of dull dread to the orange-and-blue woodwork in the house and to the trial it constituted.

On Saturday afternoons the lawn was to be mowed and raked and the edges of the flowerbeds trimmed. Inside the house, the woodwork was to be washed down and the floors of my room and passages scrubbed. Curtains were periodically removed from their rods and hung outside, and windows had to be cleaned and polished bright.

These tasks were solitary ones for Miss Tyler never asked the orphanage girls to do them, albeit she often had them in the kitchen with her and taught them how to bake cakes and muffins.

I had no companions and slept alone in a large room adjacent to Miss Tyler's. She disapproved of my referring to anything from earlier on in the presence of the girls, particularly to my travels. As I had done little else but travel with my parents prior to being taken to the orphanage by Miss Tyler, there was nothing at all to say about myself. I learned not to be present as a person. This was re-enforced by the fact that I had had no experience of being part of a group of children, which state Miss Tyler was determined to perpetuate at the orphanage.

My own trusted world was one of trees and creatures and winds and storms and running. People moved outside in worlds of their own with their own patterns and motives, in worlds in which I felt non-existent or anonymous or was an existential exile, pre-natally ostracized.

Vivian was four years older than I and was for a brief while a friend. We went to a hidden corner at the bottom of the garden where we talked. She opened up to me a new world, for she had seen her parents run over and killed by a train. Her sister had been taken in by an aunt, but she herself had been sent to the orphanage after the accident and had been there for five years without having left it even briefly or ever having had a visit from anyone.

Vivian's eyes were huge and dark and her fingers so brittle that I feared they could break at the least pressure. She never complained, yet she was branded by grief and a horror that had never been wiped out and that was going to consume her. While I was still at the orphanage she was taken away somewhere to die.

In Vivian I encountered a person whose condition in life obliterated my own experience of self-centred imprisonment and who aroused in me a feeling of burning compassion; I wanted to breathe into my own lungs and hold in there something of the air she had to breathe to relieve her grief a little.

At first Miss Tyler seemed oblivious of our connection and Vivian and I became less clandestine in our meetings. Then Miss Tyler swooped down on us and terminated everything; we were forbidden to talk to one another.

Although Miss Tyler frequently and repeatedly explained why I was not to seek contact with the orphanage girls — because they were "inferior" to me, having no parents and no background, I felt acutely inferior to them because by virtue of their circumstances, they had legitimate claims on life I did not have. The orphanage was theirs; I was there on false pretences — pretender in a realm in which I had no rights.

The only thing that was indisputably mine was Me, this thing that was set into motion before I was born and that was to go on travelling an obscure and difficult path, driven from behind without sightings of an aim, purpose or goal. As long as I was not tempted by openings for escape, I was I and belonged to my Self. There was a sense of steel somewhere behind my sternum that kept magnetic contact with the force that drove me forward, but I often lost centredness and any sense of meaning and my feeling of Self would fragment and disperse. Although I did not *think* these things at that early age, they were the keynote of my experience of existence.

As I was not permitted to appear in the vestments of my short past, I learned to do without my memories and to take each new situation at face value and let it go again. Nothing was allowed to form, to accumulate in the way of own views and conclusions, own emotions, even own motives and resistances. Complete compliance with circumstances was the only way through the needle's eye and incognito the only vestment.

Miss Tyler let no occasion pass without emphasising the difference between my status and that of the girls at the orphanage, and would explain that she did not work for the girls because she loved them, but to support *me*. I began to feel the ambivalence of my situation like the weight of chains.

She spun an airtight cocoon around my person by cutting through all threads of normal human contact. Every contact I attempted with someone other than herself was guilty in her eyes. A sense of guilt became chronic even when I only wished for contact with someone. Guilt and contact became entangled. I ceased to respond to people. Not that I became her bondsman, but I had a dim knowing that I could preserve my ultimate freedom in relation to her if I observed it in relation to everything else; the one was the price to be paid for the other.

From the outset, Miss Tyler made it clear that I was at the orphanage on an exceptional basis. I was not to take direction from any other adult on the staff except Dorothea at school — she, Miss Tyler, alone had the right to say what I should do and not do. As I had little opportunity of encountering any of the staff at the orphanage, and as they themselves — as I discovered later — exercised the greatest restraint and tact concerning my position, I met with little tension from that side.

It was harder at first to hold myself aloof from the other children and not to be part of their activities, and initially I tended to overstep the limits set by Miss Tyler. Gradually, my clumsy and shy efforts to establish myself in their company dried up and they avoided me, or at best whispered fun of my English accent and other eccentricities such as my passion for reading.

Miss Tyler began to exercise increasing control over my free time. I had to have her permission virtually to go from room to room and had to account for every minute spent outside her presence. I did my homework in her room in the evenings and when I worked outside, I knew she was watching me from her window.

As a result of her stringent scrutiny of my daily existence, I reduced my desires and impulses to a minimum, taking care not to do or want anything that would stretch the constrictions she imposed, which had nothing to do with being good or less good, but only with skimming through.

Occasionally I had time to myself when she went to Philadelphia without taking me with her. When it was raining I would find some apples and, taking a book, would repair to the attic, there to curl up on a heap of old carpets under a window and, eating apples, indulge in the book that had my current attention. Or — when the attic was too dim to read in because of a stormy sky or the approach of dusk, I simply sat and listened to the rain beating on the roof and watched a spider weaving to and fro between the beams as long as the fading light would permit.

At other times, I looked for the cat and locked myself in the bathroom with her pinioned between my knees while I mixed the contents of various bottles and tubs and jars in the bathroom cupboard to dispense to the cat in case she was suffering from any ailment. Usually the substances were apathetic, but then one substance would suddenly set off a terrific whizzing in the glass I held in my hands and was the culmination of my alchemical ambitions.

The cat lay dutifully in the vice of my knees while I perched on the edge of the bathtub and administered the potent mixture which would contain quinine, witch hazel, iodine and tonics, or I would daub its paws and nose with castor oil and zinc ointment. The patient creature would submit to my therapeutic fervour and was a willing victim of my inquiring mind until all at once, it bounded off my lap and escaped through the open bathroom window out on to the roof. What was so touching about this cat was that it would offer itself again as my companion in my search and experimentation in the world of substances.

In the garden and along the creek and on the meadow, there were mice, moles, rabbits, woodchucks, squirrels, caterpillars, garden snakes and spiders. Young rabbits nestled in the crook of my arm and squirrels fed from my hand and sat on my shoulders and did their preening. I knew where the caterpillars spun their cocoons in the boughs of the maple trees and, climbing up on the appointed day, I witnessed the emergence of the imago in a chamber of green leaves, its crumpled untried wings trembling in the sunlight filtering through the branches. I knew this world without knowledge; it was a room in the house of my existence. Only birds were alien to me; they flew.

There was an orange blossom bush at the bottom of the garden and under it, I had for a time my zoo — a contraption of orange boxes and wire netting furnished with grass. Here I kept the animals I found wounded or ailing. When one departed from life, its body was removed to the Museum — likewise under the orange blossom bush. A visit to the Egyptian section of the Philadelphia Museum with Dorothea inspired mine, and the bodies of moribund moles and mice and other creatures were mummified in leaves wrapped round with cotton thread and placed side by side as the chief exhibits.

A crisis arose because the odours that began to emanate from the Museum mingled illy with the fragrance of orange blossoms and I could hardly overcome myself to go down and attend to the creatures still alive in the zoo.

Miss Tyler appeared in my province — a rare occurrence — to discuss a possible solution to the crisis which by now was not only confined to the orange blossom bush but extended to the whole garden. She met me very properly on my own ground and I yielded to her advice and agreed to conduct a mass Funeral and bury the putrid Museum pieces.

I did so with some reserve because I felt they had betrayed my high expectations in succumbing to decay, but now next to the depleted Museum, henceforth containing coloured pebbles, sloughed snake skins and snail houses, there was the Graveyard.

There were ugly moments when I fell out of the wonderful world of living creatures and everything became unreal. In such moments insects became mechanical objects which could be dismembered joint by joint like the siliceous horsetail or crushed a worm under foot or even chased the cat. These excesses resulted in the frightening experience of my blood becoming dark brown and moving like a slimy slug through my veins, devouring all the light in my body.

The fire of shame and remorse flared up and wave after wave of heat and grief would consume me and burn in my cheeks at the thought of what I had been capable of — until my blood was cleansed and became red and luminous again. These brown blood states always followed moments of shame and later on, I perceived brown blood states in other people.

Miss Tyler was inordinately clever with her hands. She could put in new window panes, mend a broken chair or repair an iron with expediency and expertise. She had her own doctrine of independence: if you were the last person alive on earth, you would have to know how to do all these things yourself.

She was a member of the D.A.R. — Daughters of the American Revolution and attended the annual congresses of that august body. She was imbued with the spirit of her ancestors who subordinated a continent, its savage inhabitants, its wild electric nature in a generation. Her square chin had something of a bulldozer about it as she ploughed her way through situations of any practical kind. She bore down on things like a dreadnought.

She would return from Philadelphia with some dress material — green — for herself and Dorothea, cut out the pattern and sew it up on the sewing machine while Dorothea sat at her side stitching the finer hems. By evening the two dresses would be ironed and hanging up ready to be worn the next day.

She tried to teach me to embroider and I embarked upon a pillowcase designed for my father — my mother wouldn't have cared for an embroidered pillowcase. I spent long hours stitching up the seams by hand, having to undo them frequently because of puckering. The top edge was to be embroidered in a floral pattern, but in spite of much labour and repetition, the needle woman did not emerge. But Miss Tyler said: You could not start something and not finish it; the pillowcase had been my own choice — so Clotho, Atropos and Lachesis came to sit in judgment on the long afternoons I sweated over French knots which became Gordian knots and had to be forcibly cut through, while the coloured silks lost their sheen through much frantic handling. I felt as though I were being examined by Fate and found wanting. In spite of Miss Tyler's admonitions, the pillowcase never saw completion.

I had suggested to Miss Tyler that I might try the sewing machine for the seams. She said if you can't do a thing by hand, you can't do it by machine either, and taking no chances, she firmly forbade me to touch the machine or "go anywhere near it."

She went to Philadelphia one afternoon; the house was empty. I searched for something to do. It occurred to me that I might go up to her room and look at the sewing machine from a distance.

I looked. The needle came down and pinned my hand between the thumb and forefinger to the board. I froze with horror, not only at the sight of the needle through my hand, but at the swiftness of the arrival of Nemesis on the scene of a broken command. It did not occur to me to try to release myself and I sat on, a prisoner of the sewing machine like a mouse in a trap until dusk fell and Miss Tyler returned from the city.

She entered the room and switched on the light and stood for some minutes in the doorway, not uttering a word. I bowed my head, faint with fear and shame. Then she walked over, released my hand from the board and sent me to my room. A little later, the district nurse came to give me an anti-tetanus injection and I went to bed without supper. Nothing more was said, but my brief passion for sewing machines was extinguished for good.

12

I had been at the orphanage for some time and had seen neither of my parents. I was not to see them all the while I was there. I was not to see my father ever again. My father never wrote to me. My mother wrote and sent me books. She occasionally wrote that she was planning to visit me and I would live in a wild exultant hope of seeing her, until the hope went out like a candle in a draught.

I tried to remember what she looked like. My father's appearance was in my bones; I had only to sink down into my body to know my father, even to know what he felt like from inside. He moved in my movements and his flesh was mine. I never found it difficult to call up his face in my mind.

When I tried hard I could summon up in my mind my mother's small slender outline, but I was not able to focus her face in my inner vision — it was always a diffused vacuous area. This made me apprehensive lest I would not recognize her when I saw her again. Yet each time a letter arrived in her concise round script with her vivid descriptions of events I did not always quite follow — more like a conversation than a letter — the peculiar fragrance of her personality infused me with adoration and longing.

My mother never failed to send me crayons, paints and above all books for Christmas and birthdays. The arrival of her parcels was all that was needed to hallow the day. They testified of an unbroken covenant which made it possible that everything could be endured.

On my eighth birthday a parcel came from my mother. Through the brown paper wrapping I distinguished by touch two books. A premonition prevented me from opening the parcel in the presence of Miss Tyler and besides, there was the danger of her snatching up the paper wrappings to use for lighting the kitchen fire, whereas I kept every scrap of paper with my mother's writing on it in a little box upstairs.

Alone in my room, I began to undo the knots in the string around the parcel aware that my mother had tied them with her nervous slender fingers. Two books emerged out of the wrappings — squarish in shape, one blue, one cinnabar. I puzzled over the titles: the *Iliad*, the *Odyssey* — written for children by Padraic Colum with illustrations by Willy Pogany.

These titles had no affinity with those of the animal stories I so loved or with Russian fairy tales or Dr Dolittle's adventures by which I was possessed at the time. A little apprehensive of the Unknown but trustful of my mother's guidance of my mind, I opened the blue book — the *Iliad* — and read the opening lines.

There was a thunderclap in my deeper existence as out of a hitherto undivined source, a rumbling rose up out of an age-long sleep accompanied by flashes of recognition: I *knew* the events told of in this book. This was whence I had gone forth.

It was my schooling long before I was born, my legitimacy. The discovery of myself poured out over me in a flood of bliss and reunion. Yet at the same time it was a new dawn and I strode away from my beloved beasts and fairy tales towards a rising inner sun. Everything else was swept aside in the thundering roll of chariots over the battlefield of Ilion, swallowed up in the blinding dust that rose in their wake which, when it subsided, revealed the heroes who were gods and the gods who were men, whose striving was my striving, whose victories my victories, whose griefs my griefs and whose deaths I died over and over again, and whose divinities filled the waiting shrines of my mind as a cloudburst renews the springs.

I knew now whose knees I could clasp in supplication, in whose lap my prayer would germinate, whose stern hand would thrust me back upon myself when I was scattered and untrue to my sending, sustain me when I found my way again. A veil rose from Olympus: my god was born.

My parents as well as Miss Tyler were non-religious. I had not been christened and had no experience of traditional religion. The sea, the woods, shadows and the ways of different animals, the silence of trees and the wind — were manifestations of a divinity of whom I formed no image. The image now sprang into life. Zeus and Athene went before me. The magnetic needle beneath my sternum received its Polar Star and the unseen divinity around me focused and became a point of reference for my inner vision. Thus the *Iliad* and the *Odyssey* became the breviary of my childhood, the rule by which to grow.

As to the heros who became my constant inner companions, Odysseus was first, the Incognito par excellence with the grey-eyed goddess at his side, his sudden encounters with Hermes. In the identification with Odysseus, my spiritual spine began to strengthen and to sustain the values set by the event on my eighth birthday.

There were others too — Diomedes of the horses, silver tongued Nestor whose mouth was filled with honeyed wisdom, Menelaos — and Hector the enemy to whom the heart was compelled to swing over for a brief, fierce moment of breast-rending compassion to weep for the beautiful body dragged in the dust around the city walls as one never wept for Achilles however Greek he was and however much his wrath and doom were the cause of everything.

The *Iliad* tapped a well of tears not wept for myself but for old Priam pleading with Achilles for the body of his dead son, for Achilles lifting the frail old father of his mortal enemy on to his own couch for a brief rest like a tired child, himself heavy with sorrow at his own loss — Patrocles his friend — "My heart filled with the beat of tears like dancing feet" — the exquisite andante of the *Iliad*.

If the *Iliad* was the symphony of fate and death in the fulfilment of the will of Kronion, the *Odyssey* was the sonata of man's soul destined to suffer his way back to Ithaca to the fulfilment of himself. In the *Odyssey* the things of life were invested with dignity and beauty: Odysseus, king of Ithaca, ploughing his fields, carving out his own bridal bed; Nausikaa, princess of the Phaeacians, washing the palace laundry down by the sea, driving her well-laden mules homewards; Eumaeos, godlike swineherd, hosting the stranger — and the golden Homeric palaces where Helen, Arete, Penelope ministered to the needs of the guest — water in silver basins for his way-weary feet, soft covers of wool dyed purple for his spent body, the songs of the fall of Ilion and of the trials of Odysseus for his immortal soul . . .

Sing, O Goddess, of the wrath of Peleus' son, Achilles!

Tell us, O Muse, of the deeds of that far wandering hero!

Sung by the goddess, told by the Muse, the golden words in their Homeric cadence, soon read in full translation, flowed into my soul and expanded it beyond the confines of circumstances, filled it as the wind fills a sail that carries a craft forwards to its destination.

The wrath of Achilles, the trials of Odysseus read over and over again, formed the marble steps to the temple of an Unknown God. I lingered long in the archaic sunlight, ascending and reascending the gleaming steps — from the alpha of the *Iliad* to the omega of the *Odyssey* — until one day they led up and on.

13

We went to a summer camp near Boothbay Harbour in Maine for the holidays. Miss Tyler and Dorothea took a log cabin in a pine grove on the precipitous coast overhanging the sea. A corner of the cabin was screened off for myself.

Not far from the camp the mouth of a tidewater river opened into the sea and its flat muddy banks were the basking places of white seals. I spent hours just above the river watching the seals emerge out of the water and settle on the flats to lie in curved position waving their heads to and fro. The same muddy flats attracted a great variety of water birds and were a scene of constant activity so absorbing that I rarely had to look for anything other to do than lie and watch the changes wrought by the ebb and flow of the tides and the meeting of the waters, salt and sweet.

Further up the river there was an old wooden bridge at what had once been an Indian trading post. On the far side of the river on its own in a treeless landscape stood a wooden blockhouse. This solitary house commemorated an intention that had never been carried out — an intention to save a queen from losing her head. The house was still furnished for her who never came, down to the embroidery frame at the window and the basket of faded silks beside it.

We were led through the few modest and musty rooms — history that had never been, that existed only in some anonymous nostalgia — dust that had settled where there had never been life.

I looked out of the window where that queen would have sat gazing over the lonely hill far from her splendid palace across the sea. I saw her in my mind galloping on horseback over the moors, far ahead of anyone else, beautiful, fiery, excellent, a comet across dull skies, to plunge into a network of bigotries and intrigue with a gaunt hound in pursuit — John Knox — then to be extinguished like a bright torch, her head on a block — and dwelt in a jumble of undigested and not grasped historical facts picked in books. I did not realize until later that I had confused Stewart with Habsburg.

A minister and his family occupied one of the larger log cabins in the camp. Miss Tyler seemed to wish me to play with the minister's children who were five in number. When I was not watching the white seals or drawn inland by ghosts of musty royalty, I cradled myself in the branches of the pines on the cliffs, with the waves leaping up at the rocks below, and abandoned myself to the smell of sun-warmed resin and the pulse-beat of the sea, and no thought that my cradle could have been dangerous entered my mind.

I was generous enough to show my tree-cradle to the minister's children and to consider ways of sharing it with them, but the girls wore skirts and the boys acted as though it was beneath their dignity to climb trees, although when I looked down into their upturned faces below, I detected yearning and frustration in them and in the end, I climbed down from my lofty perch and went with them on ground level. They took me to their cabin where their mother was preparing their supper. She was a clean faced person with tidy sandy hair in a tight knot at the back of her head.

A huge iron pot of water was boiling on the stove in a corner of the cabin. The minister's wife said she would show me something and hauled a sack across the floor to the stove and opened it up. It was full of live crabs reaching out dejectedly over one another's backs with their scissors, not getting anywhere. I was distressed by the sight of the seething mass of frustration in the sack when suddenly with one swoop, the minister's wife raised the sack and emptied its contents into the boiling water explaining that this was the way you cooked crabs.

I was stunned and backed out of the cabin into the dusk, tears of horror and pity streaming down my cheeks. I crouched in the dark against a pine; everything in me converged on the moment of the plunge into boiling water, the extreme agony of it, the extreme agony . . . thrown alive into boiling water, boiling water closing around a living, feeling body. I suffered in mind, almost rhythmically, the excruciating moment in the boiling iron pot. In the following days even a distant glimpse of the minister's children started it up all over again.

I was in my pine tree cradle with the smell of resin in my nose and my thoughts evenly spread out around me. Anything that was nightmarish had subsided. Bees were humming.

Along the path through the woods came the minister's children and began to play at the foot of my tree as though they did not know that I was aloft. I knew though that they knew that I knew, and this destroyed the peace of the afternoon. My thoughts buzzed around the five children below like wasps aroused. The only thing was to resolve not to be the first to speak. The approach came from the other side in due course and was conciliatory enough. I responded graciously and descended from the tree to join the minister's children.

In the course of the insignificant conversation that went on, the oldest girl asked a little abruptly how a cat gets kittens. I should have been warned by the averted faces of the five and the dull flush that had not been on their cheeks before. I gave the desired information enthusiastically, describing what I had often witnessed and energetically imitating the mother cat licking each new kitten clean.

This science was received in silence; then something in the silence shifted — they had to go home for supper. The five got up and disappeared through the trees. My pine cradle seemed suddenly inaccessible. I climbed down the rocks and walked along the narrow ledge below where the roar of the waves was louder than my thoughts.

When I returned to our cabin for supper, the atmosphere was subtly charged. Miss Tyler wore an expression on her face I had not seen before. She said she wanted to speak to me after supper. Waiting was almost intolerable for I did not know what I was waiting for.

I was getting ready for bed behind the screen when she came in and told me to tell her exactly what I had said to the minister's children that afternoon — they had gone to their mother in a disturbed state and reported that I had told them unspeakably smutty things. Did I realize, Miss Tyler said, that we might have to leave the camp because of this? *What* had I told the minister's children?

Miss Tyler's face and voice, the injunction they expressed, the crabs boiled alive, the sense of overwhelming injustice and my inability to grasp the new situation erupted in a paroxysm of fury and grief. I sat on my bed in my vest pounding the mattress with my fists and howling, stammering accusations against the whole ministerial family and feeling as though I were going to explode into fragments. Miss Tyler watched and listened for some moments and then went out to return with a basin of cold water and a cloth for my head. I lay back on the pillow in the dark and let the sick headache take possession of me.

The next morning at breakfast, nothing more was said of the matter. Miss Tyler and Dorothea were brisk and cheerful, but after that whenever I saw the ministers's children from afar during the rest of our stay at the camp, I went out of their way — for me they had the moral plague. For the first time in my short life, I indulged in hating; it took me by storm. I violently hated the minister's children and especially their mother. Had I known and understood the word "Pharisee" I would have hurled it after them and it would have taken some of the vehemence out of my mind.

People asked you questions not because they wanted a truth, but because they wanted you to formulate something they did not dare to themselves. It seemed you had to pay a price for telling the truth.

14

Miss Tyler was making plans to legally adopt me. My mother had failed to contribute to my upkeep; for some reason my father was not expected to do so, yet it seemed my mother stood in the way of Miss Tyler's adoption plans.

Miss Tyler's mounting animosity towards my mother was not withheld from me. Hardly a day passed when I was not reminded that she, Miss Tyler had "born the brunt" of my education and well-being; she had "played her part," not my mother who had "shirked" her duty all along so that she, Miss Tyler, "even had to pay" for my clothing.

I became wary in referring to the things I wore, taking care to say *the* vest, *the* boots to wipe out possession of things she gave me. This manoeuvre was to all appearances lost on Miss Tyler, but through my forced detachment, I was inwardly a little free. Yet when someone remarked — seldom enough — that my frock was pretty, I blushed as though I had stolen or inopportunely borrowed it.

My books were my own; they had all come from my mother. Miss Tyler never gave me a book nor did she ever talk about books with me. Having disconnected myself from everything I received from her, I became the more possessive of my books. Luckily I was not put to the test of having to lend a book to someone else.

The dichotomy in my existence was growing obvious; Miss Tyler provided for my material well-being — my mother sustained the life of my mind, but it was beyond me to judge the merits of either or to weigh them out against one another. Preference for my mother, whatever her shortcomings, was so primary that it transcended all else.

Miss Tyler went on trying to make me "see the situation as

it was." It was like persuading someone that they were on firm ground when they know they are walking on thin ice.

One day Miss Tyler told me my parents were getting a divorce. Not quite grasping what a divorce was, I felt it was not up to her to tell me that such a thing was in the air. It was a matter between my mother and my father and myself. I asked no questions, but — where were my mother and my father and myself? A plug was being pulled out of one's existence and the water was running out.

Miss Tyler went on to explain that after the divorce, I would "belong" to my father as any court would see that my mother was unfit to have custody. My father would engage her, Miss Tyler, to be my guardian until I was eighteen and went to college . . . a steam roller of flat mustard yellow prospects was moving over my existence.

My mother's letters to me and mine to her were subject to Miss Tyler's censorship. When I saw a letter in my mother's hand lying on the table in the hall, I knew I must not take it until Miss Tyler herself had read it. Sometimes I was not given the letter I saw on the table. This caused spasms of grief I was careful to conceal. I developed a fierce kind of pride which prohibited me from inquiring about vanished mail or giving any sign that I minded whether I received my mother's letters or not.

This pride was at the root of my acceptance of many things . . . Don't show that anything can affect you. It prevented me from "stealing" my mother's letters in moments when no one was about or from ever thinking of posting a letter to her in the village, which would have meant finding a stamp somewhere. In fact, pride made me stupid and incapable of seizing opportunities, but there was something else. Above all, there was my implicit faith that I was ultimately held in an omnipotent hand and cared for; ultimately nothing could happen to me. And there was the conviction, never shaken, that my mother *knew* although there was no external evidence of her knowing. It lay in my birthright. My mother knew everything about me, she was around me, with me — her letters lay on the table in the entrance hall.

Two men in dark suits carrying attache cases came from the city to see Miss Tyler with whom they had a long talk downstairs in the parlour. They seemed to have something to do with my father and I was unusually excited by their presence in the house.

Miss Tyler came up to my room to tell me the two men wanted to see me. I went downstairs with her. She was ingratiating as she presented me to the two men. I was given a chair and she went out leaving me alone with the strangers. They said they had come to help me and to see that when the divorce — they seemed embarrassed to have to use this word — was over I would be under the jurisdiction of my father.

"But my father's gone to Chicago."

Oh, but that would be different after the divorce. When everything was over, Miss Tyler would send me to my father for a nice long holiday. I would, of course, continue to be looked after by Miss Tyler who had already done so much for me, but my father was anxious to have me with him again. Would I not like to live with my father? See him for holidays? Be visited by him? Receive presents? Belong to him?

"I do belong to my father."

"Yes, of course, he is your father, but wouldn't you like to live with him again?"

"You mean instead of with Miss Tyler?"

"You mustn't be ungrateful to Miss Tyler who has sacrificed so much for you and loves you and, of course, you'll have to go to school until you are eighteen. But you'd go home to your father for holidays and see him as often as you like. You would only have to say that you would like this and we'll put it down on paper and see that it happens."

My head reeled. To hear so much about my father all at once was intoxicating. He seemed to be present in the room — a little larger than life, laughing, boyish, beautiful. He reached out his arms; they would catch me up effortlessly and hoist me high upon his shoulders.

Somewhere in the room I sensed the presence of my mother — in the shadows, small, dark, worried, not reaching out, slightly disdainful. On *her* shoulders lay all the guilt. The two men although they made no mention of her inferred by their mission that she was the one to be eliminated.

The two men went on: my father was now in business in Chicago and was going to earn lots of money. I would have all the toys I liked and a real home to go to — even a new mother when everything was over.

The intoxication died down. My father's laughter echoing in my memory had a hollow ring, his grip tightened on my shoulder and began to hurt, his smile became a grin . . .

"I want to belong to my mother," I whispered to the two men.

The room emptied save for the chairs and the tables, the two men and myself. They were meticulously patient explaining that I was not acting in my own interests nor with the gratitude I owed Miss Tyler. They began to talk about my mother; they seemed well informed. I did not grasp what they were saying, but I felt I had moved up to the brink of an abyss. The two men sensed vulnerability — I wanted to cry — and went on urging, but I steadied and became certain of myself; I was perhaps taking my first decision: "I want to belong to my mother."

The two men dropped their patient manner. One of them got up abruptly and called Miss Tyler who was just outside the door. "This little girl is not being very co-operative."

Miss Tyler's face was livid: "She's nothing but an ungrateful little snake and anyhow, no court will take notice of what a child of her age says. We're just wasting our time."

I was sent from the room. Later I saw the two men walk up the path to the front gate, black attache cases under their arms.

I could not digest the things that were happening. The moment I woke up in the morning, excitement and tension rushed in and I would have violent stomach aches. I lived in the anxiety that my father would suddenly appear. Every ring of the front door bell, every carriage or car passing by in the street brought the frightening possibility near.

Miss Tyler was not on speaking terms with me since the day the two men came from the city; there was no one else to talk to. No letters lay on the table in the hall. I had moments of panic lest I would not be able to hold on, lest I lose my grip and be fragmented.

A fortnight later when I had finished sweeping and dusting down the staircase, I looked up and saw Miss Tyler standing behind me. A thrill of a mixed nature shot through me as I perceived she was about to speak; she had been ignoring my existence.

"I have been watching you." I began to tremble, uncontrollably. "You have not been doing your work decently" — a favourite word of hers. "Don't think you can get out of it like that. March upstairs and do it again."

I went upstairs and carefully dusted down the bannister again, aware that Miss Tyler was below, scrutinizing my every move. I was clumsy and confused and did not see clearly what I was doing. When I arrived at the bottom of the staircase, she said: "March upstairs and do it again." I said softly: "I've done it again."

"Do as I tell you." I hesitated. "Will you do as I tell you!"

"I have done it."

There was a moment of silence in the front hall, then a strange loud crack like the ripping noise of thunder. I was stunned and listened to the echo. My head throbbed. Suddenly I realized that Miss Tyler had hit me over the head with the dust-brush — it was in her hand not mine. Something outweighed by far the sharp pain that was making itself felt in my head — a primary experience of grief when one person raises his hand against another. I felt unspeakable sadness and was inwardly transplanted to the shores of an ocean of tears wept at man's violation of his own kind, experiencing my own vulnerability and innocence and a prickling feeling of pity for Miss Tyler. I sobbed. I was too overwhelmed by sadness to heed a warning contained in this incident and was not ready for what was to come.

A few days later I inadvertently crossed Miss Tyler's purposes. Quickly aware of it, I apologized. "You won't get away like that. March up to my room."

She followed me upstairs, pushed me into her room and locked the door. Veering round, she whisked the yardstick from her sewing table: "Hold out your hands!"

I did not quite grasp what I was meant to do.

"Hold out your hands, I say."

My hands went out in front of me. The brass-beaded yardstick came down on my palms, down and down.

"Turn your hands over." The yardstick flayed my knuckles; the blows made a sickening sound. Tears spurted from my eyes and released deep shuddering sobs.

I pleaded with her to stop. My hands hung swollen, throbbing with pain at my sides: "Please, please . . ."

She laid the yardstick aside and took me into her arms. I felt the woodenness of her body beneath her clothing and the faint odour of decay about her person filled my nostrils. Her chin brushed my face in a kiss; she had never kissed me before. I closed my eyes and abandoned myself to the sick headache which now came on in violence. I was excused from school and sent to bed.

In the darkened room, I sank into an abyss where my throbbing head and aching hands eclipsed all else. Again and again I vomited into the bucket at the side of the bed. I could have vomited out my very soul.

It was not only wariness that made me softer and more attentive to Miss Tyler after this. I dimly sensed she had an abyss of her own that was in some way related to my person and was aggravated by my rejection of her as someone to love and be loved by. I had to steer clear of her and everything her existence implied but I did not want to hurt. Yet other provocations followed and the scene with the yardstick was repeated with the same abject aftermath that humiliated and led nowhere. Shame at my inability to stand up to the pain delivered had to be suffered as well.

At school we were reading a book of historical studies for children which contained the celebrated account of the Spartan boy who went to school with a fox cub hidden in his chiton and who allowed himself to be gnawed to death by the cub rather than to cry out in agony and let others witness it.

I now endured the chastisements with new fortitude and had an ideal to identify with. I became able to stand the pain without wincing, without tears. There were no scenes of reconciliation afterwards. Letting the inevitable sick headache pass by, I knew I had gained some unassailability. After a time Miss Tyler had exhausted the use of the yardstick and ceased applying it.

We, that is I, found school absorbing. We were rehearsing The Priest of Horus by Lord Dunsany as the culmination of our period on Egyptian history. Apart from the rehearsals which took most of the mornings, we painted our own scenery. On high narrow light wooden frames spanned with canvas we had sized, Dorothea sketched Egyptian figures with the sideways turn at the hip, with pleated white kilts, hieroglyphics, gods with cat and hawk heads and broad borders of lotus flowers which were to be painted green and white and red and blue with gold worked in. We felt as though we were building the Temple of Horus as we perched on ladders and scaffolding in our huge classroom and painted for hours on end.

I was allotted the lotus flowers and for days I painted, leaving a trail of what I considered exquisite acts of creation. I continued painting lotus flowers in my mind at night — green and white and red and blue blossoms with the sheen of golden divinity upon them.

As the actual performance of The Priest of Horus drew near, I became obsessed by a technical problem I was convinced only I could solve. In Dunsany's play, the priest has turned away from spiritual matters and indulges in greed and good living. He gives a banquet to the dignitaries of the land and while the feast is in progress, the Nile rises up in anger and floods the temple drowning the whole company.

The River Nile! That was the problem.

I sweated to give birth to an idea how to make the Nile rise and flood our temple so that we could drown properly. I expounded my ideas to Dorothea. She listened attentively and added her own considerations, but I felt she had not fully understood the issue. I pictured a tidal wave coming up from the basement on to the stage at the right moment, if only the taciturn janitor downstairs could be persuaded to turn on all the water hydrants for the play.

"Yes," said Dorothea, "but how will you then control the water?"

"We all have to drown, don't we?"

"But you don't want to drown the whole audience too, do you?"

Dorothea continued to be biased and we didn't get much further. I remained possessed by the Nile and forgot my lines at rehearsals. Finally Dorothea took the Nile into her own hands and succeeded in switching my attention to the erection of our vividly painted temple sections over on the stage in the assembly hall.

I was enchanted by the beauty and splendour of the temple that rose up on all sides and enclosed us in an ancient sacred shrine which made one walk and talk differently, and I had to be reminded by a very firm Dorothea that there were other things to be done if we were ever to be ready in time.

For the performance our arms and legs were smeared with light brown stuff to make us look Egyptian; my white kilt was secured around my middle and the black and gold headgear placed on my head invested me with priestly dignity, for I was the Priest of Horus, and the great of the land were come to my table which was laden with fruits and good things. My place was here in the midst of the hieroglyphics, animal heads and lotuses; my dimensions swelled beyond my own skin and almost burst it; I lost any sense of my own small person; the present vanished and I was an Egyptian in ancient Egypt.

Suddenly the moment of Nemesis arrived — the Nile! I had forgotten it in my enchantment. In the wings, Dorothea was emptying a small jug of water which trickled on to the stage, barely perceptible, and signalling to us to begin drowning. We expressed somewhat belated horror at the sight of the Nile sweeping in, grimacing wildly at the trickle of water finding its uncertain way under the table, and painstakingly began to drown on the floor with loud and gruesome gulps, until the audience was in convulsions.

Punished by the Nile, we lay dead on the floor until the lights slowly faded leaving us in darkness, which rendered the hilarious roars on the other side of the curtain the more audible. The Priest of Horus was a great success and the other teachers never failed to congratulate us on our fine drowning scene.

Dorothea encouraged me to write plays and produce them. I had seen a negro performance of "Joseph and his Brothers" in a church hall in Philadelphia and became fired by this material. I read the story in the Old Testament, identified myself with Joseph and wrote the play I had seen in the church hall, including the song I had "composed" for Joseph's dreams.

The all-important factor in the Joseph drama was his coat, purportedly of many colours, which I insisted on sewing myself because no one else would achieve its fulgent splendour. Like a jackdaw, I collected bits of coloured material and cut them up to fit their neighbours and stitching them side by side or end to end. The result was a conglomeration of hideously puckered patches, a coat of many errors and multitudinous rages and tears.

In the end Dorothea came to my rescue and sewed a cloak of bands of coloured silk which was so exquisitely graceful that when it hung around my shoulders — I was Joseph in the play — I felt as though I was clothed with the rainbow.

We performed Joseph and his Brothers in one of the big fireplaces in our classroom with some of the younger classes in the orphanage making up the audience. The play was well nigh endless and during the performance, I was filled with distaste for Joseph and Joseph's father and brothers and Egypt altogether, which collapse of enthusiasm had an ill effect on the rest of the cast who lost their raison d'être: the sheaves of corn and the fat and lean kine no longer knew who they were — if they had known before — and sat and stared vacantly into the audience. In the end as usual, Dorothea came to our aid. Rising to her feet, she gave a speech of appreciation in which she supplied the end of the drama and we were all released from the ordeal.

When Joseph was well over and forgotten, I switched to the more peaceful arts, albeit equally obsessively. I worked on a lengthy opus in rhymed verse on the Twelve Labours of Herakles which I illustrated in pastels, but this opus was my Penelope's web, for whenever it was near completion, I started all over again and the consumption of materials was excessive. It was not a lack of enthusiasm or application that prevented me from finishing "Herakles"; it was my fear of finishing something that had been a kind of house for my mind to live in.

The Hanging Gardens of Babylon followed. Dorothea had told us about them in one of our history periods. She might have been less expansive had she known what was coming. When I rose from my place on the morning the Hanging

Gardens made their entry into our classroom, I was dedicated to the idea of illustrating them in a lino cut.

It was to be a very large lino cut. I asked for the biggest piece of paper in the store cupboard and set to work filling the page with the nine-tiered structure and then drawing fruit trees and vines and ferns and vegetables, grasses and flowers in minutest detail all along the terraces which began to vanish under all this lushness and under the eraser.

Always encouraging, always constructive, Dorothea could hardly control her consternation when she regarded the Gardens: "It's too big I think; you want to make a smaller picture."

"But the Hanging Gardens were bigger than our classroom!"

"But you'll never manage to reach all the corners when you come to cutting the lino if it's as big as all that."

"I can easily walk around it and cut it from the other side."

Dorothea was silent. Then: "Yes, but a very large sheet of paper won't go into the roller when it comes to inking."

I hadn't thought quite so far and suggested I start again.

"Alright," said Dorothea, "I'll give you another sheet of paper, and I'll help you a little with the perspective."

She was so quick to act that before I knew it, a fresh — and smaller — piece of paper lay before me and Dorothea was leaning over my shoulder lightly sketching the Hanging Gardens in outline.

"Let me do it myself!" My pencil magnetically traced Dorothea's lines and soon a wonderful terraced structure filled the page. I then carefully and slowly began to draw all the vegetation that burgeoned in my mind on to the paper until the unique architecture was again engulfed in the lead pencil jungles, and the eraser had to come along to thin out the vegetation so that the sheet of paper became transparent in part and I succumbed to exhaustion for the day.

The next morning, I asked for a fresh sheet of paper. "Could you start me off, Dorothea, please?" And on it went until Dorothea energetically announced a few days later that *this* drawing was going to be transferred on to the lino for cutting, and the second stage of the Hanging Gardens commenced.

If the first stage was marked by my meagre artistic abilities, the second was going to display my equally meagre manual ability. When I cut out the filigree patterns I had designed, whole fruits came away under my knife and I became the unintentional reaper in my garden, dealing devastation. Dorothea hovered behind me like a surgical nurse, a pot of glue in her hands; she was never so much with me as during the Hanging Gardens.

Finally she stated that the lino cut was finished and we pulled off print after print, washed down the roller and pulled off further prints in different colours. The prints were spread out on all available surfaces in the classroom and I wandered around not knowing which was the most exquisite. I chose a blue one to take back to the house and hang over the bed.

Not long afterwards, we went to Philadelphia to see an exhibition of children's work of the Čisek Art School in Vienna which had achieved considerable note at that time. In a small room leading off the Čisek collection, there was a little exhibition of work done by children in America. Here I saw two hideous and clumsy efforts: one, the Twelve Labours of Herakles, not quite finished; the other the Hanging Gardens of Babylon, if anything over-finished.

Adoption plans went on in a different form. The unmarried daughter of a prominent and very wealthy Philadelphia family had somehow heard of me and had expressed interest in my "case".

Miss Tyler explained to me that whatever my mother wanted or did not want concerning me made no difference because she had relinquished all her rights by not having done anything towards my upkeep. Now this Miss P. was a very rich and kind-hearted lady. She might be willing to adopt me legally and would appoint her, Miss Tyler, to be my guardian until I was eighteen. Miss P. would pay for my education and I would be going to another school and later on, to Vassar College — mecca of American amazon-hood. But first of all, Miss P. wanted to see me and it had been arranged that I go to Philadelphia to present myself.

Miss Tyler bought me a brown-and-orange tweed coat with an additional cape of the same colour and a brown felt hat for the occasion. Brown and orange and yellow were my worst colours. Miss Tyler's negro maid took me to Philadelphia on the appointed day and deposited me on the doorstep of the P.'s mansion where I was expected for lunch with Miss P. and her family.

A butler opened the heavy oak door. Miss Tyler's maid wriggled and smiled and walked almost backward down the stone steps into the street. A new maid took my cape-coat and hat. Another maid came to conduct me down a long silent passage with thick carpets to a huge drawing room and told me to wait there. I sat down on the edge of an elephantine chintz covered chair. The works in the porcelain clock on the bulbous marble mantlepiece were the only moving things in the heavy silence. Finally, yet another maid entered and summoned me to follow her to the dining- room where the family was waiting. I would have wanted to go to the bathroom but did not manage to break through the protocol the maid was observing. My eyes felt dark red as I stumbled after her, the pleats of my awkward brown serge skirt hitching up over my knees with every step.

In the centre of the room I was now led into there was a massive refectory table around which stood a number of very big people behind high-backed opulently carved oak chairs. A butler guided me to a chair over the back of which I could not see. A very big man at the end of the table murmured a few words rapidly under his breath and then there was a shuffling movement all down the table and everyone sat down. After the butler had pushed my chair with me on it into place and I had disentangled my legs from the oaken legs of the table, the person on my right introduced herself and me to the rest of the company, stumbling over my Dutch surname. I blushed and did not know what to say, but Miss P. was friendly in a casual manner and put me at my ease. She had a long full throat and fuzzy hair, a large face with coarse pores, but her hands were beautiful and so was her voice. She tactfully showed me what fork to use and instructed the butler what to put on my plate. My confidence in her grew as also the heady joy of an encounter with another person. I was beginning to feel happy.

As the meal proceeded, Miss P. plied me with questions while the rest of the company concentrated so intensely on their plates that it seemed they had forgotten that Miss P. and I were still at the table. Miss P. had heard, she said, that I had travelled a lot when I was little. Did I remember any of the places I had

Anke as a baby

In America

Tea ceremony in Japan with Yuki-san

Modelling in Vienna

Anke Weihs in the 1960s and the 1980s

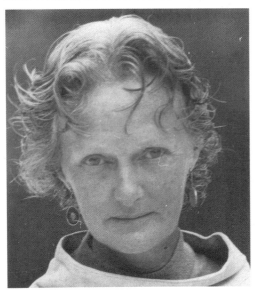

been to? I tried to present her with the geographical maze of my first six years. Occasionally, she corrected me; she seemed well informed.

Her interest in me melted all my reserves and I began to tell her things I had never spoken about to anyone else, not even Dorothea in school — about Greece.

"Surely you haven't been to Greece; aren't you making that up?"

Immediately something became a little bleak. I said without wanting to say it: "I was in Greece long ago."

Miss P. lapsed into silence. When she spoke again it was to the others at the table. The big man at the end had a loud and hollow way of laughing that held no mirth. Left out of the conversation now, I gazed up at the ceiling of the dining-room and saw a naked man lying on clouds, holding his fingertips out to a bearded personage. The naked man's muscles rolled in archaic forms, and further along there were veiled women holding books and other dim figures I could not discern. Unaware of the impossible attitude I struck, I stared and stared up at the ceiling trying to grasp the significance of what was displayed above. Much later when I once visited the Vatican, I experienced a mild shock; I discovered the ceiling in the Philadelphia mansion dining-room in the Sistine Chapel!

Suddenly I was the centre of attention again. This time the whole family was looking at me.

"You're a quaint little girl, indeedy," said Miss P. loudly and clearly, and smiled with amusement, but the core of her gaze was such that I wanted to cry.

As the family rose from the table and moved out of the dining-room Miss P. drew up alongside me: "You'll have to come and have tea with me sometime and I might take you to the zoo."

She conducted me down the long corridor to the front hall where a maid was waiting to help me on with my coat. Outside on the doorstep stood Miss Tyler's negro maid.

"Good-bye, little girl." Miss P. said and gave me one of her beautiful hands to shake.

"Oh, please may I go to the bathroom?" I had to say it. When I came out, she was gone. I went down the stone steps into the street with Miss Tyler's maid.

Some days later, Miss Tyler told me that Miss P. had thought things over and would not be adopting anyone. Miss Tyler did not seem put out.

15

We went to Canada for the summer holidays. Near our log cabin there was a sluicegate where the lake emptied into a gorge-like river-bed below. The sluicegates were usually shut while on the surface of the lake, scores of long timber stems accumulated waiting to begin their tempestuous journey down to the timberyards. The opening of the sluicegates was a dramatic event because the logs which had hitherto floated placidly on the lake became ungoverned in their fury once they had plunged through the narrow sluices and churned up the river below.

The lumberjacks with their long grappling hooks rode the logs down the current, herding them into a fierce and treacherous flock. All the summer guests and the local Indians collected in a crowd at the lake when the sluices were opened to watch the lumberjacks at their perilous task. Children were not meant to be there lest an accident happen to a lumberjack, but I managed to make myself unnoticed and witnessed the drama in full which, however, proceeded without catastrophe.

An Indian guide took the children in the camp for long hikes through the forests and across some of the old portages. We carried packs and followed him in single file. He taught us to walk with one foot straight in front of the other so that no path or ledge would prove too narrow — and soundlessly as well so that no wild creature would be alarmed. We were taught never to pick our way or deviate from the shortest route, but to move along swiftly taking roots, stones and other obstacles in our stride, yet at the same time watchful for snakes which might be lying in the sun on the open paths to all appearances like inanimate sticks, and aware that bobcats might be lying on the branch of a tree above.

By using Indian walking, long stretches could be covered with a minimum loss of energy. I revelled in the schooling the guide put us through and was prepared for it by my own continuous ramblings through the countryside at the orphanage. It did not occur to me that my place in the trail of children following the guide could be anywhere other than just behind him where, unobstructed by any other body, I absorbed his way of moving into mine.

Miss Tyler made the acquaintance of a Mr and Mrs Barclay who had a log cabin in a secluded spot down on the edge of the lake. Mr Barclay was a director of Dodge Brothers. He had a singularly shapely head and fine features and was tall, slender and dark. Mrs Barclay was round and soft and wore an expression of sweetness and gentleness on her face. The Barclays had no children.

After I went to bed at night, Miss Tyler and Dorothea often spent the evening with the Barclays in their cabin and in daytime, I was frequently sent to them on errands.

Not long after we arrived at the camp, Miss Tyler told me that the Barclays were going for a fortnight's camping trip away from everything and that they would like to take me with them. She said: Mr Barclay was a very rich man and he and his wife were thinking of adopting a little girl as they had no children of their own.

The day of departure dawned; we all rose early. I made great efforts to contain my excitement but was giddy with anticipation. Down at the edge of the lake, the Indian guide who was going with us was busy loading the three canoes. He was to take Mrs Barclay in his canoe, I was to go in the second one with Mr Barclay and the third canoe containing our tents and stores was to trail behind. The morning was radiant and the mountains and cabins and forests along the shore of the lake were mirrored in the calm water in near perfection. In all my elation, there was a dull undertone of anxiety lest in the last moment something would happen to prevent our departure.

At last everything was ready and we were ensconced in our

canoes. I turned to say good-bye to Miss Tyler and Dorothea who were standing on the tiny wooden landing place, careful not to show my happiness at going with the Barclays, but their images quickly receded as our canoes cut through the glassy water and the scene around us already began to change.

The guide and Mr Barclay paddled in silence. The drip-drip from the uplifted paddles and the gentle wash of the canoes were the only sounds to be heard in the radiant stillness of the morning. Occasionally a fish jumped. As we slipped past the more familiar parts of the lake and new scenery rose up on all sides, we began to exchange words from canoe to canoe. The guide pointed out a long wooded island which, he said, was at times frequented by moose. Maybe we could take a moonlight trip to the island from our new camp further along the lake.

The day became warm and the pristine radiance mellowed; haze trembled over the surface of the lake. At midday, we arrived at the place where we were going to camp; it was a remote corner of the same big lake. For three full hours we had seen no house, no cabin, not a single tent — only silent islands, forests and mountains closing in and narrowing the lake on all sides.

We hauled our cabins up on to the lip of a green meadow that sloped gently towards the water from the foot of a fir covered mountain. The guide and Mr Barclay unpacked the tents and other equipment while Mrs Barclay set about getting a meal ready and I was dispatched to look for drinking water.

I went along the edge of the lake with a water container towards what looked like the mouth of a stream. I soon heard the gurgle of water and found a little brook that ran from the mountain over the meadow into the lake. I filled the container. When I straightened up, I saw a tall black wooden cross standing at some distance on the other side of the brook. I cleared the brook with a leap and went over to look at the cross. At its foot there was a cluster of grey stones between which grew patches of big forget-me-nots, vividly echoing the blue of the sky. Behind the cross rose the sombre dark green mountain.

I was taken to the roots of my being; this lonely sign had a compelling power. I emulated its gesture with outstretched arms and experienced something new — a burning longing to give myself up unreservedly — to what? What was there to give oneself to? To give without return.

This silent place became my retreat during our fortnight's camp and in any case, I had to go there three times a day for water. I did not say anything about the cross to Mr and Mrs Barclay or the guide.

There was an evening when the sun was setting behind the mountain and the cross stood out against the fiery sky and the pool of forget-me-nots deepened into royal purple. The starkness of the cross was taken up on flaming wings and a minor strain became a major blast of victory. And once in the early morning when I went for water, the cross stood in the dew as though in a sea of sparkling diamonds and the clear waters of the lake rippled in the breeze that goes before the sun. The cross was a great window bar before the beauty of the world.

Life in the camp had no moments of strain or tension. I now called the Barclays Mummy and Daddy Barclay and was entirely and deeply relaxed; things that had required reserve and alertness had vanished away and for the first time in my life, I trusted that harmony would last throughout the day.

At the orphanage I was not allowed to swim in the creek where the village children swam. Miss Tyler said it was dirty and contaminated and as I got rashes from so many things, she would not take the responsibility for my swimming in the creek. There was no other place to swim and so I practised the strokes I had observed in bed which created a great upheaval in the bedclothes but gave me the confidence that when the opportunity came to swim in real water, I could do so safely.

Now on the first morning of our camp, Daddy Barclay came out of his tent in his bathing suit: "Coming for a swim?" I thrilled and went to put on my swimsuit. At the edge of the lake, I tingled with the fear of the unknown. I did not tell Daddy Barclay that I had never been swimming before. He plunged in; I saw his head rise to the surface again and plunged in after him and committed myself to the lake. Rising to the surface I swam in his wake like a fish.

A blissful sense of well-being embraced me as the soft rippling water bore up my body. Long caressing arms of invisible beings helped me forward, let me go again to take me forward once more. I caught their fleeting smiles in the ripples. Every swimming movement of mine was answered by a counter movement of theirs; swimming became a communion with another race or genii. At night after a day in the water, I felt as though I were expanded over the whole earth and tremendous panoramas and living pageants of great events rose up on all sides.

One evening the Indian guide volunteered the story of the cross on the meadow. A farmhouse, he said, had stood on that spot some thirty years before and was occupied by a minister and his wife and their eight children. The minister had come to this place for peace and solitude. He preached to the Indians at the trading post on the other end of the lake and otherwise worked the fields around the house, keeping a cow and some poultry.

One day when he had gone across the lake to fetch stores, a thunderstorm broke out and the farmhouse was struck by lightning and both it and the barn were burned to the ground. There was no one there but the minister's wife to fight the flames and in the end she and all her children save the two youngest who were playing out on the meadow lost their lives in the fire.

When the minister returned to his home, he found a charred heap of smouldering beams and planks and amongst them, the bodies of his wife and six children. That first night was unimaginable.

The next day the minister buried the remains of his family and went away with the two little ones to return some time later by himself to erect the cross over the place where his wife and children lay. After that he went away and was not heard of again in those parts.

As I listened to the guide's story, a hand seemed to reach in and squeeze my heart; I felt it physically. Standing by the cross in the evening, I sensed the presence of the minister's wife in the atmosphere, not as something that was dead, inanimate, but as living, ongoing and henceforth when I went to fetch water, the evidence of that life seemed to be the running water itself.

Daddy Barclay went fishing and I begged to paddle the canoe

for him. He sat in front with his rod and I sat behind him gripping the paddle, my eyes resting on the back of his head, my mind in a treacherous state because I did not want to see him pull fish out of the water and make them gasp for life until their convulsions quietened into death or worse, until he gave them a blow on the head, but I did want to be with him in the canoe. I paddled with might and main, the canoe zig-zagging drunkenly as a result which made Daddy Barclay roar with laughter: the fish, he said, would all flee to the other end of the lake! I was relieved for the sake of the fish but sorry that he had to return to Mummy Barclay with empty hands and was in the grip of complexities. For subsequent fishing excursions, the guide went with Daddy Barclay and what was done was enacted somewhere out on the lake out of sight, but I refused fish when it came to having it for supper.

I often sat with Mummy Barclay on the shore of the lake in the resonant sunshine and talked about whatever entered my mind. She listened with a fine little smile on her lips and by an occasional remark gave me to understand that however incoherent I was about things never spoken out before, she had infinite time as well as a warm desire to get to know me deeply. Her presence was so comforting that I sometimes felt as though I could dissolve in sheer bliss and would long for the return of the men or for something energetic to do.

One night half way through the fortnight, the full moon rose over the mountains and we set off to the moose island in the hopes of witnessing a gathering. Mummy and Daddy Barclay went in one canoe and I went in the leading one with the guide. The great round moon shed a golden glow over the lake and its surrounding mountain wall. Now and then a night bird flew its lonely flight low over the water with a sad minor cry or a fish leapt up and fell back with a plop causing fine ripples to trouble the mirror of the moon a little.

We were not far from the island, which was not far from the camp where Miss Tyler and Dorothea were, when the guide suddenly pointed and whispered: "Sssssst." At some distance a few moose were swimming, their huge flat antlers like floating branches of trees and their humps and monstrous noses so hideous in the exquisite night that I shivered in delight.

The guide laid his paddle across his knees for a bit and the canoe went on under its own impetus. This gave the moose time to reach the island. In the dark shadows of the forest along the edge, we discerned them heaving themselves out of the water. Only the knocking of antlers woodenly against one another and the soft dull thud of hooves against stones could be faintly heard.

The guide raised his paddle and dipped it in. The canoes rounded the narrow end of the island swiftly and drew close to the shore. He peered through the moonlight to find a suitable place to land and having seen one, pointed the prow of our canoe straight for the rocks. Soon we were hauling the canoes up on the fine pebbles between the rocks. Then he led the way through the forest. For a time, nothing could be heard but the rippling of the lake and the soft crackling of twigs underfoot as we passed over carpets of pine needles and cones. Moonlight trickled through the upheld branches of the firs. The smell of sun-warmed resin lingered in the cool breath of the night and wood spirits seemed to move between the trees, accompanying us as we went.

All at once the guide paused, his finger on his lips. In the centre of the island moose were roaring. We hastened on through the forest until we reached the ruins of a large stone-built house. We entered the ruin where we had a safe vantage point whence to see the moose. We took up our position at an opening which had once been a large window and peered into a clearing in the forest. To me there seemed to be hundreds of moose there. They were going through the steps of a slow dance and were in constant swaying motion. Now and then a bull roared like the blast of a trumpet. The scene proved too much for me — the moving archaic creatures, the trumpet blasts in the still night, the full moon pouring down into the clearing. I began to fall asleep standing up, leaning against the rough stone wall of the ruin — leaning against a swaying moose, moving with them, being ground, crushed in the mortar of their alien bodies . . .

Suddenly Daddy Barclay whispered: "Look, they're going!" I opened my eyes and stared into the night. In single file, the moose were leaving the clearing. They disappeared into the blackness of the forest to reappear on a ridge above over which the moon hung low. Across the moon they went, a procession of humps and monstrous noses going back in time, a trek in reverse, on and on into the stillness of the night.

In the canoe I lay cradled in Mummy Barclay's arms. I woke up fully only the next morning.

One evening the guide fried too many eggs for supper. Mummy Barclay with a faint note of annoyance in her voice, instructed him to put the uneaten eggs into the store — an orange box covered with wire netting; she would see what could be done with them the next day.

We sat and talked around the dying fire. The night was aglow with fireflies vying with the occasional upward burst of sparks from the burning wood — until it was time to retire.

Lying in my tent, I heard the Barclays talking softly in theirs. The smell of anti-mosquito oil wafted over and the stillness of the night was so intense that I could not get to sleep. After a time, the murmuring in the other tent ceased. The stillness went on.

I was about to fall asleep at long last when I heard a scratching, grunting and huffing nearby. Cautiously raising the flap of my tent, I peered out and saw two young bears in the moonlight. They had pulled over the store box and were feasting on our fried eggs; each having seized an egg would sit up on his haunches and stuff it into his maw only to fall back on all fours for another egg. I watched them with growing delight and wondered if I should wake Mummy and Daddy Barclay and tell them about our visitors.

Suddenly, without any warning, the guide came out of his tent which was pitched some way off and shooed the bears away. He righted the store box and stood motionless for a while, I supposed lest the bears or their dam return. I lay back on my bed of fir branches and ferns without a sound so that he would not know I was awake.

The next morning when the guide heard me telling Mummy and Daddy Barclay about the nightly raid, a strange look passed over his face. He was not pure Indian; he had some French blood and French was his mother tongue although apart from his Indian speech, he spoke English well. From the front his face was large and fleshy and slightly brutal. From the side it was lean and hawklike. It was a Janus face, an enigma, the face of two persons and given to staring at people from early on, I often found myself staring at him to fathom the riddle of his face. He began to notice it and, when we were alone, he put his hand on my shoulder or wrist, and sometimes smiled at me as though we had an unspoken understanding no one else must know of.

My feeling of unease mounted steadily and once it broke through into my conscious mind, it was there all the time. The daily routine of the camp having been established, the Barclays left me free to roam and to do what I liked while they went off for long walks together. I now experienced a kind of terror when they left me on the open camping ground where I could not escape from the scrutiny of the guide who, crouching near his tent, mended fishing tackle or sharpened his hunting knife. I could not get myself to go swimming when he was about.

I would try to slip away from the camping place unseen, over the meadow past the cross into the forest at the foot of the mountain, and would describe a big circle, finally coming down to the shore of the lake a good way off from the camp. From there I would approach the camp cautiously, making sure that the Barclays had returned before venturing out into the open.

Nothing untoward occurred other than the touch on the shoulder and the oblique smile, yet my fear of the guide grew from day to day. During the last three days of camping, I clung to Mummy and Daddy Barclay and begged to go with them on their walks. They welcomed my wanting to be with them. "We weren't quite sure you'd want to come with us," Mummy Barclay said.

As I walked between them, I would have rejoiced had it not been for the dark fleshy face of the guide back at our camping place. I was troubled that what had entered and possessed my mind concerning the guide was so dominating that it pushed my love and yearning and respect for the Barclays into the background just as the precious fortnight with them was coming to an end.

Nothing was clear-cut and crystalline — everything was moulded out of intricate material. It depended on the integrity of the sculptor. I had a dim feeling that I was being tested although I had no means of grasping the nature of the test; I was only nine, both clumsy and unknowing in the craft of relationships. I did not realize that by staring at people to get behind their masks, I inevitably summoned forth some kind of reaction. My interest in people was a one-way one; when on the few occasions that some mutuality of interest formed between myself and another person, it had ultimately to be undone, and so at times, I felt consuming compassion for a person as long as that compassion was not reciprocated. It was only with animals that I felt fully at ease.

On the last evening, I sat by the fire between Mummy and Daddy Barclay — the now familiar scene of the mountain-fringed lake only slightly changed by the dominating gibbous moon. This subtle moon was the sign of some subversive domain where nothing was allowed to remain clear and single, nothing was allowed to achieve perfect joy, perfect light.

Mummy and Daddy Barclay told me that they had been very happy with me. They had no little girl of their own. Would I like to be their little girl? I tried desperately not to let my affirmative sound forced by the whirlpool of longing, fatalism, relief, reserve and the keen prick of my own Self standing at one side — that filled me to bursting point.

The next morning we dismantled the tents and took to our tightly packed canoes. I went with Daddy Barclay. He paddled ahead this time and I could not see the guide who was behind with Mummy Barclay. As we pulled away from the shore, I turned to look back at the cross. It stood out black and stark against the sombre green mountainside.

16

Back at the orphanage, Miss Tyler told me that I would be spending the Christmas holidays with the Barclays at their home in Hartford. Meanwhile, there were certain departures from the usual course of events in my existence.

All the girls at the orphanage went to Sunday school and to church. I, being "private", had not been required to conform, nor was Miss Tyler herself a church-goer. But now she said I would have to begin to get used to going to church and to Sunday school because the Barclays would like me to. I scanned her face to read her thoughts. Her expression was obscure and I had a faint sense of being in league with her, although conforming to any norm always attracted me initially.

Conforming and not being different from others was one thing. The idea I had of religion was another. On occasions like Washington's or Lincoln's birthdays or other days of national commemoration, everyone in the orphanage gathered in the big assembly hall before school in the morning. Across the wall behind the platform where the principal sat was spanned the Stars and Stripes. At a given signal, the company rose to its feet, each member thrust forward his right arm and spoke the words in chorus: "I pledge allegiance to the flag, etc., etc." (from which ritual I was exempt, being a Dutch national). I assumed that the flag and the nation were objects of veneration and worship and that churches were there for the more esoteric sides of this worship. This assumption was reinforced by the sight of Boy Scouts coming out of church on Sundays in their militant uniforms or by Salvation Army officers on the streets in Philadelphia singing hymns. Militant nationalism seemed to be what Christianity implied.

My own god was Zeus. He was omnipotent; I could shut nothing away from his all-seeing eyes, not even my thoughts —

he knew them all. My mind lay spread out beneath his gaze like a sheet spread out on the lawn for bleaching. Even when I rebelled against his steadfast scrutiny and longed to hide away from it, I sought his stern corrective countenance, his cool unwavering look into the black spots within.

Zeus was not the sun; he was the infinite blue of the sky, the remote mountain peak, sharp and chaste. There was another god whose name I did not know. He troubled existence and made it swing from joy to sorrow, heights to depths, coolness to heat, hatred to love. In the end, he made everything swing to love, to loving like consuming fire that left you a little heap of ash in the morning sunlight. This god gave one premonitions and fierce moments of insight; he filled one with music, with the intoxication of enthusiasm, and he did not mind if you erred. He made you feel too big for your boots and then let you walk straight into the fires of shame. Later I would have called him Dionysus.

Zeus was the lofty Polar Star that drew the magnetic needle of my conscience to itself whether I liked it or not. He was the god to be reckoned with — the other too, but he crept up from within. Zeus was the crystalline frost that settled over the heat of confusion. He put me in my place.

The church that was to be the scene of my conversion was the little stone Episcopal church on the ridge down by the main road. On my first Sunday as church-goer, I took my place in the procession of girls walking up to the church hall for Sunday School, a new prayer and hymn book in my hand, head slightly bowed in deference to the situation and not unaware of the histrionics of the moment. (Zeus was showing his contempt, only I was not looking his way.)

Our minister stood in the doorway to the church hall smiling a welcome to his young congregation. I knew him from sight. He reminded me of the queen's wish in Snow White — to have a child whose hair was as black as ebony, whose skin was as white as snow and whose lips as red as blood. Our minister's complexion personified the queen's desire, but this by no means established him as a person in my eyes. On the contrary, I searched for some flaws in his immaculate appearance, a catch in his throaty voice and carefully chosen words, a hasty unpremeditated gesture — and found none. He irked.

Around the walls of the church hall there hung larger-than-life pictures of a sorrowful man in long garments with a rim of luminous light around his head, bending over crouching and kneeling miserable people of different races, accompanied by broad shouldered men who also wore rims of light, albeit not so luminous, who didn't seem to approve of the one who stretched out his hands to ragged little children held up in their mothers' arms. This was Jesus, the carpenter's son.

Then we sang: "Little Jesus loves me so, for the Bible tells me so." How could the sorrowful man be Little Jesus? He seemed so irrevocably adult in the pictures around the church hall. Our minister instructed us that Jesus was the Lamb of God and that we were all to become his lambs. I was bewildered. The lion cub saw no reason why it should become a lamb. We learned the creed: "I believe in God the Father Almighty, Maker of heaven and earth (this was different; I believed in Him too — he was Zeus, the One who commanded my spirit into my body), but what followed was new and alien and too sudden a reference to the sad man on the walls of the church hall whose identity I didn't grasp but who had a holy ghost. Only when the creed went on to speak of Pontius Pilate (I understood "pilot") did any gleam of recognition enter my straining mind although I didn't grasp why the terminology had all at once become nautical.

In our immaculate minister's scheme of things, inquiry was tantamount to blasphemy, albeit in one so young it must be borne with patience. As a result of our minister's patience in relation to my heathen state, the images I picked up were hard and brittle and devoid of divinity. The Holy Ghost was a querulous ancient with a wispy Tibetan beard (I was taken to a concert in Philadelphia attended by a famous veteran pianist who sat in the box of honour, at the sight of whom I murmured all too audibly: "Look, there's the Holy Ghost!") and the Little-Jesus-loves-me-so who loomed so large in the church hall settled in my mind as a public figure for whom one had to vote. As he was portrayed with Chinese, Indians, Africans and others, I concluded that he was a missionary out east (during Lent we were to forego sugar and jam for the sake of the poor starving

Chinese children) and was probably a co-worker of Ghandi's whose example dominated the social ethics of the time. Thus the "earnest expectation of the creature", the innate religious longing in the child was met by a vacuous system of sentimentalities.

My relation to Zeus was that of a potential equal in the ultimate evolution of things. What else was man if he was not to become godlike? This potential lay in the fateful, uncomfortable talent given by the Lord of the Household to his servants who were to make of it what they could and would. It was the burning issue upon which everything depended. There was no sense in life if this was not to be hoped for. Besides, men had something the gods did not have — something which aroused their envy so that they pursued, hunted down and flayed a man. It was the prerogative to sin, to err, to choose, fail, learn, to exult, to overcome — and the royal prerogative to be forgiven. No man can forgive God; God can never be a Prodigal Son.

My soul was a stringed instrument upon which the hand of the Sender played, changing minor and major strains or fierce accords and discords, and sometimes a tender lyric that assuaged the tension between that part that was indigenous to the unseen world and that part which got out of bed every morning and put its boots on to go to school.

After an hour's Sunday school, we went over to the church for the service. I sat in a high-backed pew in the dimly lit nave and the fever of inquiry abated; the atmosphere laid a cool compress of piety on my troubled brow. The discreet footsteps of the verger was the signal for us to bow our heads. Supplications bubbled from the red lips of our minister; his fervent voice, the more so to God, had a momentary somniferous effect. I clutched my prayer book and inhaled spurious virtue with the gentle clouds of incense that wafted down the aisle.

After church, the black-and-white-and-red minister stood outside in the sunshine in his robes to shake hands with his flock and flash a white toothed smile at each lamb. I would choose a longer way back to the house in order not to have to play the new part longer than necessary and to be alone.

After my third Sunday on the little ridge, Miss Tyler told me that my attendance at Sunday school and church was to be suspended for a while. She did not seem perturbed. I knew that Zeus was wearing a sardonic expression on his august countenance.

Yet Zeus was to witness another excursion into orthodoxy on my part, this time self-arranged.

A new little girl came as the tenth to Miss Tyler's house and Miss Tyler shifted my bed to make room for her in my room for a while. She was Spanish and her name was Maria. Maria had black eyes and freckles and was meticulously tidy. I felt like a Goth or a Vandal (I had just been reading about them) in her presence and watched her every move with awe and admiration although we hardly communicated with one another. She had an absorbing occupation in life which was to allow a little string of black beads to slip continuously through her fingers while she murmured: "Ave Maria, Mother of God."

Maria? Could she be referring to herself? Here was a mystery. Gradually, however, after evenings of listening intently to her exhortations spoken fervently on her knees at the side of her bed, I gathered she was addressing a beautiful lady who was a kind nurse who bestowed cool balsam on all sins one had committed during the day. This lady caught my fancy. I longed to attract her attention and feel the iron power of her gentle hand upon my brow, but I realized she would not notice me if not summoned by the magic formula: Ave Maria, Mother of God — accompanied by running beads. I became a jackdaw on the lookout for jet beads and buttons which I surreptitiously strung on a length of parcel string.

The decision to take the magic formula into my mouth was not so easy. I sensed the trespass, the tactlessness entailed, and the more I listened to Maria's prayers the more I knew that I was going to be an interloper in a territory in which I had no business to be. But the immaculate image of Our Lady and the subtle atmosphere that went with her exerted their age-old pull and one evening, an "Ave Maria" passed the barrier of my teeth and I stepped over the forbidden threshold.

The room was grey and chilly. Through the ceiling Zeus looked down on me with clear frosty eyes full of divine disgust. I looked up at him and writhed in shame. Zeus did not tolerate deviations nor was he given to mercy. I simply had to endure his contempt.

After this a single prayer remained with me, a prayer that stemmed from no orthodoxy or system and not even Zeus had the power to answer it: "O God, help me stop thinking about myself!" It was a prayer to be delivered from a curse; my thoughts circled the whole daylong like birds of prey around my own existence. They hardly ever alighted somewhere else.

I began to have obsessive ideas about death brought on by an incident in our neighbourhood.

I had been allowed to establish some contact with a girl next door although we had little in common. Her mother who was still young died and she came over to tell me that the morticians had taken out her mother's heart and insides and had pumped out her blood. They had filled her body with cotton wool and had dressed her in a pink satin dress and put rouge and lipstick on her and she was now laid out and looked so beautiful that everyone thought she was only sleeping. Would I like to come and view?

My mind bored its way into this macabre account. I pictured the morticians bending over the lifeless body, extracting parts, replacing them with cotton wool, imbuing the corpse with horrible senseless reflexes so that it would rise and walk blindly around the room, bumping into tables, overthrowing furniture — a cotton wool golem.

My fantasy became glued to the front room of the neighbour's house where the blinds were drawn for a few days (I evaded the invitation to view) and a cotton wool nightmare was rampant in my mind . . . in the darkened room, morticians were bending over their work; one held the sticky black heart in his hand and put it on the table behind him where no one would notice it and it would fall off and lie somewhere on the floor where anyone might step on it — then bales of cotton wool were stuffed into the bloody caverns — O God! Cotton wool had usurped the holy.

President Harding died in office just then and, in accordance with the nation's custom, his cortège was taken through the big cities to collect the final tributes of the people. We went to Philadelphia to see the cortègge there. The station was draped in black for the coffin was to arrive by train. Outside in the streets, flags hung half-mast and funereal drapes drooped from the windows. Most people wore some sign of mourning and the whole city had slowed down and was silent.

We took our places in Chestnut Street (maybe it was Walnut Street) and waited with the still crowds. After a time, the funeral march could be heard with its excruciating beat and gradually, the gun carriage with the coffin containing President Harding, accompanied by soldiers stepping out in slow motion, came down the street. As it drew abreast, men removed their hats and women sniffled or just looked grave as the procession moved on.

At the first sight of the gun carriage, my head began to swell for I saw cotton wool oozing out of the joints of the coffin under the Stars and Stripes laid across it and growing into huge masses that filled the streets and pushed people aside, pressing them up against the walls of the houses so that they could no longer breathe. The black drapes were dead. Thick airless cotton wool expanded into everything — no corner was safe . . . For a fortnight I lay in the house with a high temperature, a merciful reaction to something that bordered on madness.

Death came to our village again, but this time it was different. Jim and Dora, a young negro couple, were married down in the village hall. Everyone knew Jim and Dora and their wedding was the occasion for much participation and talk. People had collected furniture and a tiny white wooden house at the far end of the village stood ready for them. White gauze curtains bulged in the breeze and Dora's beaming face could be glimpsed behind them as she got her new home ready for Jim and herself.

Jim was the handyman in the village and there was nothing he could not repair or put together. Even Miss Tyler called upon his services. Dora specialized in laundering fine things for the ladies in the village and I was often sent to her with Miss Tyler's green silk blouses which were finely pleated down the front for washing and ironing.

After the marriage ceremony which took place in the afternoon — it was during school hours so that none of us could be there — Jim and Dora came out of the village hall where a decorated buggy was waiting for them. Hardly had Jim placed Dora up beside him and taken the reins into his hands, when the horse took fright and bolted, dashing madly down the long hill at the dip of which our road merged out on to the main road.

At the bottom, the buggy overturned in a ditch and was dragged on several yards by the frantic horse, which reared in its harness until the shafts broke and someone ran out and caught it by the bit.

Anxious to see something of Jim and Dora's wedding, I came panting down on to the main road. They had extracted Jim and Dora from the wreckage of the buggy. They lay side by side on the grass covered by a horse blanket. On the cobblestones a bright pool of blood was spreading and in it was a scattered broken string of Woolworth pearls. It was a revelation to see that the black person had the same beautiful luminous red blood as other people; I had assumed that their blood was as black as their skin.

The faces of the two were at ease. A wisp of Dora's wedding dress was stirred by the breeze as if it had come to summon her away. People began to crowd around the scene. I was sent off.

As I went up our street, I looked back and saw Jim and Dora being lifted up on to a hay wagon and driven away; they seemed to be more wedded than they ever could have been in the village hall.

Throughout the autumn I hummed an inner song of anticipation of the Christmas holidays I was to spend with Mummy and Daddy Barclay, but the song had to remain inaudible for any other than my own ear. Outwardly any reference to the Barclays came from Miss Tyler, never from myself.

In school we were having the history of Greece. The step from the world of Homer to Sparta and Athens was as great and jolting as the step from a Doric temple to the ground below. Before, things had been measured in the dimensions of gods and titans; now the dimensions of existence were given by Lycurgus and Solon and man became the measure of man. I suffered the pain of loss when I was torn from the womb of mythology, but once my mental feet stood on the new ground of history in the becoming, I was fired with enthusiasm.

Sparta was the overture, and over and over again I held the pass of Thermopylae with Leonidas, turned tail with Aristodemus in the face of the Persian hordes to die later with redeemed honour. But to go to Athens was to take a double step upwards again — to the Parthenon, the embodiment of the state, Pericles' state, and the roseate pillared temple of the indwelling goddess whose messengers were the salient ideas springing from one's head. The Hanging Gardens were metaphor; the Parthenon was experience.

My reading up to now had forged and tempered emotions and set standards. At this stage in my childhood — I was now nine — I began to think about thinking and knew myself as one who thought, albeit my thinking was more imaginative than intellectual. I began to put questions rather to myself than to Dorothea, having formed the notion that there was nothing I could not understand if I thought strenuously enough about it and that only what I found out through my own efforts was really mine.

I began a process of discarding what was not mine, of testing my ideas about things according to my own experience. I set out to conquer my own territory of knowledge. I thought about clay, the construction of looms, the flight of birds, the patterns created by obstacles in running water, about soil, the different grains in timber, about light and darkness. I invented a safety pin, an egg beater, even a typewriter — in my bed at night. And with the new preoccupation, I began to be able to deal with my obsessions. A potter's wheel no longer went round and round in my head becoming emboxed there. I now thought about its construction and use, laid it aside and thought about the next thing. I was now able to think about things other than myself.

Into the place of hero and half-god stepped the statesman, the leader — Aristides, Leonidas, Themistocles, Pericles. Mythology gave way to biography. I identified myself, but never wholly, with Pericles, thought his thoughts, worded his speeches, made the determined, glorious but ethically ambivalent decision to crown Athens by whatever cost in raising up the

Parthenon after the Persian wars and summoning the entire artistic world to assist in the act. Yet — the goddess had never been at his side — Pericles was not Odysseus. Sometimes I stood — it could have been at any time of day — and listened to the golden voice filling the air around the Agora with burnished meaning. Suddenly Socrates touched me on the shoulder and I was his.

High up in the peppered air to the north stood the Asclepiade. The intent gaze of the Physician lay upon his patient — a sick city, sick of the plague, sick to death, Pericles' death. Up to the clean heights where the Asclepiade stood among the Attic pines came the rotten winds from the city, pest-heavy, carrion-laden.

The Physician gave his orders; pines were to be felled and fires lit along a broad front and into the flames was to be cast the aromatic fragrance of Attica — rosemary, thyme, sage — to mingle with the glowing resin. In the face of this spiced offensive, the plague retreated, lost its impetus, weakened and died down — an asclepiad Marathon — Hippocrates!

Then Alcibiades was suddenly there. I slipped into his skin more readily than into the others. Everything was familiar; gestures, voice, the sovereign beauty of his person, the well-being of perfect form, the intoxication of vanity, the shadow of Socrates cast into deeper places, the versatility that stripped the Athenian and made him a Spartan, that clothed him again and made him a Persian, that robbed him of his only real love and made him circle around Athens, violated by his intrigues, as a wolf circles around sheep — branded by the terrible question: What have you done? The sonant echo that travelled along the central nerve of one's own existence.

To the northwest of Athens, sacred omnipotent Eleusis had its own Judas. This Judas laughed, shook his brazen curls, drunken, and cast the mysteries into the street. And when he was hunted down like a fox in the bleak wild hills of Thrace and his body was riddled by a swarm of arrows, he stepped over into Charon's boat with a burden of guilt that was his contribution to human history evolving from the mystery to the rational; a dimming look out over the enchanted sea, violet with premonitions of countless seekers of Ithaka, the choppy grey loom of the story of Europe, the wine-red libation — Aigaios.

Seawards, to the sea! The sacred summons to the prophetic act outside the city, that spun a thread into the future to the pedestal of the Unknown God — sounded: Seawards, to the sea! And the long walk through the honeyed September air to Eleusis. But somewhere along the way, the amber atmosphere was pricked by a flash of light from elsewhere, the dawn sign of Him Whose man was to come this way: You men of Athens!

Athens was a storehouse of dreams. I stood on the decks of a galley that had passed silently up the sound before dawn. The low hills bore flocks of goats; the goatherds signalled their greetings to us. The red sun rose with a gust of heat and took the day by violence. The sound was jammed with galleys fighting on a sea of splinters, the smell of resin rising from the joists, the smoke of blood baking in the sun — the firmness under foot breaking away in a sweep towards the sea, the snapping of oars. Then in the golden September afternoon, the turmoil calmed. The souls of the dead freed themselves from the wreckage and impregnated the clouds. Salamis was accomplished!

Or I dreamt that I was being carried down over the hills of Megara in the evening on a stretcher made of sticks, sick with a grave wound that sent mists coiling around my spirit, but when the physician came to my side, I knew I would live. Or — I sailed up the sound again.

Christmas was approaching and Miss Tyler said that if I wanted to buy Christmas presents, I would have to earn the money to do so — I was no longer a small child. She would give me some oranges, sugar and twelve jars and would show me how to make marmalade, which I could then sell and keep the proceeds for Christmas presents.

The twelve jars, when everything was finished, were put into a basket and covered with a cloth, and I set out into the village to sell. I sold three jars straightaway to people I knew slightly and my customers were generous over and above the stipulated price per jar. Habitually resigned to failure, I was now intoxicated by success. I went on through the village with the remaining nine jars as if I had gold to sell. I knocked at doors less and less familiar. No one required marmalade. One young housewife took a jar out of my basket — I felt as though she were taking my heart out with it — and held it up to the light of the lamp in her kitchen, but then put it back: It looks very nice, but we don't eat marmalade.

It grew darker. I went on towards the periphery of the village into parts I did not know. I knocked at doors and explained to people that I needed money for Christmas presents. This elicited obscure remarks: Think of sending a child to beg for money; anyone can see she belongs to rich folks. Other remarks were still more obscure. The basket with the nine jars was growing heavy. People were pulling their blinds down against the coming night. A chill wind blew.

I turned back. The long hill over which the main road ran lay before me. I stopped to rest in the shelter of a bare maple for the wind was piercing. As I place the basket on the stone wall behind me, I inadvertently poked a finger through the paper top of one of the jars . . . I pulled it out and licked it.

In utter dejection, I arrived back at the house with nine empty jars. The indigestion in my mind was far worse than the physical discomfort accruing from my fall and was aggravated by Miss Tyler's sardonic remarks on the weakness of my character and her real or feigned disinterest in what was to happen now.

Thrown back on myself, I realized in the fires of shame that for all my pride and untouchability, I was morally feeble; I had not firmed up inside; this seemed to be my greatest threat.

Outwardly the humiliation suffered through the marmalade fiasco did not seem to affect anything. Miss Tyler talked frequently of the visit to the Barclays and as the day drew nearer for my departure to Hartford, all apprehension I experienced was dispelled — I was definitely and unquestionably going to the Barclays for the holidays.

The day of departure arrived. I tried not to take in an awful factor that suddenly emerged as though by not heeding it, I could obliterate it. Leila was packing to go to Hartford with me.

Leila was fifteen, a big lanky girl with coarse hair in a sandy coil around her head, a long spotty face and prominent teeth in a constantly open mouth. She was cheerful and loud in manner. I always felt an almost physical antipathy to her; she was as undifferentiated as a cow. Miss Tyler had latterly taken an ostentatious interest in her and small places I had hitherto occupied in Miss Tyler's scheme of things were now taken by Leila. While I welcomed release from certain burdensome obligations, there was, no doubt, a measure of jealousy in my antipathy to Leila.

Now that Leila came in and out of my room during packing as though we had something in common, my feelings of antipathy bordered on despair. I was utterly thrown out by the violence of my emotions and bottomless disappointment. Miss Tyler clarified the situation. Leila was going with me to the Barclays because she had more right to a nice home than I did, having no parents of her own. It could be that the Barclays might like to have Leila live with them. "So, you see, you're not the only pebble on the beach."

Bending over my suitcase packing, I wondered how I was going to face what was coming. Hunger for togetherness so persistently denied to the point of almost total isolation rendered me incapable of coping with a togetherness forced on me like Leila's sharing my holiday with the Barclays.

There was nothing to do but not to *want*. I could always resort to not wanting something. In a leap forward away, I could abruptly divest myself of any desire. I had learned how not to want because I wanted so much.

In this present situation, this much-resorted-to way out did not seem to work. I prayed that something would happen to prevent me from going to Hartford. I stood in front of Miss Tyler's door ready to knock and tell her I preferred to stay back. Why? She would say with a look of triumph; it would be as she wanted it to be. A declaration of preference on my part would be a step towards further involvement I had to avoid. I turned away from her door in time.

Wordlessly I went to the station with Leila, detesting myself for my dependence on her for making the journey. Wordlessly I followed her into the train to Hartford and did not break my silence on the way.

The Barclays were on the platform of the station in Hartford. I knew they were there to meet *me*, and that Leila's presence was additional. Daddy Barclay stretched up his arms to lift me down from the carriage, but I could not overcome my hurt; I was tight and reserved. Leila's cheerfulness bridged the gap for the moment and outwardly everything seemed to go well. Daddy Barclay drove us to his house in his big Dodge; Leila sat in the front with him and I sat in the back with Mummy Barclay, my knees covered with a soft rug. I wanted to put my head in her lap and cry, but I was stony and stiff.

The Barclays sensed despair in me and did everything they could to set me at ease. They arranged to be with me separately; Daddy Barclay showed me Hartford and took me out for lunch. Mummy Barclay came into my room in the evening and spoke to me of her longing to have a little girl of her own. She said she thought I might like to grow up as her daughter. Upstairs in the attic she had chests of linen and table silver which were meant for the daughter she never had. She would be happy to think they could belong to me when I was old enough to get married.

I tried not to let her see how her fairy tale was affecting me. In the turmoil of my feelings, I began to take ribboned candies from a box downstairs in the drawing-room — taking something from people who loved and trusted me, but I felt a compulsion to destroy what was being woven around me. My raids on the candy-box were considerable. Then it dawned on me that the Barclays suspected Leila of taking the candies. I hated Leila but I wanted to *hate* not to hurt, and I stopped taking the candies.

On the last evening but one of this tortuous Christmas holiday Daddy Barclay took Leila out leaving me alone with Mummy Barclay. She had some sewing to do, she said, and if I like I could sit with her while she did it.

I sat on a low stool by her chair in her tiny rose-coloured boudoir. I wanted to put my head in her lap and tell her I loved her. My whole being was keyed to it. She was never so gentle as she was on this evening; she tenderly and purposefully began to probe my shell: How did I get on with Miss Tyler? When had I last seen my parents? Was I happy being away from them for so long? Would it not be good if this uncertainty would come to an end and I would have a secure home?

Inside, an unmistakeable voice was telling me what I anyway knew: in spite of the Barclay's love for me and mine for them, the life they offered me had nothing to do with Me at the core of my existence. It would mean a deviation for which I would have to forfeit more than I could pay. It would be they who would be more badly hurt in the end. I drew back into myself like a snail into its house. I was polite, considerate, even affectionate, but back on my own ground.

Finally Mummy Barclay rose and put away her sewing things. She was crying. A rush of pity almost forced me forward again, but then I told her that it was I who had taken the candies from the drawing-room. This was my knife for performing the surgical operation.

Our leave-taking at the station was sad and tearful. I never saw or heard from the Barclays again.

17

School began again. There were changes in the classroom. The potter's wheel, the looms, the dyeing frames had vanished. In their places there were now regular rows of desks all facing one way.

Hitherto I had not had the experience of *sitting* in school; school had been a journey, a path of discovery, a search and a finding. Now it was sitting at a desk and having the subjects presented through the pile of textbooks, all new, that heaped before me. Dorothea stood up in front and conducted the lessons. Another teacher whom we did not know sat unobtrusively at the back of the room and her presence constituted a faint threat; Dorothea seemed to be on trial. Her hair became untidy, her voice a pitch too high, her sentences trailed off. I was acutely embarrassed and pained on her behalf. Only on the days when the other teacher was not there did she regain a little of her former sovereignty as our teacher.

We now had sums and American history. No doubt Dorothea bore some responsibility for my inability to grasp arithmetic; she was too biased a humanist. She may have believed or hoped it would come by itself, but the repeated tests we now had in arithmetic revealed a complete lack of foundation in this subject which barred the way for so readily making up for the deficiency.

Dorothea doggedly took the history of the early American settlers and instructed us how to use our textbooks. In turn we read passages out of the history books in monotonous voices and tested ourselves according to the questions listed at the end of each chapter. I couldn't understand most of the questions let alone think of any answers and a sense of bleakness set in right at the beginning of this new era at school. We went on in this manner to the War of Independence, the Civil War, the Monroe Doctrine, etc., etc., (Coolidge was now president), but the ferment had gone out of Dorothea's teaching and what I retained of it was straw.

In an effort to let Dorothea know how I experienced the present circumstances in the classroom, I had the only talk I ever had with her alone, having lingered after the others had left the classroom at the end of the day. Frayed and sad, she was tidying up when I approached her and asked for some very own work to do out of school hours. She understood my need and gave me Longfellow's poems and a slender volume of Lincoln's speeches: "Learn as much as you can by heart of these," she said.

Dorothea was wise in our predicament. Although Longfellow's poems and Lincoln's speeches have long been forgotten, especially the latter exercised a strong influence on my mind because of the incomparable economy with which Lincoln was able to say the right thing at the right time.

Back at the house there was also a subtle change. A large jolly woman with an amplified knot of black hair at the back of her neck and ruddy cheeks was now the nurse in the establishment. She did far more than nursing. She had clearly taken over from Miss Tyler on a number of levels. She took no notice of my existence in the house nor did I refer to her being in the house in conversation with Miss Tyler.

Miss Tyler herself was showing a new kind of anxiousness to please the girls. She went out of her way to do things with and for them. They went in turn with her to Philadelphia and she invited them to her room in the evenings and helped them with their homework and sewing.

In all this I was brushed aside. I sensed that something was going on between the orphanage authorities and Miss Tyler and Dorothea, and that Miss Tyler's new preoccupation with the girls in her house was prompted by a fear of losing her post. Deep down I suppose I sensed that losing her post would mean losing me, but I endeavoured in no way to upset the precarious balance of her position in the orphanage by asserting my own claims to existence. The result was almost total solitude.

My lacing boots were becoming too tight. Miss Tyler usually kept a close watch over my clothing and everything I wore was in perfect condition. Her vigilance suddenly ceased. In the early mornings I sat on the edge of my bed and contemplated my boots. The decision to put them on was difficult. I tried wearing my best shoes to school. They too were getting too small — back into the boots. It took a moment to be able to stand in them — then the walk downstairs as though I had club feet. Woodenly I placed one foot in front of the other, trying to make as little movement as possible, until I slid into my chair at the breakfast table, indescribably relieved to be off my feet for the duration of the meal.

Then — how was I going to get to school with four miles to walk? Practised detachment from circumstances was of no avail. A path of agony began; circulation in my cramped toes ceased and they became numb as I limped the interminable way to school.

I hoped desperately that Miss Tyler would notice that my boots had become too small. Every day I resolved to go to her, but something held me back in spite of the blisters that turned into deeper sores on my heels. I was profoundly uncertain of what the result of an approach to Miss Tyler would be. Relief came from a new quarter.

Dr Wilson, the school doctor, a young widow, drove past as I was hobbling on the last tortuous lap to school. She stopped to ask what the matter was. I said my feet hurt. She told me to get into the car (one of the few cars in the district) and drove me to the main building where she had her office. She told me to take off my boots, my stockings as well. She took my feet into her hands and studied them. I trembled all over lest she ask questions.

She said nothing, but dressed the sores and searched around for a pair of her own shoes and when she found them, she told me to put them on. They were too big but the comfort they gave was almost blissful. As I said thank you, Dr Wilson was standing with my boots in her hand. I hurried to school.

But it went on. My skirts were getting too short and jerseys no longer reached my waistline and were too tight under the arms. Pulling at my clothes became habitual. I felt both constricted as well as exposed; people stared. Entry into the classroom was a daily ordeal. I was the walking manifestation of some complex breakdown in the background and it was not only I who was exposed; there was double exposure.

I became an object of obvious concern to teachers who had hitherto not entered my sphere of existence at all. For the afternoon hours, I was taken into the school offices where the principal herself showed me how to work the duplicating machine and the paper cutter and gave me tasks to fulfil. Later Dr Wilson came to collect me and drive me back to the house — she said she anyway had to go that way. In such unaccustomed circumstances, I dreaded lest anything be said or asked and either bubbled superficially about all kinds of odd matters or was buttoned up and silent.

Dr Wilson's daughter, Jane, who was my age, often seemed to be just where I was. Her approaches to me had a driving force which suggested that her mother was behind them. Jane was intelligent and forthright and well-mannered and we could have been friends.

One afternoon as I was passing Dr Wilson's house which lay on the far side of the highway, Jane caught sight of me and called me in. She showed me a soft blue woollen dress — it would just fit me, she said. Oh, no thank you, I don't need a dress. One thing would lead to the next; one day they would question me about Miss Tyler.

Relief again came as though arranged by an unseen agent. A large box of clothing came from my mother with a note. These were things, she wrote, outgrown by the daughter of a friend. They had been bought in England and in Paris and she thought I might like them.

I took the clothing out of the box — skirts, jerseys, underwear, stockings hardly worn of soft wool and beautiful colours. With the clothing over my arm, I knocked at Miss Tyler's door. She opened it, stood for a few seconds with a contorted expression of hatred on her face. "I'm not interested," she said and slammed the door. I remained in the passage for a moment, my heart pounding under the impact of her hatred, but knew that my right to the clothing had not been challenged. My self-respect had been restored by the person I loved most. When I wrote to my mother to thank her, I said nothing about the circumstances which the box of clothing had relieved; I assumed she knew and had therefore sent it.

A boy in the village suddenly entered my world — Buddy. He was eleven, had black curls and shining black eyes with thick lashes and his cheeks were like polished red apples. Buddy excelled in everything, I assumed, in my giddy obsession with his person which I could not keep out of my mind. I printed his name (I wished he had another) on a cardboard key tag and hung it around my neck under my vest. Every afternoon I managed to be down at the corner of the main road just as Buddy came riding past on his bicycle on his way home from school (I did not know where he lived). I hid behind a protective maple tree whence I viewed the beloved, terrified lest he catch sight of me, longing that he would, and staring into aching nothingness after he had whirled around the corner. At night I fell asleep clutching the key tag in my hand. Not a word, a glance had passed between us.

Halloween came. Down in the village hall there was a fancy dress party for children in the district and I was invited to go. I asked Miss Tyler for a sheet and went as a ghost. Almost immediately I perceived Buddy in the midst of things. My ghostly habit allowed me to feast upon his appearance without being noticed.

We were all called up for a square dance. The adored Buddy made straight for me and asked me to be his partner. I heard his voice for the first time; it was curiously grating. Stumbling over my sheet, I put my hand in his, reeling somewhat, and went to the centre of the floor. The music struck up — we danced. The sheet, still with me, twisted around my feet, but my soul soared because Buddy had preferred me before all.

After the dance, he whispered that I should come outside with him; he wanted to give me something. I followed him out of the hall with abandon, adoring his every inch as he went before me. Outside in the dark near the stables, he drew close and whispered: "You're my girl, aren't you? Here take this." Something was thrust into my hand and he was gone. I moved into a shaft of light coming from a window and held up the object to see what it was. It was a Ku-Klux-Klan badge. My mind went cold. I threw the badge over the fence into the dark and wrenching the key tag from my neck, threw it after the badge.

On an empty winter afternoon, Miss Tyler said she wanted to speak to me — I was to come up to her room. The expression on her face was not one that foreboded a scolding or chastisement — there had been none recently — but I was apprehensive. I had not seen that expression before and could not imagine what it signified. I went upstairs and knocked at her door. She let me in and locked the door behind me. Her room was airless and I was always distressed by the odour around her person. She said: "I have decided that you are old enough to be told the facts-of-life." I knew what she meant without any foreknowledge and inwardly withdrew to the defence, sensing that the imminent attack on the untouchability of my mind was going to be an insidious one, the more so because she was the one who was going to level it.

Miss Tyler unlocked a cupboard and took out a large flat book which she laid on the sewing table. "Come here," she commanded. I moved into the aura of her person; the faint odour of decay was inescapable. She opened the book.

On opposite open pages there was a naked man and a naked

woman. The sight of them plunged me immediately into turmoil because I knew they were my mother and father and that some terrifying collusion between them had precipitated my own existence which was not for me to see, to know, to see what I was being forced to see, did not want to know. I blushed and stared fixedly out of the window, but the images had burnt themselves into my mind.

"Look here," she said and turned the page. I looked again. Before me were two grinning skeletons. Their hollow eye sockets would normally have depressed me. Now they gave relief because they were entirely devoid of that terrifying flesh pulsing with life. They were as non-committal as the stones outside, so cool were the grey bones, the many big and small joints, the ribs like a basket containing nothing but space. She turned the page again. Here were two human forms filled with delicate silver network extending into each fingertip like a filigree tree branching into ever finer twigs against a winter sky. These were the nerves, she said and I experienced rising interest.

She turned another page. The two forms appeared again like two trees, but this time the trees were red and blue and the branches spread generously throughout the bodies and gave the two forms a kind of faceless royalty.

The blood systems man-and-woman were followed by a muscle man-and-woman. Here the two figures had darkened and densified but not unpleasantly. Rather they looked as though they had been modelled out of porphyry and were waiting to be polished. They reminded me of horses' chests and haunches where the play of the muscles is visible under the shining hides and is the storehouse of strength and power. It was a revelation to see that these porphyry figures were contained inside the incarnate skins of people and the interest I experienced turned into a warm and wondering glow.

Afterwards when this winter afternoon had passed and I had recovered from the final blow of Miss Tyler's onslaught, I formed the habit of imagining the silver filigree of the nervous system, the red and blue vines of the blood systems, the rich porphyry of the muscles when I regarded other people and in a curious way, it helped me to respect them however mean and unprepossessing their appearance and bearing might have been.

There was no human being who did not possess that hidden beauty within.

The pages rattled. The man and woman were there again, this time in complex form. "Here you have the inner organs" she said. The two pages were so constructed that smaller flaps could be turned back to reveal further organs deeper within. The flaps of the lungs were like the wings of a triptych enfolding the dark red heart, a tabernacle like a clenched fist of love . . .

"What is that?" I asked.

Miss Tyler looked up the reference number: "The spleen."

"What's that?"

But she was urging towards a threshold which aroused in me a sense of panic . . . NO! She fumbled at the organs which became visible when the loops of the intestines were moved aside. Pointing to them with her finger, she explained "what they were for." With the same finger she pointed to my abdomen. Pierced by a spear, I felt it long afterwards.

The "facts of life" as presented to me by Miss Tyler dyed my unready mind with an ink that did not wash off so readily and its subtle chemistry worked its way into my perceptions. Forms seen, both animate and inanimate, seemed sent to pull me back to that winter afternoon; especially animals in their pristine innocence became fraudulent and suggestive.

Earlier on, Death had placed in question the security and joy of existence. Now a more insidious and less defined force moved into hitherto inviolate places, but some own resilience helped me to establish equilibrium after a time and the natural world became free and warm again as my obsessiveness faded.

Not long after, Miss Tyler involved me in an argument about some insignificant matter. I still adhered to my mother's early admonition never to argue with an adult person, but now my own words seemed to turn against me. Miss Tyler registered horror at my seeming insolence.

"March upstairs to the bathroom" she ordered.

I went upstairs and she followed. I opened the bathroom door and she followed and locked the door. "Take off your clothes" she commanded. The tiny bathroom was filled with her stoutness and I never liked to undress in her presence. My soul was in great fear. She ran a bath; steam clouded the room.

"Get into the tub!"

I put a foot into the steaming bath and quickly drew it out again: "It's too hot."

"Do as I tell you; get into the tub."

I felt her hands on my shoulders as she forced me into the hot water. I slipped down into a bath of fire. "I can't stand it," I murmured inside myself, "I can't bear it. Don't hold on, just let go . . . let go . . . "

Miss Tyler, possibly alarmed at my sudden stillness, pulled the plug abruptly and hauled me up. "Get out!"

I could hardly raise a foot over the rim of the tub; my skin wouldn't stretch. She wrapped me in a towel and began to dry my body. I felt as though my skin would come off in big patches.

I lay in the cold room between sheets; I could not bear the blankets. I heard Miss Tyler say to someone outside in the passage: "She fell into a bath that was too hot." I fell asleep. The next morning I was alright.

Some time later I incurred Miss Tyler's displeasure. "March upstairs to the bathroom." She locked the door and turned on the cold tap. You could not let yourself go in a cold bath; you were convulsed with shivering and uncontrollable chattering of teeth. Cold is an anti-force which compels you to jig like a marionette. Cold is utter dejection. The cold bath was a frequent occurrence. It left no traces on your skin but it could not be got used to; it was indignity.

Another nightmare began. I did not like parsnips; the very smell of them caused upheavals in my stomach and Miss Tyler never made me eat them. She now seemed to have forgotten my difficulty or revised her attitude to this idiosyncrasy and would heap my plate with parsnips. Everyone in the dining-room would be distressed by my inevitable retching and the room would become still. I was told to take my plate and go into the next room. In the chilly orange-and-blue parlour I put the plate down and stared out of the window. When the others had finished, Miss Tyler came in.

"Eat your dinner up at once!"

She thrust the plate under my nose. My stomach heaved in revolt.

"Eat it."

She fed me, stuffing my mouth while she held my nose. The result was disastrous and shameful. I fetched a bucket and mop to clean up.

For a time I scarcely had a normal meal in the dining-room. I spent the mealtimes in the parlour with a plate of parsnips in front of me. The same plate was there at supper. It came on to the breakfast table the next day.

At school we were having ancient history with a new teacher whose name I never took in. Our textbook was Breasted's history of the world. This world began with a whirling nebula like some super-dimensional separator ejecting clots of cosmic cream into space where they went on spinning around while — this was my own deduction — the leftover skimmed milk became the Milky Way.

With Dorothea the world began with an egg which was hatched releasing its golden yolk of the Sun whence all light and life and warmth was derived. Or it began with the union of Gaia and Eros — or with the Elohim breathing upon the infinite waters, the Elohim whose breath breathes on in every living creature — the driving Pneuma of the Spirit.

With Dorothea the various mythologies were not in contradiction with each other — Eros was the great Elohim of life; Aton, the golden yolk of the Sun sending its rays into every being and rousing it to evolution. We became Iknatons under Dorothea's tutelage.

Now — one of the spinning clots was the earth which was mud, the progenitor of cells which begot amoebas, dinosaurs, frogs and men and plankton. Was the earth a divine excrement? And what begot Me who was trying to understand? Who knew I was trying to know?

History proper, so we learned, began in the land-between-the-two-rivers, advanced to Egypt, from there to Greece in gradual stages of primitivity in which ignorant superstition created gods and theogonies and mysteries.

Dorothea had taught that the gods were forces which earlier men were able to perceive and communicate with and enlist their help in building their wonderful temples, obelisks, colossi — because men themselves were nearer their origins as spirit — conceived in the image of God. She inferred that modern men were much more clever, but far less perceiving of the real world and that history had been a long, long story not only of advance but of loss too — loss of divinity.

Now, so I learnt, only with the Romans, who, although they had no ideas of their own and had to copy Greek religion and Greek Art, created the Law and were good organizers, did men begin to emerge out of their erstwhile rudimentary state and become civilized to the extent that they could no longer be regarded as primitive. (I had not yet encountered Plato or Aristotle.)

I had taken history as my own biography on a world scale extending back to the beginnings and continuing into the future to the final consummation of evolution. With world history I myself reached from Alpha to Omega and there was nothing for which I was not potentially co-responsible, nothing in which I had not been in some way participant.

In the new approach, history was objective, the mechanical, predictable continuation of an initial spark-off. Its only goal that of technical advance. I abandoned ship as far as history lessons were concerned, preferring to go down than to land on the bleached shores of materialism.

Spring came. We had Botany. We learned (not from Dorothea) to discern the mechanisms of the facts of life in the plants. We went for botanical walks and collected flowers which we were taught to dissect in the classroom to discover the male and the female functional parts.

Birch trees dangled their catkins and lusted for one another. At the Resurrection, men and women do not marry, it said somewhere, but are like angels in heaven. If the trees would marry, they would uproot themselves and fall into each other and die bringing all else down with them.

The injunction that Nature was lascivious brought me near a kind of madness for a time — because a young child is by his inherent nature an arch humanist. He will become a scientist or rationalist or materialist in his own good time — early forcing is trauma.

18

The summer was unusually hot. Miss Tyler made no plans for going away for the holidays. The days were spent in trying not to move more than was necessary because of the humidity.

Chicken pox was going around among the girls. Those who caught it were quarantined in an empty wing of the house the existence of which I had hardly been aware; actually it was the other half of a semi-detached structure.

We (I had chicken pox too) were supposed to stay in bed, but the sheets got damp and clung to our bodies and the nurse's supervision was sporadic and so we made free use of the adjoining cold shower. As a result some of us became really ill, myself included, because the pox spots turned in on themselves and became infected. I ran a high temperature for a few days until the spots erupted like miniature volcanoes and oozed all over the bedclothes. When the nurse came and whisked back the sheets, she seemed revolted by what she saw.

One by one, the girls recovered and left the isolation room. I remained alone. I asked the nurse for my books. She went to inquire about them. "Books" meant the *Iliad* and the *Odyssey*. Miss Tyler suddenly appeared in the sickroom; I had not seen her since I had been in quarantine. There was a strange little twist around her mouth: "You were asking for your books? I had to burn them in the furnace because they were infectious."

"All my books?"

"Why, yes, all your books."

A long-drawn-out state of apathy followed this illness. When I was up again, I was given a basket and a kitchen knife and sent to the garden to pull beetroots. When the basket was full, I rested in the shade of the orange blossom bush. My melancholy mingled with the heavy fragrance of orange blossom and became painful; the mood of tombs was around me. I drew a beetroot out of the basket and held it head up. Its rich green yet bloodshot leafage trailed downwards like robes. I laid its head on a flat stone, raised the kitchen knife and decapitated it ; it bled as it toppled over.

I beheaded another beetroot and another. I was the executioner and the kitchen knife the guillotine; the beetroots were aristocrats condemned to die. Gradually I myself was beheaded over and over again and in the speeches I delivered before execution, things were stated I could not otherwise say — they accused where I had to be silent; they mourned for what I dared not think of. They pronounced judgment on one terrible act I would not name to myself, one act of bereavement never, never, to be made good.

Towards the end of the long and humid summer, Miss Tyler made a sudden decision to spend ten days in the Pocono Mountains. We had little rooms on the third floor of a "rustic" boarding house overlooking a tiny lake in the rocks. Miss Tyler and Dorothea had work to do — they were drawing up some kind of report — and I was left to myself. We met for meals in the dining room where there were a few other guests. Miss Tyler was breezy at the table; even Dorothea was conversational. I never experienced them as strangers so strongly before.

There was a tang of autumn in the air and the shadows slanted obliquely across the lichened rocks. The rugged terrain of the Poconos, the many herbs containing etheric oils, the wild azaleas growing among the pines, the transparency of the air and the sunbaked solitude in the woods were healing and reconciling.

When the legacy of summer withers and dies away, there is a new quality of light over the earth which is an intangible source of strength and buoyancy. My personal New Year began in the autumn when my sense of "godness" was restored and I moved into His Presence.

I walked for hours around and beyond the lake into distant forests, and scaled cliffs. I formed resolves as I walked: I would not hanker after something that could not be regained — one blue thing, one cinnabar thing. A breviary long practised becomes part of the flesh of the mind and can never be burnt away. Only external things go up in flames. "Heaven and earth shall pass away, but My Words shall not pass away" are not words of comfort, but fanfares to battle against possessing and being possessed by material things. Only the extract, the resonance remains as the single nerve of inner existence. Yet it was difficult to say whether the things of the earth such as I mourned for were of heaven or of earth, for although they were books, they had given me heaven.

I walked and thought off my grief in dialogue with myself and any desire to pay back the hurt dealt faded. Purged by the autumn air, my mind turned to major things; it had dwelt on the minor all too long. For the first time in many weeks I looked forward to the next day.

But this was not all. I climbed up a steep rock and on the top, I pillowed my head on a clump of lichen and stretched out in the sun. The air vibrated with the scent of wintergreen and dry pine needles. A sense of well-being spread throughout my being in spite of the discomfort of the sharp rock under my spine. It was the bliss of the ecstatic walking on burning coals.

A tiny adder slithered up over the edge of the rock and paused, peering at me. Behind it was the abyss of the forest below. The little forked tongue flickered like an infinitesimal flash of lightning and electrified the atmosphere. I experienced a curious sense of fear mingled with expectancy and raised myself up on my elbow to watch the adder.

The countenance before me grew and grew and filled my field of vision. I stared into the face of an angel — grave, beautiful, forbidding. I saw nothing other than his gaze upon my own Self, earnest and dangerous. Under this gaze, I felt myself filling up like a spring from below with exultation and immense promise and pride, so great that mine were the only dimensions experienced in that moment.

There would be no comfort from this angel, but there would be ferment, the bursting of bonds and the intoxication of beauty and talent and unchallenged superiority in many things. I knew in a flash that if I dedicated myself to this cold angel, nothing in the end could hurt me, for I would possess the means to hurt more than I ever could *be* hurt . . . the countenance quivered, faded and was gone. The tiny adder lowered its head and vanished over the edge of the rock, leaving a faint draught of danger behind.

19

The new school year began differently from all others, but auspiciously. Bernhard Newman came to talk to us about his travels in the Far East and opened up strange and lovely worlds with his projected coloured photographs. Dan Ghopal Makurji, a disciple of Ghandi's, came to tell us about his book, *Mother India*, in his fine dedicated manner. All this provided exquisite nourishment as well as relief from the one-sided orientation to all things Greek.

Paul Robeson and his choir sang negro spirituals in the assembly hall to the whole orphanage. There were men and women in the choir whose voices ranged from unbelievable heights to glowing dark base tones that made one think of big barrels of burnished honey. I sat up in the front row with Dorothea's class and was enthralled. At the end of the programme, Paul Robeson, bowing to our tumultuous applause, offered us an encore of our own choosing. Up went a forest of hands and wishes were shouted out. Paul Robeson was looking down at me: "And what would *you* like, little girl?"

"Please sing 'Ise got shoes'," I whispered.

"Then you come right along up here," he said and helped me on to the platform. The choir assumed places again and Paul Robeson lifted me on to his knee. They began to sing as though setting sail on a deep rocking ocean of warm sound. He made a movement that I was to relax and I leaned back against his chest and felt the resonance of the rich warm voice all down my spine; a child on the lap of the All Father listening to music from the depths of the universe. Below on the earth there was the blur of many faces — far away. When at the end of the song, he released me out of his embrace, it was like falling out of heaven.

Back in the house, things were going well too. Miss Tyler was cheerful and pleasant and struck a balance between the girls and myself so that I was almost one of the group. I frequently helped her in the kitchen and learned to bake bread and muffins and cakes. I ran messages for her, was attentive, even affectionate. We began to have little jokes together; there was a new and easy familiarity between us.

I had not heard from my mother for a long time; she was away in Europe. Miss Tyler never mentioned her and she sank down into my unconscious existence. I was absorbed by the immediate present.

Yet as the weeks passed into deeper autumn, something began to wear thin. The report that Miss Tyler and Dorothea had drawn up seemed to have failed to achieve its purpose, whatever it was. Miss Tyler lost her equilibrium in dealing with the girls and me; either she devoted herself doggedly and exclusively to my needs or she turned to the girls with a rough kind of vehemence and I was cast out.

She began to distrust me when I was out of her sight and acquired the habit of cross-examining me in front of others as to what I had been doing, which imposed a strain on everyone because there was a boring madness in it. In these moments, she had a little frown over one eye which I grew to regard with dismay. She seemed to want to demonstrate publicly that I was her possession but that she did not value what she owned, yet was willing to go to any lengths to secure her ownership. She not only forbade me afresh to enter into any contact with other people; she seemed to dread it.

I avoided the teachers at school. I abandoned my tasks in the school office and hurried back to the house after lessons to show Miss Tyler that I had not wanted to stay with anyone else, but she often thrust me off brusquely when I returned as though shaking off something repulsive or — she overwhelmed me with suffocating affection which forced me into my own defensive for I dreaded her kiss most of all.

One November afternoon, I heard Miss Tyler shouting

angrily downstairs — someone had stolen a banana from the larder. I listened. I had seen a banana skin in a certain place and knew who had taken it, but I did not stir from my room. The angry hollering grew louder; Miss Tyler was summoning everyone downstairs. I obeyed and joined the group gathering in the hall. She looked across at me: "What do you know about the missing banana?" I was silent. She was staring at me with icy blue eyes. I began to tremble. "Come on, say what you know about the banana!" (Was she accusing me of having taken it?) I blushed hotly.

"March upstairs to my room!"

Upstairs in her room, she locked the door and told me to take off my shoes and stockings. With uncertain fingers, I took them off. Before I realized what she was going to do, a short black whip lashed around my legs. "Now get out and go to your room!" I picked up my shoes and stockings and waited for her to unlock the door and went to my room. I could not pull on my stockings again because of the weals. I sat on the edge of my bed. It gradually got dark. The maid came in and said it was time for supper.

"I don't want any supper, thank you." I sat on in the dark.

Nothing was said the next day. But it came again. I excused myself from gym for fear the weals on my legs would be seen when I wore bloomers. Dr Wilson sent for me. Why was I staying away from gym? I did not feel well, I said.

"What's that on your hand?" There were two oblique weals on the back of my left hand that were open and angry. I put my hand behind my back and blushed. Dr Wilson scrutinized me and frowned. She took up my hand with a certain energy and dressed it. No further word was said, but I tried hard after that to keep out of her way.

I was brushing snow off the path in front of the house. Dr Wilson came along in her car and stopped at our gate. Jane was in the car with her mother. I pretended not to see them, but Dr Wilson called out telling me to show her my hand. Reluctantly I walked up to the gate and held out my hand. "It's alright," I said.

"Yes, it's better." She drove off; Jane turned round and waved.

The moment the car had gone up the street, a window was flung open. "Come up to my room at once!"

Upstairs she shook me by the shoulders: "What were you talking to Dr Wilson about?"

"Nothing," I said. "She just stopped and said hello."

"How often have you been seeing her?" Miss Tyler was trembling all over.

"Hardly at all." I was not telling an untruth; I had avoided her where I could.

"Take off your shoes and stockings!"

I tried to take them off — my stockings were stuck to the open weals from before. As I pulled, the woollen fibres tore away any new tender skin and blood ran down my legs. There was no resistance left.

The whip lashed. And lashed. I was standing in a pool of blood. "Now get out of the house altogether!"

I pushed my feet into my shoes and took my stockings in my hand and went out. Blood ran into my shoes as I went down the staircase. The black maid came into the hall and flung her hands into the air: "Lord Almighty!" And vanished.

I went through the empty hall and opened the front door. The cold air blew against my burning legs and the blood congealed. But my shoes left a red imprint in the snow on the path. I had no coat on.

I went up the street without aim. The snow was very white and the houses lining the street were transparent. I knew what the people inside were doing but they and the things that motivated them were far away. I knew everything but it had no bearing at all on anything to do with me. I walked on into a white blank.

All at once I heard Jane's voice: "Gracious, what's happened?"

"Nothing."

"Something's happened — wait, I'll fetch my mother." I heard her running over the ice on the sidewalk. I turned and went down a lane out of sight. Cold twilight came down. Car lights shone behind me and came nearer. A car pulled up. Dr Wilson leaned out and told me to get into the car. I began to run. The car caught up with me. I ran faster. I fell headlong into the snow and could not rise.

Two voices — Dr Wilson's and a man's: "Would you mind

taking her into your house?" I was lifted up and taken into someone's house. Dr Wilson followed behind.

Inside I was laid on a sofa. Dr Wilson knelt beside me and the sight of my legs brought forth an exclamation: "How did you get these?" I shut my eyes.

"Tell me, don't be afraid." The gentleness in her voice was unbearable. Tears poured.

"I went through a barbed wire fence." I sobbed.

When she had bathed and dressed my legs, Dr Wilson took me back to the house and told the black maid to put me to bed. From my bed I heard raised voices in Miss Tyler's room. The black maid opened the door to hear a little better. Her eyes rolled. When she heard Dr Wilson leave Miss Tyler's room, she quickly followed her downstairs. Dr Wilson drove away some time later.

The next morning I was told that Miss Tyler and Dorothea had gone away for a few days to visit someone. I did not know that they had anyone to visit. I was to stay in bed.

Later on Dr Wilson came with Jane. They stayed for a while and I enjoyed their visit save for the strain of having to avoid any talk about myself. I need not have feared. Dr Wilson and Jane were full of news about the village, Jane's school, the car — and so on — until it was time for them to go.

I was up and about when Miss Tyler and Dorothea returned from wherever they had been. Miss Tyler was pale and quiet and hardly took notice of me. We continued in a vacuum until Christmas.

20

"Here we come a-wassailing" — we sang from house to house in the village, holding storm lamps to light the way through the snow and wrapped up to the ears against the cold. Up and down the main street we went and along outlying roads at the end of the village. When we stopped to sing in front of a house, the blinds went up or shutters were pushed open and the people inside came to the windows to listen, and afterwards one of the singers went up to the front door to collect coins in a tin for the missions. Sometimes we were given mugs of hot cocoa. Human warmth pervaded the cold winter evening and the comradeship among the singers young and old had a glow as comforting as any great stove.

Sometimes I was pushed out in front to sing "O little town of Bethlehem" in a high reedy voice while women behind me fell in with a hummed accompaniment. I put my soul into the little song and vividly saw the town I was singing about — a cluster of lights in the valley below like a constellation of stars fallen out of the night sky to the earth.

We were drawing near to the house. I begged the company to sing for Miss Tyler. We took up our positions in the snow beneath her window. There was light in her room — the curtains were not drawn.

We began to sing to the emptiness of the room above. Was she not there? Why didn't she come to the window and look out? Anxiously I sang staring upwards. A shadow passed — all at once she stood at the window. She seemed shrunken and old and curiously helpless. A wave of compassion swept over me. I sang, fighting back the tears I wept for her.

The next day the feeling of compassion persisted and gnawed at me. I tried to think of a Christmas present for her. I had planned no other Christmas presents that year; I did not know where my mother was.

I attempted a lamp-shade, I hemstitched a handkerchief, cross-stitched a face-cloth. Everything went wrong because these were things I could not do without her help. I then drew flowers as they appeared in the course of the year. I tried to model General Tyler in clay but could not remember what he looked like; he had been so long in an Old Folk's home — or was dead. Finally I wrote a poem for each month of the year (I had always wanted to do that for my mother) and asked in the office for permission to type them out which I did laboriously. When I had finished, I stapled the sheets together and made a little book of the poems with a blue cover.

On Christmas Day, I put my present for Miss Tyler — it was for Dorothea too — underneath the Christmas tree. We all gathered in the parlour which was lit by lanterns the soft light of which mitigated the glare of the coloured light bulbs on the tree. Cider and cakes were served. We sang carols and opened our presents. I had a small parcel from my mother containing a tiny Italian painted pot. I was intent upon the moment when Miss Tyler would discover my present to her and would open it. She sat in her rocking chair and opened parcels and read cards from the girls. Dorothea sat on a stool at her side and shared in her presents.

My flat little blue parcel lay where I had put it. Didn't she know I had put it there?

The enchantment of Christmas leaked away bit by bit. The bare features of the parlour stood out without any magic to redeem their bleakness. I felt a sick headache coming and asked to be excused. As I went out of the room, a sidelong glance at the tree confirmed that my parcel had not been touched.

One morning in February, I woke up into a thin white light reflecting in my room from the snow outside. I felt as though I had no skin. The cold white light went through me and blanched everything inside. I looked out of the window while I was dressing. A thin white wraith drew upwards out of the snow on sharp pointed wings –a white witch trailing rags of blinding ice, shrieking soundlessly as she rose up, bigger and bigger, her cold laughter filling the fallow sky. She was declaring war.

At school I vomited after the break-time biscuit and was sent back with a sick headache. On the way I walked into the territory of the enemy and no one knew where I was. The blinding snowfields stretched out to the horizon like blanched sheets. The fence posts, each one in desolate isolation, intensified the glare and a labouring sun stared across the white wastes like a single relentless eye.

All contours, roads, bends, hummocks — were levelled out under the snow; only the telegraph poles, stark against the empty sky, indicated the direction in which I was going. Red flashes flickered across the vacant sky and in and out of the black wires. I was beginning to walk upside-down. Barbed wire surrounded me and was hemming me in. I was getting lost in the endless snow, but I did not mind, felt no panic, just walked and walked . . .

I lay in another room on a long hospital bed heightened at the head-end. In the open window there was a screen of fine silk. Something burned in a tin on a blue flame in the room like an offering. It was still. Folds of darkness kept coming up and blotting out the whiteness. I sank down into the dark . . . whales filled the room and swam round and round until the bed under me dissolved, my body dissolved and I swam round with the whales in their ponderous tenderness. The universe focused on the pinpoint I had become in a cosmos of primary existence — the pinpoint became more and more concentrated until it exploded outwards into the periphery in an outpouring of love and the great big fearsome earth was a tiny thing in my hand . . .

I sat in an ebony boat crossing a deep blue lake. Beneath the keel whales were swimming but none lifted up the little boat on its great back nor endangered it by churning up the water, but conducted the boat to its goal, circling round so that their shadows passed over the bottom of the lake like gentle hands . . .

The boat drew near to the other side where a mountain rose topped with gleaming silver snow. Silvery streaks ran down into the crevices roseate with the glow of an unseen sun. As I stepped out of the boat, a red rose lay at my feet. I picked it up with a feeling of bliss as the talisman I had been waiting for — its fragrance filled the air, filled me — I began to ascend the mountain . . .

It was evening. I saw everything in the room with closed eyes. I could not feel my body at all: it had the weight of a petal. People were in the room. Miss Tyler, old Dr Lawse and someone with honey-coloured hair in white the touch of whose hands was infinitely tender. Dr Lawse was bending over me: "She might not live," he whispered over his shoulder . . . The summit of the silver mountain drew near gleaming in unearthly splendour. I strode on upwards like the wind . . .

The blinds went up with a clatter. Polly, the day nurse, was busy in the room. She looked like a chicken with her long, raw red neck. Her starched apron crackled. She thrust a cold bedpan under me with a rude joke and wore an expression of scepticism on her face as though she knew I was pretending to be ill. I had no defences; everything went right through.

Outside the watchful white evil laughed in league with Polly, and the laughter rang out in brazen silence through the bare skeletons of the trees. My soul turned to the wall and sought in anguish the still lake where the whales circled — but could not find it. Fog had come down between me and the silver mountain — I could not find the red rose; the sense of loss was piercing.

The head-end of the bed was lowered. I lay flat. I lay on the rock bottom of existence, flattened to nothingness — not separated from non-existence.

At night the honey-haired nurse filled the room with gentleness. In the dimly lit room, she shone from within. The coming of the next day broke it off. After a time she was no longer there in the evenings to stay with me during the night. Polly was the last person in the room at night and the first in the morning. She banged about as though she were shutting down kennels and her thrusting the cold bedpan under me was the thrust of the enemy.

I fought against tears all day long; I was too sad to speak or open my eyes to anything. When Miss Tyler came in, she seemed to share Polly's disbelief in the severity of my illness; she adopted the attitude that I was simulating: "There's no need to make any fuss" she repeated with an odd kind of reproach in her voice.

Old Dr Lawse sat on the edge of my bed and bent over me. The smell of tobacco on his whiskers was almost too powerful, but the kindness and concern in his brown eyes was comfort. I lay on the pillow and felt his big warm hand on mine and my eyes filled with tears. "You've fought a brave battle, little lady."

As the gentleness of the nights receded, the daylight grew more intense and with it, the sounds from the street outside beginning with the milkman's cart, the heavy bang of the front door below, the greengrocer's wagon rattling up the road — caught me again in the net of things like a fish — day after day, but as my body grew stronger, my soul shrank.

Polly entered the room carrying a large parcel wrapped in brown paper which she set down at my bedside with a bump: "Someone sent this to you," as though it was incomprehensible that anyone should send anything to me. I looked at the writing on the parcel and knew before I saw it that it was from my mother and thrilled as the rundown battery was suddenly recharged.

When I was certain that my voice would be steady I said: "I need some scissors, Polly, please."

"You'll have to hold your horses — do you think I've nothing to do but wait on you all day long?"

I lay back with my hand resting on the parcel my mother had sent me. After an interminable time Polly came with some scissors.

I sat up against the pillows and took a long time over each knot. When I opened the last, I had to lie back and rest before I heaved myself up again to undo the wrapping. Cold sweat broke out all over. I lay back once more, my work unaccomplished. I was assailed by panic lest I would not last long enough to open my parcel. I slept. I dreamt of my mother; it was night and she was in the room just behind Dr Lawse who was bending over me — Mummy, Mummy — she had been there in the room all the time — I loved her so much — there was nothing else in the world . . .

Suddenly restored, I sat up and unwrapped the parcel. Miss Tyler came into the room: "It's high time your mother did something for you, although she would never get into a train and come even when we thought you were dying."

My hand dangled inside the box, feeling its contents, but not exploring further while she was in the room. She bustled about, straightening things — Polly only came for an hour now in the evenings.

My hand still dangling inside the box, I dozed until I heard her shut the door. Then came the exquisite moment of seeing what my hand had guessed at — the box was filled with little parcels done up in paper of different colours. On top lay a note in my mother's hand: Darling, I hear you have not been well and that you are to have a long rest in bed, so I am sending you a little parcel for each day of your convalescence, twenty-four in all, and hope you will be well enough to be up when you come to the last parcel. I am sorry I have not written for so long, but I have been very busy and had to go to Italy . . .

With the delectable discipline laid upon me by my mother to restrain from opening all the parcels at once, I recovered my joy and capacity for anticipating the coming day. Each morning after the maid had brought my breakfast tray and I was alone again, I took another little parcel out of the box, opened it and placed its contents in the bright array of things set out on my bedside table. There were tiny Italian dolls in costume, little painted dishes, notebooks, crayons, handkerchiefs — all chosen with the fine sense characteristic of my mother.

Miss Tyler entered the room: "Hattie would like some of your packages; she's ill in bed too and has no one like you to send her things to cheer her up."

Hattie was thin and wiry. She was the thief and liar in the house; she always had her hand where it shouldn't be and did not mind being seen and her mouth was a wet smear. Her existence was a source of distress to me: what was coming now could not be — I was speechless. "Well, if you can't share your things with others, I'll have to assist you."

Miss Tyler plunged both her hands into my box and drew out a heap of little parcels. Some fell on the floor: "I'm going to give these to Hattie." And went out of the room.

My tears flowed uncontrollably; I was too smitten to stop them. They came from a deep well which having re-opened could not be stemmed. A new darkness followed.

Polly disappeared. Instead there was an elderly nurse who seemed to have a big body without a face. She was in the room all the time for a while but I could never tell what she was doing; it seemed to have nothing to do with myself.

I began to recover a second time through a kind of bitter resilience. I felt hard and stubborn and urged to inflict hurt. I was allowed out of bed for increased periods every day and sat in an armchair by the window. Everything was still covered with snow outside, but beneath the snow water ran and gurgled and hollowed out the drifts. The sky was fallow. Empty winds gusted — a fading wraith of enmity withering over the tired snow in the vacant interval between winter and spring . . .

I heard someone playing the piano in the neighbouring house — a high melody cascading downwards. Outside thin new snow was falling from an ashen sky. The descending notes hit my nerves with the touch of snowflakes at the end their fall. Crystals danced on my open nerves, a little wild, till I felt their icy caress creeping up to my heart. My heart quickened to the cold, leapt up, became a snowflake in the misty flurries of some wind's fancy. It danced off over the tops of houses out of sight. Later I found my ice heart scarcely discernible on the steely tracks of a train. I held it in my hand panting faintly in the frosty air. I was pervaded with the singular warmth of extreme cold, exquisite cold which shot through my limbs and made them quiver — an ice faun, and I went dancing on twinkling feet driven by tiny hammered notes, given to the homeless flurries of snow sighing beneath the low branches of firs . . . the weary opal sun hangs heavy in the sky, but too many currents are humming in the frosty air for the sun's wan light to hem my exuberance and I grow sharper, pointed, keen and keener, and flit, icy wanderer bobbing through blue-green shadows of snow-laden pines on and on . . .

This was the first time I ever danced — danced in my mind.

Soon I was up for the whole day, first in my room and then about the house and finally, I went back to school. It was the end of March.

The damp spring winds and running water and open earth weighed me down. I had no buoyancy. I had to walk to school slowly because of the strain on my heart. The bright red scooter my mother had sent me was locked away. Everything smarted like salt on raw flesh. I could not maintain my icy calm; tears seemed to be waiting for the slightest provocation.

Dr Lawse called to see me. I went straight into his arms and wept. His big warm hand held my head against his breast until the storm was over: "You need a tonic, little lady."

A bottle of tonic came from the drugstore in the village and was placed on a shelf in the bathroom. It was to be taken at meals in a glass of milk.

At lunch a tall glass of brown milk stood on my place. I sipped it and put it down with some alarm for it contained creosote to which I was violently allergic. When I rose from the table Miss Tyler stood at my side: "You have not taken your tonic."

"No, it's that fence post stuff; I can't drink it."

"Nonsense, fence post stuff or not, you're going to drink it right now."

I raised the glass to my mouth and drained it, but I could not keep it down.

At supper a glass of creosote milk stood on my place. The same glass was on my bedside table when I went to bed. I put it on the windowsill so as not to smell it during the night. It was downstairs on my place at the breakfast table.

Dr Lawse called. I told him about the tonic. "Well, little lady, we're not here to make your life unpleasant. I'll send you another tonic you'll certainly enjoy."

A big new bottle came from the drugstore and stood on the bathroom shelf, its contents a rich Burgundy red.

I went up to my room to have the prescribed rest after lunch. I had almost dozed off when Miss Tyler came into the room with a tall glass of brown milk in her hand: "You're going to drink this."

"Dr Lawse said I needn't; there's a new bottle of tonic on the bathroom."

"You're going to drink *this*."

She held the glass under my nose. My stomach rose in revolt

and I warded off her hand. She forced the rim of the glass between my lips — the smelly brown liquid ran down over my jersey and soaked my pillow. I retched and retched. I heard Miss Tyler put the glass down on my bedside table and go out of the room. For a moment I lay paralysed on the vile pillow.

Then — a string snapped bringing everything down around me. It kept coming from behind and there was no more holding on in the violent torrents sweeping me away. I sprang off the bed, seized the pillow and flung open the door. Miss Tyler was about to go downstairs. I threw the pillow after her — then I slammed the door and lay down across the foot-end of my bed.

There was an uproar in the house — the maid talking loudly, Dorothea's shrill hysterical voice rising above all else. Cars came and went. It got dark.

Late in the evening the maid came into my room with a bowl of bread and milk. "When you'se eaten you'se to pack yo tings — you'se leaving tamarra."

"Where am I going?"

"Ah dunno, folks who done such tings has mostly nowhere to go."

"What have I done? WHAT HAVE I DONE?"

"You'se broken Miss Tylah's leg."

I reeled. The maid left me alone. After a while she came in again: "You'se not touched yo bread an' milk honey."

"I'm not hungry thank you."

"Lawd Almighty, Ah knew it would come to a bad en'. No human chile can stan' that yeah afta yeah."

The tide had turned. Why? What had happened? She was bursting to discuss things. I liked her, but I remained silent.

Packing was brief. Everything Miss Tyler had bought me was to be left behind. There remained the few books that had accumulated since the burning and what was left of the clothing my mother had sent the year before. It all went into a cardboard box which was tied up with a string.

It was still dark when I was woken the next morning and given something to eat in the kitchen by the maid. No one else was about. The maid was tearful. Then Dr Wilson came with her car to take me to the station. When we drove off I did not look back; my feelings were locked up. I only wondered how I would manage the change of trains in Philadelphia by myself.

But now Dr Wilson was very direct and very firm. She asked hitherto not-asked questions about Miss Tyler. She seemed to know a great many things, things I did not know and did not want to know. My composure was being undermined. I made a desperate attempt to ward off exposure. When an account is settled, nothing more is needful.

The nearer we drew to the station, the more centred I became. I regained the sense of steel inside; any longing for understanding and commiseration bounced off it. Grey daylight was coming — the train was pulling in.

Dr Wilson hurriedly bought me a ticket for New York and helped me on to the platform with my cardboard box. Suddenly before mounting the high step into the train, I caught up her hand and kissed it.

Inside the train I shut myself in the washroom until the train was in motion. My five and a half years with Miss Tyler had come to an end.

INTERLUDE

21

Measured in distance, the train journey from Philadelphia to New York is not long. Measured in experience, it was a nameless interval without bridgeheads. What had taken place was too enormous to be contained in my mind. For what lay ahead, there was so little to bank on that even my imagination, never much at a loss, could not see into the fog. I stared out of the window with inwardly blind eyes.

Finally the train plunged into the tunnel under the Hudson River (my father used to ask if I could hear the river rushing) which signified the approach (it came back now) to Pennsylvania Station in New York.

Memories shot up out of oblivion — the spiky skyline, the long high dingy streets, the ruthless rumbling of huge carthorses on the cobblestones down by the wharves, the smell of decaying green groceries. A sharp thrill streaked along my nerves: I was about to see my mother again.

She would be on the platform when the train pulled in. Would I recognize her? Would she know who I was? How would she know?

I stared into the vacant faces of the people on the platform when the train pulled in and jerked to a halt. I could not see her. I was pushed along the passage of the coach by the pressure of grown up passengers behind me who were in a hurry to leave the train and disgorged out on to the platform clutching the string of my cardboard box. I did not dare to look this way or that for fear I would see nothing.

The crowd of passengers and those who met them formed a dense mass motivated by alien compulsions that shuffled them along to the exit. I tried to stem against the lava flow scanning each face that passed. According to its own laws, the crowd thinned out and a new crowd surged on to the platform servient to a new set of circumstances, and I became a straggler.

"What you'se lookin fo', missie?"

I said to the big round black porter: "My mother."

"You'd bettah look upstahs; maybe she's waiting up deah."

On the way to the ticket barrier, I knew she was not there — she did not know I was coming — she was away and not expecting me — she didn't know where I was. I trembled so violently that I could hardly hold out my used ticket to the ticket collector.

In the big central hall of the station there was a vast crowd of standing, shifting, hurrying people. All eyes were fixed on some point behind me. I faced a wall of non-concern, a battery of blankness.

Somewhere in the cardboard box I had my mother's letters. The knots were tight but if I could get them open, I would find my mother's address. Then I could take a taxi. I was almost sure I knew how to take a taxi. I put the box down and began to tug at the knots in the string. I was surrounded by a forest of trousered legs as though my father had advanced in legion. I couldn't loosen the knots that held the box and panic took possession of me. I picked the box up and wormed my way feverishly to the exit.

All at once I was fixed by a grey gaze. I slowed my steps; the blood pounded in my temples. The box slid from my fingers. I reeled. I saw her — through a mist and wanted to slip to her feet and give up my separate existence: "Mummy," I murmured.

"Oh, there you are."

It was the voice I knew — the beloved English inflection — but it sounded closed off. I wrenched my gaze upwards and looked into her face, my own distorted by the anguish of seeing her again.

"Come along, we can't stand about here."

I picked up my box and followed her out of the station. She hailed a cab and we got in. All the while we drove downtown, her mouth was set and she did not say a word but stared fixedly ahead of her. I glanced sideways at her hands, tense, nervous and to me always moving, and longed for their touch. There was a faint familiar fragrance about her (her letters always had a whiff of it) which made it difficult for me to hold on to myself, but I did not want to annoy her by looking at her — only her hands.

The cab pulled up at a kerb. My mother got out, paid the driver and went into a house. I followed with my cardboard box. By the time I reached the door, she was already on the first floor landing. There were four more flights of stairs. The house was dingy and dismal. When I reached the top floor, a door stood open. I entered a large room with grimy windows. My mother stood at a window with her back to the room. I shut the door behind me and waited.

Suddenly my mother wheeled around: What did I think, being sent back to her like this with nothing but the clothes I stood up in? What a disgrace? What did I expect her to do about me after the unspeakable performance I had given? Who was going to want to have me now? What had I to say for myself?

I could not take my eyes off her face — my mother. But I was sundered as though by an axe. A sick headache seized me with violence and I asked if I could lie down. My mother signed to the sofa. She drew the blinds in the room and went out.

The sofa was suffocating, the springs broken (it became my bed and gave me bedfellows — bedbugs against which we conducted a fierce campaign). The headache lasted three days and was so intense that I could not react to my mother's presence or to her occasional inquiries as to whether I needed anything. From time to time, she rinsed out the bucket at my side.

The day I got up my mother received a large white envelope from Philadelphia which she opened and read with exclamations of horror. Her attitude changed radically; she gazed on me with incredulous pity: "My poor little darling."

She began to question me — for hours on end over meals, sitting on the edge of the sofa at night when I had gone to bed or out in the street when we went to the grocers at the corner. The days were interlaced with her interrogations.

During my five and a half years with Miss Tyler, I had not once doubted that my mother knew, that what happened to me happened to her, that we were in unquestioned communication even where things were unstated to myself. She was the omnipotent protective being whose wings were spread out over me all the while. Now in these hours of interrogation, I discovered she knew nothing at all. We had had separate existences. Words were no substitute for something one had never had.

Her pity was embarrassing and painful. I told my mother nothing about Miss Tyler and was on all scores evasive. Her cross examinations took on various forms and I grew to recognize the expression on her face when she was about to renew her efforts to extract information from me. It went from cajoling to threats, up and down the scale. I longed for respite. The more she tried to get me to speak, the more out of place it seemed to mention even the slightest inoffensive detail of my life at the orphanage. Gradually her interrogations ceased, but more letters came from Philadelphia. I read some of them when my mother was out. I did not understand all the terminology used and they told me more than I knew myself. I could not deal with it all in retrospect and then — there was the curious fact that the letters seemed not concerned with me but with some kind of vindication against something that had nothing to do with me. It was no longer my situation.

The subject of Miss Tyler and the orphanage was finally dropped. Much later when I would speek more freely to my mother about my years at the orphanage, she herself would look remote and be disinclined to listen.

The only time Miss Tyler's name was mentioned between us was when, some while later, a note came from Dorothea saying that Miss Tyler had not been well and had asked to see me. Would I be able to pay them a short visit?

I showed the note to my mother and asked for permission to go (I had managed the journey to New York — I could now manage the journey back to Philadelphia). The idea was highly distasteful to my mother. She reminded me that after all the whole affair had had to go before the police. Would I want to go back on her efforts to clear this matter up?

I tried again a day or two later. Could I please visit Miss Tyler? I could go quite alone; I knew the way. Surprisingly my mother gave me some money and said that if I insisted, she would not prevent me from going although she found it perverse of me to want to see Miss Tyler again. I was to be back in New York on the fourth day.

I went to Pennsylvania Station by subway, bought a return

ticket and caught a train to Philadelphia. The train went through the tunnel under the Hudson River and emerged in New Jersey and went on — retracing steps.

The train I had to take in Philadelphia was the same we used to take to the village where the orphanage was, but now it was to take me beyond that village to another village further north. I recognized all the stations on the way — but they could not possess me now. It was not even tempting a forgotten fate — I was not apprehensive.

When I came out of the little station in the village where Miss Tyler and Dorothea were now living, I perceived no omen, no sign that this was a device of destiny to entrap me again. The place was entirely nondescript. I asked the way to the particular street.

Dorothea stood at the front door of the tiny white wooden house. She must have been waiting. She led me straightaway upstairs to Miss Tyler. It was not difficult to face her again because I did not recognize her. She was frail, shrunken and thin and confined to a wheelchair. I was immediately assured by both that this had nothing to do with what had happened — their sentences trailed off and they looked smilingly and beseechingly into my face.

I was shy of their being so apologetic and went out of my way to be polite and informative and responded to Miss Tyler's timid questions as to what I was now doing willingly (although I did not really know what I was now doing), but all the while we talked, the curious experience of not recognizing her persisted.

I stayed with them for three days. Downstairs in the kitchen, Dorothea and I seemed to be in league with each other. She talked and laughed continuously (but never referred to the past). I helped her with the cooking and laid trays for Miss Tyler and carried them upstairs when they were ready. I sat by Miss Tyler when she ate. Mostly we sat in silence — occasionally she would turn around to me and smile like a little child. I felt very much her senior.

It was an odd experience to look at her as I had never looked at her before; her existence had lain too heavily upon me that it could be looked at. But now I was out of reach and she herself defenceless. I did not look at her now with curiosity; only with freedom.

When she finished her meal, I would take up the tray and return to Dorothea in the kitchen. She had laid the table for both of us. Over the steaming dishes, she seemed to be talking in order that nothing be said. I fell in with her and contributed banalities where I could.

When I lay in the cool narrow bed upstairs in the sterile little attic room next to Miss Tyler's, I felt nothing at all — perhaps only faintly something like a curtain having come down on what had already receded into the past. When the three days were over, I left them as easily as I had come. I heard from neither again.

22

The room we lived in had reputedly once been O'Henry's but that was its only distinction. I have mentioned the bedbugs. The two grimy windows looked out on to the backyards of like dismal houses walled off from one another by blackened brick walls, embellished along the tops with jagged pieces of broken glass to keep out thieves and cats.

These walls were the meeting, eating, courting, fighting places of innumerable cats which sat gingerly on the broken glass or picked their way fastidiously along the top of a wall to the next wall. Their petulant growling and sing-song wailing in the misery of courtship rose to a crescendo and sank back to the previous petulance, to rise once more to a hideous pitch and was a regular feature of the nights. Windows were flung open and buckets of water accompanied by invectives were ejected out into the night to result in brief respites.

In my mind there was a powerful after-image of green trees and meadows and the activities of many creatures whereas the grime and din of the city was unreal, yet it was where my mother was.

She was doing sporadic reporting for one of the big New York newspapers and was often called out at night to the scene of a fire or a crime or accident which, as she was sensitive and morbidly inclined, constituted soul-searing ordeals for her. She never said anything about these nightly excursions to me, but swallowed everything into herself, but I grew to dread the fire sirens as they screamed through the streets after mid-night and the telephone that inevitably followed calling my mother out.

After these calls, she would return to our room in the early hours of the morning and in the dim light before dawn over the city, although I pretended I was still asleep, I saw her haggard face and the traces of the horrors she had witnessed as she bent over her typewriter (the same she had in Tokyo) putting it all down on foolscap sheets of yellow paper. When she had finished her report, she hurried out to the newspaper office to return later, either relieved to have had it accepted and to have been paid for it, or in utter dejection because another reporter had got there first or had done it better.

When my mother thus earned some money, we went for a meal to a nearby Italian cafeteria and indulged in large plates of pasta. Only — eating lots is conducive to hunger. I was all the hungrier the next day.

On occasions a wealthy friend of my mother's, a novelist who had written one bestseller, sent her butler over to us with a three tiered thermos container of food, but there was a disturbingly erratic element in the appearance of the butler who often did not come for days on end.

My mother tried not to discuss food with me. There was an unspoken agreement between us neither to indulge too freely when there was food nor to give any sign of distress when there wasn't any. Yet it was the nervous undertone of our life. My mother's self esteem was undermined by her not being able to provide a regular living for us both. It was probably easier for her when she was alone.

I had always devoured meals with voracity and tended to eat a lot, although I remained as thin as a stick. Small and irregular amounts of food rapidly weakened me and I became lethargic. In order not to irritate my mother by my constant presence in these circumstances, I went out to the park where I vegetated in the pale sunlight until it was time to go in and go to bed.

One day when I was sitting on a bench in the park, a peanut vendor passed by. His little cart with its charcoal roaster trailed a delicious fragrance. Someone hailed the vendor, and he went back around the corner to see who wanted him leaving his cart unguarded in front of me. The smell of roasting nuts was enchanting and produced a sense of euphoria in my system. I thought: I could fill my pockets with peanuts and disappear and no one would know a thing. How many peanuts would one have to eat? I wondered if the peanut vendor were poor. I was still sitting and contemplating the perfect crime when the peanut vendor reappeared and continued on his way with his cart. I leaned back against the bench with unsullied or was it indolent innocence? I had done nothing; it could have ended there, but it didn't. I was faced with the new question: Were ideas, however immoral, not guilty as long as they did not become actions? Could ideas engender evil? Was I evil for having hypothetically considered theft? Was my having let an opportunity go by due to some kind of inbuilt conscience or due to indolence and ultimately cowardice? The absoluteness of childhood was being replaced by the ambivalence concerning moral questions with which one was going in one way or another to spend the rest of one's life.

The park was a respectable square downtown. It was usually quiet and empty and one could sit on a bench in the sun undisturbed, half dreaming, half watching the pigeons with their disconcerting strut and nurses pushing prams and old and gentle vagrants with shabby down-and-out jackets sucking their yellow teeth. But on occasions the Park became a scene of drama.

Men in dark shirts waving red flags, followed by their women with big sorrowful eyes holding infants close, poured into the park causing the pigeons to fly up and the park folk to fade away.

The Internationale would strike up from somewhere and stocky dark men with melancholy mien would leap up on to benches and deliver fiery orations denouncing the rich and proclaiming the advent of bolshevism, communism, anarchism, terrorism and the freeing of the workers all over the world with a frenzied — and I thought inspiring — shaking of fists.

The general nationality of social deprivation and suffering seemed to be Italian, but at times, the park filled up with other "reds" whose nationality could not be determined. It was a nationality of despair and violence — a host of Princeps washed up on the shores of the Land of Liberty.

Sometimes the rallies were distinctly Russian. The Italian Reds were so unremittingly obsessed with social injustice, but the Russians came singing so that you shivered all down your spine at the beauty of it and even when they were at their wildest in the park, one or the other would notice you staring and would look at you with a twinkle in his eye as though he were about to invite you into his house. Then the singing came again and the song the Russians sang soared upwards and expanded out over everything like a vault of sound.

The inevitable termination of the rallies was the sirened appearance of Black Marias, the efficiently brutal hand-cuffing of the leading men, the silent resentment of the women and the age-old look of suffering in the eyes of the old men with their finely lined faces and bent backs. I was always distressed by this part and wept as the Black Marias sirened off up the streets, while the rest quietly dispersed. Soon the park heaved a sigh of restored respectability.

At times the park was the haunt of a band of older girls one of whom was the daughter of my mother's wealthy novelist friend, but we never acknowledged our tenuous connection.

When these girls appeared, it was expedient for me to withdraw as inconspicuously as possible at which a sense of self-preservation made me apt. From a safe vantage point on the far side of the Park from behind shrubs, I observed the sinister mysteries they enacted on the tarred paths. Hopscotch was the name of one malignant ritual from which the band seemed to derive awful power. I was Orpheus spying on the priestesses of Hecate.

The enemy invariably made for my hiding place to continue their evil rites during which my presence behind the shrubs could no longer remain unrevealed. Prompt and speedy retreat from the park was my only course of safety at this stage and I was always indescribably relieved to have escaped intact.

One day — it had to come — I was caught. The leading girl — my mother's friend's daughter — espied me as I was attempting to liquidate myself. I was bidden to remain on the spot and surrounded. I knew that the pounding in my heart could be heard by them all and that they despised me for a rabbit.

I was told to state my accomplishments: Could I play Hopscotch? Skip rope? Play ball? Alas, for these my years at the orphanage had not trained me. I had to confess — I was an intruder on hallowed ground.

"You must be able to do something," a lifeline was scornfully thrown out; I was being given a last chance.

"I can jump," I stammered

"Then jump!" came the iron command.

I looked around wildly for opportunities to display the ability I claimed to possess. My indecision was quickly registered by my captors. My harrowed gaze travelled to the statue and up its stony grey torso and rested upon its massive shoulders.

"Jump off the statue!" shrieked the sacrificial adepts.

The inexorable presence of fate left me no further choice, but I appealed for a condition. It was deemed fair and all agreed that if I jumped off the statue first they would all follow suit.

I was edged to the base of the Statue by the phalanx of maenads and assisted in scaling the initial protuberances. Slowly and with an icy clear mind, I climbed out of their reach. The buildings surrounding the park, the wrought iron gates, the garbage cans on the other side of the street — stood out in disinterested animosity.

I reached the flat unbreathing breast of the personage commemorated in this place and crouched upon one shoulder. I straightened up carefully; the certainty that it was folly to think of taking such a risk as to jump from here to the ground made me slightly silly. I laughed down into the upturned faces below. Then — I was suddenly deflated and sad — everything was grey and far away.

I lay face down on the gravel path. I neither knew where I was or how I got there. It flashed across my mind that I had lost both feet and hands, for where they had been was aching nothingness. It was chilly. I shivered violently.

I could only pick myself up by contracting in the middle and rolling on to my side. I then discovered that my feet and hands were still attached to my body for they were coming out of their numbness. My palms and knees looked like raw meat; the sight of them caused nausea. I slowly got to my feet, my teeth chattering uncontrollably as I hobbled to the gate.

I was reticent about my afternoon in the park when my mother came home in the evening. I said I had wanted to see if I could jump off the statue. My mother seemed to think I was slightly deranged. I stayed on the sofa for a few days because my palms and kneecaps teemed with alien life and throbbed at night and the glands in my armpits and groin were enlarged.

Yet this jump was of importance; the impossible remains impossible but with a different condition of mind, one can jump from the possible into the impossible, from one dimension into another without a bridge to walk on. There was a magic in one's ultimate attitude to circumstances which opened ways where there were no ways. One might have to lose a little of oneself, but one could get through where there was no way through — always.

These were the Prohibition years in America. My mother's widening circle of friends — journalists, writers, actors — belonged to those who pitted their wits against the anti-alcohol laws that prevailed, and tremendous ingenuity and risk were involved in the illegal obtaining of wines and spirits from over the borders to Canada.

The black night porter on the Pullman train between New York and Buffalo moved like a god in my mother's circles. He came to us in the evenings accompanied by his wife, both enormous people in evening dress, his tuxedo studded with diamonds, diamonds decorating her broad black neck, and bargained with my mother over the couple of bottles of wine he produced from inside his voluminous evening cape.

"Take it or leave it" he would say with a broad benevolent grin: "If you don't like the price, I can sell it somewhere else." In the end my mother would take the bottles.

She gave drinking parties in our room at night. I would be sent to sit outside on the landing where there was a wooden chest under a gas-jet to read. From there I witnessed my mother's guests coming up the stairs out of breath from the many flights, bottles concealed under their coats. Some of them were well-known personalities. The risk of being discovered in the possession of alcohol was great and penalties severe.

These men and women passed by without looking at me and disappeared into our room. I was not there to them, but they were there to me — I saw into their minds, saw their frightened motives, their lumps of guilt, opportunism and abject weaknesses, but censorship or indignation had not yet distilled in me; I simply steeled myself to face what came up from below and what was going to be the aftermath.

When the last guest had mounted the five flights of stairs, the door to our room closed. The faint roar of traffic in the streets overlaid any sounds from within. The gaslight was too dim to read by: I leaned back against the wall and waited and dozed fitfully.

At about three o'clock in the morning, the door to our room opened and a familiar but no less terrifying spectacle emerged. My mother's sodden guests staggered out followed by waves of acrid air and sought the staircase. My mother leaned foolishly against the doorpost with a maudlin leer on her face. Farewells were muttered, sometimes bawled. Faces were blotched and bloated, their silver incarnate tarnished.

A big man — I knew who he was — vomited copiously at my feet and collapsed in a sprawling heap. I thought he was dead. Several men and women half carried, half dragged him down the stairs, they themselves barely able to stand upright. My mother urged them on imperiously. The shuffling and hoarseness lasted interminably until they seemingly had him out on the street and the bang of a cab door could be heard. The mess of vomit lay unattended on the landing.

After one such party when my mother was leaning against the doorpost as her guests were departing, another "she" stepped out of her side and stood separately at a discernible distance from her. This Other was coarser, earthier and had a leering smile which was not unattractive, somehow more clever and compelling, more capable — magnetic and sinister at the same time. The blood in this "double" ran brown and thick. In comparison my real mother looked slight and transient and anxious. The two stood in the doorway for a moment, an ominous bond between them, until the one became the other again and there was only my mother.

The discovery that my mother contained a powerful and dangerous and brown-blooded double in herself, that she walked about with it inside her — was horrifying. I wanted to throw myself between her and this other and protect her from it when it emerged out of her at night, to sever the sinister bond, but was terrified lest I make an enemy of my mother instead.

I became very thin and could not throw off a cough remaining from a cold. My mother said I was too much a creature of the country to be shut up in a room in the city; I would have to return to the country. Besides, I would have to go to school again — no eleven year old child can simply stay away from school. "Can't I go to school in New York?"

"No, you must have country air to get rid of that cough and put on weight."

The thought of leaving my mother filled me with desperation on her behalf. How would she manage without me? I made her tea, cleaned the room, laundered her clothing and ironed her silk blouses with their fine pleats all down the front. I ran messages and shopped. I polished her shoes and had begun to make just the right little jokes when I sensed she was going to be depressed.

Money was coming in a little more regularly now and our life was more ordered. I contributed to that order by carrying out so many necessary chores with dedication. It was unbearable to think that my mother would have to do all these things herself.

And in the stifling nights, the brown atmosphere, the lowering Other in the dark, I wanted to be near lest she be alone with it, delivered to it.

Yet the idea of my going to school in the country was gathering momentum. My mother was clearly trying to manipulate me into accepting a decision she had already taken. One morning when she opened her mail, she said she had found just the right school for me; she made a studied show of enthusiasm designed to infect me. The school was upstate, the fees were reasonable and I would be able to come home for occasional weekends if the principal would allow it. I was to go in a week's time.

We did some meagre shopping. My face was set, my thoughts reduced to nothingness in an effort to master the grief and worry that had taken possession of me; she would be all alone when I went.

The moment the train pulled out of Grand Central Station and the slight figure of my mother had merged into the crowd on the receding platform, I abandoned myself to tears and wept all the way upstate.

The school I was going to was a small boarding school for girls, about two hours' train journey from the city. I was met at the country station by the principal of the school, a gaunt red-faced cheery woman with a flat chest and bobbed hair. She was oddly deferential; my mother must have impressed her.

The farmhouse in which the school was housed was bare and clean. It smelled of cold soap water. As I entered, in one corner of the dining room which served as classroom and common room, a sandy-haired girl with a spotty forehead was practising Schumann's "Wild Rider" very slowly on a tinny upright piano. The uninspired dirge could be heard throughout the house and proved to be inescapable.

I followed the principal up the bare wooden staircase, blinded by a sick headache, the inevitable consequence of weeping. It was a fallow afternoon.

I asked if I could lie down and went to bed in one of the six narrow beds in slightly damp sheets in a dormitory. The smell of cold soap water was all-pervading, the fallow daylight blinding and from downstairs came the thumping of the Wild Rider.

Later when it got dark, some girls came up and went to bed in the dormitory. I drew the sheet up over my eyes and heard their muted voices as though from a great unbridgeable distance.

The next morning I woke up to the Wild Rider whose wildness was still only a promise and had perforce to open my eyes. It was a fallow morning. Five girls lay in their beds discreetly observant of the newcomer. They all had the same pubertal complexions and sandy hair. They were all older than I, but my hair was not far from being sandy.

Some law of inertness seemed to keep the girls wide-eyed and quiet in their beds, but this changed abruptly when the door opened and the principal looked in with a cheery "Good morning, girls!" Then came a melee of vests and suspenders and combs and blouses, tooth brushing and sitting on toilets with open doors, which collective activities were new to me.

Breakfast was the occasion to see the school in its entirety. This consisted of twelve girls and four gaunt cheery teachers. I shivered for cold at the table and began to weep, an unusual outlet in most circumstances which now had something of an accomplishment about it.

The principal took me into her bare chilly office after breakfast for a talk. She had a degree in psychology. Outside, the passage resounded from the efforts of the Wild Rider to advance. The efforts of the principal were washed away in my newly discovered ability to produce floods of tears. I wept for a fortnight.

Only once did I stop when the Wild Rider, hobbling along on the piano below, so thumped on my every nerve that in a paroxysm of rage, I tore what I had on into shreds. Luckily, I was alone when I did it and was able to repair the signs of my extremity before anyone else saw them.

Exactly two weeks after my arrival at this school, a letter came from my mother saying that I was to leave — things had not worked out. She was not sure how much of it was my fault, but in any case, there was no point in staying on.

The floods receded. Having no further cause to weep, I felt firm and centred and my self again. I was driven to the little country station by the principal who was polite but a shade less cheery. I apologized and thanked her and departed.

My mother was reasonable and refrained from much comment. When I reported on my fortnight at the school and its stodgy accompaniment on the upright piano, she was amused and sympathetic, but she made it clear that as soon as she found another school, I was going to go.

After only a week in the city during which I worked for my mother like a Trojan (I never quite grasped why Trojans provided such a durable example of working fervour), she said she had found the ideal school. By a trick of fate, this new school was on the other side of the small town upstate where the school was I had just left.

The new school had a Latin name.' I shall call it Freedom which is near enough to its real name.

I needed none of my mother's persuasive powers to win me over to consenting to going away to school again for I felt completely apathetic. The fact that, in my case, the fees were going to be halved did not impress me nor did I want to understand the implications. (My short sojourn in New York coincided with an abrupt betterment in my mother's economic situation.) I was neither sad nor glad. I mended my clothing, packed my suitcase and left on the appointed day for the country once more. It was the end of May.

PART 3

23

Something in the winding seclusion of the valley where the white farmhouse stood, in the rustle of the leaves on the lawn, in the swift flow of the river past the mill-house, in the rising of the conical wooded mountain on the other side of the stream, in the intensity of the sky above that place — aroused in me a sense of ferment the moment I set foot in Freedom. Over the generous boughs of the maples that shaded the lawn, over the narrow dirt road that ran through Freedom along the steam, there hovered a magic transparent veil that deepened into burgundy in the evenings, into amber or etheric blue in the changing afternoons or darkened into saturated green — but was never grey. When the wind was raced by running feet, the secluded valley was vibrant with exuberance. In moments of stillness one knew that that exuberance was being recharged. When one caught a glimpse of the conical mountain on one's way back to Freedom after an excursion, one saluted it as the guardian standing watch over the place where the ideals were the sunlight and enthusiasm, the warmth in which its charges lived and grew.

The wealthy farmer of four sons had founded Freedom to give his sons the opportunity to go to school with children of differing social backgrounds in a progressive and unbiased atmosphere. Freedom was one of the earliest, if not the earliest, co-educational boarding schools in the country.

Some of the boys and girls at Freedom came from families who had fled the revolution in Russia. Others had parents who were bolshevists or communists of Balkan origin (people of the Park). There were children of orthodox Jewish families, problem children from the city, (was I one of these?), a small number who could not be classified (or one of these?), one or two whose parents were bohemians and lived in Greenwich Village (except that my mother had now moved uptown). For a time, I was the only blond child at Freedom, whatever that may have signified. There were no negro children while I was there; there may have been some before. Pauline, our nurse, was the only black person at Freedom.

The youngest son of the founder of the school, Jack, was still at Freedom as a pupil. He was fifteen and a rheumatic cripple, confined in the best of times to a wheelchair. His racked and twisted body housed for us the Palladium of Freedom. There was an unspoken but common awareness of this and everyone knew too that Jack was approaching the end of his life. As long as his flame flickered, Freedom was safe.

Jack took part in everything and his presence on all levels went without saying. When he had to stay in bed for longer periods, he was still fully included in our deliberations. Outwardly no distinction was drawn between Jack and ourselves and no pity was shown. We wheeled him from place to place, vying with each other in discreet manner as to who should push him where, but in reality, he walked before us, was our torch bearer.

Freedom had student government. Our teachers were there as experts in their respective academic fields, but not as representatives of authority. Authority was vested in the school's Assembly which comprised all the pupils save the very little ones of whom there were few at Freedom. Office bearers were drawn from the senior boys and girls.

The school's Assembly established the code of discipline which regulated a wide range of human propensities from essential ethical behaviour down to "don't-stick-your-chewing-gum-under-the-dining-room-table." Transgressions of our (it was "our" from the first moment) self-established laws or the adoption of anti-social attitudes or individual undertakings that were not in the interest of the whole organism were referred to in the school's Assembly and dealt with there in candour and seriousness. Few problems of this kind were carried over; the Assembly digested them quickly and social buoyancy was always re-established after each meeting.

We were fierce in our allegiance to the code of Freedom

and the whole school suffered when any one of us forgot, besmirched, misused or violated it. Yet I myself was, from the beginning, compelled by an often uncontrollable drive to challenge just the code I so loved, to test it to the utmost in order to discover that its strength and virtue were stronger than my own weaknesses. This was to lead to my downfall two years later.

Freedom used the Dalton Plan in its educational programme. By means of this method, the pupil himself was made responsible for achieving the appropriate knowledge and ability in the respective subjects taught. The teachers offered their wares — the pupils were to avail themselves of these wares on their own initiative and sense of responsibility. Every month, large cards were issued to the pupils with columns of units to be filled out in each subject according to the achievements of pupils within that month. This had its implications.

If a pupil wrote his essays, read the relevant study matter, managed his test papers — say, in history — within the given period or even prematurely, he was issued with a fresh card and could proceed at his own greater or lesser speed to meet the next month's allotment of historical material, but it did not follow that his units in other subjects were filled out at the same time. Nor was it of primary importance that a pupil attend regular lessons. Some of the more brilliant pupils (there was a high proportion of brilliant pupils at Freedom) had their cards filled out months in advance and were hardly ever to be seen in the classrooms. The less gifted pupils who doggedly attended all the lessons often found themselves in a class of advanced pupils far younger than themselves together with a number of very mature ones who lacked ambition. In such uneven circumstances, the average pupil often failed to advance and had to suffer a gradual snowballing of not-filled-in units in all his subjects.

This plan designed to release and foster initiative and responsibility in children at school resulted in a very mixed harvest at Freedom. Even with the integrity of the atmosphere there, the method of academic education engendered unbalanced ambition at too early an age, fostered opportunism as well as fatalism in many and in a few like myself, non-co-operation.

It also presented hazards in our relationships to our teachers because, although all of them exercised great tact and endurance and were convinced of the merits of the educational methods they had adopted, there were some who could not stand up to our arrogant selectiveness and sporadic attendance at lessons and who became victims of our ruthless derision.

Not in its student government but in its use of the Dalton Plan lay, I believe, some of the roots of Freedom's short duration as a school, for not long after I left, it closed down.

As far as I was concerned, my schooling at Freedom was a failure from the start. I adored the freedom at Freedom but could not deal with it. I could not get myself to attend lessons, not because I was idle but because I found so much else to do, and the teachers more or less directly concerned with me did not manage to gain my co-operation or arouse my sense of responsibility towards my own education.

During my two years at Freedom, I achieved a few units in one or two subjects, but had a yawning deficit in mathematics and the sciences. No teacher insisted that I sit down and work off this deficit so I went without half the activity of the young learning mind. In a sense, I was becoming a mental cripple, limping along on one foot as far as my general knowledge was concerned. The lack of that discipline the study of the sciences creates made me sanguine and superficial even in relation to those subjects in which I could have excelled had I been taught to learn. In spite of the richness of experience opened up to me by Dorothea, my house of learning was built on sand and my self-education through reading, indiscriminate. The progressive educational plan pursued at Freedom did not serve to consolidate its foundations, but left it permanently fragile.

But Freedom was a school of another kind — a schooling in enthusiasm and community spirit; it was a schooling in knighthood — in brotherhood.

I arrived at Freedom late one afternoon at the end of May. It had been raining. A sweet spring wind was beginning to lift the clouds away from the earth and they inhaled like sails hoisted for a journey out to sea. The rain was still dripping melodiously from the eaves of the big farmhouse. I immediately sniffed the soul of Freedom.

I was taken upstairs to the dormitory where I was to sleep. Everyone was out on some cross-country adventure. The dormitory was a large low-ceilinged room with two box windows looking out over the front lawn, which proved to be the Agora of Freedom where everyone met often during the day, where multitudinous comings and goings converged for brief exhilarating moments of mutual enquiry, where meals were taken in warm weather, where newcomers and guests were welcomed.

The dormitory was furnished with Spartan economy; there were few traces of individualism in the sparsity of objects that lay around between the beds, and it proved that the dormitory was never a haven to return to, but always a barracks to go out from. Mine was the eighth bed.

Dusk fell as I was unpacking my suitcase. Suddenly the silence in the empty house was rent by shouts, banging doors and laughter. There was a noise of someone skating along the upper passages and thunderous moving about downstairs. Into the din fell the resounding summons of a huge gong. Someone whirled round the doorpost of the dormitory: "It's suppertime!" and out again.

The fact that I was painfully and inordinately shy had not dawned upon me before coming to Freedom because of my having spent so long in isolation. Now in an onrush of self-discovery, I realized that I had a formidable handicap to contend with and a new searing experience of my uncertain identity: Who are you to say who you are?

All around as I descended the stairs there was a closely-knit, seething and vibrant inter-communication between the bodies sliding down the bannisters. Everyone was shouting, gesticulating to the other in a synthesis of exuberance and goodwill. The atmosphere was charged with mutual interest, enquiry and pleasure in the other person. These boys and girls who had been together the whole day long now met in the narrow passage at the bottom of the staircase with a renewed urge to discover one another as though the other were a boundless source of information, meaningfulness and delight.

My own sources of information, meaningfulness and delight

had been my books and their heroes. It had not been my experience that live human beings could be this source. I had always assumed that like Ariadne, I would marry a god when the time came. The impact of live people and the terrifying prospect of relationships with them was, on that first evening at Freedom, overwhelming. It was the impact of a heaven on earth, whereby a bookish and abstract heaven was by far the safer. In all the new tremulousness that rushed in upon me, my inborn fatalism made itself felt: would I ever become an *in*sider?

I reached the dining-room where I was told to sit down at one of the long bare tables in the large L-shaped room. (Why was everything here painted in blue and orange? Ugly memories forced their way into my mind. Later I learned that blue and orange were the colours of Freedom.)

I sat with my back to the dining-room. Opposite me sat two boys. The one was slightly dwarf-like in that he had an insignificant body but a large head with the strongly developed physiognomy of an adult under a shock of rich brown hair. This was Victor. He was Jewish, brilliant, talkative, brazen and he spoke with a succulent Yiddish inflection. His deep wolf's eyes missed nothing and everything he observed inevitably received his sardonic and witty comments.

The other boy — although he was sitting beside Victor on the bench — seemed to be sitting behind him. This was the constant impression the two gave wherever they went — the one just behind the other.

Randal had a flat round face like a pale moon and light brown eyes. There was a faint constellation of freckles on the bridge of his nose which fanned out over his high cheekbones. He was reticent. At first one was inclined to dismiss him as Victor's shadow, but then one discovered that he was the more formidable of the two — ruthless and at the same time infinitely compassionate.

Victor lost no time in impressing me that the voice of Freedom spoke through him. I found out later that although his actual age debarred him from bearing office in the Assembly, he was regarded as a kind of senior advisor; an age-old mature mind rested incongruously in the body of an eleven year old boy — but his voice had deepened.

During this my first meal at Freedom, Victor played with me benignly as a cat plays with the mouse it is going to devour. I floundered and flushed, spilt my milk, blurted out odd scraps of concepts that weren't really mine and at which Victor's deep-set eyes gleamed with unholy amusement. He deftly drew the attention of everyone in the dining-room to my oddities. Randal looked on with Mongolian detachment.

When supper was over, I tried to creep away unnoticed, to hide somewhere in the unfamiliar house, but Victor's voice with its Yiddish timbre held me back: "Now let me introduce you to everyone at Freedom."

With his hand firmly gripping my elbow, he paraded me around from pupil to teacher with mock courtesy, repeating with pointed innocuousness the things I had spluttered out during supper. I looked into the shut doors of faces in legion. My eyes blurred and something began to throb inside like an old wound opened up. "Leave off, Victor." — a dry almost rasping whisper came from behind.

The first thing that shot through my mind when I woke up the next morning was a thrill of anticipation at the thought of seeing Victor and Randal again. With a quiver of expectation and apprehension, I rose to meet my first full day at Freedom.

Einar was a Dane. He ran the farm at Freedom and work on the farm was a major factor in our lives there. To work under Einar was being part of a saga — a saga of the seasons, of the seven fat kine, Homeric kine, for Einar was our Odysseus and the farm his Ithaca.

Early in the morning before breakfast, we gathered in the barn to receive his instructions for the day. Although he knew that not all of us attended lessons, he never allotted us tasks during school hours. Erik was the only exception; he worked all day with Einar and studied at night. He was the oldest boy at Freedom.

Einar's instructions were lucid and laconic, as long as we were in the barn to hear them. He showed no displeasure or annoyance when we overslept or were too late or too indolent to be on the spot — we simply no longer existed. We would creep into the barn behind the others and his gaze would pass over us as though we were air. Gradually we wrested back our self-respect, our willingness, our usefulness, and one morning we were again included. It was not that Einar received us back with any show of welcome; the light blue eyes would simply rest upon us gravely and we were told what we had to do that day.

We handled Moses, our huge Holstein bull, who was kept in a high reinforced concrete pen. We fed him, watered him, arranged his marriages with business-like efficiency, and loved him. One day we found his enormous body lifeless in the pen. Silently we hauled his carcass out of the pen with winches into the back of the truck and drove him away. The iron gate of his pen stood open and stillness filled the place that had been charged with his minotauran vitality. The autopsy revealed that he had swallowed a large nail which had travelled through his massive body to lodge in his heart.

We helped to milk our twenty-four Holsteins and ten Jerseys cows by hand, kept the dairy, drove the surplus milk to town, mixed mash for the cattle and swill for the pigs, filled the horses' mangers with corncobs and scattered crushed corn kernels to the hens.

We spent long hours at the silos, feeding the silage cutter with cornstalks and pouring barrels of molasses down after the cut stalks into the depths of the silos out of which heavy sweet fumes rose up, causing us to feel slightly tipsy.

At haying time, we were joined by everyone in the school including all the teachers out on the hay-fields and had thick slices of bread and peanut butter and milk to drink at the edge of the fields instead of going back to the house for dinner.

In the winter, we cut ice on the ponds and used grappling hooks to heave the blocks of ice on to sledges to take them back to the ice sheds behind the barn where they were stored in sawdust and salt.

Einar expected us to contribute to the work on the farm, but he never overtaxed us nor did he blame us for anything that went wrong as long as we did our best. Human frailty was a sudden squall — it had to be reckoned with. Whenever a greater or lesser disaster occurred on the farm, Einar went about restoring order and at the same time, if the disaster had not been the direct result of negligence or foolhardiness, restoring our confidence in ourselves.

We, for our part, were convinced that nothing could really happen as long as Einar was there. Yet he evoked no emotional relationships. Communication through the spoken word was brief and referred solely to the needs of the farm. On rare occasions he smiled and we were relieved to know that he had a sense of humour.

Einar's impersonality had the effect of relating you to yourself, of assessing your own merits. Illusions, ambitions, even ideals had no place in Einar's realm. There were no thrones — only the sober responsibility for the farm and its animals.

There were riding horses at Freedom. I discovered Ginger, a highly strung red mare, soon after I arrived. Only those pupils who knew how to ride and to look after horses were allowed to use them. I had occasionally handled buggy horses, but had never ridden, yet the moment I mounted Ginger, I became a rider and from the moment I became a rider, I had a passion that could not be curbed. Although my riding had not been sanctioned by the school's Assembly, I monopolized Ginger; she was my horse.

I took my first long ride on her early one Sunday morning. We rode into unfamiliar parts of the country several miles away. Stillness lay over the fields and up on the edge of the forest hovered the same sabbatical silence. Not a leaf nor a blade of grass stirred; Ginger's slow tread on the stony track was the only sound to be heard as we rode upwards.

High over the rising hills ahead, storm clouds were beginning to churn and flashes of dull orange lightning sheeted across the darkening sky. Thunder rumbled as though from the roots of the hills. Below us the breathless air quivered over the rippleless cornfields. Sweat ran down our bodies in the humidity. A black turmoil of storm clouds was rolling down over the crest of the hills into wooded gullies. There was a faint sulphuric smell in the air. Ginger was nervous and danced about on the track.

Just as we reached the edge of the forest, a wild whisper whistled over the cornfields and in through the forest, whipping up the treetops and the great branches swayed around in circles. The storm broke.

Lightning played over the forest accompanied by drums of

thunder and swathed in sheets of rain. The whole forest rose up in applause and received the rain. Until — the storm weakened and passed on over other hills, leaving the forest gently dripping and the sweet corn glistening in the shy sunlight that followed in the wake of the storm. Ginger was wet and shiny all over and my clothes clung to my body. The forest breathed forth freshness.

Up there on horseback at the edge of the forest, I had a fleeting vision: Marathon, Bannockburn, Borodin — knots and nodes in the tapestry of history, battles fought in the flow of human events, myself in the flow of human events . . . I turned Ginger and rode back to Freedom, feeling curiously thoughtful and composed, the low hanging wet branches of the maples brushing my face as though in a caress.

However far I rode Ginger, there was always a magnet that drew me back and the sense of expectancy increased the nearer we came to the farmhouse. Something had taken root in the soil of my soul and was growing there. It was the experience of being part of a context, of belonging, a certainty that when I was away, there was a gap in the ranks of Freedom, ultimately that I was loved freely without binds.

It was what shot through me on my first morning when I moved into the place that seemed to be waiting for me — between Randal and Victor.

Randal and Victor were my Scylla and Charybdis. I could never pass between them without leaving something of myself behind and taking a sharp imprint of them with me. Being a girl, yet not yet a girl, my place in the trio was both subordinate and sovereign. The fact that I was one year older than they was not essential.

They claimed my soul and spirit. "Tell us what you've been doing" — Victor's deep voice would command, Randal lowering enigmatically behind him. I knew that they knew what I had been doing. I had seen to it that they knew for they were my constant inner point of reference in whatever I undertook. My life from morning till night was an almost uninterrupted dialogue with them. We knew of each other because we were each other's Other, but our protocol demanded verbal confession. Not only that — we longed to pay for every minute we spent in each other's company, only we did not permit ourselves to show it.

I laughed insolently: "What's that got to do with you?"

"I said you were to tell us what you have been doing." The Yiddish inflection was pronounced and sent waves of delight coursing along my nerves. I laughed more pointedly and was as taut as a bow, suspended for a moment, then I bolted so suddenly that the two were taken off their guard and began the chase at a disadvantage.

Sometimes my route of escape lay through the house, but Randal and Victor were deadly strategists and I was prone to losing my head in the face of their mental superiority and was soon captured. But outside, with open stretches of field or road before me, I was at a distinct and acknowledged advantage for I was able to outrun almost everyone in the school.

I streaked up the road with Randal and Victor gradually falling behind. They would suddenly lose all interest in the chase. I saw the expression of feigned disdain on their faces although I was far ahead. I knew it was there; it was part of our agreement. Casually and with detached demeanour, they sat down on the stone wall and studied the wayside herbs. I sat down on the same stone wall further up and studied the crop of gourds in the field. We sat. When I got up, they got up in lethal imitation. I sat down again. They sat down again. The stone wall conducted an electric current between us which mounted in tension and exquisiteness until I could stand it no longer; I shot off the wall with Randal and Victor in pursuit.

Once I stretched the game beyond its limits. As long as I kept my prowess in running in check, Randal and Victor would concede a truce after a time and our relationship became blissfully relaxed. But this time, I did the impermissible and took a leap off the wall, making off over the field. When I reached the far side, I looked back hopefully, but there was no one behind me. They had not pursued me. When I got back to the road, I saw them in the distance entering the school grounds.

I was indescribably hurt by what I had done and went down to the school with yearning and remorse in my soul. Too bereaved of their company I loitered around the barn doing odd little things, but later in the evening, having become more composed, I sauntered into the common room where evening activities were in full swing. Randal and Victor were playing chess in one corner of the room. They did not look up as I entered but a warm smile spread over Victor's face as he concentrated on the chessboard and I knew that he knew that I was there.

When our clashes came and I chose the house once again as my route of escape, the other pupils abandoned the passages and staircase to us. It started downstairs: "Tell us what you've been doing!"

"Why should I? Am I your slave?" With the usual show of insolence, I made a dash for the upstairs bathroom, slamming the door in the face of my pursuers so that the walls shook. When the bathroom was occupied, I was lost. An iron grip closed on shoulders and ankles and I was carried out of the house bodily and thrown into the brook with all my clothes on.

But when the bathroom was free, it was different. I slithered off the rim of the tub through the tiny square window out on to the gabled roof of the house over which I sprang, sure-footed but a little silly when I thought of Victor and Randal struggling through the bathroom window — knowing what was coming, for I possessed a unique trump.

I was the only pupil at Freedom who dared to jump off the kitchen roof, possibly because of the jump off the statue in the park earlier on. Poised on the edge of the steep roof, I was well aware of a new and insidious urge to show off (I had never experienced such an urge at the orphanage). I permitted my pursuers to advance within victory and then jumped — self intoxication lending me a certain buoyancy — down into the courtyard below.

Rising to my feet and always a little incredulous that it was I and not someone else who had performed the feat, I looked up to see Randal and Victor peering down with open admiration and all three burned with a kind of love for all three of us.

I rarely encountered Randal and Victor in a classroom, not only because my own attendance at lessons was so sporadic, but because they both belonged to the category of pupils who worked off their units far in advance of the stipulated period, young though they were, and therefore we had little common ground for meeting on an academic level.

One day though, I was attending a Latin lesson and was in an unusually studious frame of mind. An oral translation of Cicero was underway and I was making a laboured contribution to the efforts of the class when Randal and Victor entered the room, stating in subdued voices that they had come for extra translation practice. Room was made for them and they sat down in the circle, not glancing in my direction. It was my turn to continue. I bent over the book, my face aflame. I didn't really manage Cicero at all and I knew that Randal and Victor had come with the sole purpose of putting me on the rack — their innocent mien was too meticulous.

Randal was one of the most advanced pupils in Latin and Victor composed Latin doggerels and quoted Ovid on all occasions. The oil leaked out of the precarious machinery that emulsifies two languages into one meaning; wrong words and faulty constructions tumbled out of my mouth and I lost the thread of what I was meant to be translating. I put the book down and announced that I had a headache.

Our teacher asked Victor to take over where I left off. He began to translate fluently and rapidly, his voice metallic but agreeable, resounding in the flabbergasted silence in the classroom, his astonishing prowess and the incongruity of his Yiddish accent rendering the performance all the more fascinating.

My solar plexus glowed with admiration and pride, but I knew the danger of giving myself away and tightened up my mind in order to contain my love, and fanned a rising sense of indignation. What right had they to come to a Latin lesson when everyone knew that they were only pretending to practice? It was only to prevent others from learning, the conceited pigs! I rose, calculated my aim and flung Cicero's speeches at Victor's head and took flight.

With the throb of righteous indignation coursing through my veins, I sped to the stables to saddle Ginger. I saw the tips of her ears twitch expectantly over the top of her box. Suddenly I was seized from behind and before I could defend myself, I was hauled swiftly and deftly up the wooden steps to the empty grain-room.

The grain-room was lined with galvanized tin to keep out rats and mice and it had no windows. I was thrust inside and the door was bolted on the outside. I lay for a while on the floor where I had fallen and slowly recovered composure. The air in the completely dark grain-room was dusty and stifling so that I could not inhale deeply but had to take shallow little gasps which made me light-headed after a while. The darkness was unrelieved.

The grain-room was insulated against sound as well. When the great outside dinner gong was struck (a sledge hammer was used to strike it), it was muffled and came to my ears as though from a very great distance. I could hear no nearer sounds of anyone moving in the stables below.

Breathing became increasingly difficult and I was near to succumbing to panic; I would bang at the door and shout to gain release from this awful place . . . but I didn't. Perhaps I was already too light-headed. Yet I realized that not only was I very hungry but I had other needs which were becoming acute.

The room lightened up and I saw into all its corners which were now illumined by a delicate reddish glow and were so vast that the angles of each corner were far out in the universe and I a pinpoint in the centre. I marvelled at the splendour of the immense cube and perceived that the glow was intensifying so that the walls, ceiling, floor, myself were dissolved in radiant light shining out into infinitudes.

After a time, I was aware of a peripheral gaze focused upon myself and knew it for my Self; I was gazing at Me. The universe filled the spaces between Me and myself . . . then the peripheral Self faded away taking the radiance with it, leaving me in the centre a little black clot — negligible . . .

A cool draught stirred in the utter darkness of the grain-room. Carefully and thirstily I filled my lungs with fresh air. A hand groped for mine and pulled me to my feet. The same hand helped me to climb down the dusty wooden steps and below on the threshold of the stables, I was released out into the night.

I acquired two pages, Sammy and Manny, beautiful, curly-haired, Jewish identical twins. It was a singular honour to have the twins in my following for they were regarded by the whole school as human treasures. They gave me my first experience of feeling sisterly and I was much concerned with their welfare, albeit I learned to distinguish between what was good for them and good for me and in as much I achieved some wisdom, they were my teachers.

As long as I felt harmonious and integrated, I kept Sammy and Manny (Samuel and Manuel) at my side and was secure in the approval of others. But in moments of oncoming dissonance when I felt unaccountable and volcanic, I learned to dismiss them in time so as not to submit them to the consequences of what was going to consume me. In any case, these were moments in which I needed to be alone.

The summer holidays came all too soon. My mother now possessed an old farmhouse in Connecticut and went there for the summer months with a friend. Noel and Milly were there as well; the threads of connection between our mothers had persisted over the years — but we did not have Freedom in common and I found it difficult to enter into companionship with them.

We had a collie named Petroushka, a perfect example of his kind with his fawn coat and white ruff, black-tipped and plumed tail. His nose was long and slender and inquisitive. Petroushka accompanied me on my long walks when I communed with the spirit of Freedom and thought of the day of return.

Petroushka was a great hunter or rather chaser and often came back smelling of skunk and had to be ostracized to the woodshed where I brushed down his coat with paraffin until he was deemed respectable again. He often had encounters with porcupine and we would hear him wincing at the door. He would lay his riddled muzzle on my knee and suffered me to draw out the quills one by one, but Petroushka, though beautiful, was stupid — he would go off and snuffle at porcupine again.

Our neighbour had twelve cows which grazed in an orchard up the road. No one tended the orchard and the apples fermented on the ground and were eaten by the cows. This made them tipsy and in late afternoon, they came swaying down the road and just before they reached the gate to our neighbour's barnyard, they would fan out in all directions and disappear into the woods opposite.

I would dash over to the neighbour and offer to round up his cows and would wade through swampland infested by adders and through dense thicket to encircle the inebriated animals and conduct them safely home.

Milly and I went swimming in the millpond. When we emerged out of the water, we were covered with leeches. We would spend the next half hour pulling them off our arms and legs only to return once more to the water day after day.

I waited for the return to Freedom all summer. I chopped firewood and stacked it in the woodshed, right up the wall. My mother, her friend who was a writer, Milly, Noel and I had supper in the rickety old dining-room. I had cooked most of it on the rickety paraffin stove in the kitchen next to the woodshed. My mother had given me an Italian cookery book to go by. Milly, Noel and I were allowed to stay for a while by the fire in the front room and read as long as we were quiet, but I offered to wash the dishes to be alone. I was waiting to go back to Freedom.

24

Some of us met already at Grand Central Station. We were back in the golden stream.

The founder family of Freedom occupied the mill-house by the brook. We were always welcome there when we paid our visits to Jack who was now permanently confined to his room upstairs. His window looked out over the mill stream on to the conical mountain that stood guard over Freedom. His bed was surrounded by small tables laden with books and there was an air of enhanced mental activity in the room in spite of Jack's obvious and prolonged bouts of pain, and the smell of medicine. He could scarcely hold a book in his knotted fingers nor could he raise his head far off the pillow. His eyes were hollows of pain. Yet his mind was master in his house and we always went away from him stimulated by his interests, although the impression of his increasingly stricken body went with us too. These were Jack's last months.

Downstairs in the drawing room of the mill-house rhythmic dancing lessons took place every Friday afternoon. A fair-haired, soft-voiced teacher came from the city once a week to give these lessons which were attended only by girls. My Amazon status among the boys did not permit indulgence in female pastimes and I wholeheartedly contributed to the chorus of derisive catcalls which accompanied the girls who surreptitiously hurried across the lawn to the mill-house for their rhythmic dancing lessons.

Not only did we have important business just in front of the mill-house on Friday afternoons; we seemed to have no other purpose in life but to crouch beneath the drawing room windows in the flowerbeds and to hoot at and imitate the girls inside as they bent their bodies to music, clad in short silken tunics. The sight of them waving like reeds irritated me beyond control and spurred me on to ever more extreme manifestations of contempt. Randal and Victor regarded my attitude to rhythmic dancing with satisfaction and my mandate to declare myself an enemy to all "soft" activities was confirmed.

I was just descending the stairs in the mill-house after having knocked at Jack's door and being told that he could not have visitors that day. Down in the big drawing-room, the dancing lessons were in progress. I heard the teacher's voice instructing the pupils — and then I heard —

It was not that I was stirred by the memory of what had once struck me like lightning. It was simply that the lightning struck again. I stood on the staircase and listened and felt as though I were being called by name. I had a powerful experience of being *sent*, not to do anything spectacular in life, but rather sent out of a former state of existence into the present. I was where I was meant to be — not locally but existentially. I would only have to remain in tune with the sending. The desire to acknowledge this flash of awareness filled me with a religious urge to make my existence sacramental, to make every step I took a prayer, a hymn of praise. I went downstairs, knocked at the drawing-room door and asked the teacher to allow me take part in the rhythmic dancing lessons. I was astonished that she showed no apprehension at including me. Afterwards I wrote to my mother for a length of bottle-green silk to make myself a tunic.

The demonstrations of derision now directed towards myself on Friday afternoons seemed paltry compared to the musical experience I had in the dancing lessons. Never having had the opportunity to handle a musical instrument, I discovered that the body itself can be a musical instrument and the person inside it the musician. After a while, the demonstrations of contempt ceased and I continued in the rhythmic dancing lessons as long as I was at Freedom. It had a bearing on my future.

Downstream, at some distance from the farmhouse, we set out to construct a dam so that there would be sufficient water in the brook for swimming. The lack of swimming facilities at Freedom was one of its few drawbacks. We chose a spot where the bed of the stream widened and deepened naturally and worked hard for almost a week on our dam which was beginning to be effective. We inspected it frequently and ascertained where our construction would have to be improved upon. Then we lost incentive for a few days and were otherwise engaged.

When we returned to our dam construction site, we were confronted with a scene of destruction: beavers had dismantled the dam, making of it an unrecognizable mess of debris, and had used our material to build a dam of their own further upstream. The sight of this sabotage filled us with wrath and indignation. Furiously we undid the beavers' work and hastily rebuilt our dam on our chosen site. During the night that followed the beavers with characteristic diligence removed our their sticks and reconstructed their dam on the site of their choice. We retaliated the next day by destroying it and restoring our dam, muttering threatening incantations to all beavers while we laboured.

I rose early next morning to see how our most recent efforts had survived the night. Our dam was intact. The pool had begun to fill up. There was no trace of beavers. The place was forsaken and curiously empty.

An overwhelming sense of shame suddenly invaded my mind and I realized the enormity of what we had been doing; I had been a ring-leader in an ignominious campaign against an unequal contender and should have known better — did know, deep down.

A brown Beaver Spirit with small grave eyes hovered close in front of me, regarding the writhings of my conscience with elevated calm. I was the dumb one-sided creature and he the universal one with a wisdom that welled out of the deep foundations of existence. In great humility, I stood before the Beaver Spirit and confessed my moral inferiority. When he had vanished, I broke up our dam and admitted it to the others when they saw the renewed destruction. The brown Beaver Spirit wrought his work upon us all. Henceforward, we referred to that spot in the stream as the Beaver Dam and regarded it rather as a sanctuary than as a place for sport.

Reciting long narrative poems was a feature of our intercommunication at Freedom. We had a big repertoire — Macaulay, Longfellow, Walt Whitman, Poe, Masefield, Kipling. I never had to learn a poem by heart because at a glance, a page of poetry imprinted itself so vividly on my mind that I simply "read" it off again from an inner page, I was useful to the group because of this as I could always supply the cues.

We recited while we washed the dishes, cleaned the rooms, raked leaves, shone our shoes and especially when we went on full day hikes across country. At the time, a Yiddish satirist, Milt Gross, published a Yiddish parody of Longfellow's *Hiawatha* in serials in one of the New York papers. We waited voraciously for each new stanza to appear and after a while under Victor's expert tuition, the whole school was able to recite the Yiddish Hiawatha with unbounded relish. It was our collective obsession. Vestiges of Yiddish in my English accent were the first factors to undermine my mother's good opinion of Freedom, although she had so far not visited.

I developed an urge to drive fear out of my system and was regarded as fearless which was not really the case, but the strong undercurrent of fear always with me was suppressed by a growing vanity and an irresistible desire to show off. Avoiding the ultimate encounter with my Self, I sought out and provoked situations that were ticklish, even dangerous, in order to steel myself against cowardice and to demonstrate my courage.

We had parents' visiting afternoons once a month at Freedom always on a Sunday. An odd array of unmistakeable city folk, uneasily carrying picnic baskets, often barely able to speak English, trudged in pairs or singly up the country road to Freedom and sat about on the lawn with their progeny after having been duly shown around the school grounds, until it was time to catch the train back to the city.

An older boy, Gene Levine, had a tiny mother who wore a black shawl over her head and could not speak English. Gene led her around and explained everything to her in Russian and treated her with great gentleness and consideration. His father was often jailed because of political agitation, but when he was free, he came to visit Gene and would recite Pushkin in Russian to all of us listening spellbound on the lawn.

Victor was afflicted by his entire clan of Yiddish shopkeepers of whom his father was the most wily, regarding us and all the visitors as prospective customers and ready to make a deal at all costs on these Sunday afternoons. While he abandoned himself to this commercial zeal, Victor's mother and numerous other female relatives chortled in Yiddish over their "golden boy" and Victor would suffer excruciatingly and was, for once, helpless. We did what we could to rally to his aid and keep his "old man" in check.

Randal's mother was a pale care-worn little widow who worked as a cleaning woman in the city. She brought Randal little cakes in a tidy round basket and they sat on the lawn off to one side and were never observed to exchange a word.

My own mother would have electrified the company with her elegant figure and dress and her wit and I would have had something to be very proud of, but she never came on those visiting afternoons however much I begged her to — just once.

There was a bridge over the millstream, the iron girders of which rose to a considerable height above the river-bed. The angle was steep till they levelled off at the top, not being quite a foot in breadth. The girders were secured at intervals by large round bolts which allowed one with concentrated effort to scale the girders, run across the top of the bridge and down the other side.

On one of the parent's visiting afternoons, I resolved to display my fearlessness. Having ascertained that everyone was on the front lawn whence there was a clear view of the bridge, I sprinted forwards, ran up the girder, along the top and down the other side, taking a flying leap to the ground because the angle became too steep to maintain a foothold on the bolts. Lingering for a moment to pull down my middy, I tasted the delectable impression I must have made on the crowd on the lawn before disappearing into the woods at the foot of the mountain.

In the evening when all the parents had left, I sauntered in for supper with an air of detachment. This did not prevent me from perceiving the equally studied air of indifference that met my entry. I firmly suppressed an impression of something like compassion in the expression on some faces.

Showing-off was regarded with contempt at Freedom and I was rapidly developing a reputation as a show-off, but I could not control the urge. If I didn't thrust myself into the arena of attention at this stage, I often had no experience of myself at all; I was not.

I was aware that I was becoming an actor on a stage all day long, playing to an audience, acutely conscious of the effect I was having on others. I played different parts with different people in different situations. I was losing immediacy in my relation to my environment. The effect of my exhibitionism on my own integrity was silenced by myself. I did not allow myself to raise the issue. I became addicted to effect. Emergencies provided the only relief from this addiction when I could forget myself and give my energies unstintingly with no thought of anything other than the matter in hand. These emergencies occurred mostly on the farm and the farm became the only place where I could at times be myself. After the emergencies were over however, the insidiousness of self-consciousness came stealing back into my mind and once having entered it, clouded my momentary innocence and I would again become intoxicated by my seeming bravura.

I was restless, hardly ever in the dormitory, ruthlessly disregardful of the other girls with whom I shared a room. I was insatiably hungry for everything at Freedom, had to be everywhere, in everything, and there was a constant throb of grief in my soul when I missed out on something.

Then followed paralysing periods of self-recognition. I knew that my erratic behaviour was a source of dismay to my comrades and teachers. They were witness of constant wastage on my part. I knew that I was a danger to myself. I knew, too, half consciously, that I could claim justification for all this disturbed and disturbing behaviour which could exonerate me from responsibility. But in the depths of my existence, I knew there was no real justification for my erratic way-of-being other than my own lack of morale, that in the face of my own scrutiny of myself it was impermissibly cheap to make use of a set of circumstances now left behind to elicit sympathy or understanding from others. Besides, pride prevented me from regarding myself as a victim of or handicapped by what had been earlier on. Perhaps what I did not know was that this fierce independence of Self was in itself a handicap.

I took long solitary walks up the mountain wrestling to get through to the stern seat of judgment only an encounter with my Self could provide, but even this Self seemed to have withdrawn as though it wanted to deny any association with me. In all the wonder and delight of Freedom, I felt at times completely alone, a convicted outsider. Yet occasionally, I was to some degree morally restored when I came down from the mountain and could step into the common stream again.

We planned a cross-country fox-and-hound chase. When it came to drawing lots for sides, a demon took possession of me and I refused to accept my lot and tried to force other means of decision. Not able to overcome my stubbornness in time, I was ignored and left behind.

The chase started off: my soul went with it with longing. I knew the route the foxes had taken and the strategies the hounds would adopt. I knew every ditch, wall, field and wood across the country. I knew too, that a mammoth cake had been baked for the winning side to share with the losers in the chase. The cake was waiting on a shelf in the storeroom behind the kitchen. In a black mood of retaliation, I resolved to remove the cake and hide it.

Most of us were practised larder-raiders at Freedom (Randal expounded the Spartan doctrine that the only crime of the thief was to be discovered in the act, although he was never one of the active larder-raiders) and I met with no difficulty in taking the giant cake from the store with the cooking staff well in the vicinity.

I intended to hide it in the grain-room where it would be safe until I chose to produce it. I had not foreseen where the real danger in the undertaking lay; this was the terrible unthinkable shame — it was the whole cake.

When the chase returned, the absence of the cake was soon discovered. Sensitive as we were to one another, everyone immediately realized what had happened. Randal and Victor averted their eyes when I passed by, my own full of sickness and supplication. The look on their faces was not studied; I was not spoken to by anyone for two days.

On the evening of the second day, there was a school's Assembly. I went alone and sat alone. As matters proceeded, I sank into a grey oblivion and was beginning to feel I did not exist. As a last effort to save myself from disintegration, I raised my hand and asked to speak. There was utter silence in the room when I rose to my feet and told the Assembly what I had done (although everyone knew I had done it) and apologized with tears running down my face. I loved Freedom very much in this moment; there was nothing on earth more precious.

And Freedom's love for me came back like a great wave of fresh water washing me down. After the meeting, Randal and Victor stood at my side and everyone, including the teachers, came to say how indescribably relieved they were that I had spoken as I did in the Assembly. A cloud that had hung over us all was dispelled.

Winter came and as a consequence of not being outside all the time, the classrooms were more frequented.

Our English teacher was a poetess of some repute. Small, short-sighted and sandy-haired, she had a keen mind and a dry sense of humour and was a disciplined person. The imagery in her poetry was strong and unfeminine. I took pleasure in her tuition and began to find grammar an ethical schooling. It was she who introduced me to the Russians, above all, to Tolstoy.

For the first time since my arrival at Freedom, I put in an appearance in the science room where Richard, our handsome science teacher, demonstrated in biology. I learned to hold a frog deftly in the fingers of one hand while I destroyed its cerebral nerve with a scalpel in the other to observe the mechanical almost epileptic jerking of the disassociated frog body in the palm of my hand.

I had been unable to inflict injury on living creatures hitherto without undergoing deep and distressing feelings of guilt and now had the experience of legitimate torture in the name of science, but this was not a classroom I frequented because our handsome Richard did not explain life in terms that were meaningful to me. In fact, I found it difficult to reconcile his clinical approach to biology with the intense humanity of Freedom.

Our history teacher, Gloria, was rather young, dark, very fat and untidy and was, even for Freedom, too easy-going. Yet she was respected by us for being an excellent teacher with great powers of engendering enthusiasm for her subject. In our sessions with her, we did not primarily acquire historical information but rather historical thinking. She did not hand out dry bones, but flesh and blood and spirit and a sense of responsibility in the individual for the course of history; she continued where Dorothea had to leave off. Gloria also taught us Latin.

Her husband was our geography teacher as well as Greek teacher. He was much older than she, and was a gaunt, austere, dour man with a desperate glint in his eyes that made us tend to avoid him. I was never in his classroom, but as he worked part of the time in the school office where mail and pocket money and the like were dealt with, I had perforce to encounter him.

Our mathematics teacher was a young Jew with a pronounced lisp. He had been brilliant at college and had graduated with distinction, but suffered from a sensitive and highly romantic nature, the manifestations of which provoked merciless teasing on our part. He was extremely susceptible to the feminine sex whatever the age or description and regarded it *in toto* as a hierarchy of lofty and unearthly beings. There was something saintly in his innocence that endeared him to us all in spite of our maltreatment of his person. I myself always had to stifle a pang of pity when I witnessed how ruthlessly he was teased.

His name was Bernie and once, at a masked ball, to which I went dressed in black as a widow, he asked me shyly for a dance, not knowing who I was. As we passed by Randal and Victor neither of whom ever danced, I heard Victor whisper: "Give him the works."

I was twelve and Bernie was one of the teaching staff. I led him by the hand into the courtyard outside and took off my black veil and hat: "I can't really dance, Bernie, I'm going riding."

He took the disillusionment well and suddenly looked kindly. Whatever little I learned in mathematics at that stage, I learned or tried to learn from him.

This was a period in Freedom when my unit card was within reach of being partially filled out and I was not so readily distracted by activities outside the classrooms. But the old trouble of regular sick headaches interrupted continuity in study and my belated efforts to learn were frustrated because of this as well.

We played ice hockey on a frozen flooded field on winter afternoons. Enthusiasm made up for my lack of skill and competitiveness and I was always called up to fill a gap when the teams were being drawn up. Ivan, one of the older boys, a Russian Jew, played forward with tremendous speed and efficiency. He had a warm personality and would encourage us all, regardless of sides, to keep up the game and his highly reddened round cheeks were a beacon of general cheer.

It was he who inadvertently let fly his hockey stick which

struck me across the larynx. Falling to my knees, I gasped and gasped under the sudden shock. The bare trees outlined against the snow moved sharply into the foreground; my diaphragm was convulsed in a concave cramp and everyone stared at the visible contraction beneath my sweater. Extinction seemed close — beyond the trees the blinding whiteness — then I experienced a distinct intervention as something like a hand seemed to pass soothingly over my convulsed diaphragm releasing the cramp so that I could breathe freely again. I felt a great rush of gratitude to whatever agent had intervened and back in the dormitory I fell into a deep sleep.

On moonlit nights, the older pupils went sledging after the younger children had gone to bed. It was a transgression even the most responsible older pupils reserved for themselves. I included myself in this exclusive infringement of our self-made laws, and met with no objections on the part of the others.

The hill we sledged on was a long gradual slope that levelled out gently and opened up into a wide, flat meadow. We only had to loosen a stretch of barbed wire fencing between two posts to gain access to the meadow and to close it up again when the night's sledging was over because the meadow did not belong to Freedom but to the farmer down the road.

One night, a diffuse moon hung limply in an opaque sky. There was no perceptible wind or frost and the snow was a dull white. We climbed the hill, pulling our sledges behind us to coast down and climb the hill once more.

Most of us had our own sledges. Mine was borrowed from a shy, studious boy whose father had lots of money (which fact caused some reserve towards him on our part), but who himself was a modest, undemanding boy. I had borrowed his sledge so often and so exclusively that I had virtually appropriated it, particularly as this boy never seemed to want to use it, although he always came along with us on our nightly adventures. He had grown up in the city.

I had already accomplished several descents and was climbing the hill for yet another when I saw his slender form at the edge of the slope half-way up: "Come on, we'll go down together!" I called out. At the top of the hill we arranged that he lie beneath me and steer while I lay on his back. Just as I kicked off, another sledge came whizzing down from behind and zigzagged across our path as we gathered momentum downwards. My companion was thrown into confusion and in spite of my shouts of warning, steered the sledge in a careering course which came to an abrupt stop as we crashed into a fencepost.

The sledge turned over on top of the boy who scrambled to his feet unhurt. I was thrown forward over his head and thrust out my arm to ward off the impact of the oncoming fencepost. After the crash, I remained lying in the snow feeling sick. Some of the other pupils who had come down the slope saw me lying and ran to assist me to my feet. Ivan grasped my arm. I fainted. When I came around, Ivan had rolled back my sleeve and by the ashen light of the moon, we saw it dangling at an angle.

There was a quick counsel and the decision was taken to drive me to town to our veterinary surgeon, Dr Burton. Some of the big boys went to fetch the truck from the farmyard, rolling it down to the road with loosened breaks so as not to waken anyone. Helped along by a small band, I joined the truck while the others restored the barbed wire fence to its usual state, collected the sledges and took them down to the school. I was cold and faint and not quite part of events.

Dr Burton was still up but drunk as was to be expected. Ivan took me in and held me firmly while Dr Burton set my arm in a splint, breathing alcoholic fumes into my face. The pain of the long clumsy procedure was excruciating and my spirit whirled around in despair. I vomited and fainted once more.

Back at school in the cold night, I managed to get into my bed. Before sinking into the oblivion of sleep, I insisted that we should not give away anything of our illegal nightly activities, and was convinced I would manage to conceal my splinted arm.

In the morning I woke up racked with pain and fainted in the bathroom. Ivan was called; he wanted to tell the teachers. The others agreed, but I insisted that to tell the teachers and not to stand the consequences of our transgression would be to betray Freedom itself: "Why shouldn't one bear a little pain?" I stated with bravado. I went down to the dining-room with the others for breakfast, a jacket slung over my shoulders to hide the arm. I managed to swallow a mouthful of cornmeal mush and no more. I was sick and fainted, sliding off my chair on to the floor. Ivan explained. I was wrapped in blankets and put into the back of the truck again and one of the teachers drove me to the hospital in the town where my arm was found to be wrongly set. It was re-set under chloroform. Nothing further was made of the incident and I was able to use the arm, my right, in due course.

Yet the enforced inactivity resulting from an arm in splints thrust something forward into my conscious experience. My sense of balance and movement was so thrown out through incapacitation of a limb that I became aware of the extent to which balance and movement were dominant elements in my existence. I discovered that I could make a much more fundamental statement of my Self, at least to myself, through movement than I ever could through words and formulations. When I was in tune with myself, it was with a being of balanced movement rather than with one who thought clearly or was manually creative or skilled.

Earlier on during one of the holidays, my mother woke me up late in the evening: "Hurry, come down to the studio and present yourself to the great Isadora." In my flannel nightie and with tousled hair, I stood before Isadora Duncan who seemed broad and pear-shaped and tragic and who embraced me saying: "My child, you must become a dancer."

Isadora Duncan saw the dancer in all children and her injunction made no impression on me. It did on my mother though, and later on, I was sent to all kinds of dancing teachers in New York and abroad, achieving slightly above moderate virtuosity in the accepted modes of the time.

Inwardly I was a dancer from the moment music broke upon me through Beethoven. Then there was that peculiar forward stride I learned from the Indian guide in Canada which became an experience of flow from a dynamic pre-natal source of movement into the future, knowing no insurmountable metaphysical barrier or obstacle. I could have said had I known how — In the beginning was Movement and Movement was God and God was Movement . . . (Much later I danced to an audience in Berlin that consisted of SS men. Hitler and Goebbels sat in the front row. I danced — not as Salome before Herod, but as David before Goliath and knew that I had made a potent statement. Afterwards an elderly friend of mine said: "I didn't know that *Agape* could be danced." It was the highest tribute I ever received.)

I formed a friendship with Frieda who was two years older than I. Her family were orthodox Jews. Frieda had a womanly figure and flowing black hair around a mature and kindly face. She was a buffer between my chafing spirit and others at Freedom. She did little things for me such as mending awkward tears in my clothing and I derived an immense comfort from her sisterly concern.

Frieda invited me to her home in the city during the Christmas holidays when my mother was out of town or abroad, although my mother never failed to express disdain at my spending so much time with Jews, albeit her own circle of friends and colleagues was almost entirely Jewish.

We had a reunion of city pupils from Freedom at Frieda's house. Randal and Victor (Randal was not Jewish), Sammy and Manny the twins, Ivan and his sister came with a few others. Gene Levine came too.

It was an oddly stiff occasion. Randal was embarrassingly deferential to Frieda's mother (we couldn't understand why), Victor grimly and meticulously polite (even to me), Ivan and his sister ill-at-ease in their city clothes and I felt guilty at being ashamed of my best friends.

Gene Levine was the only one to remain above the situation we had created for ourselves. He was quiet and considerate. He had a way at all times of not relating things to himself, but of relating himself to things or people, which made him appear unusually free and self-contained. Yet we were all vastly relieved when the reunion drew to a conclusion and we parted company.

Frieda's mother was an older edition of her daughter — kindly and concerned about my welfare, cooking no end of good dishes to fatten me up. The Friday evening Sabbath rituals at which I was occasionally present as a "goy" and which she conducted with so much dignity and joy were a source of religious experience and moral steadfastness to me which I have never forgotten.

By this time my mother had obtained a steady and highly

remunerative job in the advertising department of a big shipping line of which she was subsequently to become the head. Her style of advertising was original and distinctive and had considerable influence on the advertising world of the time. She frequently took recourse to using her own photographs of Japan, Holland and other places in many of which I figured as a child. I would pass a big travel agency in Fifth Avenue and see the face of my childhood looking through the huge show windows from the posters on the walls inside, or I would pick up a magazine somewhere and experience the multiplication of my image with ambivalent feelings. In spite of the pride my mother tried to fan in me at having a public image, I never overcame the persistent sense of having no legitimate past of my own.

The Christmas holidays came to an end and we gathered once again at Grand Central Station to take the train back to Freedom. Gene Levine was on the train.

All at once he stepped over the threshold of my experience and from that moment, I was possessed painfully and exclusively by his person.

Gene was the most responsible pupil in our system of self-government although he was not quite the oldest. Yet he was oddly apart — whether because of his reserved temperament (he could be extremely funny) or because he was not outgoing (on occasions he was the life of the party; in fact, no party was complete without him) or because his father's unconventional political allegiances (which shouldn't have created prejudices at Freedom) or possibly because he aroused envy in others — I could not say. Although they called upon him on all levels of life at Freedom, even the teachers were not entirely at ease with Gene. It could have been his peculiar degree of self-containment — he did not need others to the same extent that others needed him.

Gene had represented to me the upper stratum of older pupils at Freedom whereas I moved in the middle stratum with Randal and Victor and there was an unspoken, natural gulf between us. The common denominator in all of us was our total commitment to Freedom's ideals and the love we had of that total commitment in each other.

As far as I was concerned, Gene as a person had been remote. It never occurred to me to address him nor had he even appeared to take any notice of me. In my more blatant attempts to show off, I tended to make sure he was not present. His presence in the barnyard or anywhere else constituted a stricture on my wilder moments and the limelight was not so brilliant when he was about. I harboured a silent admiration of his many gifts, but remained in the assumption that our ways would never cross.

All this suddenly became a gnawing, terrible and beautiful obsession.

Soon after our return to Freedom, Randal, Victor and Ivan, who was actually older than ourselves, founded a debating club and because membership included some younger individuals like Sammy and Manny and myself, it was decided to embark on themes that were not too exacting, at first.

We began by debating the relative merits of the Greek and Roman personalities of *Plutarch's Lives* and according to the code of the club, we were never to proceed from a biased premise, but were to debate purely for the sake of argument. For me to favour a Roman, however, even only for the sake of hypothesis, was an impossibility. It had to be a Greek. Thus my membership to the new club was from the outset a prickly matter and Ivan spent much effort in trying to persuade me that I would lose nothing by learning to become a little more objective in my outlook.

My one asset to the club was my minute knowledge and memory of the facts in *Plutarch's Lives*, Roman or no. I was a living index as to details and could be consulted in the midst of the most heated debate as to correct facts and the chronology of events.

The debates were to be weekly ones, but because we rarely came to conclusions in the given time, we continued debating during the day and into the next night when the others had gone to bed. We were convinced that our debating held alive the mental and spiritual life of Freedom.

Gene sometimes attended the regular weekly meetings and his participation was both mature as well as stimulating and the level generally reached when he was there, was heightened. But

I suffered on these occasions because Gene was dispassionate and clear-minded and pursued a path of inquiry, whereas my own path was littered with scraps of passionate Hellenism which tended to turn into defiance when he joined the debates. He would pass over my arguments as an adult would pass over the ignorant and untimely utterances of a child and would frown faintly when I became persistent and dogged as though I were presuming to take up too much time (which I was). Yet at the same time, these occasions were an opportunity to hear his voice, to be in the same room, to take in the full impact of his personality, and the attraction grew ever more consuming and agonizing.

An almost intolerable tension developed in me at the intrusion of Gene into my experience. His image so possessed my mind that my own sense of identity tended to crumble in the vehemence of my wild young love. I became unpredictable and unreasonable, unable to resist the urge to provoke others, to break up meetings, to upset laws. It was no longer showing off; it was a desperate and dumb need to express something new in my life.

At the same time I was beginning to sense depths and dimensions in my existence that seemed to hold dark yet joyous promise as though I were going towards a supreme moment which inspired in me an almost sacramental readiness to give myself, offer myself at some unknown altar. I had been cast into the churn of puberty.

I spent hours on Ginger's back, galloping her ruthlessly through the countryside. I wanted to ride through mounting barriers and banks of bewildering mists, to ride through zero point — to some kind of promised land. I stayed out till dusk one afternoon and then galloped back on frosty roads. Just outside the school grounds, Ginger slipped and sprawled on the ice, throwing me clear. By the time I got to my feet, she was struggling to hers. I saw that she was badly shaken and that she had a slight limp. I led her gently back to the stables, unsaddled and groomed her, smarting with remorse that I had caused her fright and pain, but I was in a phase of isolation and withdrawal and did not speak to anyone about Ginger's fall.

The next evening there was a school's Assembly. It had been especially called. Gene presided. The main point to be discussed was the ruthless treatment of riding horses by persons unknown — for Ginger had been found limping and no one had come forward to account for it.

The spirit of Freedom clearly challenged me to rise to my feet and state my responsibility for Ginger's condition, but a new ambiguity undermined my impulse. Had Gene not been there, had he not been president, I would have spoken. I would have done anything to win his understanding and gentleness, but I could not risk not winning it.

By a unanimous vote, the resolve was passed that Ginger should not be ridden for the remainder of the term and the meeting passed on to other matters. But the resolve concerning Ginger contained a personal indictment and — a warning.

I plunged into an abyss of shame and self-accusal and for days I spoke to no one, barely ate meals, took no part in activities. My continued silence as to what had happened to Ginger imposed a strain on all my bonds. Randal and Victor passed me by as though I were a stranger. Nothing more than formal communication took place between all others in the school and myself.

I wandered aimlessly up the road along the stream. It was cold and grey. The brook gurgled plaintively under the ice blocks. It was February. I could have walked off the edge of the world.

Ahead of me on the road I perceived a transparent, glowing globe emanating warmth. A deep force drew me towards the quivering globe. The moment I entered it, I knew what it was. It was my Self receiving me with infinite love and forgiveness. It fell around me like protective a cloak, investing me with dignity and courage and comfort, and I walked back to the school restored and singing to the world of my gratitude and joy.

I had often experienced this Self as a stern and unpitying judge. I now sensed that it was something given to me on trust by an ultimate Lender who did not disclose what he exacted in return other than a realization that this Self was not responsible to me; I was responsible to it. Transgression against the Self was ultimately persecution of the Lender.

Pauline, our nurse, instituted a first aid team at Freedom the primary principle of which was never to hesitate to go to the aid of someone in need whatever the circumstances. Yet she never allowed us to lose ourselves in the fascination of bandages, tourniquets and vaporous feelings of pity. Compassion to her was the disciplined overcoming of reservations and prejudices as well as indulgence in false sympathies. The injured person was the sufferer; the feelings of everyone else concerned were immaterial. The intelligent and dispassionate necessary action was what had to be cultivated in order to be a member of Pauline's first aid team. She was her own example; therefore she was the only member of staff at Freedom who had unwavering and undisputed authority.

Pauline's influence on me came just in time for I was entering a phase of fastidious aestheticism in which imperfections, abnormalities or conditions of disease in human flesh were beginning to affect my relationships. A relationship to someone not physically intact or harmonious of build, to someone who had spots or dandruff or any slight uncleanliness about his person was becoming impossible, but Pauline sowed a tiny seed of compassion which ultimately helped me over this phase.

The drama group at Freedom was rehearsing Shaw's *Arms and the Man* for the end of term. There were no suitable girls for the leading female part and so Gene decided to play it himself. Those who were not in the play were permitted to be present at rehearsals which took place in that part of the large barn which had been adapted as stage and gymnasium.

In this barn ropes and rings had been hung from the rafters for us to practice trapeze and it was a favourite pastime to swing back and forth over the heads of others below, to let go in mid-air and grasp the next ring and in this wise, to travel around the barn aloft. The taut body, the suspended moment between one ring and another, the indescribable relief to have caught the next ring firmly were a source of a kind of bliss — like flying.

Rehearsals of *Arms and the Man* were well advanced and the scenery had already been put up. I went in to watch a rehearsal. The moment came for the leading lady to appear. Gene came on to the stage wearing a long dress and a wide-brimmed lace hat. He wore little make-up for his skin was naturally brown nor did he wear woman's hair to augment his own curly dark hair. He relied on the genius he always showed when he acted. His low and agreeable voice gave to the lady's part singular charm. Napoleon entered; repartee began.

I was completely unnerved by a jumble of feelings of wild admiration, identification, jealousy, longing, hopeless inferiority and exclusion which whirled around inside at the sight of Napoleon and the lady. I wanted to dash out into the night. Instead I scaled the ladder affixed to the wall of the barn, seized a ring dangling at the end of a rope and began to swing back and forth while the rehearsal continued. The actors on the stage below showed no sign of annoyance or of being aware that I was on the ropes. I increased my efforts, became rash and performed feats I had not yet attempted. I became dizzy and detached from gravity. In a moment when the lights dimmed down on the stage, I missed a ring and had the sensation of hurtling towards a bottomless pit. I crashed into the scenery at the far end of the barn and brought it all down around me.

I regained consciousness from the concussion three days later. Consciousness brought home the fact that something had happened in my body, It had come in violence when I was not on the alert. It filled me with fierce pride and the anticipation of mythological power, but also with shame and regret. It had come like a thief and taken away my childhood.

Pauline gave me cool and objective instructions. My mother had been called to the school because of the concussion and she arrived in a state of alarm and reproach. It was the only time she visited me at Freedom. She wanted to talk with me about the other thing that had happened, but it embarrassed me to speak about it with her.

A day or two later, I was allowed up for a short while to show my mother around. Her only comment was: "I don't like places that use broken milk jugs."

25

We returned to Freedom after the Easter holidays. I was as enthusiastic and as expectant as ever, but aware of a new tenderness towards animals, flowers, stones and towards people. Strong currents of love flowed through my eyes when I stood at a stone wall and gazed over a field sprouting corn, or at cows grazing, or the sun going down behind the hills.

The trio I formed with Randal and Victor entered a new phase of mental stimulation which supplanted the old fights and chases and was no longer an unsettling element. Randal and Victor were often solicitous and protective towards me in a gruff, restrained manner which made me very happy yet caused embarrassment because it was directed to the girl in me.

Yet my bouts of withdrawal still came and when they did, I resorted to the mountain on the slopes of which were two sets of caves. The first set was half way up. These caves were large and deep and used by us for sheltering and hiding in on organized chases. Above these, the mountain became steep and somewhat intractable and the path upwards tentative and precipitous. Up there the second set of caves was concealed by cliffs. These caves were shallow and actually not more than ledges under protruding boulders that looked as though at the slightest nudge, they would loosen and crash down the mountainside.

From the slightly precarious position of these ledges, there was a wide view out over the country in which the grounds of Freedom seemed an insignificant patch in the foreground. Far to the south, trains bound for the city trailed faint ribbons of white steam. Clouds rolled up over horizons far beyond my ken and somewhere on the giant chequerboard of fields, woods, towns and hamlets, the tiny dirt road leading to Freedom began its meander and could be followed with the eye right up to the mill-house down below.

Up here I breathed the air of another freedom which was rare and calm and where turmoil came to rest. Sometimes the Freedom below at the foot of the mountain seemed to look up at me like a Medusa's head and I was startled that something one so loved and was so much a part of one could have another cold, destructive face — or — and the question was formed with some fortitude — was that hard white face my own looking at my blind rash existence at Freedom? There was only one ear into which the question could be spoken — into the ear of the Other who alone knew me and had the right to judge. To see yourself as others experienced you was to look into the face of the Medusa and become stone . . .

I wrestled for truths up there on the mountain, but by the time I had descended to the foot and breathed air of Freedom again, all clarity was submerged in a tidal wave of life and relationships that swept one up and carried one over to the next day.

I had an odd moment while climbing up to the higher caves near the summit of the mountain. It was warm and I was barefoot, picking my way carefully over stones and roots. As I was seeking a foothold in the crevices of rock, I looked down and saw the long, slender, brown foot of a man. The hem of a saffron robe fluttered about the ankle, blown by the wind, and there was a fleeting vision of twisted pines and the winged roof of a monastery higher up . . . That night I dreamt I had died and that my body, lying in a sideways position, was being carried up a mountainside where there was a vast cave in which many other bodies were lying around the walls in sideways position. I was placed among them. Incense was burning in brazen vessels and I rested, infinitely at peace, in the sweet dimness of that remote cave waiting . . .

The summit of the mountain was round and bald and I had never been up there. It was a dumb place and never called me. But one afternoon I rose from the ledge where I was sitting and went on up. A strong wind blew around the crown of the mountain. When I reached the top with the wind snatching my breath away, I came upon a grassy plateau which fell away from the summit into a broad green hollow to rise again to a second summit, higher than the first, invisible from the foot of the mountain.

I went down into the hollow over clumps of springy grass out of the path of the wind and saw an array of bleached cattle bones lying in the sun like marble fragments of some forgotten temple. Among the gleaming white bones there lay a perfect skull, the sickle moon horns of a cow still in their sockets. An endless procession of teeming ants hurried in and out of the huge eye hollows of the skull. Staring at them, I saw them as the ideas and associations of billions of minds seeking their labyrinthine way through the rocky skull of the earth since the beginning of time in the pursuit of understanding the "Why?" of human existence. It was as though I were seeing mankind on earth through cosmic eyes; I was the mountain top, the wind, the clouds, I was the sun and the endless deep infinite of the sky — I was in the forehead of God, and one of the tiny hectic ants was me, so easily crushed under heel . . .

This grassy plateau became a sanctuary visited when I felt the need for creating my own personal Sunday, and I took care that no one, especially not Randal and Victor, knew that I went up there.

Only once did the old aggression flare up between Randal and Victor and myself. It was during a debate on Dion and Brutus and it was as though the atmospheric circumstances had arranged the setting for what turned out to be a heated and opinionated argument on regicide. The evening was sultry and humid and dull orange sheet lightning flashed intermittently across the night outside. The atmosphere was charged with tension.

I was in an apocalyptic frame of mind and thoughts of "wars and rumours of wars", dictators, subjugations of peoples grew so real to me that in the end, having left Dion and Brutus with their problems far behind, I tried to convince everyone that we, at Freedom, would have to be ready to do anything, even to commit regicide, tyrannicide, to save the world. (The Munich *putsch* had already taken place and Hitler had written *Mein Kampf*).

Nobody could accept my presumptuous behaviour and efforts were made to guide procedure back to the point of departure — Dion and Brutus. Lightning crackled like a hissing snake and the lights fused. The room was pervaded by an ominous sulphuric smell. Drums of thunder beat overhead and a fitful orange script appeared in intervals on the wall of the night. I continued to try to express what was moving me. Victor was sardonic and others laughed in derision. I became desperate. Rising to my feet, I flung a cushion at Victor and leapt through the open window on to the lawn and made for the stables with Randal and Victor in pursuit. As I ran, I thought: Why this old stuff again?

They caught me in the stables and fettered me with straps and ropes to the post of an empty horsebox and left me there. The storm broke; my war had started. Lightning sizzled down the sky, thunder burst the heavens and the rain beat like bullets on the roof of the barn.

Ginger and the other horses were restless and shifted about in their boxes. The dark silhouettes of their heads jerked up when the lightning ripped up the sky with a sound like tearing silk. Their purple spirits broke loose and crowded together in the congested darkness, ponderous yet shadowy, and they communicated in deep primeval language, oppressive because it was so far removed from the human yet so near that it enveloped me. I was inside it, inside horsehood in the porphyry chamber of their big dark hearts, animated by their spirit who was neither good nor evil, but terrifyingly big and undifferentiated.

The storm moved on although rain continued to beat on the roof. Above the din of the rain I heard the clanging of the great gong in the courtyard. This gong was an iron ring about seven feet in diameter and six inches thick. It hung from a sturdy wooden frame and was struck with a sledge hammer. It gave forth a resounding tone of singular beauty, albeit deafening for the one who rang it, and it could be heard for a considerable distance in the surrounding country. It was struck three times daily for meals and for other routine occasions, but it was also rung as an alarm in emergencies. One required an intuitive ear to discern its message because the resonance of each blow lasted so long that a distinct code distinguishing routine from emergency could not be maintained. When it rang at unusual times, we knew that something unusual had happened. It was the summons to everyone at Freedom.

Tied up in the horsebox, I immediately jumped to the conclusion that the house was on fire now that the gong was ringing in the night, and was seized by panic: "Let me loose! Let me loose!" I wailed, and tugged and tugged at my bonds. No one came. I sobbed with great grief and fear. Everything would be burnt down and I would not be there to help. I would be the only one left, I and the horses and cows, and out there in the night there would be a smouldering heap of charred remains of everyone I loved and the wind would lash across what had been lovely, vital, warm Freedom . . . I fell asleep hanging on the post, my hands tied behind my back, and had violent dreams of wars and revolutions and killings — fire and grief and mechanical horses and tears . . .

In the grey light of the early morning, someone entered the stables. It was Gene. Without saying a word, as though I were one of the horses he came to attend to, he loosened the straps and ropes and set me free. I stumbled as I stepped stiffly away from the post. He caught me up and set me on my feet. I did not dare to ask him about the catastrophe of the night.

I stepped over the threshold of the stables and the cool fresh morning breeze bathed my face. The white farmhouse shone in the rising sun.

26

I went again to my mother's country house for the summer holidays to long and to wait for the return to Freedom. Milly and Noel and I had for some obscure reason to share a large double bed in the back part of the house. We undressed in the dark and gingerly took our places in the bed; Milly in the middle, Noel and I on either side. Milly always went to sleep first while Noel and I debated *Plutarch's Lives* (prompted by gnawing nostalgia on my part) over her oblivious body.

Noel was unusually precocious and immensely erudite for his age. (He was to achieve considerable distinction in adult life as professor of ancient and modern languages, and kept open house for intellectuals and poets and politicians in Istanbul where he ultimately died.) His donnish enthusiasm for facts made me think of him as an old man, particularly as at the age of fourteen, he had lost his childhood beauty.

Our debates were mere shadows of the debates at Freedom and were entirely devoid of heat, yet they taught me a lesson. Noel was at least as biased towards ancient Greece as I was, but I now found myself having to raise the Roman Standard in the face of his sophisticated and dry logic and for the first time, the question of principle versus necessity dawned in my mind. I took the first tentative step out of my house of absolutism which snuggled up against the rock of the Acropolis and ventured into the Imperium Romanum, secretly even to myself, relieved to shake off the Greek obsession for a bit.

We discussed the Greek in the Roman State — the individual in society — and my concepts widened, less impeded by my hitherto emotive modes of reaction and defence against adding anything to what I already knew. Indeed, Noel was more of a teacher to me than many of my teachers.

During the day, Noel spent his time reading while Milly

and I went riding. We had been given permission to use our neighbour's horses provided we caught them and returned them in proper condition. These horses, a brown mare and a big black gelding, grazed out on a large pasture. They were both imbued with a demonic sense of independence and it often took Milly and me the best part of a morning — armed with carrots and apples and sugar lumps — to bend their unholy wills to ours. The moment when the black gelding finally nuzzled into the open palm of my hand and let me take his halter to lead him over to the fence where our saddles were hanging always moved me profoundly, and tenderness and respect wiped out any urge to triumph over the animal. He was called Thunder. His mouth was somewhat insensitive to the bit and it needed a great effort to pull him up once he was in the flow of a gallop, but he was a cheerful and willing horse in spite of his powers and seemed to take pleasure in making good his initial intractability — or so I imagined.

An Irish farmer's family lived up the road. The farmer himself was fair-haired, burly and of few words. His wife was a tiny, slender woman with no grey in her jet black hair. Her eyes were gentian blue. These two were the parents of eighteen sons and five daughters and their family name was Useless. You could tell a Useless anywhere because they all had their mother's gentian blue eyes. There was a Useless in the Post Office, one in the grocer's store in the village; the village blacksmith was a Useless. He was as grimy as Hephaistos and when we went to have the horses reshod, it was startling to catch a glimpse of his blue eyes beneath his shaggy brows — there was something other-worldly in their colour. The Useless family was the woof and the warp of the village.

Up at their farmhouse, the diminutive matriarch sat on a wooden bench in the sun, a gentian-eyed infant on her lap. We never knew whether it was one of her own youngest or the child of a grown-up son or daughter. Some tongues wagged that she wouldn't know either. She was the still centre around which the whole family revolved, her smile enigmatic, still a girl to her husband, her mark upon her entire clan.

One of the younger Uselesses was Wayne, a youth of seventeen who was serving his apprenticeship in his brother's smithy. In the summer evenings, he strolled about in the village with a gang of other youths on the lookout for girls. The village girls leaned in the open doorways of their houses and derided their would-be suitors as long as the sun was up. As soon as dusk fell over the village, girls and youths vanished into the lilac bushes.

Milly, although she came from a sophisticated and wealthy city family, often went into the lilac bushes with Wayne and his like. It would start when Noel went to the drawing-room after supper, to read. "Come on, let's go for a walk to the village." Milly would say. It would still be light when we arrived on the village green and the gang would be playing baseball as though nothing else existed in the world. Dusk descended and the scene changed. Bats and wickets disappeared and we would be surrounded by the gang. Milly's cheerful repartee kept the gang at bay and everybody waited for the fall of darkness which would obviate all further necessity to uphold ritual — and the lilac bushes became alive with giggles and whispering. This was my cue to go home. I walked up the road inwardly and outwardly in the dark, not knowing whether to envy Milly and what to envy her for. Wayne Useless was a lout for all his gentian eyes and wouldn't fit at all into Freedom — yet I felt excluded.

There was a chest in the attic of my mother's house containing old clothing left behind by the former owner. Milly and I often dressed up in the things in the chest. Among them were widow's weeds — a sweeping black bustled skirt and a jet bespangled bodice with a wasp waist and a broad floppy black lace hat.

One Saturday afternoon when I was alone in the house, I put on these things and went into my mother's friend's bedroom to look in her mirror. A ravishing — or so I thought — young woman was looking back at me. I used some of my mother's friend's make-up and found the image under the shadow created by the floppy black hat tantalizing. Hitching up the voluminous skirt, I hurried downstairs and over the lawn to the pasture where Thunder was grazing, taking his bridle from the stables on the way. He must have been overawed by my appearance because for once, he was immediately at hand and let me swing myself up on to his saddleless back without ado.

I set off for the village with the bustle billowing out at the back and my skirt sweeping Thunder's black sides. The gang was idling on the village green. I cantered Thunder around the green, holding the brim of my hat with a black-gloved hand. The wolves gathered. I reined in Thunder and looked down into their upturned faces, conscious of my ravishing appearance, and saw in their eager eyes — a new element had entered Wayne's eyes as though the blue were shot with fire — that I could be a factor to be reckoned with in the village, one that would alarm. That is what I wanted — to alarm and to go again. I flicked the reins and galloped off, not looking back because my mind was already ahead and intent on other things.

That evening I went to the drawing-room to read instead of going down to the village with Milly. Later on, the darkness outside was disturbed by catcalls. I went on reading. Finally the catcalls died away, but the onslaught continued for a few days and it was some time before I could make an unnoticed appearance in the village.

One evening I rode in late on Thunder and groomed him in the neighbour's stables while the light was fading. It was almost dark when I came out on to the road. Someone was walking behind me. I felt ill at ease and walked faster. The steps behind me accelerated. Instinct prompted me to run. The one behind me broke into a run and was gaining on me.

Just before our own gate, knowing I would not reach, it I leaped over a barbed wire fence into a deep ditch and up over the other side and across the swamp, springing from one clump of swamp grass to the next, heading towards the woodlet further up. I heard the squelch of my pursuer's tread behind me. I gained the woodlet and plunged through the undergrowth and up the steep pasture behind it. It was very dark now.

The dead twigs crackled in the woodlet. I ran on up sensing that something deadly was in pursuit. All at once, I stumbled over a tuft of grass and fell headlong. My pursuer came up like a predator about to pounce on its prey. In sheer terror, I struggled wildly to fight it off. A torch flashed into my face and as I thrust it away, I caught a glimpse of gentian-blue eyes — merciless. A great fear came over me. " Aw shucks, you're only a bawling child, but don't you come down to the village any more like the other day! D'you hear?"

I began to read avidly and widely with no other guidance than greed: Tolstoy, Dostoevsky, Proust, Stendahl, Hemingway, Sinclair Lewis, Dreiser — William Morris and Shakespeare and Wodehouse. There was a shelf of books in the drawing-room which was taboo for the three of us. Milly evinced no interest in them — she wasn't a reader. Noel wasn't interested in them because he had other things to read, but when the opportunity presented itself, I read some of them and discovered that I seemed to understand some of the basic theses. These were the works of Freud.

When my mother and her friend discussed Freud over the supper table in lowered voices so that we could not take in what they were talking about, I followed silently (we were not meant to participate in any grown-up conversation, but wait until a subject suitable to our juvenile status came up) and often I felt I knew more about what Freud was getting at than they; they were both so "literary" and in their attitudes still experienced an all too sensational element in Freud.

The summer passed slowly, so slowly that I lost some of the intensity of my yearning to be back at Freedom, even lost Freedom out of my conscious mind. I spent days doing nothing at all or I went for long walks with Petroushka, automatically putting one foot in front of the other.

My mother and her friend went away for some days taking Milly and Noel with them. I did not want to join their trip and my mother allowed me to remain behind alone, saying I would be useful in looking after the house.

One afternoon a thunderstorm broke. I put on my green silk tunic and played Toccata and Fugue by Bach on the gramophone by the open window and danced to it on the lawn in the rain. Beethoven would have thundered down the storm to earth, but Bach's music soared above the storm, rising upwards like the spire of a cathedral in the titanic outburst of the elements — the articulate voice of man singing, crying out to his Maker. And in the music as I danced, three crosses became experience and imprinted the signature of the Passion in all its countless and infinitesimal variations in human existence on my being. It was a kind of Damascus; Bach's statement, new and too big for me, opened up another dimension in my musical communion with the Sender. The old dialogue with Pan seemed to fade away like a wraith dissolving in the winds. In this hour with Bach I experienced my childhood like an outworn garment.

On my last Sunday we went down to the millpond to swim; there were crowds of people there for a village fair. At the end of the pond there was an old disused mill-house with a huge iron millwheel between it and the waterfall which poured over the top of the dam out of the pond. Below the level of the dam, there was a hidden sluice pipe over a yard in diameter. No one ever swam near it because the suction from the pipe was powerful and dangerous. A big dog had once been sucked into the vortex and down through the pipe and was spat out by the torrent issuing from the other end of the pipe and was dashed to bits on the rocks below.

On this Sunday, one of the ladies on the shore not far from the mill-house dropped her hat in the water and was visibly distressed. I swam over and retrieved the hat and threw it up on the grass at her feet. As I wanted to swim away, I felt a curious, gentle yet relentless grip on my lower limbs and struggled to free myself, but the grip strengthened and was drawing me down. I realized in desperation that I was near the sluice pipe and that realization drained me of all my strength . . .

My mother carried a slender bamboo walking cane with a silver knob. This cane now reached out to me. I grasped it and held fast. Two forces were pulling — from below and from above. Suddenly the pull from below relaxed its grip and a moment later, I was standing on the grass. My mother was looking at me with an odd expression on her face. With a tremendous pang in my soul I remembered how much I had loved her and wished I could love her again — above all else. As I walked up the road alone afterwards, I wept for gratitude to her, for pity and for my lost love.

27

When we gathered at Grand Central Station, the news went round that Jack had died during the summer. We were stunned. The train journey back to Freedom was our funeral procession for Jack, our demonstration of mourning. Not a single word was spoken the whole way.

The school truck fetched us from the country station. We drove into the valley where Freedom lay, acutely aware of what had befallen it and ourselves. The forsaken mill-house (the family were still away) was a lamp that had gone out. The millstream flowed swiftly over the stones as alive as ever, not heeding the human condition of loss, unfulfillment and anxiety. The empty mill-house was a memorial to everything that couldn't be finished.

At supper we talked about Jack in subdued voices. Gloria, our history teacher, told us about his last weeks, hours — and finally of the funeral which was attended only by his family and one or two of Freedom's teachers. We felt cheated of Jack's death — it had not happened in our midst as we always thought it would. We did not concede full rights to his family, for *we* were the community to which his spirit belonged. We were profoundly taken aback and experienced in our grief a rising resentment against the family who had claimed Jack for themselves.

The next day life at Freedom went on, but there was a faint underlying current of desperation as though we knew we were on a bridge that threatened to break off in mid-air, but we covered it up with bravado and induced sparkle — until it was no longer acute.

We founded a new club to debate Plato's Dialogues. Gene and Ivan were president and vice president, Victor and Randal the convenors. Like every innovation at Freedom, our new club's activities became absorbing to the exclusion of many other things. My own mind was entirely taken. I had to make a great effort to understand the gist of the Dialogues and to live up to the mental demands of the club, which had a sobering as well as stimulating effect. It was the Socratic method of inquiry rather than the Platonic concept that made a strong and lasting impression on my mind. There could be nothing either of God or of man that could not be stripped to its essentials or regarded as yet to be born. There was no teaching that need be static, no statement that need remain categoric — everything was in the becoming, generative — Socrates was the eternal midwife, delivering the Man from the womb of himself.

Autumn deepened and with it, our relationships and our ideals. For a while the harvest claimed us. Days were declared free from lessons and pupils and teachers alike under Einar's guidance worked on the fields from morning till evening. At midday, steaming pots of stew with bread and butter were brought out to us and we sat along the edge of the field we were just harvesting to eat and rest a while, to go on again binding the sheaves of wheat behind the horse-drawn cutter, stopping only for an occasional drink of water from pails carried from the well in the courtyard.

In the slanting autumn sunlight, I seemed to sense a presence shining over the fields, eyes grave and encouraging, transcendent and summoning, cleansing. With the falling grain, the light that had helped it to ripen seemed now released and available for individual enlightenment, for the catharsis of everything that afflicted the buoyancy of one's onward striving, onward striding. This same light was the light of our brotherhood at Freedom.

When the sun was going down, we gathered up our tools and went back to the farmyard where potatoes were roasting in the embers of a fire and corn-on-the-cob dripping with butter was ready. We sat in a large circle around the fire and had our supper and afterwards we sang our school songs and many other songs in different languages, a lot of songs in Russian, and lingered long, watching the sparks fly upwards until they could no longer be distinguished from the stars.

Early the next morning we were out on the fields again. I went out before the others because I wanted to hear the corn whispering: "Cut me down, cut me down" — in the yearning to give itself for the good and sustenance of other creatures.

Everything falls in the autumn — the sap to the roots, leaves to the ground, nuts and apples to the earth with the throb of an invisible pulse. Down over the fields of the mind too, float the golden leaves of the Tree of Knowledge to cover the heart with the humus of ideas and impulses. The autumnal earth was a temple of fired will and one could be more oneself in autumn than in any other time of year. Freedom was an Order of Autumn.

All through the harvest, I worked in Genk's team and therefore he often spoke to me. As a result the vehemence of my preoccupation with this person evened out in the amber stream of warmth that flowed through us all in these days. Even when he singled me out and listened when I made suggestions, I did not react with a violent upsurge of feeling. Rather I allowed myself to be carried in a smooth current, hoping there would be no sudden halt, no change.

Erik was the oldest boy at Freedom. He looked like a Viking with his wavy fair hair and blue eyes and handsome, somewhat soft face. He was immensely reliable and steady and was Einar's right hand on the farm. Yet we all knew that he studied long into the nights because his father wanted him to have a brilliant career after college. We regarded him as a being from a better world, above the things most of us had to contend with. He was our beloved Outsider.

Respect bid me pause in the doorway before passing Erik who stood in the front entrance under the light of an electric bulb that shone on his fair hair like a halo. "Hallo, Erik" — I wanted to squeeze past him but he placed a hand on my shoulder: "You are only a child now, Pan, but remember, one day I am going to marry you." His blue eyes looked vacantly into mine for a moment, but I knew they didn't see me.

We were not alone; everyone was in the front hall listening to this sudden and uncanny betrothal. I looked around for help. Erik was staring at the floor as though he were listening to a distant sound. I saw Gene; would he not do something to dispel the queer atmosphere? But he was looking at me with accusation in his eyes as though I had provoked Erik into saying what he had said and was making use of something fragile in him for my own purposes. I saw it all and saw his look of accusation turn into contempt. I spun round and dashed out into the night.

For days I was spiked on my love for Gene, realising that he had little reason to trust me. An ocean was widening between us although we had never drawn close. My sense of loss was acute and I had to do something to relieve it. I overheard someone say that Gene was in the stables. I resolved to go to him there to tell him that at heart I was not superficial and wanton, to seek his understanding. I went out through the door.

The summit of the mountain became visible as I climbed up to the higher caves. The school buildings, the barn to one side, the mill-house, lay below in the valley. On the windswept ledge the Other was waiting. We sat in the cold — it was November — and had our singular communion.

"You want something you cannot have," said the Other "You are like a moth fluttering around a flame. Give it up, Pan, cut it out of your mind; it is not to be."

Why? Why? Because some things are permissible, others are not. But why is this impermissible? You know perfectly well that there is a pre-determined veto. Pre-determined by what? The Other was not more coherent, but I knew it anyway.

Everything was poured back into the well whence it sprang and the well was covered up — a wishing well, bubbling with delicious water, clear and fresh but not for me to drink.

"The wind blows where it wills; you can hear the sound of it, but you do not know where it comes from or where it is going."

The wind can shake through and through but you cannot hold it fast. You can only let it blow through you and know you will be different afterwards. If you try to hold it fast it will shatter you. Some relationships are like the wind. They take you by storm and you tremble, but you must let them go for they will not be possessed. Gene was a wind blowing through — and on.

When I came down from the mountain, the first snow was falling.

Life went on at high tension as always at Freedom, but there were no new challenges, arbitrary or sent by fate. I made little headway in the classroom and had the peculiar feeling that I was not going to learn any more at Freedom. But the debating club continued and there were the hours in which we recited — Shakespeare, Milton, Keats — and the songs . . .

During the Christmas holidays, Erik hung himself in his father's house. Our teachers told us when we returned to Freedom. We were dumbfounded. When we recovered from the shock, we asked: Why? They said because his father had expected too much of him; his mind had not stood up to it — he had become deranged.

None of us spoke about Erik — it was as though he were still vulnerable. But on walks alone, I tried to follow in thought Erik's pathway into the despair that prompted his final act, to enter into his broken mind as it approached the abyss from which he had not returned. I saw the fair head with its sheen of light like a halo hanging over one shoulder — a plucked flower. A light had gone out in Freedom — another one.

A new girl came to Freedom after the Christmas holidays. She sat somewhat apart with her father in the train that took us to the country. We resented her coming to Freedom because she was, to us, of the bourgeoisie, and her father although he was a doctor looked like a bureaucrat, which was unforgivable. Her name was Sarah. She had no mother.

Sarah, who was a month younger than myself, was placed in our dormitory. Her hair was red and silky and her skin fine and transparent. Her hands and feet were tiny and fragile, although her body was plump and ungraceful. She possessed too many clothes and other personal objects for Freedom and wore dresses on all occasions (I cannot remember having worn a dress at Freedom). She had knock-knees and couldn't race. We could not digest her in the stomach of Freedom. Yet we saw that she was unhappy and were even concerned about her, but we could not help her — she was too alien.

About three weeks after our return from the holidays, Sarah sickened. She was removed to the little white house upstream where Pauline presided over sickroom and surgery. Visiting the surgery to have cuts, scratches, burns, boils and stings treated was a daily event, but we collectively managed to keep out of the sickroom; to be sick meant missing too much. But Sarah's removal there struck an ominous note. We heard hat she was very ill. She had scarlet fever.

Her father came to be with her and as soon as she was able to travel, he took her away from Freedom. But she left a legacy — a virulent epidemic that swept through the entire school. Pauline's little white house was over-occupied and the dormitories in the farmhouse were turned into sickrooms. Our teachers nursed day and night under Pauline's supervision.

Sammy and Manny and I seemed to be spared. We were moved to our history teacher's room to free our own beds for those who were sick. We slept with our teacher on camp beds and helped where we could, although our teachers did not want to overtax us lest we, too, should fall ill. But we did what we did to the point of exhaustion.

It was February and very cold. When some of the pupils began to recover, a few parents came to visit on Sunday afternoons. Sammy and Manny and I went for a long walk on one such afternoon. When we started back, darkness was beginning to settle. We were on the other side of the millstream at some distance from the bridge. As the stream was blocked with huge blocks of ice, we decided to make use of them and to cross the stream on the spot.

Sammy and Manny picked their way over the ice successfully. I was tired and lagged behind. I could not see my way clearly. Sometimes the ice flashed in blinding whiteness. Between flashes I groped through inky darkness. When I reached the middle of the stream, the ice block I was standing on shifted under my weight. I tried to leap on to the next block but the one I was on rose at a steep angle and I slid into the icy water. Blocks of ice closed over me and I was terrified lest I be decapitated. Then darkness was complete.

Einar passed by and gathered from Sammy and Manny that I was in the river.

I became aware of rafters that stretched into the infinite. I got out of bed to see where they went. A firm black hand pushed me back against the pillow and drew the bedcovers up. The bed was very long; the foot-end was in fog. I got out of bed to see where the end was. Pauline's hand thrust me gently back again. My mind was drawn out into great distances — it stretched so far that for moments I did not recognize it as myself when it entered me again . . .

When I was able to focus myself, I perceived that I was lying in the big attic in Pauline's house with ten others — boys and girls. Large patches of livid red formed a geography of their own all over my body. We were all too wan to talk much to each other. Only Sammy and Manny were spared.

It was well into March before the epidemic began to abate and we began our wholesale convalescence. There had been no fatalities although the epidemic had been severe. Yet we were weakened, tender and raw, and our teachers were exhausted. We realized, in a quiet unspoken way, what they had done to pull us through.

March was a month of swollen streams and soft low winds. Everywhere wetness gurgled and seeped in the pastures. Furrows were open, waiting, and beneath the leafmould in the woods, spring violets were unfolding their first tiny green banners.

Everything was transparent between us and our teachers and the bond so inward that it was almost unbearable. The Easter recess brought the necessary relief.

28

When we returned to Freedom after the Easter break, we immediately sensed a change. When an army becomes thinned out, it has to rearrange itself to meet the final onslaught. Our teachers had obviously been seriously concerned with the survival of Freedom in our absence.

We were met with their decisions: our system of student government was to be maintained, but the educational plan was to change. The Dalton plan was tacitly withdrawn. Our teachers emerged as an authoritative group and attendance in the classroom was to be obligatory. Those pupils who had not advanced according to their age were to undergo extra coaching and tuition. Monthly examinations were to be introduced ; intelligence tests also. But it was too late.

Freedom had schooled us to individualism; its soil did not engender conformity — only community. We rose as a group to any occasion; we were a united brotherhood and Freedom was our degree. Antipathy to conformity, to averages, was ingrained in all of us. It was all too obvious that we were now expected to conform to a standard school system.

These last months — weeks — in Freedom were oddly lonely ones. We seemed no longer to know of each other but laboured under a shadow of doubt and uncertainty we did not manage to bring out in open communication. As for myself, I responded to the changes with my former means of protest — with anarchy, which was dooming from the start, because a new challenge, however uninspiring, demands a new response, however unheroic on the surface. A heroic response to an uninspiring challenge overshoots the initial problem and can be wastage in the extreme, but I was compelled to pursue the heroics of anarchy — because of disappointment, grief and fear.

Was the deep reality of Freedom proving a chimera? The question gnawed. Subversiveness became a habit. By being apathetic in the classroom, I forced my teachers into the defensive. By being over-meticulous as to human rights, by being all too just or all too tolerant, I drove others into seeming bigotry for which I flayed them with derision. To arm myself against the end, I drove a wedge between myself and Freedom.

Six younger children became my bondsmen. They followed me blindly and were the unwitting instruments of my anarchy. Because of this a second warning, which was in effect an ultimatum, was delivered to me in the school's Assembly. If I could not abandon my policy of disruption on all levels, I would have to face the consequences. I could not continue in the delusion that everyone felt the same about the issues in Freedom as I did. "Oh, but you do! You do!" was my silent anguished cry. "Don't forsake me now when all our puzzlement and insecurity come down on me and I am forced to demonstrate what we are all labouring under." Was that a delusion? I found no response, only bottled up worry.

I had started a splinter group of our debating club which could no longer contain me. I loathed the splinter group but led it doggedly and managed to get it regarded as a political minority, the only constructive value of which was to unite all the others against it — me. My club met likewise at night after the lights were turned out. I staked claims on the library knowing that it was the established meeting room of the club proper. After raucous encounters relating to our respective venues, I withdrew in indignation, having undermined the equanimity of the others, and repaired to the roof of the farmhouse with my followers.

This was cruelty, for my young flock possessed neither group nor personal fearlessness nor the lust for risk, and found the steep roof and gables in the cold night air a veritable nightmare; and even when they perched along the roof with a foot stemming hard against each side, their teeth chattering for cold and anxiety and I felt like a murderer knowing that like this I would never kindle the fire of ideas in their minds, I steeled myself and led them on.

I had by now alienated everyone. Randal and Victor and Ivan and the staff left me in my isolation as though I were suffering from an infectious disease. The more my relationships narrowed, the fiercer became my final stand.

Only Einar was left, but one couldn't cling to him. He was beyond the pale of subjective relationship. Yet the time I did not spend on disruption, I spent on the farm, working hard, always alone and often long after the others had gone in. There must have been some agreement that the farm was the only place where I found some peace in myself, and no one prevented me from being there.

I began to experience a slight derangement of which I was conscious. I was losing control over my actions which were no longer calculated, but unpremeditated, disjointed, eruptions out of the vacuum in which I moved. I could not account for myself to myself. Day after day no relief came. I formed bizarre fixations, the over-riding one being to lead my little band up to the caves by night where we would all be transfigured so that everyone could see our light and know that we were saving Freedom.

I had to go up the mountain. I spoke of it to the band. There were apprehensive giggles: What if we were found out? That's not the point; once we were on the mountain, everyone will see — see . . .

We would go by night after all the lights had been turned off. I would waken them, we would dress and take the stable lamps and biscuits in a box and would cross the bridge to ascend the mountain. Sometimes the goal in my mind was my sanctuary of bones in the dip beyond the first summit, but it was mostly the upper caves where the sky was open and it was from the open sky that IT would come and change everything.

Towards the middle of May I made the first attempt. I lay awake in bed long after the lights had been turned off and towards midnight, I woke the small band and told them to dress while I went to the barn for the stable lamps. As I groped my way in the dark to the kitchen door, I passed the stairs under which our box of graham biscuits was hidden.

The night was soft and warm and the stars somewhat faint and withdrawn. It was very still. I took three stable lamps from their hooks near the horseboxes and hurried back to the house.

I lit one lamp and put it on the kitchen table and went upstairs to summon the band. They were all deeply asleep in their beds.

I went out into the dark with the stable lamps and put them back on their hooks. Then I crossed the bridge and entered the wood at the foot of the mountain. I sat on a fallen tree and was vacant.

The drive to go up the mountain by night became ever more obsessive after that — as if everything depended on it being carried out. I thought of nothing else — and tried again.

This time the night was wild and windy. Rain lashed over the barnyard in sudden squalls. When I returned to the kitchen, the little band was waiting there with big frightened eyes. Doors banged and the wind howled around the eaves.

We took the lamps and the biscuits and with myself in the lead went out into the night. As we rounded the corner of the house, a blast of wind extinguished one of the lamps and as we crossed the bridge, the second one went out. My own lamp flickered fitfully but gave a little light. Yet the night was not black; somewhere above the storm clouds, the moon must have reached fullness, for the forms of trees and boulders stood out like wraiths in ghostly silver.

I led the shivering flock swiftly upwards along the broad path to the first set of caves. It was now raining steadily. The wind drove the rain into our faces like a barrage of pins and we were wet to the skin.

The wind continued howling and bent the treetops to and fro in its rage. Twigs fell across the path and tripped us up, but I would not permit the group to falter. The path levelled out at the approach to the first set of caves. A tremendous gust of wind blew around the rocks and my lamp sputtered and died. It was dark now as we groped towards the mouth of the biggest cave.

Inside it was dry and the sound of the wind was muffled. We huddled together to share what warmth there was in our shivering bodies and I passed the biscuits around. We munched in silence. I said we would wait before going up to the higher caves.

Someone was snivelling. I was horrified. Crying! I stared into the dark not moving a muscle. Bit by bit, the snivelling in the cave gave way to deep rhythmic breathing and heads became heavy on one another's shoulders. My own eyes began to sting and I dozed.

I was suddenly wakened. The great gong was sounding in the valley below — ringing urgently. It was an unmistakeable alarm. I stood up and went to the mouth of the cave. The wind had died down but the rain continued and by the secondhand light of the night, I saw the water running down the path in rivulets.

I felt the urge to run up towards the summit, but was gripped by the sight of many lights down below. As I watched, the lights gathered and formed a procession which was approaching the foot of the mountain. They disappeared for a while in the trees but re-emerged further up and were coming nearer and nearer. I did not wake the others but stood in the opening of the cave, waiting. Then I heard voices and distinguished raincoats, ropes, picks and stretchers by the light of the torches they carried. Something in me wanted to shriek out into the night.

Richard, our science teacher, headed the rescue party. He was the first to see me — or perhaps he didn't see me, for he brushed past me roughly, holding up his flashlight to shine into the cave. When he saw the little huddle on the floor of the cave, he called out: "They're in here!"

I stood back against the rock at the opening and they all brushed past me as though I was not there. They wrapped the six children in blankets and gave them hot cocoa to drink out of flasks. Some of the children cried with relief. Then they were lifted up and carried out, each in the arms of someone who was bigger, and the procession began its descent.

I was left leaning against the rocky mouth of the cave. For one wild and terrible moment, I wondered if they had not seen me, could not see me, because I was not. I was the night, the darkness, the baleful wind, everything that was desolate, only not I. I felt I was about to explode into fragments. But the moment passed and I went down the mountain in the dark. Before I reached the bottom, I heard the gong sounding and recognized its message: We've found them and they are safe!

Our English teacher met me as I entered the farmhouse. "You are to come to my room." Her room was low-ceilinged under the attic roof and was lined with books. She indicated that I was to sit in the armchair in one corner of the room. She herself sat down at her writing desk where a subdued lamp was burning and began to write, from time to time referring to one of the many books piled up at her side. In this wise, we spent the rest of the night. Not a word was exchanged.

When day dawned, my clothes were still wet and I needed to go to the bathroom. She went with me and stood outside in the passage until I came out. Then she conducted me back to her room. Later, when the breakfast gong sounded, someone brought her a tray and she breakfasted at her writing desk with her back to me. Afterwards she went on with her writing.

In the middle of the morning, some of the teachers came up to talk with her and she went out into the passage with them, leaving the door to her room slightly ajar, but I did not hear what they were saying.

The lunch gong rang and a tray was brought up laid for one. She rose and brought me her bowl of soup. But I could not touch it, because her act was unbearably compassionate and loosened a flow of tears and I had all I could do to weep silently.

We sat on into the afternoon. It got dark and she lit the lamp. When the supper gong sounded, someone knocked and asked what she wanted for supper. "I'll have it downstairs." She went out. She trusted me — there was nothing more I would have done.

Later she came up and said that a school's Assembly had been called; I was expected to attend. She had a few things to do — then it was time. I followed her over to the Assembly room in the barn; everyone had already gathered. I entered behind my English teacher, my clothes rumpled from the night having dried on my body, my hair unkempt. I was as I had returned from the mountain.

The president of the Assembly opened the meeting. It was Gene. A grave decision lay before the Assembly, he said; it concerned the well-being of Freedom. The matter was outlined. I listened and heard the proposal. Gene called for a vote. All hands went up. I was asked to stand.

Without raising his eyes, Gene told me that I was expelled

from Freedom. I was to leave by the first train on the morrow. My mother would be informed.

I did not raise my eyes either. They could not see. They were wells of sorrow. The room was utterly silent. I turned to go. "Oh, God, wipe all this out and let me stay! I love this place!" was my silent outcry.

My English teacher took me back to her room. She brought me my night things and made up her bed for me. I do not know where she spent the night.

I lay in the dark. I had been through this before, but this was different. I knew why it is said that a heart can break.

The next morning, my English teacher woke me. I washed in the bathroom with the others and went to my dormitory to dress. The gong sounded for breakfast. I went downstairs with the others to the dining-room. On my first evening at Freedom, I was not yet one of them. Now I was no longer one of them. The distance between me and Freedom was already expanding. It would go on without me like a river. How would I go away from it?

I took my place at the table. Breakfast began. Why is it that the sharing of food is so unbearably brotherly? The moment I ate the same food as they did, my reserve broke. I hung my head and could not control the tears. Silence fell in the dining-room. I heard more than the sound of my own weeping. We were mourning together.

As I packed my belongings upstairs, I thought: "I am going into exile, but I will ask to come again." I knew that was what everyone was thinking. (Only, when I could have applied for re-acceptance in the autumn, Freedom was no longer in existence; it had been given up — the brave and inspiring adventure.)

My departure was befitting to Freedom. No sentiment was shown, but everyone was there. I shook hands with them all. With Randal and Victor, Ivan. With Gene, with the teachers.

Einar drove me to town to the station in the truck. When we passed the gates to Freedom, I experienced grief like the blow of a sledgehammer. But Einar drove on.

I arrived in New York in the midst of the tickertape welcome for Charles Lindberg who had achieved the first solo, non-stop flight over the Atlantic. I was thirteen; my childhood was at an end. What would I be able to make of it? Where would I go from here?

Epilogue

The rest of my schooling in the United States after my expulsion from Freedom was an anti-climax except for one thing. As a punishment for being expelled, my mother sent me to the summer camp in Connecticut of a school of dancing based on platonic ideas founded by Florence Noyes who, according to Gladys Hahn, was known to and respected by Rudolf Steiner. She herself had died before I went to her school.

What was intended as a punishment turned out to be pure bliss. We spent the mornings in an open pavilion improvising to music, but maintaining the integrity and discipline of the underlying platonic system, and the afternoons were given to rehearsing a pageant of Eleusis. It was a re-entering of my spiritual homeland. Young though I was, I saw my vocation in this school. It was not to be. My mother wanted me to be a ballet dancer and, back in New York, I was sent to Serge Lifar, one of the great dancers of the Diaghilev era. I continued, however, in the Noyes school clandestinely, and it has never lost its influence on me.

My mother had by this time reached the top of the journalistic ladder, was the head of the advertising department of Cunard Ship Lines, of the most exclusive fur shop in New York, and editor of "Town and Country", a high society magazine. As a result she had become a wealthy woman and now planned to take a year off in Europe.

For the last four months before we left for Europe, I worked in a country hotel run by an acquaintance of my mother's, where I waited on people like Theodore Dreiser, Sinclair Lewis and Richard Hughes, a Welshman of "High Wind in Jamaica" fame among others, but when September came, we boarded the ship that was to take us to Europe. I was now sixteen.

We were now joined by Natalie, a friend of my mother's. On her mother's side, she stemmed from the enormously rich Jewish Schiff and Warburg family of New York. Her father was an Irish officer. Both parents lost their lives when the Lusitania was torpedoed by the Germans in the First World War, leaving Natalie a millionairess. She was a beautiful, slightly plump, childlike person.

She and my mother had rented Tiberius' villa on the island of Capri where we were going to stay for a while.

Our ship docked in Plymouth on September 29. I rose early to catch this first glimpse of Europe before sailing on to Cherbourg. While I stood at the railing watching passengers disembark, the thick fog suddenly cleared and the hills of Cornwall shone out in unearthly emerald green. I had a vision of white knights riding up to a castle until the swirling fog obscured the picture, but the vision came back to me when we entered Camphill in 1940. Meanwhile, however, the next eight years were to be strangely digressive and superficial.

I caught a cold that morning in Plymouth which by the time we had reached Paris had developed into a full-blown bronchitis. My mother, nonetheless, insisted on my seeing the sights of Paris and for the next three days, I was whisked around that city.

We then boarded the luxurious sleeper train bound for Italy. By the time it reached Munich, my temperature was very high and I was no longer quite in possession of my senses. When we reached Salzburg, my mother became worried. The train was held up, a doctor was called and bronchial pneumonia was diagnosed. I was taken off the train, not to a hospital, but to a respectable old hotel — the Österreicher Hof — in the centre of the town, where I remained under the care of the doctor and the hotel staff until I recovered, my mother having left a sum of money behind to cover expenses.

Of all this I was not aware until I opened my eyes one morning while still in bed and looking out of the window, I saw a huge medieval fortress on a massive cliff. Although I had no idea where I was, I had an overwhelming experience of coming home. The portly butler who looked after me explained in stilted English that this was Salzburg in Austria.

After a while the doctor said I must take the air. A horse and carriage came for me and bundled up in blankets, I was taken by the driver daily through the town, until its churches, museums and precincts became familiar in all their Baroque beauty, and all the while catching glimpses of the wonderful mountains that surround this exquisite old town which then had not yet seen the post-war urbanization which turned it into a sprawling tourist centre.

One day the driver took me up a steep street to a somewhat chilly and bleak church and showed me a gravestone there with the name "Paracelsus" inscribed on it. The name struck a deep inexplicable note in my soul.

In time, a letter came from my mother saying I was to move

to the dancing school of the revolutionary dancer, Isadora Duncan, run by her sister just outside Salzburg.

So I moved to Schloss Klessheim, a beautiful Baroque palace built by the celebrated Fischer von Erlach, but now in a badly neglected state. The Duncan School consisted of four persons: Elizabeth Duncan, elderly and confined by rheumatism to a wheelchair, Director Merz, Jarmilla, a pupil from Prague, and myself. It seemed that further pupils were expected. Meanwhile there was nothing to do. I went for long walks in the rundown old park as well as outside its walls and gradually ventured into Salzburg every day where among other things, I had discovered a tiny but exquisite pastry shop.

One afternoon, I left the park by a rusty back gate. A swift river flowed immediately along the wall. There was a tiny bridge over it guarded by a single gendarme and beyond there was a sun-mottled birch wood. I asked the gendarme where that was: Deutschland — he said.

Having been at school in the United States, I knew the histories and geographies of America, England and the ancient world. Of European history and geography I was innocent.

After the War, Schloss Klessheim was renovated and became the venue for high power summits. The famous meeting between John Kennedy and Nikita Khrushchev took place there.

Meanwhile, the domestic staff of the Duncan school were making almost daily inroads into my clothing. I was too shy to tell Director Merz, but wrote to my mother that I would soon have virtually nothing to wear. A letter came back to Director Merz instructing him to put me immediately on a train to Vienna.

My mother and Natalie had meanwhile conceived the idea of undergoing psychoanalysis as patients of Freud himself and as a result of their preliminary negotiations, my mother heard of a friend of Anna Freud's who wanted to take one or two young girls into her home.

This was Eva Rosenfeld, known as Muschi, wife of a Viennese lawyer, Wagner enthusiast and Goethe specialist. Two sons had died in the First World War as children. The only daughter, aged nineteen, had died that summer mountaineering near Salzburg. It seemed that I walked into the empty heart of Muschi and the love between us was almost consuming, only I could not yield to being possessed again even by someone I loved, and the relationship remained mutually painful until very much later when Muschi had established herself as a leading analyst in London and Thomas and I often visited her.

The Rosenfelds occupied a very spacious villa in a lovely old district of Vienna. An enlarged summer house at the bottom of the big garden housed a small school for children of the Freudian circles, with two handsome young teachers, one of whom was a blond Danish artist, Erik Homburg, who became Professor Erik Erikson when he later moved to America.

Erik asked me to write and produce a play with his children, to be performed on the occasion of Freud's seventy-fifth birthday. Why I chose the theme of Beowulf would not bear analysis, for I had always disliked this legend intensely.

We performed the play in Freud's large drawing-room, after which I was asked to sing some English folk songs to him. This was occasionally repeated. Never did Freud establish contact with me nor thank me, but withdrew silently and unsmilingly. I did not realize that he suffered from cancer of the jaw. He did, however, give me a little alabaster pot from his famous Egyptian collection, which I later gave to Tilla König. Having become friends with one of Freud's grandsons of my own age, I was often in and out of the Berggasse 19.

I was almost pathologically shy and spoke little, although I had begun to speak German, and the consensus was that I needed psychoanalysis, but although I tended to be vulnerable and defenceless, I knew that even if I had to leave my skin behind, I would get through this Scylla and Charybdis without psychoanalysis.

My mother and Natalie had arrived in Vienna and had approached Professor Freud who refused to take on my mother, but saw in Natalie a person in need and advised her to go to his great Hungarian disciple, Sandor Ferenczi, so my mother and Natalie moved to Budapest where they rented a large villa and Budapest became the back-drop of my life for the next three years.

My mother insisted on my continuing to dance and I finally entered the school of the Master of Ballet of the State Opera in Vienna. This man possessed a phenomenal beauty of body and face, was a kindly but exacting teacher and I became a devoted and striving pupil.

My mother, however, found Vienna too provincial and I was sent to Berlin to study "proper" ballet under Egorova, a Russian dancer from the St Petersburg State Opera. I stayed with Muschi Rosenfeld's mother, Omi, a wonderful, dignified and humorous old lady with a great heart for young people. I did not thrive under Egorova, but discovered another Russian teacher, Gsovky, to whom I went in the afternoons, so for a while I was virtually dancing all day. Later I went on some tours with a small group Gsovky tutored.

I met Peter St— among Omi's young friends. He came from Vienna but was studying with Hindemith and was already then tipped to be one of the great pianists of our time. This was not to be because of unconquerable stage fright but he is an honoured and senior music critic and Wise Man of today's musical world in London.

Peter was impecunious at the time. Having large sums of pocket-money at my disposal, I engaged him as my accompanist when I practised and benefitted tremendously from his outstanding musicality.

Already in Vienna, Muschi had taken a second girl into her house in the person of Kyra Nijinsky, daughter of the famous Russian dancer who, however, was confined to a psychiatric hospital in Switzerland at the time. Natalie had adopted Kyra.

Kyra could be startlingly beautiful with her pointed, catlike face and slanting green eyes, but her body was muscular and she was small, although as a dancer she could have been very gifted. She and I, the same age almost to the day, had a stormy love-hate relationship, swinging from extreme to extreme to the dismay of our fellow men.

While still in Vienna, our seniors decided we were to have instruction in history of art, and a Dutch teacher, Elsa van Houten, was engaged to take us around the old imperial city and its churches and museums. Only much later when Thomas and I met Laura Grimmond, wife of former Liberal party leader, did I discover from Laura that Elsa van Houten was an anthroposophist, for Laura had spent some of her own girlhood in Vienna and had had the same teacher.

Kyra and I were both sent to Omi Rosenfeld in Berlin where, for a while, we continued our turbulent adolescent relationship.

My mother had connections to Max Reinhard, the famous theatrical producer of pre-War times and had obtained for me small non-speaking parts in some of his productions. In his production of Kleist's *Prince of Homburg*, I had a tiny speaking part as a lady-in-waiting to the old princess in the play. Little did I know that she and her husband, — the elderly acting couple, Helena Fedmer and Friedrich Keyssler, were anthroposophists and friends of Christian Morgenstern. In theatre life, they were non-condescending and cool.

Max Reinhard had an outspoken antipathy to myself, no doubt because my mother was far too pushing of a daughter devoid both of acting gift as well as ambition. My final encounter with Reinhard was dramatic. I had received a typewritten slip signed by Reinhard's theatre manager of the "Deutsches Theater", engaging me for a small non-speaking part in the "Salzburger Welttheater", a sophisticated revue with a text by Hugo von Hoffmannsthal. I was to report to the mistress of costumes at three o'clock on a certain day for my costume as the Archangel Michael and be on the stage for the rehearsal beginning at three thirty.

It was curiously still when I reported upstairs and the costume mistress was agitated: "You're late," she said. I showed her my signed slip. She bundled me into my suit of armour and in the cumbersome gear, I managed to get downstairs on to the stage only to find that the rehearsal was in full swing with Reinhard sitting out in front directing.

Some of the actors signed that I was to take my place with the other hierarchical beings who were standing up on the scaffolding. I tried to comply without attracting attention, but to climb a flimsy scaffolding in a bulky suit of armour was to prove my undoing. Halfway up I missed my footing and crashed down on to the stage in front of the whole company. Reinhard roared: "Who's that?" When he saw that it was I, he roared again: "Out of my sight and don't ever set foot in this theatre again!" After that, I was affectionately known among theatre folk as the Fallen Angel.

More serious things were happening. I was in Berlin when on January 30, 1933, Hitler came to power. I witnessed the flames of the burning *Reichstagsgebäude*, Hitler's first public parade went through our street; and living in Jewish circles, I witnessed from the first day the other side of Nazidom. Jews, socialists, Communists and others fled the country, anti-Semitic demonstrations began and there were rumours of the concentration camps which were already there for those who could not get away.

I had achieved a certain modest standing in the dance world and received an invitation to give a solo evening in one of Budapest's largest theatres, and with Peter St— as my accompanist, I worked hard at the programme and at designing my own costumes.

In Budapest, Sandor Ferenczi had died of a brain tumour, leaving Natalie in a highly disturbed state in which she made several attempts to take her life. In the end she succeeded.

My mother, who had begun to drink heavily in Budapest, had, at one juncture, to be admitted as an involuntary patient to a private sanatorium just outside Vienna, where she recovered remarkably quickly, only to begin to drink again after her release.

This was in February 1934, the month in which the Austrian right wing "Heimwehr" — home guard — under Prince Stahremberg decided to crush the Austrian socialist movement, the only factor that could have upheld Austria's independence from Germany. A bloodthirsty few days of civil war took place in Vienna, destroying any strength the socialists had. Visiting my mother daily at the sanatorium, I had to pass through the barbed wire barriers and saw the destruction Prince Stahremberg's right wingers wrought in the socialist housing estates.

Although I had become a young adult, I found it very difficult to be of any real help to my mother. She had never really accepted me as a person and I had no influence on her whatsoever, although as her only relative, I signed the documents for her release from the sanatorium. But now my big evening in Budapest drew near. I looked forward to it with an almost religious feeling of responsibility. I wanted to dance the human saga of sorrow, joy and love, to make a statement.

My mother came down to Budapest and for the evening sat in the audience in a prominent place. Less than halfway through the programme, she rose to her feet and produced such a drunken scene that the curtain came down and the evening ended in disaster.

Apart from the unholy relish of the Budapest press, I had difficulties with money implications. In the end, I agreed not to take a penny and went back to Vienna where I wrote a letter to my mother thanking her for what she had done for me, but stating I would henceforward live my own life and not accept a penny of her money.

I do not know if she was hurt. She went to England, bought a beautiful Elizabethan house in Hertfordshire where she lived till her death in 1947. Dr König insisted I maintain contact with her and so I visited her once a year from Camphill. She died penniless, abandoned by all her old friends; I was the only one to walk behind her coffin the day before my birthday.

In Vienna, my freeing myself from dependence on my mother occurred at a difficult time. Through spending so much time in Berlin, I had become a stranger in the Viennese dance world. I had no work and no money. I spent some months sleeping on a bench in a common wash house on the top floor of an apartment building. My diet was sour cocoa and stale buns which could be had for practically nothing. Had it not been that I was now and then invited by friends for a proper meal, these months would have been a greater ordeal.

At last I found work, but not dancing. I met two young men who were photographers for an exclusive Viennese woollen firm, who were looking for a model. I entered an agreement with them and modelled the most exquisite pullovers, suits, ski outfits and the like and was very well paid. I could once again rent a proper room and provide my own meals.

My state of health improved and I was then engaged by a leading dancer of the State Opera to join her troupe of eight dancers who went on tour dancing Schubert, Strauss and the like. I became the soloist and was often partnered by leading male dancers from the Opera. Being Dutch and not Austrian, there was no chance of joining the Opera staff itself.

I was very well paid by the dancing as well as the modelling and would have enjoyed some private pleasures such as holidaying in countries I wished to see, but Peter St—'s mother, a widow, had a subtle way of relieving me of a considerable portion of my salaries to feed her own family, so that instead of being able to afford private pleasures, I had to keep working round the year.

I enjoyed work, however, especially on tour — the orchestra rehearsals, the discipline of the stage, the practice, the rehearsals, the acclaim and the lovely suppers when the day's work was over. We toured in Hamburg, Hanover, Frankfurt, Berlin and other German cities, Czechoslovakia, Budapest, Sopron and Debrecen in Hungary, towns in Normandy, Brittany, the Riviera in France, Rome and London, meeting fascinating people and human situations on the way — Anthony Eden, Lord Beaverbrook, Eva Curie, Franz Molnar.

That the actual dancing never touched the profound ideals and hopes in my soul, I could not allow to trouble me too much. My life in these years was altogether superficial.

A friend of mine in Vienna was the painter, Erwin Lang, son of Maria Lang whom Rudolf Steiner mentions in his life story. Erwin had been married to Grete Wiesenthal, the famous Austrian dancer of the time, but having been detained for a further ten years in Siberia after the First World War, he returned home only to find that Grete Wiesenthal had remarried, but his and her families remained closely befriended and it was through Erwin Lang that I met and was received by Wiesenthal.

She had been a solo dancer in the State Opera Ballet, but had broken away radically from ballet, because of her intense musicality, and created an own form of movement quite unlike anything else in the dancing world. She herself was like a delicate early Gothic wood carving; her body was a musical instrument. Unforgettable was the experience of dancing Schubert's *Forellen* (Trout) *Quintette*, each of us one of the instruments. With Wiesenthal I found what I had been looking for.

In July 1934, the same year of the February civil war against the socialists, Chancellor Dollfuss was assassinated in Vienna by Nazis. I happened to be walking over the Ballhaus Square in front of the Chancellory when police appeared, clearing the square of all civilians. It was obvious that something very serious had happened. From that time on, Vienna ceased to be a place for striving, future-orientated, artistic youth. It became spiritually suffocating.

I spent a few of the autumn months of 1934 in the Hague and in Leiden with members of my father's family, as I had spent three and a half months the previous years in Paris with Russian teachers. In London, I went to a concert shared by three young musicians —

Peter St—, Franz Reizenstein, and a shy awkward Englishman. Peter stole the evening with a Schubert sonata, but the shy young Englishman was Benjamin Britten.

When I was back in Vienna, Alban Berg was to give the first performance of his violin concerto on the Viennese radio with himself playing the solo part. Peter St— knew a well-to-do young man with a good radio and on the evening of the performance, we gathered in the large flat of the Weihs family. Other people were there as well, among them Tommy Weihs's inseparable friend, Peter Roth.

From then on I saw the two not infrequently as they were doing obstetrics in a hospital near my dancing studio. All three of us were twenty-two. I was impressed by their freshness and civility, not always too obvious in young men about town. Before that and quite independently, Carlo [Pietzner] and I had met at an artist's party, and Alix [Roth] and I met when she worked as an assistant to a well-known photographer who did a series of photographs of me.

Meanwhile, my life and various relationships were becoming painfully meaningless and I developed a violent and dramatic form of urticaria. Consultations with specialists, diets, modern medicines all seemed to aggravate the condition and I ended up in fairly poor health.

My two young medical student friends insisted the only thing to do was to go to Dr König. I have described this encounter in Dr König's Memorial Number of *The Cresset*, Michaelmas 1966. His treatment necessitated twice weekly injections which were to be given me by Tommy Weihs, so I went to him and his family twice a week. He was at that time engaged to a young Swiss girl, Helen Stoll, and he, Helen and Peter and I sometimes went out together. Never did either Peter or Thomas suggest I join the study evenings they attended in Dr König's house.

Just before Christmas 1937, I went once again on tour to Berlin. Our little group of eight dancers, all of whom save myself were Austrian and now openly pro-Nazi, was enthusiastically fêted in Berlin for it was an established fact that Hitler was preparing the annexation of Austria and everything Austrian was made much of.

One day between afternoon and evening performance, when we usually remained in the dressing rooms mending, reading or writing letters, the director of the theatre came asking us to dress hurriedly in the beautiful old black Tirolean costumes in which we danced some medieval dances, as we had been invited out to supper. Two black Daimlers with SS drivers were waiting at the stage door to take us to the Chancellery where, after being let through gate after gate, we entered a large low-ceilinged room in which a big round table was laid for supper. Various notables from the theatre and film worlds were there, and one big, slightly florid, very handsome man, President of the Berlin Police Force, Rosenberg — to me the only sympathetic person present. He was later to participate in the officers' attempt to eliminate Hitler in 1944 and was hung for so doing.

But our host that evening was Hitler himself. He welcomed us and went around the table serving each one personally. I was completely frozen as if in a nightmare, and was the only one in our group he didn't address. It was known that Hitler had blue eyes, but I could have sworn his eyes were yellow. His posture was sagging, his shoulders narrow and chest hollow. Later we were photographed with him. I kept the photograph, which caused me some trouble in wartime Britain.

On March 11, 1938, Nazi troops crossed the Austrian border and on Sunday 13, Hitler triumphantly entered Vienna in an open car with Rudolf Hess at his side. I stood by the Opera with many others and witnessed the end of Austrian independence.

For most of my friends, the time to leave the country had come. Thomas married Helen and as he could not take his finals at the University, he went to Switzerland where he qualified and where he worked for a while under Ita Wegman. Peter had an invitation to Britain where he went in June 1938. I accompanied him. Dr König and his family came over at Christmas of that year, likewise Alix, and on March 30, 1939, the saga of Camphill began.